JENNIFER SLATTERY

Evelyn Frey

When
Dawn
Breaks

A CONTEMPORARY ROMANCE NOVEL

JENNIFER SLATTERY

When Dawn Breaks

A CONTEMPORARY ROMANCE NOVEL

NEW HOPE
PUBLISHERS
Gospel-Centered. Missions-Driven.

BIRMINGHAM, ALABAMA

New Hope® Publishers
P. O. Box 12065
Birmingham, AL 35202-2065
NewHopeDigital.com
New Hope Publishers is a division of WMU®.

Library of Congress Cataloging-in-Publication Data

Slattery, Jennifer, 1974-
    When dawn breaks : a novel / Jennifer Slattery.
        pages ; cm
    ISBN 978-1-59669-423-1 (sc)
    I. Title.
    PS3619.L3755W48 2015
    813'.6--dc23

                            2014038087

Cover Design: MTW Studio
Interior Design: Kay Bishop

ISBN: 978-1-59669-423-1
N154102 • 0115 • 2M1

DEDICATION

To my favorite railroader,
my love, my greatest supporter,
and my closest friend.
Steve, you know I adore you!

ACKNOWLEDGMENTS

FIRST AND FOREMOST, I want to thank my Savior, Jesus Christ, for giving His life so I may live. If not for His transforming grace and mercy, I would still be on the streets of Tacoma (if not in jail or dead). May everything I do, write, and say proclaim the gospel and point others to Jesus Christ.

I want to give a special thank-you to my husband, Steve Slattery, who continually supports my writing endeavors even if that means eating leftovers three days out of seven (and burnt ones at that!). This novel was especially fun to write as, being a railroader as the hero in *When Dawn Breaks* is, my husband played an active and crucial role in the writing of this novel, sharing industry insights, verifying accuracy of details and authenticity of plot lines, and spending a great deal of time brainstorming possible scenes and scenarios. Love you, Slattery!

I also want to thank Jesseca Randall, my sister and a strong woman in the faith who has been involved in the foster care industry in various capacities for almost a decade. Her passion has bled into me and stirred within me a desire to write this story. I also want to thank a sweet sister in Christ named Gale Perkins who, while in her fifties, sensed God calling her into foster care. Not shrinking from that call, Gale showed us all what can happen when we say yes to God. Watching her raise up children who've been placed in the system, like Gavin and his sisters, I was continually reminded that lives can in fact change, and each one of us can be a part of that life change.

I also want to thank insurance agent Leon Van Berkum for sharing his wisdom regarding insurance claims and processes with me. Your help proved invaluable in the writing of this novel.

I want to thank Joyce Dinkins, my editor, for her insights, encouragement, and guidance. Every time I get off the phone with her, I am reminded anew of my call and purpose. Behind every published book you'll find a team of very talented and gifted staff, and this is true a hundred fold for New Hope® Publishers. It's been such a blessing to work with a publishing house who is gospel-centered and missions-focused.

Thanks to the myriad of critique partners and beta readers who combed through this novel, helping me to make it as strong, impactful, and authentic as possible. Eileen Rife, Henry McLaughlin, and Kathleen Freeman, thank you.

CHAPTER 1

JACQUELINE DUNN STARED at her television, reading for the fourth time the alert scrolling across the bottom of the screen. *Hurricane warning for Southeast Texas: Mandatory evacuation in effect for the following areas.* Six zones followed, including hers. Was everyone overreacting?

She crossed the room and peered out the window. The sandy beach stretched before her, frothy waves tumbling in. Dark clouds hovered near the horizon. Not unusual. Except that Hurricane Gita had grown to a Category 4 storm, and it was headed straight for the Gulf Coast.

She glanced back at the television. The news shifted from the radar map to Lowe's Highway. Loaded vehicles inched forward at what looked to be a five-mile-per-hour crawl. Which meant if she left now, she might make it out of Crystal Shores before the storm hit.

There was no sense delaying the inevitable. Sucking in a deep breath, she gripped a packed suitcase in one hand and her computer case in the other. Stepping around partially packed boxes, she headed toward the front door. A stack of mail lay on the entryway table. She shoved it into the side pocket of her computer case then marched into the garage.

Lord, please stay this storm. I can't afford to start over. Not at my age.

With a sigh, Jacqueline loaded hastily packed belongings in the back of her car and cranked the engine. She started to set the global positioning system (GPS) then stopped. Gripping the steering wheel, she stared at the white cement wall in front of her. Where to? Staying in a hotel, for only God knew how long, would eat her savings. But what else could she do? Her parents lived too far away, and her daughter—

The muscles in her neck tensed as she thought about their last conversation. No. A hotel was her best option, expensive or not.

She glanced at the clock on the dash—8:30 a.m. According to the National Weather Service, the storm would hit in five, maybe six hours. That didn't leave much time for debating. Right now she needed to focus on one thing—leaving town.

Two hours later, stuck in a major traffic jam, her phone chimed. Her car's Bluetooth picked up the call.

"Hi, Elaine." A hot flash ignited Jacqueline's pulse and triggered sweat glands. She turned up the air and positioned the vents toward herself.

"Don't tell me you're still at home thinking this thing will pass."

"No, I'm taking the slow, scenic route." She leaned forward, stretching her chin to allow optimum ventilation down her itchy neck. It didn't help. "What about you?"

"Just entered Kentucky."

"Where you going—Canada?" Keeping one eye on the road, Jacqueline angled her face toward the dash. Cold, dry air pelted her eyes, making them water, no doubt sending rivulets of mascara down her cheeks.

"Indiana. What about you?"

"Great question. I'm actually hoping to make it to a hotel before everything within a day's drive of the coast gets booked."

"Have you thought about—?"

"Delana's? Briefly." Hovering near spontaneous combustion, she searched for something able to double as a fan. She settled on a plastic map and flapped it in front of her face at sound barrier speed.

"She's so close. Willow Valley is five hours north, right? An hour from Texarkana?"

"Six . . . but it doesn't make a whole lot of sense to leave one storm to head into another." Tossing the useless fan, she gave her shirt a tug then glanced toward the window, ready to thrust her head outside.

A man in bifocals stared back at her from the car idling in the next lane. She straightened and focused on the long line of vehicles in front of her, certain her face resembled a bad case of measles.

"I thought you two were doing better," Elaine said.

"If by better you mean forced niceties and two-sentence conversations, then yeah, we're great."

"Maybe this is what you both need—some time together. To reconnect."

"Maybe. Do you have a bucket list?"

"A what?"

"You know, a list of things you want to do before you die."

Elaine laughed. "It's a hurricane, not the next world war. And now that you've decided to listen to me, the mayor, and the weather officials, you're going to be fine."

"Define *fine*. Does it include a dwindling bank account and no retirement plan? With nothing to show for the past five decades of my life but a long list of debts and chamber meetings? If that's fine, I want the upgrade. Do you ever wonder if there's more to life than commission checks and designer hand bags?"

"More than purses? Says the girl who once joked about opening a boutique."

It wasn't a joke. An impossibility, perhaps, but if she had it to do over—

Although right now she'd be happy to salvage a portion of the assets she left in Crystal Shores, soon to be inundated with massive amounts of water. "I'm just taking stock, you know?"

"Sounds like you need to lay off the melatonin. I've heard it can make people depressed."

"I'm sharing my midlife cheer is all."

"Honey, you passed midlife eons ago." Elaine paused. "So, are you going to your daughter's or what?"

"I'll contact her." What was the worst that could happen? Stupid question. The better one: How long could two headstrong women coexist before strangling one another?

With a heavy sigh, Jacqueline searched through her contacts for her daughter's number.

Maybe she should wait. Until when? She showed up at Delana's doorstep with suitcase in hand? No. Her daughter needed time to process and maybe even throw a fit or two.

She hit call then wiggled against the seat back to relieve a sweaty itch. Her nerves fired with each ring.

"Mom."

Jacqueline exhaled. "Hey, sweetie. How are you?"

"I'm good. I meant to call you. You OK? I saw the news."

Was that genuine concern? A good sign. "I'm fine, sweetie. On the highway with all the hurricane evacuees. In fact, that's why I'm calling."

"Uh-huh?"

A hint of tension. Not good. "I haven't seen you in . . . Wow, almost two years?"

"Yeah?"

"I miss you."

Dead air.

"I figured I might as well make a vacation out of this."

"Uh-huh?"

"I thought it might be nice for you and me to spend some time together."

"Meaning?"

Jacqueline swallowed. "You're so close, and as long as I'm driving north . . . I figured I'd head your way. Stay with you for a few days." Or weeks, depending on the severity of the storm.

"You what?"

Jacqueline flinched at the venom in her daughter's tone. "Is that a problem? Because I could always check into a hotel." At $150 a night?

Her daughter sighed. "No. It's fine. You can stay in my guest room." Her voice held the warmth of a salamander.

FOURTEEN-YEAR-OLD GAVIN RALLINGS sat on the edge of the couch, picking at a fingernail. How long before Hurricane Gita hit? Too soon—he knew that much. They needed to leave now. Only they had nowhere to go and no way to get there. Mom's boyfriend sure wouldn't help them. The only person he cared about was himself.

Gavin's pulse quickened as the dude stomped about the apartment, shoving dirty clothes in a gym bag.

Mom chased behind him. "What're you doing? Answer me when I'm talking to you!"

Ace scowled. "Stupid cow, lay off me."

Mom hurled insults in return, clenched fists trembling, while Gavin held his breath, waiting for Ace to unload.

Gavin's eight-year-old sister, Adele, hovered near the hallway, wide eyed. His other sister, eleven-month-old baby Jaya, sat on the floor in the corner. With her peach-fuzz head turned to the side, she chewed on a remote control. Saliva dripped down her chin, and snot bubbled from her nose. Gavin wanted to go to her, scoop her up and hold her close, but he stayed frozen, staring, waiting.

"Where we going?" Mom wrapped the belt of her robe tighter around her thick waist.

Ace whirled around. "What do you mean, 'we'? You're grown. You do what you want."

Mom fired another string of curses and hurled a coffee mug across the room. Gavin flinched when it hit the wall and shattered onto the floor in jagged pieces.

Baby Jaya started to cry. He hurried to pick her up. Shushing her, he grabbed her pacifier and poked it against her pink lips. She turned away, scrunched her pudgy face, and let out an ear-splitting wail.

Ace spun around, narrowed eyes targeting Gavin. "Shut her up, already!" He took a step forward. Snake-like veins bulged on his forearms.

Gavin lifted his chin and leveled his gaze. "She's just a baby." Holding his sister close, he rocked and hummed softly.

Mom's boyfriend sneered. "Listen to you. Thirteen-year-old runt trying to act like a man."

Fourteen! More of a man than you'll ever be.

The wailing continued, so Gavin stood and started to pace until she settled into a hiccupped whimper.

Mom moved in front of Ace and crossed her arms. "So you're leaving, just like that?"

"Just like that." With his bag in hand, he pushed her aside, marched across the living room, and threw open the door. "Check ya later, Teresa."

Mom chased after him. Gavin followed to the doorway and peered around the frame. People moved through his peripheral vision, lugging boxes and armloads of clothes down the apartment hall, but they barely registered. His vision, his thoughts, zeroed in on one thing—Mom freaking out, on the verge of losing it, which meant Gavin needed to step up. Only this time he didn't know how.

"Wait! What about us?" Mom's shrieks echoed through the narrow hallway, and a few neighbors poked their heads out.

Without so much as a backwards glance, Ace disappeared into the stair well. Mom called him a bunch of nasty names then slumped to the floor. She covered her face, rocked for some time.

A woman in heels and shorts passed by, pulling a bulging suitcase. She glanced at Mom and shook her head. More apartment residents passed, some by themselves, others dragging whimpering children behind them.

And still Mom sat.

Adele tugged on Gavin's arm, looking up with wide brown eyes. Her chin quivered as tears welled behind her long lashes. "Are we going to leave, too?"

He inhaled and exhaled slowly. *Stay strong. Calm. Don't let her see your fear.* "Don't know, but we'll be all right."

A door creaked open and Stella, their nearest neighbor, emerged from her apartment carrying a sagging box. She rolled her eyes. "Teresa, whatcha doing sitting on that nasty ol' floor crying like a crazy woman?"

Mom lumbered to her feet and wiped the dust from her backside. She looked from Stella to the stairwell, shoulders slumped.

"That loser done took off on you again, didn't he? I told you he was no good. You better get on the bus and get outta here. The news said Mayor Carson's shipping folks to a shelter in Houston."

Arms crossed, Mom shook her head. "I'm not going to no flea-infested shelter." She moved out of the way as another tenant passed by with two gym bags.

Stella glanced from Gavin to Mom then threw her hands up. "Come on. Y'all can ride with me."

"Where you going?"

"Does it matter?" She laughed. "Got me an old boyfriend north of Tyler."

"Texas?"

"No, Saudi Arabia." She rolled her eyes then checked her nails, a smile emerging. "He'll be real happy to see me, too."

"Happy enough to let us stay?"

She shrugged. "Probably."

Mom blew out a puff of air. "All right. Just let me grab a few things."

"Make it fast. If you're not at the curb in three minutes, I leave without you."

CHAPTER 2

SITTING IN STELLA'S CAR, heading north on Lowe's Highway, Gavin slumped against the side door. Mom sat kitty-corner from him, holding baby Jaya in her lap. Beside him, Adele dozed with her head drooped on his shoulder. Rain splattered the windshield. Wind rocked the vehicle and bowed the trees lining the road.

Feeling trapped, Gavin hugged himself and stared at the long line of cars, trucks, and vans barricading them in. He craned his neck and leaned forward to check the speedometer. Ten miles per hour.

They passed a rusted pickup stalled along the side of the road. A handful of women and children sat in the back, surrounded by drenched boxes and miscellaneous furniture while two men bent under the hood.

"Can't see a thing." Stella cursed and hunched over the steering wheel. The windshield wipers screeched a steady rhythm.

Mom cracked her window, funneling spray into Gavin's face. "Not like we're going anywhere, anyway."

Adele stirred with a moan and shifted away from the splatter. Baby Jaya started to fuss.

Stella glared at Mom. "What're you doing?"

"I need a smoke. This is stressing me out."

"Uh-uh." With one hand on the steering wheel, Stella stretched across and rolled up the window.

Mom muttered under her breath then flopped her head against the back of her seat. "This is stupid."

Stella glared at her. "You want out? Because I can pull over right now."

"Whatever." Mom huffed. "How much farther we gotta go?"

Stella grabbed a tattered atlas from the dash, studied it, then tossed it back with a shrug. "Three hundred fifty miles?"

"Great. Let's hope traffic picks up; otherwise, we won't get to your boyfriend's until midnight next Tuesday."

"If we're lucky."

"He knows we're coming, right?"

Stella shrugged. "Can't get a hold of him. Must have changed his number or something."

"What do you mean he must have changed his number? When was the last time you talked to him?"

"A few months back. Maybe six."

Mom cursed and shook her head.

Gavin's stomach knotted as he thought of all the guys who had come and gone in his mother's life, some staying for little more than a night. Most likely Stella's boyfriend wasn't any different. If he was even around at all. Not that Gavin could do anything about it, except keep his mouth shut. He didn't want to add to Mom's stress.

No one spoke the rest of the way. The rain unleashed its fury with a thunderous riot then slowed to a steady drizzle. As darkness fell, he pressed his temple to the cool glass and drifted into a fitful sleep. Snapshots of flood waters, uprooted trees, and abandoned women and children filled his dreams. He woke to a sheen of sweat covering his clammy skin, the low hum of an engine idling, and Jaya's fussing.

He rubbed his eyes and peered into the darkness. The rain and wind had stopped, and stars dotted the sky. In the seat in front of him, his mother held his wiggling sister while poking her head through the opened window. The driver's seat was empty, and angry voices sliced the night air.

Through the windshield, he watched two forms standing beneath a faint porch light. On the stoop, Stella had her back to them, hands jammed on her hips, head cocked. A hunched figure, small and thin, stood before her.

"I told you, he ain't here. Took off months ago. No good-bye, no note." A hoarse older woman's voice.

"Stupid good for nothin'." Stella said. "What're we supposed to do, huh?"

"Why's that my problem? There's a shelter downtown on the corner of Broadway and Ellington, but they're probably closed for the night. Gotta get there by five if you want a bed."

Stella cursed, and so did Mom.

A man, tall and bulky, joined the woman. "The church down the street's taking people."

"Boy, how you know?" The woman flicked his arm.

"I seen 'em. Plus they got signs in their parking lot, something 'bout hurricane victims. Might be all filled up by now, though." The man started to give directions but Stella whirled around, stomped down the stairs, and into the car. She peeled out of the drive.

The stench of burning rubber stung Gavin's nostrils, tightening the band around his chest. Digging his fingers into his thighs, he studied his mother's shadowed profile. She didn't move. Just stared straight ahead, rigid. *Don't lose it, Mom.*

He clamped his dry mouth shut as a rush of bile flooded the back of his throat. Baby Jaya's whimpers turned to wails. His mother alternated between shushing her and hurling bitter words about no-good, good-for-nothing men. Gavin stared into the night sky, focusing on the full moon partially hidden in wisps of clouds.

Adele turned to him with moist eyes. "I'm scared."

He held his breath and waited for his mother to unload. Instead, she reached behind her seat to touch Adele's knee. "It's OK, Adabear. Everything's going to be OK."

Adele slumped in her seat and faced her window while the riot within Gavin raged. How he longed to believe Mom's words, to trust that everything would be OK, but he knew better.

Stella slowed near a small brick church. Two men dressed in reflective vests over red ponchos stood on either side of the parking lot entrance, guiding cars onto the property. Many more vehicles lined the asphalt, enough to fill the tiny building two times over.

When they drew near, Stella lowered her window. "You got room for five more?"

The attendant, a wiry man with a hooked nose, smiled. "We've always got room. Go ahead and park along the back, and go in through the double doors. Irene, our women's ministry leader, will get you all set up."

Stella followed the string of automobiles around the church where two more men stood in the center of a grassy area directing traffic. Following their lead, she pulled onto the lawn, bouncing over muddy potholes, and parked behind a dark-colored sport utility vehicle.

"Grab your stuff." She got out, rounded the vehicle, and threw open the trunk.

Gavin grabbed his backpack with his comic book, toothbrush, and a change of clothes.

Standing on the asphalt, Adele rubbed her eyes and stared about her.

"Come on." Dangling a sleeping Jaya over one arm, bulging diaper bag slung over her shoulder, his mom grabbed Adele by the wrist and jerked her forward.

Gavin followed, weaving around parked vehicles and dodging those still coming in. Stella marched ahead of them, clutching a rolling suitcase in one hand and a lumpy duffel in the other. When they reached the curb, his sister tripped, sprawling against the cement. This unleashed the floodgates, and sobs quivered through her small body. Gavin lunged forward, ready to help his sister up, but Mom beat him to it.

Shoving the sleepy baby at Gavin, she knelt on the wet ground, pulled Adele close, and kissed her cheek. "Shh. It's OK. Everything's going to be OK."

Holding his sister, Gavin stood beside them while people streamed past. They stayed like that for some time, Adele sniffling, Mom soothing her. Soft voices drifted toward him, raising questions, suggestions. But nothing registered outside of his sister's cries and Mom's words.

A woman dressed in jeans and a blouse moved into his peripheral vision and knelt beside Mom. "Ah, the baby's sleeping. I imagine it's been a long night for all of you. Come on inside." She placed one hand on Mom's back and the other under her elbow. "Let's get all of you settled. Would you like a cup of coffee?"

Mom glanced up, face scrunched, gaze shifting from the opened doors in front of her to the woman beside her. Finally, she nodded and lumbered to her feet.

"I'm Irene." The woman tossed Gavin a smile, and the sparkle in her eyes drew him.

He quickened his step, as if staying near this woman would somehow make everything better, or at least deaden the ache in his chest.

Irene led them down a narrow hall lit by flickering fluorescent bulbs into a large room lined wall to wall with cots. Basketball goals hung on opposite walls. Mobs of people stood in corners and in front of a rectangular table lined with cups and jugs. A woman with thick, curly hair that puffed around her head like mounds of cotton clutched a crying baby to her chest. She swayed and stared straight ahead, as if in a daze. A kid with glasses sat cross-legged on the cot beside her with his chin propped on fists. He glanced up as Gavin passed.

Irene lifted a clipboard and pen off a small folding table. "Let me get you all signed in. I imagine you're here because of the hurricane?"

Mom nodded and pulled Adele close, her head swiveling as she looked from side to side.

A lump lodged in Gavin's throat as he watched. *Hold me too.* Only he was too old for that. Besides, Mom's hugs wouldn't last. Someone would say something, do something, and she'd snap. Maybe even ruin their chance of staying.

"Your name?"

"Teresa."

"And who's this cutie?" The lady lifted Adele's chin.

"Adele. And this is Gavin. This here's baby Jaya." She raised her arm slightly, rustling the baby, then glanced around. "Where can I smoke?"

Irene's lips pressed together, looking to the baby. She offered a tight smile. "You'll have to go outside for that."

Mom nodded, shoved Jaya into his arms, and left, pulling out a pack of cigarettes as she went. With one hand on Adele's shoulder, Irene looked at Gavin. "Let me guess, ninth grade?"

Gavin swallowed, thinking of his essay paper tucked in his backpack and the B scrawled on the top, the one he hoped would get him into accelerated English next fall. "Eighth. Going into ninth." Would he return home in time for school? Would they even have a home to return to?

CHAPTER 3

JONATHAN COHEN STOOD in his office with his back toward the railroad yard. Train brakes squealed behind him. He grabbed the framed photo of himself and his wife taken fifteen years previously. With the Hawaii skyline behind them, their hair wind-stirred and eyes smiling, they were an image of marital bliss. Married fresh out of college, they'd made it twenty-eight years, two shy of their pearl anniversary.

Someone knocked on his door. Bart Lundquist, his former boss and lifelong friend, entered. "You're really going to do this, huh?" He sat in the black leather chair in front of Jonathan's desk.

Jonathan nodded and dropped the photo into a partially filled box. Beneath the picture lay plaques and framed certificates recording twenty-five years of service. "It's time."

"Is there anything I can do to change your mind?"

He shook his head. "This has nothing to do with you or this job. It's time for a change. And to move closer to my family. Where I want to retire."

"It won't be easy, coming in as the low-man. This railroad might be small, but everyone knows you, respects you. You won't have that at Central Rails."

"I know." That was one reason he wanted to move—to get away from the deep history surrounding him in Alta Loma. So he could finally move on, learn to live again. Even if that meant living alone.

"They give you a moving package?"

Jonathan nodded. "Typical new-hire contract. They pay my expenses, give me a moving allowance for incidentals."

"Nice." Bart leaned back and rested folded hands across his stomach. "I heard that shop has some shady dealings. Rumor says the general director's not exactly on the up-and-up, if you know what I mean. Might be rough. Like heading for a derail."

"You know what I think of rumors." Machinists had spread more than a few about him.

"Yeah, well, if you change your mind . . ."

Jonathan smiled. "I know where to find you." But he wasn't coming back. This phase of his life was done.

THE SUN HAD JUST STARTED to peek over Willow Valley's horizon as Jonathan drove to his first day at Central Rails. The yard was ten times bigger than the one at his old job. With his new title as senior manager, he'd be in charge of two hundred fifty men. He was running with the big engines now. He'd find out soon enough if he had the horsepower to pull it off.

Needing a diversion, he skimmed through radio stations, finally settling on something that sounded local.

"With so many storm refugees flooding our city, we're bound to see some sort of backlash." The host spoke with a thick Texas twang. "A storm of this caliber wreaks havoc on the economy. Would you agree, Mr. Pierce?"

"Certainly," the in-studio guest replied. "With coastal businesses devastated and refugees flooding surrounding areas, I expect the unemployment rate to rise. Unskilled, minimum-wage workers will be hit hardest as they fight for jobs that aren't available. For some, this could create a vicious cycle of poverty and dependence."

As the men talked about an overburdened welfare system, Jonathan thought about the storm refugees sheltering throughout Willow Valley. The in-studio guest predicted perpetual gloom and hopelessness for these people. But surely there was a way out. Some skill or trade they could learn.

Mentally sifting through potential solutions, he followed a dike past a recycle yard and a row of factories. He continued along a two-lane highway until stretches of track dotted with locomotives came into view. Black smoke swirled around the train engines and clouded the sky. A long metal fence secured the rail yard, centered by a security gate.

An odd flutter filled his stomach, the kind he used to get in high school speech class. Which was crazy. He had nothing to fear. His manager, Darren, and the crew would realize soon enough that Jonathan could hold his own.

Unless the rumors Bart mentioned were true; if so, he was in for quite a storm.

Slowing to a stop, he rolled down his window and punched in the security code. The rusted gate clanked open, and he eased through. He stopped outside a lone brick building. The windows were dark, and a thick haze hovered over the yard.

Tucking his safety goggles and protective earplugs into his front pocket, he grabbed his hard hat and stepped out. His steel-toed boots crunched on the gravel, and a gust of humid air carrying the scent of diesel fuel swept over him.

Once inside, he paused to study an evacuation map tacked to the wall beside the stairwell. First floor: cafeteria and lockers. Second floor: foreman, nurse's office, and on-duty manager. He debated stopping by to say hello to the foremen and their guys, but then he thought better of it. He should meet with his boss first then check out his office, make sure he had everything he needed for the morning conference call.

Foregoing the elevator, he climbed the metal stairs two at a time and emerged into a dark hallway. After groping the cement wall, he flicked a switch. Two office doors, both closed, stood in front of him. The door on the right read: *Darren Web, General Director, Locomotive Repair Facility.* The name badge had been removed from the other door, which meant it probably belonged to Jonathan. He tried the knob. Locked, and he didn't have a key. He checked his watch. Odd that Darren wasn't here yet.

Jonathan sat in a metal folding chair in the hall and crossed an ankle over his knee. He pulled out his smartphone for a quick game of solitaire.

Ten minutes later, Darren barged in carrying a leather briefcase. His protective earplugs dangled from a cord around his neck, and something white and crusty splotched his shirt collar. Toothpaste?

Jonathan rose to meet him. "Good morning, sir."

Darren grunted with a quick nod and dug his hand in his front pocket. "Welcome to Central Rails." He studied Jonathan for a moment as if sizing him up. "I'll have Lynda make you a copy of your office key this afternoon."

Jonathan nodded. As he moved aside to allow the man access to the lock, a phone blared inside the neighboring office.

"Excuse me." Darren shoved his briefcase under his arm and moved to the adjacent door. Jonathan returned to his folding chair. The phone rang again.

A moment later, Darren's deep voice bellowed, "I don't care what he says. Just take care of it. You're smart. I'm sure you can figure it out."

When the call ended, Jonathan stood and ambled to his boss's open door. Leaning against the frame, he cleared his throat.

Darren looked up. "Your office. Right." He stood to his feet, he followed Jonathan back to his office. With a click, he unbolted the door. "Conference call's in an hour."

Then he left.

Perched on the edge of a leather chair, Jonathan swiveled to glance out of the long window behind him. Locomotives lined the yard, and a switch crew manned the track. Everything gave the appearance of a typical shop, but his tightened gut told him something wasn't right. Thanks to Bart and his gloom-and-doom stories, which was exactly what they were—stories.

Besides, he only needed to stick things out for five more years. Then he'd have his 30 years in, his company pension, and his house in the country. Now all he needed was someone to share his happily-ever-after with. His stomach soured, and his gaze fell to his bare ring finger.

Evie, I haven't forgotten you, darling. I'm just tired of being alone.

JACQUELINE PEELED BACK the fluffy blue comforter and sat up. Early morning sun filtered through the partially opened blinds, casting beams of light onto the beige carpet. The rich aroma of coffee drifted into the room, signaling her daughter was awake.

Hopefully Delana was in better spirits this morning. Last night, Jacqueline arrived well after midnight. Her daughter, dressed in a silk robe, hair pulled back, had answered the door with little more than a tense smile and short sentences. Although Jacqueline told herself Delana was just tired, their history said otherwise.

She slipped out of bed and wrapped a thin bathrobe around her stiff frame. She paused in the mirror to inspect her puffy eyes. Smudged mascara had settled into the wrinkles, giving her the appearance of a haggard bag lady. Quite fitting, actually. She chuckled, thinking of a conversation she shared with a co-worker about her middle-aged son moving back into the house. *Way to flip roles, Jacqueline. Keep climbing that ladder of success.* But this wasn't permanent, and she certainly wasn't mooching off her daughter.

She crossed the room and poked her finger through the blinds, widening the slats. Pale blue stretched across the horizon, giving no evidence of last night's storm. Of course, she was almost 400 miles from landfall.

In the kitchen, she found Delana leaning against the counter, talking on the phone in a hushed voice. Dressed in scrubs, she wore her cinnamon-toned hair pulled back with her bangs that swooped to the side.

Meeting Jacqueline's gaze, Delana's silvery-blue eyes widened, and color crept into her face. "I gotta go." She snapped her phone shut and tucked it into her pocket. "You sleep well?" Casting a glance Jacqueline's way, she reached into the cupboard, pulled out a mug, and filled it with steaming coffee.

"I did, thank you."

Delana set the cup in front of Jacqueline. Her thinned lips twitched in what was probably meant to be a smile. "Cream and sugar, right?"

"You remembered."

Delana shrugged and strolled to the fridge. "Any news on the storm?" She pulled out a pint of creamer, grabbed a spoon, and brought both to her mom.

Shaking her head, Jacqueline doctored her coffee and watched steam rise from its surface. Why did she feel like a teenager begging her parents for a handout? Maybe it was because she was a grown woman with a sad bank account and an unsuccessful career, sleeping in her daughter's guest room until she could return to what was quite likely a flooded and destroyed home. Yeah, on her way up. Worse, considering most of her real estate listings lined the coast, she probably wouldn't climb out of this mess for quite some time.

Delana wrapped both hands around her mug. "So, how long are you planning on staying?" Her eyes narrowed, cold.

Jacqueline's gaze shifted to the window. "Uh . . ." *Lord, does it have to be this hard? I know I made mistakes. A lot of mistakes, but Your Word says I'm a new creation. Help Delana to see that. Help her to forgive me. Or at least not hate me.*

Her daughter tuned to the morning news on a television mounted under the upper kitchen cabinets. Images of extensive flooding and uprooted trees floating in murky water filled the screen. It transitioned to footage of the coast guard pulling a woman from a storm-damaged roof then to the downtown area before zooming in on the shattered windows of the Troy Towers.

Delana snapped off the TV. Gripping the counter, she stared out the window above her sink.

Jacqueline traced her finger along a crack in the table. "I can always stay at a hotel." If there were any rooms left.

"Quit playing the martyr, will you?"

Jacqueline blinked. "Martyr?" She sucked in air. *Hold your tongue. No fights on the first day.* Operating on six hours of sleep didn't help. "I'm sorry you see it that way." She stood and smoothed her hair from her face. A surge of anger spiked her temperature, but she refused to give in to it. She wouldn't slip into old behavior patterns. Lifting her chin, she forced a smile that stretched across dry teeth. "I'd really like to—"

"I know. Make amends, work things out. Start fresh." Delana grabbed her purse and slung it over her shoulder. "Listen, I've got to go." She reached the door in two strides.

"Delana?"

Her daughter paused with her hand on the knob.

"Would you like me to leave?"

She sighed, her shoulders rising before settling into a slump. "No. You're fine."

The door clicked softly behind her.

Exhaling, Jacqueline shuffled back to the guest room and plopped onto the bed. She stared through the blinds at the rising sun reflecting off low-lying clouds. A gentle breeze stirred the leaves of a willow oak centered between her daughter's condo and a man-made pond.

She grabbed her Bible and hugged it to her chest. *Should I leave? Go to a hotel, or maybe join Elaine with her grandkids.*

No. She'd bailed on her daughter once before, and she refused to do it again. Not without a fight. Besides, didn't the Bible say something about God turning the hearts of children to their fathers?

Did that also include mothers? And terrible ones at that?

Her phone rang, and checking the number on the screen, she smiled. Elaine. Always Elaine. How did she know just when to call? "Hey, good morning."

"Morning, fellow refugee. How's the war zone?"

"You want the Sunday School answer or honesty?"

"That bad, huh?" Children giggled and sang in the background, high-pitched voices merging with what sounded like a folk song. "Remember what Jesus said about losing family?"

"Um . . . not really." Elaine had told her so much over the past year, from how to accept Christ as her Savior to how to grow in Him. But Jacqueline couldn't remember her saying anything about how to restore past relationships.

"Give it time. She'll come around, and if she doesn't, you can always stay here. My daughter's got a lumpy, saggy futon with your name on it."

"As tempting as that sounds . . ."

"What are your plans for the day?"

"Besides obsess over the news and stare at walls, maybe shave lint off a sweater or two?"

Elaine laughed. "Full schedule. Don't let me keep you."

"I'll call you tonight." She hung up and dropped her phone on the bed. There'd be no sweater-shaving or wall-staring today. No. She might as well find something more useful to do, like clean the house. A little vacuuming and a nice, hot dinner would counter her daughter's negative attitude.

With an Internet radio station blaring from her cell phone, she started in the living room dusting furniture. Swinging her hips, she hummed an old Bee Gees tune. Next, she moved to the half bath, then to the kitchen, eventually finding her way into the laundry room. So this was her daughter's "must-do-later" chore. Clothes spilled from an overflowing hamper in the far corner, and designer outfits were draped over a folded ironing board.

Moving from the Bee Gees to Simon & Garfunkel, Jacqueline continued her private concert and sorted through dirty garments. Halfway through the hamper, she pulled out a slinky, red, lace bustier. Beneath it lay what appeared to be matching panties made from scant fabric.

Oh!

She tossed them back in the hamper and grabbed the pile of clothes already dropped into the machine. After shoving everything back into place, she returned the items exactly where she'd found them then dashed into the kitchen to wash her hands.

Sitting at the table a moment later, she tried to wipe the image of the lingerie from of her mind. That wasn't sleeping attire.

Clearly her daughter had a beau, and a serious one at that.

CHAPTER 4

GAVIN WOKE TO THE SMELL of coffee and bacon and the constant noise of shelter life. A few rows down, two teenagers fought over a stupid pillow. A bunch of ladies gathered near the hall, chattering and cackling. A baby cried. For once, it wasn't Jaya, although she'd woken three or four times during the night, thanks to the constant influx of refugees. Now she slept on a nearby cot, barricaded by rolled blankets.

Lying on his back, he rubbed gritty eyes and stretched. His ankle pressed against the metal bar of his cot and his right arm hung over the side. Sitting in the adjacent cot, his sister played with a miniature doll with matted hair while Mom surveyed a line of people weaving around the perimeter of the room.

"Don't these people ever sleep?" She jumped up, got tangled in the mess of cots, then fell back on her rear. "We gotta get out of this place."

Sitting kitty-corner to Adele, Stella checked her reflection in a compact mirror and ran a brush through her hair. "I'm starved." She craned her neck.

Gavin followed her gaze to a rectangular table covered in steaming metal tubs. People held out plates while men and women dressed in white aprons scooped out food. Irene stood off to the side studying a clipboard.

Stella dropped her brush in her tote. "How many people you think they got up in this place, anyway?"

Mom glanced around. "Too many, and none of 'em know how to keep their mouths shut."

Jaya stirred, whimpered, then kicked her feet. Gavin scooped her up before she started to cry and scanned the mounds of bedding for her sippy cup. Empty. She began to fuss.

Mom closed her eyes and rubbed her temples. "Not again. That child's getting on my last nerve."

"Excuse me?"

Gavin glanced up to see a woman standing beside Mom. She held out a ziplock bag of cereal. "For your little one."

Mom stared at the woman who continued to hold out the snacks, smile intact, left cheek twitching.

He shifted Jaya to his other arm, studying Mom's pinched expression. Baby Jaya squirmed and whimpered. He swayed and hummed the Oscar Mayer bologna song, the only tune he could think of.

Take it, Mom. Why wouldn't she just take the stupid Cheerios?

Mom cocked her head, eyebrows plunging as if the woman offered a decomposing snake. She shrugged. "Sure. Whatever."

The woman handed it over, ruffled Adele's hair, and left.

"Here." Mom tossed Gavin the cereal and stood again, this time stepping carefully between the cots. "If we want some of that foul-smelling food they're hawking, we better get in line before everything's eaten up." She grabbed Adele by the arm and pulled her to her feet. "Come on."

Holding a contented Jaya, Gavin followed Mom, Stella, and Adele around the mass of people. They moved into line behind an old woman with a hunched back and long gray hair that hung in a loose braid. She glanced over her shoulder and smiled, revealing swollen gums lacking teeth.

The line crept forward. Mom pulled Adele close, resting her hands on his sister's tiny shoulders and her chin on Adele's head. "Someone needs to find some deodorant." Wrinkling her nose, she tickled Adele's ribs, producing a giggle.

Stella lifted her arm and sniffed her pit. "Not me." She laughed and tried to raise Gavin's arm. "What about you, boy? You foul this morning?"

A smile tugged on Gavin's face, and he squeezed his bicep to his side. "No, ma'am."

Stella raised her eyebrows and thrust her chin toward a man with a scraggly beard that reached to his midchest. "I bet I know where the stench's coming from. Someone bring in a hose already, and a big ol' jug of disinfectant."

The guy hovered a few feet away rubbing his hands, body jerking as if charged with electricity. Or more likely, meth. A man with a bloated stomach and clumps of hair protruding from a greasy scalp stood beside him sucking on his bottom lip. "Bet it's Mr. Twitch over there. Or his buddy, Inflatagut."

Mom swore and shook her head. "I'm not hanging out here all day; I can tell you that right now."

Gavin's stomach clenched as he studied his mom, her tight lips, the smudge of mascara beneath her eyes, the hair hanging about her face.

"Yeah?" Stella planted her hands on her hips. "So where you gonna go?"

A man wearing a faded T-shirt turned around. "The church lady said there's public transit. I'm going to the library after breakfast to talk to my insurance guy."

"Insurance?" His mom snorted. "I don't got no insurance, but I sure would like to get out of this place and get me a burger or something. Only, you need money for that."

Stella twirled a lock of hair around her finger. "You're right about that. We do need money." She angled her head and the corners of her mouth lifted. "I know how we can get some, too."

Mom frowned. "You talking about what I think you are?"

Stella's grin widened. Heat flushed Gavin's cheeks as he looked from his mom to her friend. Surely they wouldn't . . . she wouldn't . . .

Mom shook her head. "You're crazy."

Gavin exhaled. He knew Mom wouldn't try anything stupid, which was all Stella ever did—stupid stuff.

Stella's face hardened. "I'll tell you what's crazy. Staying in this nasty place, that's what. I told you this was my old stomping ground." She shrugged. "Unless you'd rather hang with the twitch-and-stench crew."

Mom rubbed a finger over her lips, gazing ahead.

No. Mom, don't listen to her. Please.

JONATHAN PULLED INTO his sister's driveway and parked behind a cherry-red convertible—his brother-in-law's latest toy. He pictured Walter cruising down the highway, exactly four miles over the speed limit, bifocals balanced on his thick nose, and his curly, silver hair puffed in the breeze. Maybe tonight Walter would take Jonathan for a spin. Then two old geezers would light up the highway.

Before stepping out of his vehicle, he called the shop to see how many engines the crew planned to release overnight. Their response wasn't impressive, promising a hectic morning. But worrying about numbers wouldn't help the mechanics move any faster.

He started to tuck his cell phone into his front pocket when a text message alert caught his eye. He clicked on it and smiled. It was from his daughter, Stephanie.

Hope you're enjoying your new job. Miss you!

She ended her message with a heart shape, one of the many emoticons she'd learned to create. Warmth radiated through him as he thought of all the notes, texts, and hand-made cards his princess had sent him over the years. She was always so thoughtful. Just like her mother.

He responded with what had become a common phrase, one birthed after Stephanie's first job: *It beats cleaning toilets. Love you, too.*

Phone returned to his pocket, he grabbed the store-bought pie lying on the passenger seat—his contribution to dinner—and got out. His boots scuffed the cement walk as he made his way toward the front steps.

The adjacent window curtain fluttered, and the door opened before he could ring the bell. Jeanne-Anne engulfed him in a hug, her rose-scented perfume mixing with the aroma of roasted garlic. He licked his lips. It'd been quite a while since he'd enjoyed a home-cooked meal, assuming canned spaghetti and sausages didn't count.

"Hello." She ushered him in. Her silver hair, chin-length, shimmered under the light of a bronze chandelier. Walter stood behind her wearing a striped polo and khaki shorts.

He gripped Jonathan's elbow as they shook hands. "So, how was your first day at Central Rails?"

Jonathan followed him into the living room. "Interesting." He perched on the edge of a floral couch.

Walter sat across from him while his sister scurried into the kitchen, saying something about basting a pot roast.

"Interesting—how?"

Jonathan shook his head. "Something tells me my new boss is acting shady. Worse, I get the feeling he's less than thrilled the chief marketing officer (CMO) hired me."

"Tense, huh?"

"Slightly."

"Do you regret taking the job?"

"Doesn't matter. According to my hire-on contract, they can sue me for a hefty sum if I quit within the first twelve months." Of course, they wanted him to stay on long term but had only specified penalties for early termination. Maybe they assumed the first year was the hardest.

"I wouldn't worry about it much." Jeanne-Anne swept into the room carrying cheese and crackers on a silver tray. "I'm sure you'll settle in soon enough. You always do." She deposited the snacks on the coffee table between the two men then sank into a navy blue recliner. "Although, you'd be much more comfortable here." She studied him. "Why you insist on staying in that hotel is beyond me. We've got plenty of room."

"I know, Beannie, but I don't want to intrude." Plus, as much as he loved his sister and brother-in-law, he needed his space, and the hotel was on the company's dime. Part of his relocation package. "Besides, I told you how unpredictable I expect my schedule to be. I could get calls all hours of the night. I'd wake you both up."

"Nonsense." Jeanne-Anne flicked a hand. "If I can sleep through Walter's snoring, a few late-night phone calls won't hurt me none."

"Hey, now!" Walter pushed his glasses up with his index finger, a hint of a smile betraying his feigned offense. "Don't pester the man, Jeannie. He said he's fine."

She nodded, hands cupped over her knees, and turned to Jonathan. "So long as you know you're welcome. Always."

He smiled. "I do, and I'm grateful."

"So," Walter reached for a chunk of cheese, "when do you start house hunting?"

"I should meet up with the company realtor sometime next week." If the woman would ever return Jonathan's calls. Thinking of Evie, he cleared a lump from his throat and brushed some crumbs from his hand. "Truth is, this is where I've always wanted to retire. Moving here on my own would've cost quite a penny." He paused. "What about you, Walter? When do you think you'll head for the big R?"

"That's what I've keep asking him." Jeanne-Anne grinned.

Jonathan's stomach growled. He grabbed a handful of crackers to stave off the monster. "Think of all the golfing time you'd have, my man. I could always use a partner."

"Speaking of—" The corners of his sister's eyes crinkled.

Jonathan leaned forward, elbows propped on his knees. "I don't like the sound of that, or the mischievous look in your eye."

She and Walter exchanged glances, her smile growing. "I've got a friend—"

"Oh, no!" Jonathan shook his head.

"She used to play golf. Well, she did once, anyway, and had a good time."

"Uh-uh."

"She likes NASCAR."

"I don't."

"And baseball."

"Not interested."

"And is almost as lonely as you."

Jonathan laughed. "Meaning she's desperate."

"No. Meaning—available."

"No blind dates. No matchmaking."

"Jonathan, I worry about you. We worry about you."

Walter raised his hands, laughing. "Don't drag me into this one. I'm nothing more than an innocent bystander."

"You, innocent?" Jonathan chuckled. "When has that ever been the case?" His sister meant well, but he wasn't ready for the dating scene. Not yet, maybe never.

Jeanne-Anne's face sobered. "Evie wouldn't have wanted you to spend the rest of your life alone; you know that. And I can't picture you frequenting a local bar."

Jonathan shifted, feeling like a spotlight radiated above him.

"Just give her a try," she urged.

It beat Internet dating and joining the local bingo hall. Besides, what did he have to lose? "Fine."

Jeanne-Anne squealed and jumped to her feet. "Great! I'll call her right now. She'll be so excited."

"Wait a minute! Excited?"

But she had already launched into a phone conversation.

AFTER MEANDERING AIMLESSLY through Delana's condo, resisting the urge to snoop, Jacqueline drifted to the guest room and a stack of real estate listings printed on glossy paper. Ten of her properties sat along the coast, most likely saturated by floodwaters.

She dropped the documents onto the bed and removed her mail from her computer bag. Tossing aside the junk mail, she sifted through the bills. Next month's cable and home security, services currently unnecessary but part of a two-year contract. Did they have a get-out-free-due-to-an-act-of-God clause? Knowing her luck, probably not.

She grabbed her purse and rummaged for her insurance card. Of course, it wasn't there. That meant it was back in Crystal

Shores in her home office, soggy or swept away. If only she could remember the terms of her policy—or at least had had the foresight to grab the documents explaining them.

Picking up her phone, she typed her agency's name in the Internet search engine then pressed on the accompanying number.

An automated voice followed. "Your call is very important to us. Due to heavy call volume, you may experience longer than normal wait times. A customer service representative should be with you in an estimated thirty-two minutes." If it took that long just to reach a live person, how quickly would they be able to review her claim?

After the voice invited her to visit their website, where she could "find answers to many of her questions," elevator music came on.

Breathing deeply in an effort to still her churning stomach, she turned her cell phone on speaker and scooted back against the bed pillows. She spent the next twenty minutes wading through information presented on the insurance company's website. Step one: list all the damaged property.

Considering she hadn't returned to survey the destruction, she had no idea. But even so, she could make note of her belongings.

She started with the living room. A couch, loveseat, and a handcrafted glass-top table she'd purchased at a craft fair. An oak television console storing recorded sitcoms and family videos, including those containing Delana's first steps.

Tears burned her eyes as other items came to mind. A ceramic dish Delana had made in elementary school, a safety pin and paper clip bracelet, also made by her daughter. Notes Jacqueline had saved in the drawer of her bedside table for safekeeping.

Dropping her phone on the bed, she closed her eyes and rubbed her face, a deep ache building in the back of her throat.

Snippets of Bible verses she'd heard over the past year resurfaced, but her memory of them was too vague to bring comfort. So instead, she picked up her cell and clicked on

Pandora. Closing her eyes once again, she focused on the words pouring from the online radio.

> *Our God is like a mighty mountain*
> *Our God will never fail*
> *His love is like an endless fountain*
> *A shelter through the fiercest gale*

The tears she'd been holding spilled out, streaming her face. It was as if God were speaking directly to her, comforting her, through the words of the song.

Oh, Father, You are so gentle and kind. Help me to make it through this. Show me what I need to do from here.

Her phone chimed with an incoming call, and she glanced at the screen. She didn't recognize the caller. Unfortunately, in her attempt to answer, Jacqueline inadvertently disconnected with the insurance company. After twenty-two minutes of waiting. Feeling as if bricks pressed upon her shoulders, she sighed.

"Hello?"

"Hi. Can I speak with Mike please?"

She closed her eyes again and pressed the palm of her hand to her forehead. "Wrong number."

"Oh, sorry."

As if having wasted twenty minutes of her morning listening to Lionel Richie wasn't enough, by the time she dialed the insurance company again, the wait had increased by another fifteen minutes. And her phone battery was running low.

She'd call Monday. She probably also needed to get her mail rerouted, unless the city cleanup crew worked miracles. Because last she saw, ninety percent of Crystal Shores remained submerged, and the rest lay in shambles. According to official estimates, storm damage was millions and mounting, and the death toll continued to climb. She shivered, thinking how close she had come to staying.

Thank You, Lord, for moving me out of the hurricane's way, even if it did land me in another storm. But these things took time. Surely her daughter would warm up to her eventually, once memories kicked in—the pleasant ones, anyway.

What she needed now was a king-sized candy bar, or a tub of mint-chocolate chip ice cream. Exiting the room, she proceeded down the hall and to the kitchen. Bare cupboards and an empty fridge spoiled her plans. No problem. She'd go shopping.

She grabbed her purse and dashed out into stifling hot air with enough humidity to melt her foundation. Typical July weather in the South. Across the parking lot, her car baked under a metal carport, still loaded with clothing and other hastily packed items. She needed to bring her things in, eventually. Although that might irritate her daughter further, suggesting Jacqueline's stay could become extended. It likely would, unless Delana gave her the boot.

As Jacqueline crossed the melting asphalt, a man on a Harley-Davidson motorcycle pulled into the adjacent slot. A wisp of a man, he wore all leather, fringed, with metal studs dotting the back and shoulders. He revved his engine before cutting it, slid off his helmet, and tucked it under his arm. Leaning with one arm on his handlebars, he tossed Jacqueline a crooked smile.

Unruly, gray-streaked eyebrows protruded from behind dark glasses. "It's a hot one."

With a raised eyebrow, Jacqueline suppressed a giggle and nodded instead. In full-leather garb? Yes, it was.

"You must be new because I would've noticed a woman like you. Did you just move in?"

"I . . . no. I'm visiting." Searching her purse for her keys, she turned away from him.

"That's what I said when I came out here ten years ago." Carrying the distinct scent of analgesic cream, he closed the distance with an arthritic-John-Travolta swagger. "I think you'll find this place and its people grow on you. How long you staying?"

She threw open her car door and slid in, hot air engulfing her. "I'm not sure, but it was nice to meet you." Pressing her lips together, she didn't unleash her laughter until she turned the corner and pulled out of the complex.

And to think she remained single when so many eligible men—in leather, no less—waited to be caught.

Tossing her purse onto the passenger seat, she used her GPS to find the nearest supermarket, Sunflower Produce. An hour later, she returned with two bags of groceries, a recipe magazine, and a rented comedy DVD. By 5:30 p.m., a honey-glazed, stuffed pork loin roasted in the oven, a green salad decorated the table, and two glasses of ice water started to sweat.

Her daughter breezed in, dropped her purse on the counter, and headed toward her bedroom.

Jacqueline chased after her. "I'm glad you're—"

Delana's bedroom door slammed shut.

"Home."

Jacqueline sat on the couch, thinking back twenty years. How many times had she hurried home after work, passing her daughter with little more than a smile, before slipping out again? Either to meet a client. Or some man.

Chewing her bottom lip, she flipped through her cell phone, her gaze shifting between the screen and her daughter's bedroom door.

When it opened again, she offered her best smile. "Hey."

Delana had traded her scrubs for a summer sundress with thin straps. Its hem hit her midthigh. Powder blue platforms with straps wrapped around her ankles added at least three inches to her petite frame. Silver hoops dangled from her ears.

"I made dinner. You hungry?"

Delana glanced at Jacqueline as if noticing her for the first time. "Sorry. I've got plans." She pulled a tube of lip gloss from a cocktail purse draped over her shoulder. "But I probably won't leave for a few minutes. How was your day?" She perched on the edge of an orange leather chair, her knees pressed together, her dress growing three inches shorter.

"Do you have a date?" *With a man who likes slinky, red lingerie?* Once again, thoughts of her past—of all the men she'd allowed to sully her, to use her—came to Jacqueline's mind, causing her heart to ache. Great role model she'd been.

"Something like that." Dropping her gaze, Delana shifted and scratched her ear. Jacqueline studied her daughter's face, the taut skin around her mouth and eyes, and the way she ran a tongue over her bottom lip. What was she hiding?

Jacqueline wanted to press further—to ask where Delana was going, whom she was seeing, and what she'd done with the rest of her outfit. But that would instigate a fight.

Delana's cell chimed a text and she pulled it from her purse. The corners of her mouth lifted and she sprang to her feet. "I may be out late."

Jacqueline followed her to the kitchen. Funny, she hadn't heard a car pull up, although maybe he parked some distance away. Still, he couldn't come to the door?

After smoothing her hair and applying another layer of lip gloss, her daughter dashed out. Standing at the kitchen sink, Jacqueline rose on tiptoes to peer out the window into the parking lot. Empty cars filled the slots, engines off. No one stood outside the door or on the walk and a moment later, Delana appeared beside her car.

Jacqueline frowned and shook her head. Some Romeo. Interested enough for lingerie but not to pick a girl up?

Like it was any of her business. Besides, Jacqueline had forfeited her right to play the parent long ago.

CHAPTER 5

SITTING AT A LONG GLASS TABLE in the conference room, Jonathan straightened the stack of papers in front of him. Senior Manager Ron Fisher sat to his left. Manager Gary Wilson sat across from him casting frequent glances from his watch to the door.

Darren marched in less than two minutes before the conference call. Dark circles hung under his eyes, and a heavy frown deepened the crevices in his face. They were fifteen units over their goal, and yet another engine had broken down the night before, raising their monthly count to forty. Shaffer wouldn't be pleased.

Darren eyed each of his managers in turn, his gaze lingering on Jonathan. "On the call, I'll do the talking."

They nodded without making eye contact.

Jonathan cleared his throat. "I spoke with the floor supervisor." Now probably wasn't the time, but he had no choice. Darren needed to know. "Unit 3678 needs air break valves for the triennial inspection, but he said we don't have any. Would you like me to call Secure Air Brake, see if I can get some ordered? I think we can get the part in by Friday."

Darren cursed and raked his hands through his hair.

Jonathan shifted. "And the supervisor said we need new exhaust stacks because the old ones are cracked." Adding one more locomotive to those already awaiting repairs. Not good.

Darren glanced at the clock on the wall then reached for the phone in the center of the table. "We'll talk about that later." He punched in numbers to join the conference call.

Mr. Shaffer's deep voice soon spilled from the speaker. "Ned, Midwest. Great shop count and no road failures yesterday. Good job. Tim, you've got five three-day-olds. How many of them are going today?" He addressed each shop, asking questions, raising concerns, until he got to Armstrong Yard, then his tone hardened. "Darren, what's the deal with that road failure last night?"

"I, uh . . ." Darren pulled his ear, a vein bulging along his temple. He and Ron exchanged glances, the senior manager visibly stiffening.

"Check the work order, and figure out what's going on."

"Yes, sir."

"And what about all those engines you've got collecting dust? You're fifteen over goal. What are you going to do about it?"

Darren leaned forward. "I've got six extra people coming in for day shift, and I'm going to call more guys in for second."

"Uh-uh. No more overtime. You've got a full crew. Make it work."

Darren rubbed his forehead until his skin turned red. "I've got five engines coming, and we'll try to release seven out of here today."

"Try? Not good enough."

"We'll take care of it."

Apparently satisfied, Shaffer moved to the next shop before concluding with a question on safety concerns.

When the call ended, Darren stood. "We're getting too much heat. No more babysitting. I want you to ride your men. And get unit 3678 out of here. I expect it to be gone by morning."

"Will do." Ron nodded and followed Darren out of the room.

Jonathan hurried after him. "But sir, we don't have the part. There's no way we can get those units released until we do."

Darren whirled around, his eye twitching as his tense expression smoothed into a tight smile. He opened his mouth as if to say something but then clamped it shut. He turned to Ron. "Fisher, my office."

The senior manager cleared his throat and nodded.

Jonathan returned to his desk and slumped behind the computer. Now what? No one would be able to get them air brake valves by the end of the day.

He called the first of their two suppliers. "We need an air brake valve ASAP. Any way I can talk you into an overnight shipment?"

"Sorry, but we're short of cores."

Great. Jonathan hung up and called Secure Air Brakes, only to receive the same answer. Best he could do was move on to problem number two, reducing the amount of road failures. The numbers indicated something wasn't right. Either the guys were signing off for work not done or someone was getting lazy. Or both.

He spent the rest of the morning fielding phone calls, looking at the budget, and dodging union reps. At noon, he took a tour of the shop before heading to the foreman's office. He found Phil Qualls sitting behind his desk staring at a computer screen.

"Hey, boss." Phil swiveled to face him. "What can I do you for?"

"The big dog asked about the unit that failed last night. We had it in the shop two days and checked it for leaks. I want to see who signed off on the pressure test."

Phil rubbed his forehead. His gaze looked past Jonathan's shoulder then back.

"Is there a problem?"

Phil cleared his throat. "No. No problem." He turned toward his computer, typed, then scrolled down the screen until he hit the appropriate unit and date. "Tollhouse."

"Haven't met the guy." Jonathan pulled a small spiral notebook from his back pocket and scrawled the name. "He been here long?"

Phil shifted. "He . . . uh . . . think he came in as a fireman and oiler."

"Thanks, Phil."

"Anything else, boss?"

He tucked his notebook back in his pocket. "Not for now."

He scanned the shop through the glass window. Everyone appeared to be doing what they were supposed to, running inspections and making repairs. Why the large numbers and frequent failures? He needed to find out. They couldn't fix the problem until they understood the cause.

He found the senior manager in the hall outside the locker room. "Hey, Ron, know where I can find Tollhouse?"

Ron frowned. "What for?"

"He signed off on the work order for that road failure yesterday. I want to follow up with him. See what he did, what he found."

A tendon in his jaw twitched. "I'll take care of it."

"I appreciate that, but I'd like to talk to him myself."

The man's eyes intensified. "I'll let him know you're looking for him." He clamped a massive hand on Jonathan's shoulder. "You heard Shaffer, right?"

Jonathan nodded.

"Seems to me you've got better things to do than waste our machinists' time digging up old work orders."

CHAPTER 6

JACQUELINE SCRAMBLED EGGS on the stove. Bacon sizzled in an adjacent pan. The rich aroma of freshly brewed coffee surrounded her, and the early morning sun filled the kitchen with a warm glow. She paused, inhaled, and recalled her morning devotion. No matter how hopeless or dark things between her and her daughter appeared, there was always hope in Christ, the God of reconciliation.

Footsteps shuffled behind her. She turned to see Delana, wrapped in a purple bathrobe, hair tousled. She glanced toward the stove. "What's all this?"

"I did a little grocery shopping." Jacqueline smiled. "You hungry?"

"I appreciate the offer, but I'm on a diet."

"Yeah, me too. Only I keep forgetting." She chuckled and returned to the stove. Platter in hand, she removed enough eggs and bacon to feed the southern United States.

"I thought you hated cooking." Delana filled a mug with coffee.

"Things change." With a wink, she scooped food onto a plate. After pouring herself some coffee, she joined her daughter at the kitchen table.

Delana raised an eyebrow. "You're all dressed up this morning. You going somewhere?"

"Church. Any suggestions of where I can find one?"

"Hardly."

"I take it you don't go?"

Delana snorted. "Not a fan of condemnation."

Jacqueline forced a smile. "Actually, I think the Bible says, 'You're not condemned in Christ Jesus.' Would you like to come? I'm sure we can find a noncondemning church to attend."

"In the Bible Belt?" Her daughter's face scrunched. She wrapped both hands around her mug, peering at Jacqueline through the steam. "So, I'm guessing you're still doing the Jesus thing, huh?"

Jacqueline studied her daughter, not sure whether to extend the conversation or leave it for another day. "If you change your mind . . ."

"Sounds tempting, but I've got an appointment with the bathroom and a toilet scrubber. Would hate to disappoint."

"Speaking of dates, how did your evening go?"

Delana straightened, and her lips pressed together before smoothing into a tight smile. She rose with a shrug, her slippers thwacking her heels as she padded across the tile floor.

"Delana?" Jacqueline stood and crossed the kitchen.

Her daughter paused, turned.

"I know things haven't always been good between us. But I'd like to . . ." *What? Start over? Undo the mess I made? The pain I caused?* Life wasn't that easy and some messes left permanent heart stains. "You want to go to lunch today? My treat."

Delana's face softened, a hint of a smile emerging. "Sure. We can do that." With a yawn, she swiveled back around and plunged her head into the fridge.

It was a start.

GAVIN SAT CROSS-LEGGED on his cot, breakfast balanced in his lap. Hundreds of voices echoed against the shelter's concrete walls. Babies cried, children fought, and mothers snapped as people tumbled out of bed and moved toward the food line.

Others filled the hall leading to the nasty smelling bathroom with its bulging trash cans and clogged toilets. One of them had overflowed during the night, and Gavin awoke to foul-mouthed yells as a woman dressed in flannel pajama bottoms and a long T-shirt ran out waving her hands. By the time the verse-spouting, stiff-dressed churchies arrived with plungers, half the shelter, including Mom, was freaking out. Things hadn't settled down until an hour later.

At least Jaya had slept through most of the night. Now she lay beside Gavin, sucking her thumb.

Adele sat beside him, picking at a lump of oatmeal.

"Quit playing and eat." Mom frowned and nudged Adele's shoulder.

Nose wrinkled, Adele plopped the plate beside her and crossed her arms. "I'm not hungry."

Mom shoved it into Adele's hands. "Do not make me feed you."

Sighing, Adele slumped and plunged her spoon into the goop. When she raised her spoon, a trail of slime followed.

Someone whistled, and the clamor faded to a low murmur as Irene stood at the front of the room, surveying the crowd. She wore a cream-colored blouse tucked into a knee length skirt, a sharp contrast to the gym shorts and T-shirts all around her. A man in a collared shirt and slacks stood beside her.

"I hope y'all had a restful evening." With a toothy smile, Irene looked from one end of the room to the other. "I want to invite all of you to church this morning."

Someone shouted amen, and a few people sprang to their feet while others cracked jokes about grabbing the wine and taking a dip in the holy water.

Irene pressed her hands together, but her smile never wavered.. "Service starts in an hour. To get to the sanctuary, follow the hall on the right," she pointed to an exit beyond her shoulder, "and up the stairs. Children are welcome to join our Sunday School classes on the second floor."

Irene left, and the voices rose once again.

On the cot beside him, a lady stood. "Don't know about attending no service, but I could sure use a break from my kids."

She grabbed a curly-haired toddler by the wrist and yanked him to his feet. "Come on, let's find your classroom."

Gavin watched his mother. She hunched over her plate, eyebrows pinched together, hair falling around her face.

She looked up. "Whatcha staring at me for?"

He shifted, swallowed. "Can I go?"

"Why you wanna do that? You thinking they'll give you some of that wine those people were talking about, huh?" Chuckling, she shook her head. "Boy, you're something else. You know you got to join some kind of club, sign your name in blood, for that sort of thing."

She turned back to her food and shoved a heaping spoonful into her mouth. When Gavin continued to watch her, she dropped her spoon and looked him in the eye. "What is it, boy? You're giving me the creeps."

"I want to go to the Sunday School that lady talked about."

"Why?"

Tugging on a loose thread in his cot, he shrugged. Why did he want to go? To get away from the chaos and stench of the shelter? To meet more people like Irene with her frequent smile and soft eyes? To find a distraction, anything to make him forget he was homeless, with nothing more than a duffel bag of clothes and his favorite comic book?

Inhaling, he lifted his chin. "Just want to, is all. I'll take Jaya and Adele."

Mom frowned. "I don't care what Irene says, those church folk don't want our kind." She glanced toward a line of people waiting for the showers. "Besides, you stink. Come on. We better go before those losers take all the towels." She reached across her cot to jab Stella who sat, hugging her knees, with earphones jammed in her ears.

Stella's eyes popped open. "What?"

Mom jerked her head toward the bathrooms. "I'm going to go for my assembly line clean up. Watch Jaya for me, will ya?"

Stella yawned. "Got nothing better to do, so long as I don't gotta change dirty diapers or nothing."

Mom laughed. "All out of diapers anyway. Gonna see if Ms. Do-gooder's got any." She flicked Gavin's arm. "Let's go."

Taking Adele's hand, Gavin followed Mom. They wove past two teenage girls dressed in skimpy tank tops and boxers and around an old woman with greasy, white hair sprawled on her cot. A splotch of wetness spread beneath Adele's hips, and the stench of urine made Gavin gag. Her gaze met his, her eyes dull, her skin slack and sallow, and Gavin's heart wrenched. He reached out to touch her hand, her fingers like ice.

"Momma, wait!" Adele lurched forward, pulling Gavin with her, as their mother disappeared in a mob of people.

He quickened his step, tightening his grip on Adele's hand. "We're OK."

A shirtless man with thick shoulders and a dragon tattooed across his chest eyed Gavin, sending a chill down his spine. Avoiding the man's shadowed gaze, Gavin hurried to catch up with Mom.

Standing in line, she crossed her arms and cocked her hip. "Can you believe they've only got two showers in this place?"

Gavin glanced at the mob of scowling refugees behind him, then toward the front of the line, inching its way around the corner.

A woman with jet-black hair streaked with gray turned around. "You should be grateful. We could be floating through the mess back home."

Mom scowled. "Was I talking to you?" She crossed her arms, eyes bulging. "I suggest you start minding your own business before I mind it for you."

With a humph, the woman turned back around, and Stella burst out laughing.

A man with saggy skin emerged around the corner, hair dripping onto bony shoulders, towel tied around his waist. The line inched forward. Ahead of them, a brunette lady wearing a loose braid stood on the outskirts. She held a sleeping toddler on her hip while smoothing the hair of a young girl standing beside her. The child, who looked maybe seven or eight, clung to the woman's leg with her cheek pressed against her thigh.

Gavin picked at a dried cuticle, a drop of blood seeping along the edge of his fingernail. When would they be able to leave this place?

As if in answer, a radio flicked on, blasting news of the storm damage.

"Rescue workers continue to lift people from homes and roof tops, transporting them from the storm-ravaged city to overcrowded shelters in the tristate area. The death toll continues to rise as more bodies are pulled from the flood wreckage. Hurricane Gita reduced homes, buildings, entire neighborhoods, to piles of rubble. With three-fourths of the city underwater, preventing cleanup for what looks to be quite some time, many residents are talking about permanent relocation. This could create a population surge in the outlying areas, leaving small towns scrambling to accommodate the massive population influx."

The news guy transitioned to a farm town an hour east. He introduced a local principal who talked about a huge number of school registrations for the coming fall. "We are discussing ways to deal with the increased student population now."

Gavin thought of his essay paper shoved in his backpack and his dream to earn a college scholarship. "Mom?"

She whirled around. "What?"

"Are you going to register us for school?"

She snorted. "Boy, how do I know where we're going to be this fall?" She huffed. "This is stupid. Don't nobody need a shower this bad. It's not like we've got anyone to impress, anyway. Gavin, hold my place."

Hips swaying, she sauntered across the room and back to their cots where Stella sat surrounded by a group of guys dressed in tanks and cutoffs.

Not wanting to watch his mother flirt with strangers, Gavin turned away and nudged his sister forward.

She looked at him through teary eyes. "How long we got to stay here? In this shelter?"

Gavin gripped her shoulders and pulled her close so the back of her head rested against his chest. "I don't know, but it'll be all right."

"Promise?"

He turned her toward him. "We're fighters, Adele. You and me. Nobody and no storm can get us down less we let 'em, you hear me? You know I'll watch out for you. Don't I always?"

She nodded, lashes fluttering over teary eyes.

CHAPTER 7

ARRIVING AT ABIDING Fellowship, Jonathan found Jeanne-Anne waiting in the foyer, eyes trained on the entrance. Walter leaned against the brick wall, phone in hand.

Jonathan strolled over. He offered his sister a grin and shook hands with his brother-in-law. "Sorry I'm late." He scanned the quaint lobby lined with cushioned chairs, a coat rack, and a rectangular table covered in glossy magazines and brochures.

After enveloping him in a sisterly hug, Jeanne-Anne pulled away, frowning. Jonathan followed her gaze to his big, hairy toes poking out of plastic flip-flops. He chuckled, shoved his hands in his Bermuda shorts' pockets, and rocked on his heels.

Her lips pressed into a tight line. "You couldn't wear something a little nicer?"

"Didn't know there was a dress code." He shot his brother-in-law a wink. "Came for Jesus, not a fashion shoot."

Jeanne-Anne crossed her arms. "The least you could've done is shaved."

Jonathan rubbed his hand over his two-day beard. "Want to tell me why you're so concerned about my appearance this morning? Or did I miss the, 'Thou shalt not wear cotton' commandment."

"Your sister lined up a little meet-and-greet for you after service." The tug-of-war that had been yanking on his brother-in-law's mouth gave way to a full-fledged grin.

Jonathan raised an eyebrow. "A meet-and-greet?" Then he remembered his sister's matchmaking plans. "Wonderful." He exhaled and shook his head. "About that . . ."

"Oh, no." Jeanne-Anne planted her hands on her hips. "Don't even try to get out of this one. You gave your word."

"I did no such thing. If I remember correctly, I didn't fight you with bared teeth."

"Exactly." She looped one arm through her husband's then cupped Jonathan's elbow. "Which is a concession if I ever encountered one. You don't want to turn into another Uncle Harold, do you? We both know what happens to single old men who spend too much time in isolation. Besides, you'll love Maggie. I promise."

"Maggie?"

Before he could protest further, she whisked him through the double doors and into the cathedral sanctuary. People sat elbow to elbow, most in their Sunday finest, a few in jeans and golf shirts. A formal choir fanned the stage. They sang an old hymn while a large man dressed in a black suit that appeared at least two sizes too big pumped his arms, a baton in hand.

Standing between his sister and brother-in-law, Jonathan searched for an empty seat. He spotted a few sprinkled here and there.

He turned to Jeanne-Anne. "Looks like we'll have to divide this morning. How about we meet up in the lobby after service?"

She frowned then shrugged. The three started to diverge but were intercepted by a silver-haired man in a gray suit and colorful tie. With a quick nod, he led them down the center aisle then stopped midway beside a straight-backed woman decked in antique yellow.

The usher leaned toward her and whispered. The woman frowned and nudged the man sitting beside her. This created a domino effect of tight-lipped stares, nudging, followed by shifting. The end result—four empty chairs side by side sandwiched between Mrs. Priss and an old couple dressed in vintage polyester.

Jeanne-Anne gave Walter a shove, and he maneuvered past the old couple, apologizing as he jostled their knees before sliding into the farthest chair. Jonathan started to follow, but Jeanne-Anne pulled him back and wiggled her way in. With a sigh, he sat beside her, leaving an empty seat on his left. One he presumed would soon be filled, if Jeanne-Anne had her way.

He felt like a speed-dating participant misplaced in a house of God. Not exactly an act of piety, although not something he'd vigorously oppose, either. Truth was, his sister was right. It'd been a long five years, and loneliness was beginning to roost in his soul. Living near his sister and within three hours of his daughter would help, but the occasional dinners and family get-togethers were poor substitutes for a heart-to-heart companion. Nothing screamed lonely old man like a night spent in an empty hotel room zoned out to the sports channel and lame reruns.

GAVIN SAT WITH HIS BACK to the wall, hugging his knees. He closed his eyes, straining to hear the words floating toward him. The man spoke of purpose, despite the storm, and a God who could turn all things to good. A God who loved each person, from the old and crippled lying in a hospital bed to all the victims affected by the storm.

The man's voice stopped, and singing, soft and sweet, took its place. Resting his cheek on his leg, Gavin closed his grainy eyes and let the music sweep over him. He sat like that for quite some time, blanketed in peace, surrounded by a warmth that extended to his very depths.

A touch on his shoulder startled him. His sister knelt beside him.

He glanced past her down the hall toward the shelter. "Momma know where you at?"

Adele lifted her chin. "She know where *you* at?"

He laughed and pulled her into a sideways hug. "You hear what they singing in that fancy church?"

She angled her head then nodded.

"Like it says, this here's our valley, but our mountaintop's coming, know why?"

She shook her head.

"Because there's only one way to go from here—and that's up." Things certainly couldn't get any worse. Now all they needed was someone to throw them a lifeline.

JACQUELINE STOOD AT the back of the sanctuary, hands folded in front of her. Heads turned as the usher led her forward to what appeared to be the lone empty seat next to a broad-shouldered man with a two-day beard. In his beach attire surrounded by men in suits and ties, he stood out like a hairy wart at one of those brand-name cosmetics shopping parties.

He offered Jacqueline a slight smile, flashing a pair of red-carpet celebrity eyes beneath thick brows, before turning his attention back to the preacher. A woman with wavy blonde hair, most likely the man's wife, sat beside him, spine pulled straight, chin lifted, knees pressed together. In fact, couples spanned in every direction, shoulder-to-well-dressed-shoulder, like images from a greeting card.

Intent on proving she wasn't the only fifty-something single woman in the evangelical South, Jacqueline craned her neck and made a slow visual sweep of the sanctuary. Couples, families, moms cradling young children in their arms.

Three rows to her left, a head swiveled, and a man's gaze met hers. The corners of his mouth lifted, and his head, with its spiked mullet, dipped. Heat flooded Jacqueline's face as recognition surfaced. It was the leather-loving man from her daughter's condominium. The frequent glances he cast her way suggested he would zero in as soon as the service ended.

Doing her best to ignore him, she focused on the big screen ahead where Ephesians 5 was displayed.

The preacher gripped the podium, his deep voice echoing from the rafters. "Each day, God gives us countless opportunities to serve Him. To choose to live lives of purpose or futility." He closed his Bible and stepped to the front of the stage. "We've all seen the news. All those bodies floating on the water, pulled from the wreckage, countless lives, entire cities, destroyed. Hundreds of fancy beachfront houses, leveled."

The pastor paused, and a solemn hush fell over the crowd. "Those individuals who survived the storm are left to start over. Many of them lost jobs. I imagine a lot of folks feel like God abandoned them, like things are hopeless, beyond repair. But sometimes God has to strip everything else away to help us see His big picture plan. Remember what He did with Joseph? How about Moses? Esther, the exiled Jews? With God, nothing's wasted. Everything, everyone has purpose."

Jacqueline leaned forward, latching on to the words with every part of her has-been, jobless being.

"Like Esther, God put you here, now, for a time such as this. But the choice is yours. You can keep chasing the American dream, padding your bank account and stock piling for retirement, or you can spend your time and energy on those things that matter. For eternity." He paused. "And here's my question, one I hope you'll think long and hard about: how's your obituary going to read?"

That I sacrificed my daughter for a flopped career and died alone, having accomplished nothing?

When the preacher launched into a story about a burger-eating contest he won in college, which somehow tied into the rapture, she used the time to peruse her bulletin. If God wanted her to make the most of her time, she needed to spend less of it moping around Delana's condo and more pouring into the lives of others. Otherwise she'd turn into one of those clingy old maids who sucked the life right out of their children. A fine line existed, it seemed, between being available and hovering. Based on the exasperated look her daughter shot her this morning, Jacqueline neared the hover stage, which would only propel her daughter in the other direction.

What she needed was a women's group or ministry to join, anything to keep her occupied while she waited for Delana's heart to soften and city officials to resurrect Crystal Shores.

Interesting. The church had a singles' group. She surveyed the sanctuary again, found a handful of college students sprinkled along the perimeters and a few old men sitting by themselves. Once again, she glanced at Mr. Mullet, and her cheeks heated to find him watching her. What was it with this guy? With her luck, he'd be in charge of the singles' group, if it weren't filled with people who were decades younger than her.

No, thank you. Besides, bored or not, there was no sense dabbling in romance. This phase was just that. By the end of the month—at the most, two—Crystal Shores and her life would return to normal, or more accurately, a new normal. Regardless of what happened, one thing she knew for sure, she was *not* returning to property sales.

This thought initiated a second prayer request. She needed a career change, not an easy endeavor at fifty-one. Stewing on all the what-ifs swirled around her age and dipping bank account, she forced her attention back to the rest of the message. Ten minutes later, the preacher concluded with announcements, followed by a plea for shelter volunteers.

"Many of you are aware of the large number of Gita victims sleeping in our church basement. We are desperately in need of donations and volunteers. If you are interested, you may contact Irene Ford. Her phone number is in today's bulletin."

After he closed in prayer, people spilled from their seats and into the aisle.

Trapped beside the elderly man fumbling with his cane and his wife blocking the exit beyond him, Jacqueline cast a nervous glance toward Mr. Mullet. Although a mob of people hid him from view, it was only a matter of time before he sauntered her way. Hoping to exit to her left, she whirled around to stare into a pair of hazel eyes flecked with green.

"Excuse me." Clutching her Bible to her chest, she peered over the man's shoulder at yet another stagnant crowd blocking the far end of the row. *Seriously, people, this is not a social gathering.*

"Looks like we hit a traffic jam, huh?" The man grinned.

"Apparently." Maybe being barricaded was a good thing if it kept her out of Mr. Mullet's reach. "Is this church normally this busy?"

The guy shrugged. "Don't know. This is my first time. I'm Jonathan, by the way." He extended a hand.

His grip enveloped hers, warm and strong. "I'm Jacqueline. Are you—?"

"Here because of the storm? No. Just moved as a new hire. Came to church with my sister and brother-in-law." He indicated the woman standing by his side. She faced forward, looking all about, as if searching for someone. "You?"

Jacqueline nodded with a nervous laugh. "Displaced refugee."

"Here comes Maggie." His sister tugged Jonathan's sleeve. "You'll love her. I promise." She waved a hand and called above the clamoring voices. "Over here."

Dressed in a red blazer, a lady with short black hair waved back and wove her way through the crowd. Eyeing her escape route, Jacqueline finally made her way into the aisle, casting one last glance toward Jonathan. Handsome, in a just-rolled-out-of-bed, grabbed-some-clothes-off-the-floor, sort of way.

That glance cost her. She whirled around and bumped into Mr. Mullet, dressed in a velvet green shirt accented with tan fringe.

"Fancy meeting you here." He fell into step beside her.

"Good morning." She lengthened her stride, focusing on the sanctuary exit.

"Like the preacher said, God never wastes a moment." He pulled a toothpick from his shirt pocket and stuck it into his mouth, working it as he talked. "I imagine He expects the same from us, wouldn't you say."

"I suppose." Something told her she wouldn't like where this conversation was headed.

"Seems the good Lord keeps placing you and me in the same vicinity. I'm beginning to wonder if He has a purpose in that."

"I, uh—"

In front of her, a woman veered to the right, creating a narrow passage into the lobby. "Excuse me, but I need to talk to someone about the shelter." She pushed through the door.

Unfortunately, Mr. Mullet followed like a heat-seeking leach. "You need to speak to Irene. Follow me. I'll introduce you." When he turned to scan the lobby, Jacqueline used the opportunity to make her escape.

"Thank you, but I need to—"

She dashed around a group of people, down a hall, and around the corner. Standing with her back against the wall and her hand to her neck, she exploded in laughter.

Regaining composure, she smoothed the front of her blouse and turned to leave when something caught her peripheral vision. She turned to see two children sitting against the far wall, watching her with wide eyes. The older of the two, a boy perhaps thirteen, maybe fourteen years old, had auburn hair with bangs swooped to one side, hazel eyes, and a splattering of freckles on his nose and cheeks. The girl bore a strong resemblance with lighter, almost carrot-toned hair and double the freckles. Her eyes were a beautiful mixture of chestnut and green. Based on their shadowed expressions, damp hair, and rumpled clothing, they came from the basement shelter.

"Hey, there." She chewed her bottom lip, at a loss as to what to say but unable to turn away from their big, beautiful eyes.

The two looked so . . . broken. Probably like she felt every time she watched a news broadcast, only she had years of pulling up herself up by her bootstraps to carry her through and a Savior who promised to always stay by her side. What about these kids? Who did they have?

As if in answer, a heavy-set, scowling woman barreled toward them. Upon seeing her, the children scampered to their feet.

"Where have you been?" She grabbed the girl by the arm and yanked her forward. Her icy gaze flicked to the older boy who cowered before her. "I've a mind to beat you, child. Get your sorry selves back downstairs. Now!"

Jacqueline watched them leave with a heavy heart, memories of the past and the woman she once was, flashing through her mind. She thought of the morning's message, not of Esther the delicate queen who saved her people through an act of courage, but of Moses. A murderer turned liberator, used by God to set captives free and point them toward the Promised Land.

Sucking in a breath of air, she stood staring, as the angry woman pulled the two children around the corner and out of sight.

The pastor said God never wasted a moment or tear, that every life had purpose. Could God use a woman who had dashed the hopes of her own child to bring hope to someone else's?

CHAPTER 8

JONATHAN FIDDLED WITH his fork, moved his glass. Fighting a grimace, he nudged the salad-impersonating weeds on his plate in search of the candied pecans. Clearly the only thing edible in this place. Even the crackers resembled cardboard. In color, flavor, and texture.

Maggie sat across from him, nibbling a portabella-eggplant sandwich. Jeanne-Anne and Walter filled the remaining seats, acting as liaisons, or more accurately, conversation prodders. They were failing, not that Maggie gave them much to work with.

She dabbed the corner of her mouth with her napkin and glanced around. "Isn't this restaurant wonderful? And everything is completely organic."

"So I noticed." Apparently the owners had an obsession with the color pea green. Everything in the place glowed like a radiation-exposed football field, from the walls to the wait staff uniforms, tablecloths . . . and food. A sliver of pecan poked out from under a chunk of foul-smelling cheese. He wedged it between his fork prongs. "Do you come here often?"

She nodded and grabbed her glass of yeast-laden orange juice. It looked like frothy vomit and smelled equally revolting. "Most other restaurants load their food with preservatives and toxic chemicals. Here they let me order what I want, how I want it. I always order my food raw." She stabbed a potato with her fork then proceeded to saw off a chunk. "Cooking food kills enzymes, you know."

Jonathan nodded, not because he had any clue what she was talking about, but because he didn't want a biology lesson. He got one anyway.

"Live enzymes help our body digest food. Take steak, for example."

Jonathan would love to—or a burger, or big ol' plate of chicken wings slathered in Buffalo sauce.

"Meats are so hard to digest. Hard on our bodies in a lot of ways. Places like Burger Haven and Hamburger House are nothing but cardiac arrest triggers. With the obesity rate as high as it is, the government really should step in, make those places post warnings or something. Like they did with the cigarette companies." She stopped with her fork in midair. "But we all know the food and pharmaceutical companies are in cahoots." She shook her head. "They're not interested in fighting obesity any more than politicians want to lower spending."

Jonathan cocked an eyebrow and sipped his water. That was one he hadn't heard before. He glanced at Jeanne-Anne and Walter who appeared to be waging war with a fit of giggles. Color seeped up Walter's neck, and tiny veins bulged in his right temple as his twitching lips pressed together. Jeanne-Anne's eyes danced, her mouth also squished shut, the corners tugging upward.

Maggie sipped her frothy beverage, brown foam clinging to her upper lip. "Cancer's a multibillion dollar industry, you know."

She went on to talk about the money pharmaceutical companies made from chemotherapy, how much universities received each year for "research," and why the entire medical system was part of an elaborate conspiracy. Then she transitioned to food companies and how they deliberately contributed to the American obesity rate. "You know, MSG makes people hungry. Of course, all that processed food lining the grocery stores don't help any. Have you ever read the labels on the back of cereal boxes and crackers?"

"Uh . . . can't say I have." He cast his sister a pointed look. Sitting beside her, Walter chuckle-coughed, covering his mouth with a fisted hand.

Maggie flashed a toothy smile. Bits of alfalfa sprouts stuck between her teeth, giving her the appearance of a dairy cow.

"You should always read the ingredients of everything you eat. You'd be surprised the kind of garbage food producers sneak in."

Jeanne-Anne cleared her throat. "Maggie, I told you Jonathan worked on trains, right?"

Maggie frowned. "Yes, and I am sorry to hear it. But I'm sure he can't help all the nasty fumes and pollutants created by diesel engines. After all, everyone needs a job."

The conversation tumbled from there, moving from air pollutants to skin irritants, to why Americans shower too much. According to Maggie, frequent showers only washed the vitamin D off your skin. Jonathan fought against a burst of laughter. Trying to hide it behind a drink, he sent a spray of vitamin-D-stripping water Maggie's way.

She inhaled and jerked back, her face elongating as her mouth and eyes rounded.

"Excuse me." Dabbing at the mess with his napkin, he spoke through his snickers. "I'm sorry to . . . disrupt . . . your . . . vitamin . . . D." At this, Walter and Jeanne-Anne joined him, leaving Maggie to stare between them with pursed lips.

"Well." She blinked twice and grabbed her napkin, which she used to dab her face, no doubt careful not to disturb her vitamin layer.

Jonathan glanced at his watch. "It has been . . . interesting, but I've got this . . . a thing." Strangers in the hotel lobby to stare at? Spam emails to go through? A date with his toenail clippers? And since they paid when they ordered, there was nothing to keep him. He rose, smiled, and waited for Jeanne-Anne and Walter to slide out of their seats.

"That it has." Maggie took one last bite of her potato, topping it off with a parsley sprig. "I'll call you. Perhaps we can meet for tea later this week."

Jonathan and Walter exchanged glances, and Walter looked ready to lose the war, his cheeks bulging and the skin around his eyes crinkling. Everyone said their good-byes and Maggie left, purse draped over her shoulder, arms swinging staunchly at her sides.

When the door chimed closed, Jonathan gave a low whistle. "Beannie, what were you thinking?"

Her mouth twitched, as if fighting a severe case of the giggles. "Apparently she's more eccentric than I realized."

"You think?" He shook his head. "I appreciate your effort, but me and my remote control are doing just fine."

"I hear you." Walter clamped a hand on Jonathan's shoulder.

"These things take time," Jeanne-Anne said. "Give me one more shot. I'll ask for—"

Laughter broke up her words. ". . . dietary information next time."

Jonathan raised his hands. "No more."

"Just one more. I know the perfect woman for you."

"Perfect like old Maggie Moo?"

"No, seriously. Her name's Cayenne."

"Like the pepper?" He rubbed his forehead.

"She's very sweet. Lost her spouse, like you. Works for the city, has her own place and four grandkids. Maybe five, I can't remember. And she cooks a mean steak."

Jonathan stared through the window to the street beyond. Cars streamed past, and pedestrians flowed down the sidewalk, some clutching packages, others strolling hand in hand. At the curb, an old man with a shiny, bald head helped a woman out of the car. After closing the door, he draped one arm over her shoulders and placed the other under her elbow. The two shuffled down the sidewalk. He and Evie always said that would be them: old, hunch-backed, shuffling side by side.

His sister touched his hand. "One more try. I'll do better next time. Promise."

"Why do I have a feeling you'll nag me until I concede?"

"Ah, childhood memories."

"And then you'll leave me alone?"

She nodded.

He sighed. "Fine."

"I CAN'T EAT ANOTHER BITE." Jacqueline pushed her plate forward and leaned back in her chair. She and her daughter sat at a two-person table outside a small Italian café, surrounded by classical music and the rich smell of garlic marinara. A warm breeze stirred, and Jacqueline smiled. For once, she'd gone almost an entire day without a hot flash. Miracle of miracles. Maybe God was working in her favor after all.

Tossing her napkin onto her plate, she glanced at her daughter's half-eaten meal. "You had a light appetite."

Delana sipped her water. "My hips are fat magnets." She set her glass down and plopped her purse onto her lap. As she inspected her reflection in a compact mirror, Jacqueline thought again of the lingerie buried beneath a pile of dirty clothes and her daughter's Friday night departure. But now wasn't the time to ask her about it. Not that "the time" would come, considering the state of their relationship. And yet, Delana was here, and so far, the meal had been relatively pleasant. No arguments, bitter words, or accusations.

Delana snapped her compact shut and dropped it into her purse. "You watch the news today?"

Jacqueline nodded. "Crystal Shores is still flooded, and rescue workers continue to find bodies."

She stirred her straw in her water glass, her heart heavy as she thought about all those who had lost loved ones, and those who were still waiting to hear if their missing family members were among the dead. So much devastation. In truth, she should feel grateful she made it out safe, and that she had a place to stay. But even so, she couldn't help but think of all she herself had lost. Her house—her dream house—back in Crystal Shores. All the time and money she'd put into it, all the memories it contained.

But she was here now, and she planned to make the best of it. And if she and her daughter could rebuild their relationship, it'd all be worth it.

Swallowing, she looked up and forced a smile. "I appreciate you letting me stay."

"No big deal."

"I can't imagine sleeping in a hotel for any length of time. Or in a shelter." She folded her napkin and ran her fingernail along the edge. "You know, the church I went to today is hosting storm victims in their basement."

"Really?" Delana's glassy-eyed gaze drifted to another table.

"I'm thinking of volunteering. It'd give me something to do while you're at work."

"Uh-huh. That's a good idea."

"The message today really hit me. It was about living a life of purpose."

She picked at a fingernail. "Interesting."

"So, how is work going?"

"Good. Cleaning teeth, scraping tarter. You know."

"You still thinking of going back to school?"

Delana shrugged. "Maybe in the future."

"Yeah. What would you major in?"

She studied Jacqueline for a moment, rubbing her index knuckle against her chin. "Fashion design."

"Really? That's wonderful." Jacqueline smiled. "I can see you doing that."

This appeared to zap the tension from the conversation, and by the time the waiter brought the check, they had even shared a few snippets of laughter.

After paying, Jacqueline stood and observed the boutiques and flower shops lining the street. "You up for an afternoon of window shopping?"

Delana checked her phone.

Conversation drifted from the adjacent tables. A horn beeped, and a family of four strolled past, the youngest pausing to glance at a plate of nachos.

Jacqueline shifted and shoved her hands in her pockets. It wasn't like she was asking her daughter to give up a kidney. But ice often melted slowly.

Delana glanced at her watch and shrugged. "Sure. Why not? I've got nothing better to do anyway."

Leaving the café, they strolled along Fawn Street past an old man cleaning a convenience store window, a couple sitting on a park bench eating a soft pretzel, and a used bookstore. The rich aroma of roasted pork drifted from a corner pub, bringing with it the twang of a banjo. When Jacqueline paused to decipher the nasally lyrics, a handmade sign taped in the adjacent store window caught her eye.

Boutique for sale.

Inquire within.

She moved closer, studying first the sign, then the hodgepodge store behind it. Strands of beads hung in the window and along the orange walls. Vibrant wraps and scarves, some depicting ocean scenes, others marbleized splotches of color, hung from mannequins and wall displays. Sequined flip-flops adorned the far wall, and racks of costume jewelry filled the center. Eclectic figurines and other knickknacks cluttered metal tables, and books lined two shelves flanking the counter.

"I wonder how much something like that costs." More than she had in the bank, but surely she had a sizeable insurance check coming. If her agent would ever get around to returning her call.

Delana shrugged.

"I'll be right back." Jacqueline dashed inside and headed toward a woman with long, wavy hair that draped her shoulders. She wore a smock tent dress and thick bands of gold around her neck.

"Good afternoon." The clerk grinned. A long black whisker poked from a mole below her left nostril. "Can I help you find anything?"

"Yes, ma'am. I saw the sign in the window. Are you the store owner?"

"Nope. That'd be Sky Rainbows."

Jacqueline clamped her mouth shut as a giggle bubbled in her throat. Sky Rainbows? Add a few Stars, Raindrops, and Sunshines and they'd have a regular hippie fest. The moment her thought concluded, she felt a twinge in her heart as she realized how judgmental her reaction had been. And just that morning she'd asked God to help her view others through His eyes. Through a lens of love. *Sorry, Lord. Please help me do better.*

She offered a more genuine smile. "Can I speak with her?"

"She's not in today. Would you like to leave your number?"

"Yes, please."

The woman nodded and sashayed to a counter covered in candles, incense sticks, and various chocolates. Feather dream catchers and glass wind chimes decorated the wall behind her. She handed Jacqueline a slip of paper and a pen.

She scrawled her number and handed it over. "Thanks."

The woman offered a business card in return.

Outside, Delana waited with crossed arms. "What was that about?"

Jacqueline glanced at the for-sale sign again. "I feel like I'm at a crossroads."

"Meaning?"

"Meaning, it's time for a change."

"Like buy-a-boutique kind of change?"

"Maybe. To be honest, I don't really know, but what I do know is I'm done with the real estate business." She turned away from the store and started to stroll down the sidewalk, assuming her daughter followed.

"Oh, no."

She spun around at the edge in her daughter's voice.

"Do not tell me you're thinking of relocating to Willow Valley."

"Why not? Besides, I can't afford to go anywhere else."

"Contact one of those head hunters. See if you can't find a new employer, one that'll pay your moving fees. I have a friend who could help you. Want me to call him?"

"Wow."

"I'm not trying to sound harsh, but we'd drive each other crazy. You know that. I mean I love you and everything . . ."

Did she? It'd been decades since Delana had said as much, not that Jacqueline blamed her, considering their history.

But her daughter just needed time. Today had been a good start. They'd actually shared an entire meal with minimal sparks. That meant something, right?

CHAPTER 9

JACQUELINE SMOOTHED HER blouse then entered the large, carpeted church office. Soft music drifted from speakers mounted in the corners, and the faint scent of hazelnut filled the room.

A thin woman with short, black hair sat behind a mahogany desk decorated with family photos. "May I help you?"

Jacqueline glanced at the clock on the wall. "I'm here to see Irene, but I'm early."

"Have a seat." The woman motioned toward two leather armchairs to her right. "I'll let her know you're here."

Jacqueline obliged and picked up a magazine. On the cover a woman with dark skin and soft, delicate features cradled what appeared to be a sick child. Other children ranging from toddler to teenagers gathered behind her, clothes ragged and dirtied, eyes wide. The caption read, *Missionaries bring much-needed medical care to orphans in war-ravished Sierra Leone.*

Jacqueline frowned, thinking of the children in the picture, the kids she'd met in the church hallway, and the countless others like them. *So much pain, Lord. So many in need. Please show me what I can do.*

She started to turn to the article when her phone rang. Glancing at the screen, she smiled. "Elaine!" Standing, she checked the time again—she still had another ten minutes before her meeting—and moved out into the church foyer. "So you finally decide to return my calls, huh?"

Elaine laughed. "Sorry. Chasing a bunch of sugar-infested kids around wears a body out."

"Uh-huh. And where are they getting the sugar?"

"You sound like their parents."

"Well, someone has to be the adult in this relationship."

Leaning against a glass wall, she failed to contain her grin. She really missed their silly banter. Missed Elaine, period. "So, how are the grandkids anyway? Besides near comatose from junk food?"

"Adorable as ever. How about you? Any major catastrophes to report?"

"One hurricane is enough, thank you." She paused. "But on the relational front, things may be looking up." She told Elaine about her lunch date with Delana. "I'm hopeful our outing was the first of many."

"That's wonderful. I've been praying for you. For both of you."

"Thanks, Elaine. You're a great friend." She breathed deep, running a hand along her forearm. "Hey, do you remember the time we went to Le Claire, Iowa?"

"To see the that antique-hunting television show. Absolutely! What a wonderful trip that was. I'd really like to go back, spend more time looking through the boutiques. When things settle down, of course." She sighed. "You know, I really should've bought that pendant. The jade frog with sapphire eyes."

"To go with the ginormous turtle broach and lizard earrings. I agree. Why stop at one amphibian when you can have them all?"

"Lizards are reptiles. So are turtles."

"Whatever." Jacqueline glanced back at the church office. The secretary was on the phone and Irene still hadn't emerged. "Remember how I talked about one day owning my own boutique?"

"Right! So you could give me all the free jewelry I wanted." The laughter in Elaine's voice warmed Jacqueline's heart, made her wish they were back in Crystal Shores sipping coffee at their Miss Nora's café.

"What would you think if I actually did that—bought a boutique, I mean?"

An extended pause followed. "Why, what's up?"

She told her about the for sale sign she'd seen downtown.

"So, you're planning on staying in Willow Valley for good, then?"

She let out a slow breath. "Maybe. For Delana."

"You don't want to sell houses anymore?"

"I could. I still have my license, but . . . I don't know. I guess I feel like maybe this is my second chance, you know? With Delana, with my career, my life—everything."

"You prayed about it?"

Jacqueline smiled. Sweet Elaine, always the voice of wisdom. "I'll do that." She glanced up to see a petite blonde talking with the secretary. Irene? "Listen, I gotta go."

"Love you, friend."

"You too." Oh, how she missed that woman! Slipping her phone into her purse, she straightened her spine and returned to the church office.

The blonde glanced up as she entered. "Jacqueline?" Dressed in white capri pants and a floral blouse, she approached.

"Yes. Hello." Jacqueline accepted the woman's out-stretched hand.

"Good morning. I'm Irene, and I'm in charge of the shelter. Come with me, and we'll get your paperwork filled out. A pain, I know, but a requirement for all church volunteers."

Jacqueline followed the woman into a small office painted lilac and adorned with verses and inspirational posters. She sat in one of two chairs positioned in front of the simple oak desk. "Does it matter that I'm not a member?"

"At this point, we'll take all the help we can get." Irene laughed, taking a seat behind the computer. "As you can imagine, we're not prepared to deal with a catastrophe such as this. In fact, our 'shelter' is nothing of the sort. Until recently, it was our multipurpose room. But we're doing the best we can with what God has placed before us, trusting Him to take care of the rest." She pulled documents from a file cabinet and handed them over. "You can fill these out at home and bring them back."

Jacqueline scanned the papers. "Thank you."

Irene folded her hands on her desk. "Currently, our volunteer list is sporadic, but I'd really like to see some stability and long-term commitment. Relationship building, that sort of thing. Now, how about I show you the shelter area and introduce you to some of our volunteers?"

Jacqueline stood with a nod. "That sounds great, thank you."

Irene led the way downstairs and through the hall. They ended at a storage area filled with food boxes, tubs of baby formula, and other items.

"Everything in here has been donated by community members. Without them, I don't know what we'd do, except perhaps pray for a loaves-and-fishes miracle." She glanced about, her eyes softening. "Let me show you where we're housing the storm refugees."

They continued into a large room packed with cots and people of all ages and ethnicities. Stuffed duffel bags filled the corners, others protruded from beneath the cots. A foam football with a jagged chunk torn off its end lay on the floor beside a pair of orange-and-green flip-flops.

The stench of stale urine mixed with body odor stung Jacqueline's nose. She shivered, scanning the many hollowed faces and slumped shoulders around her. If not for Delana and her meager savings, she would be one of them, sleeping on stretched canvas, surrounded by strangers, dependent on people like Irene for her next meal.

Blessed to be a blessing, wasn't that what her old pastor always said? Never a moment, a tear, or a hurricane wasted. A dull ache filled her heart as she watched an old woman with sagging skin and a caved mouth struggle to her feet.

Lord, show me what You want from me. Why You brought me here, through this storm and to this town filled with broken people.

She glanced from Irene with her pressed outfit and manicured nails to the handful of church volunteers scattered throughout the room. They stuck out like china at a hillbilly picnic. Most of them probably knew the Bible by heart, their worst sins being the occasional gossip or rush to judgment.

Here she was, a newbie believer, and already thinking she could serve. That God would want to use her. But these people . . .

Observing a young mother standing a few feet away holding an infant and gently swaying, tears sprang to Jacqueline's eyes. Ill-equipped or not, she couldn't walk away.

"It breaks your heart, doesn't it?"

She glanced over to find Irene watching her with a soft smile. "Yes, it does."

A woman with short brown hair feathered around her face approached. "Irene?" She wore a striped blazer buttoned over a coral blouse and tan slacks. A string of pearls adorned her neck.

"Hello, Kathleen," Irene said. "Do you need something?"

"Yes, ma'am. The manager from Food Bargain is on the phone. Would you like me to take a message?"

Irene's smile widened. "Oh, good! I'm coming." She turned to Jacqueline. "I hate to do this, but can you excuse me for ten minutes? This is an important call, potentially worth a great deal of baked cheese crackers."

"Certainly. I'll just . . ." Jacqueline looked for a place to sit. Mounds of bedding and luggage occupied nearly every square inch. "Wait right here."

Irene left with a nod. She and the other woman scurried along the room's perimeter like a pair of children chasing the neighborhood ice-cream man.

At the sound of soft chatter, Jacqueline glanced behind her to find the young girl she'd met in the church hall the day before. She sat in the corner playing with a one-armed doll with matted hair. The girl's brother sat beside her, manning an infant, a book spread before him. The baby, who looked to be nine or ten months, sat with her legs spread in a V, anchored by a round, pudgy belly. She chewed on a set of plastic keys.

Jacqueline closed the distance between them and plopped down onto the floor. "Such a beautiful little girl." She ran her hand over the baby's soft head. "How old is she?"

The boy looked up with a slight frown. "Eleven months."

Jacqueline tickled the baby under the chin, eliciting a high-pitched squeal. "And happy-almost-birthday to you, little one."

She glanced at the comic book opened on the floor. "Is that *Valiant Vayan* and the *Inter-Galactic Invaders*?"

The boy nodded, his frown smoothing into a faint smile.

"My cousin collected the entire series. I can't believe those things are still around." She flipped to the cover, noting the date printed on the top right hand corner. "Wow, is this an original?"

The boy shrugged, the corners of his mouth twitching as if fighting a full-fledged grin.

"Where'd you get this?"

"My English teacher. For my birthday last year."

"That's quite a present. You must be a good student."

His gaze fell, and his shoulders settled back into their slump.

"What's your name?"

"Gavin."

"And who's this beautiful princess sitting beside you?" She turned to the girl who had abandoned the doll to inch closer. "What's your name, sweetie?"

"Adele." Her voice barely rose above a whisper, and her green eyes never quite met Jacqueline's.

"I'm Jacqueline. I'm going to be hanging out here from now on, and I could really use a friend."

Adele's eyes widened, and a smile bunched her cheeks.

Jacqueline suppressed a giggle and turned the conversation back to comic books and superheroes. By the time Irene returned, Gavin's grin broke loose and Adele had turned chatty.

"Sorry about the disruption." Irene smiled, first at the children then at Jacqueline. "Where were we?" With hands on hips, she glanced around. "Oh, let me show you the kitchen."

When Jacqueline stood to leave, the children's faces fell, and they hunched forward once again as if about to lose their best friend. Perhaps, their only friend. Their broken faces mirrored the one Jacqueline's daughter displayed twenty-five years ago when Jacqueline sent her to live with her dad. She couldn't change the past, but she could make better choices now. Grace and love-filled choices.

Squatting, she touched Adele under her chin. "I'll see you later? If not today, then tomorrow."

GAVIN WATCHED JACQUELINE leave, thinking of Mrs. Rust and all the other adults at school who looked him in the eye and treated him like he was worth something. Not all adults stunk. But she wouldn't stick around. The nice ones never did.

He rolled up his comic book and tucked it back into the inner pocket of his duffel bag next to two old birthday cards. One was from Mrs. Rust, given to him when he turned thirteen. The other was from Mr. Axhelm, the man who owned the corner store Gavin and his sister passed each morning on the way to school.

Most likely the store was gone, its beams splintered and buried in muddy floodwater. And what about Mrs. Rust? Would he ever see her again? Probably not. He gave a shuddered sigh and searched the shelter for Mom. She sat on a cot halfway across the room, her back to him, surrounded by men. Always surrounded by men.

"Hey."

He glanced up to see the girl he'd met in the shower line standing in front of him holding a deck of cards. She'd pulled her chestnut hair back in glittery barrettes. Thick lashes framed almond eyes. "Want to play?"

He shrugged. "Guess so." Although he'd never enjoyed card playing, he needed a friend, even if it was a girl.

"My name's Ami. What's yours?"

"Gavin."

Ami sat cross-legged in front of him. Baby Jaya clawed at his arm, trying to stand. Or climb over him, which would keep her occupied for a while.

Holding Jaya by the waist, he scooted back and moved his duffel bag to his side to make room for their card game.

"Where you from?" Ami brushed a stray lock of hair off her forehead.

"Crystal Shores. You?"

"Thirty minutes from Galveston." She spread the cards face down on the ground and stirred them with her hand. "I don't know how to shuffle. Is this OK?"

"Don't matter to me."

Baby Jaya fell on her rear. She started to crawl away but Gavin grabbed her around her middle. He plunked her back on her bottom and wiggled her toy keys in front of her. She squealed, grabbed hold of them, and shoved them in her mouth.

After a thorough stir, Ami gathered the cards and started to deal them, then paused, looking at Adele. "You want to play?"

Adele nodded and, clutching her doll, wiggled over until the three of them formed a circle that doubled as a baby-barricade.

When Jaya started reaching for the cards, Ami giggled. "Maybe this isn't such a good idea." She leaned forward and tickled Jaya's feet.

Jaya shrieked and kicked, then shrieked again. Then she swiveled her torso and grabbed hold of Gavin's shoulder, struggling to her feet. He pried her off and set her back on her rear. She shot forward, crawling toward the aisle framing the sleeping area. After reeling her in for the third time, only to have her wiggle from his grasp, Gavin gave up.

"I better take her for a walk." Holding her hands in his, he helped her to her chubby feet.

Ami sprang up. "I'll come."

"OK." Back bent and pointer fingers strangled in tiny hands, he glanced at Adele. "You coming?"

She shook her head and returned to her doll, one of three toys packed in her sequined purse. All she'd had time to grab before they left their apartment. Luckily, Gavin snatched up a pile of dirty clothes lying in her room.

Jaya bounced on her toes, tugging forward. Gavin followed her jerky lead as she swayed and tottered across the floor.

"Can I help?" Ami touched one of Jaya's hands.

He nodded and released his grip, now able to stand a bit straighter.

Ami glanced around. "How long do you think it'll be before we can go back home?"

He shrugged. What home? According to what he saw on the news, all that remained of Crystal Shores was a mess of flood-waters, uprooted trees, shattered glass, and destroyed buildings.

Pattering feet followed, and soon, Adele fell into step beside them, staring about her with a wrinkled brow.

Gavin stopped. "Everything OK?"

She sucked in air, clutching her doll with both hands. "Some man started talking to me, asking me where my momma was."

Muscles tight, Gavin craned his neck to see behind him. He made a visual sweep of the area. A large number of men—tall, short, hairy, bald—crowded the room, some standing, others sprawled across their cots or sitting with their backs pressed against the concrete wall. "Who?"

Adele followed his gaze then shrugged. "I don't know who he was."

"Stay with me, then."

Ami looked at Gavin. "Your daddy here?"

"No."

"Mine neither. They haven't found him. Least, I don't think they have. Not sure if I'd know if they did, with all those people they're pulling out from under collapsed buildings and floating in the river and all." She blinked as moisture pooled behind her lashes.

He wanted to comfort her, but didn't know how. "I'm sorry."

"It's OK."

"We don't got a daddy." With crossed arms, Adele cocked her head and lifted her chin, a comical imitation of their mother.

"I'm sorry." Ami's face softened, her obvious pity raising Gavin's temperature.

He huffed. "Yeah, well, I'm not. What do I need someone else nagging on me, telling me what to do all the time for anyway? I got my momma for that."

But later that night, as he lay upon his mat watching baby Jaya's chest rise and fall, he thought about Ami and her daddy and wondered what it'd be like to have one. Not the mean, nasty men his mother brought home, but the good kind he saw on TV. Except men like that didn't exist. Least, not for a kid like him.

CHAPTER 10

JONATHAN DROPPED HIS cell phone onto his desk and rubbed his face. Maybe it was time he invested in a sleep aid. Between his trilling cell phone and a couple fighting in the adjacent hotel room, he'd slept maybe a total of four hours last night. To make things worse, the local chairman called first thing to line up a meeting. Based on the edge in the guy's voice, the unions were stirred up again. And Jonathan had only been on this job one week.

He sifted through the reports on his desk. Their in-shop engine number continued to climb as the railroad sent more road failures their way. He called the clerk to find this Tollhouse guy, whom he still hadn't located.

"Yes, sir?"

"Morning. This is Jonathan Cohen. Who's this?"

"Barbara Lotus."

"Hey, Barbara. Have you seen Tollhouse?"

"Who, sir?"

"Tollhouse. A machinist working second shift last week."

Dead air. When she spoke again, her voice sounded strained. "He doesn't work here anymore, sir."

He rubbed his temples. Great. Now he had to track the guy down. "That was quick. What'd he do?"

"I'm not sure. If I remember correctly, I think he retired."

"I don't remember a retirement party."

"It was two years ago."

"That doesn't make sense."

Another extended silence.

"Thanks, Barb. I have all I need."

He'd never been a conspiracy theorist, but things were getting pretty weird. And yet, a company this big? No, there had to be an explanation. A typo or something.

This job was going to steal his sanity. But he had to at least finish out his probationary year—fifty-one weeks left to fulfill the terms of his contract. Then he could quit without getting sued.

Except he'd never been a quitter.

He swiveled to his computer. Moving to the service archives, he clicked through each train unit number—a month's worth—one by one. He read the work done and jotted down the name of the man who signed off on it. Now to call the planner to check on a unit shopped for routine maintenance.

He tucked the sheet in his briefcase for future examination and picked up his office phone. "Hey, Arnold, this is Cohen. I'm calling about unit number 3985. They need it down in Barnhart. When's it going to be ready?"

"Tai's looking at it now."

"What other engines do you have coming?"

He made notes as Arnold relayed all the units coming into the shop for repairs and inspections. His pulse climbed with the number. Already they were fifteen over goal. "How many do you think you'll release?"

"Hey." Darren poked his head through the door. "I need to talk to you."

Jonathan nodded and raised a finger, listening to Arnold complain about being short a machinist.

Darren's frown deepened as he crossed to Jonathan's desk, a large vein in his neck pulsating.

Jonathan cleared his throat. "Listen, Arnold, I'll call you back. And see if you can't get me contact information for Tollhouse." He hung up and propped his elbows on his desk, keeping his face smooth while heat seeped up the back of his neck. "What can I do for you, boss?"

"Don't place any more units."

"What're you talking about?"

"It's simple English. Leave 'em in the yard. Don't place 'em."

That meant fudging the numbers. "We can't do that. It's not right."

"That's where you're wrong, Cohen. It's exactly the right thing to do." He crossed his arms. "Headquarters is breathing down my neck, and the union's threatening to strike." His hot breath carried the stench of stale coffee and onions. "You want to explain to our crew why they're out of a job when the shop goes under?"

Jonathan exhaled. Surely it wouldn't come to that, but even so, it didn't matter. "We gotta be honest and work our way through this."

Darren gave a cynical laugh. "You think you know better than me how to run the railroad?"

Jonathan looked away to keep from blurting something that could quite likely get him fired. A moment later, heavy footsteps clomped out and down the hall.

What a jerk.

Jonathan let his head fall against the seatback. He raked his hands through his hair, thinking of his signed contract, his retirement plans, his dream home, and Bart's warning on the day he packed up his old office.

Had he made a mistake in taking this job?

Fifty-one weeks—357 days, 8,568 hours. He glanced at the clock, fighting against a brain-numbing headache. Make that 8,564 and counting.

AS SHE DROVE THROUGH TOWN, Jacqueline tried to focus on the words drifting through her radio speakers rather than the ever-tightening knot growing in her stomach. No matter how busy she attempted to be, she kept thinking about her home back in Crystal Shores—whatever remained of it. Visions of items left behind—the quilt her grandmother had made, back when she was alive; the family photos lining the upstairs hall; that goofy coffee cup Delana had painted in elementary school.

How much had been lost? If the images she saw on television were any indication, a lot. Maybe everything.

Though tears threatened, she refused to give in to them. It was time she focused on the positives, like the opportunity God had provided for her to reconnect with her daughter. That was worth a lot more than a picture or mug.

Inhaling, she lifted her cinnamon dolce frozen cappuccino tucked in her console cupholder, breathing in its soothing aroma.

Thank You, Lord. Thank You for showing me every storm truly does have a silver lining.

As she neared L and North Fifteenth Street, her gaze shooting from her rearview mirror to the now empty crosswalk in front of her. Her phone chimed as she eased forward, and she glanced at the screen. She didn't recognize the number, but it was local.

"Hello?"

"Good morning, this is Sky Rainbows from the Silver Sky Boutique."

"Yes, ma'am. Hello." She turned down an alley and idled. "I stopped in to inquire about the sale of your store. Is there a time I can talk with you?"

"I'm available now. Would that work?"

"Certainly! I'll be there in . . ." She surveyed her surroundings, mentally retracing her steps. "Fifteen minutes or so."

"Perfect."

She hung up before thinking to ask for an address. Oh, well. That's why she'd purchased a smartphone. After a quick Internet search, she found the boutique and followed the directions presented by her maps app. Ten minutes later, she strolled into the store with her head held high and a professional smile in place.

A musky aroma tinged with jasmine assaulted her, stealing her breath. She crossed the boutique to where a woman stood lighting display candles. Raising the match, she moved with a swaying rhythm, as if performing an ancient rite, long dreadlocks reaching to the center of her back.

Jacqueline cleared her throat, feeling as if she had stumbled upon a private moment.

The woman turned and offered a smile, revealing a smudge of plum lipstick on her front teeth. "You must be Jacqueline." An orange shawl edged with red and purple tassels draped across her shoulders. She extended a hand, large stone rings glimmering in the florescent lighting. "I'm Sky Rainbows." Grabbing Jacqueline's other hand, she closed her eyes, leaned forward, and inhaled. "You have great energy!"

"Thanks . . . I think."

"Would you like a tour?"

"More than likely, yes, although we should probably talk price first."

"Of course. Follow me." After turning her shop sign to closed, the woman led Jacqueline through a beaded curtain to a small room. A laptop rested on a lace-covered table.

Sky settled into a wooden chair and motioned for Jacqueline to sit across from her. "Never saw the need for formal office furniture." She handed Jacqueline a stack of stapled paper. "You looking to lease-to-own or buy outright? Because I'm flexible."

"Uh . . ." Jacqueline glanced at the store brochure. Four images were printed on the top sheet. "How about I take one of these with me?"

The woman shrugged. "Be my guest. But you should know, I plan to sell fast. Getting too old to be running a business, know what I mean?" She pushed up from the table with a grimace, flashing long, painted nails. "My health is not as it should be."

Jacqueline nodded, noting the price printed on her sheet. It'd help if she knew how much insurance money she'd be getting.

"Come." Sky motioned toward the doorway. "I'll show you the upstairs apartment."

The woman led her down the hall to a narrow flight of stairs leading into an eclectic living room. As they moved from the small kitchen and into the master bedroom painted a pale blue with candles dotting every surface, the place suddenly became more appealing. The apartment needed work, and a bit of redesigning, but it was spacious. Conveniently located.

Two more rooms flanked the end of the hallway: one painted butter yellow, the other a pale green. Both filled with boxes. She could turn one into a guest room and the other into a home office. No more traffic, no more finicky clients with upturned noses. Most importantly, no more hurricanes. Yes, this would do nicely. Although cobwebs clung to the corners and a layer of dust covered the windows, a heavy cleaning and a few cans of paint, and this place would be perfect.

She'd call her insurance company tomorrow.

After a thorough tour, Sky led her back to the shop entrance. "My number is on the front page of the flyer. And the price is negotiable."

"Thank you. I'll get back to you."

She considered calling Delana then thought better of it, adding another request to her prayer list—namely that God would soften her daughter's heart. She needed to prove to Delana she was here for the long haul. Buying property was a great first step. Jacqueline wouldn't allow their bitter past to get in their way. No. She'd walked away from her daughter once. Not again.

CHAPTER 11

GAVIN SAT IN A CORNER with one eye on baby Jaya and the other trained on the hall leading to the church sanctuary. Another toddler sat to his left. The child's mother, a thin woman with frizzy hair, occupied a cot behind them, talking on the phone. Adele and Ami sandwiched him, the former playing with miniature dolls provided by one of the church ladies. He didn't know where Mom and Stella were.

Would Jacqueline come today?

Ami snapped her magazine closed and tossed it onto a pile of books. "Who you looking for?"

Gavin turned toward her. "What do you mean?"

"You keep staring at the hall like you're expecting someone."

He shrugged, not willing to admit he waited anxiously for a total stranger, one who probably wouldn't even remember his name. All because she had looked him in the eye. Spoke to him like maybe he was somebody. But it was almost 2 p.m. She wasn't coming. Most likely she'd found something better to do than hang out in a nasty-smelling shelter.

Someone whistled. Gavin turned to see a gray-haired man dressed in slacks standing beside Irene. He held a clipboard.

The room stilled, minus the whining of a few children.

"As many of you well know, our gym reached maximum capacity some time ago. In an effort to reduce some of the chaos, we will be assigning daily chores in exchange for a bed and food."

People moaned, complained, and shouted out protests. Baby Jaya squirmed in Gavin's arms, whimpering on the verge of a wail. He searched for her pacifier, found it on the ground, and popped it into her mouth. She spit it out and scrunched her face.

Mom appeared out of nowhere. "Uh-uh. I am not cleaning up anybody else's nasty old mess. No way."

A bony man with a scruffy beard glanced over his shoulder at her. "So you'd rather make someone else clean up after you, is that it?"

"Was I talking to you?" Mom's face hardened. Fire radiated from her eyes while curses flew from her mouth.

Gavin tuned her out and focused again on the man with the clipboard.

"We are also going to be starting morning devotions, hopefully next week."

More groans and swearing. A few snide jokes, quickly silenced by the man's booming voice.

"Of course, if you don't like our rules, you're welcome to leave at any time." He made a slow, visual sweep of the area. "Breakfast will be served as normal, followed by devotions. We are still working out the arrangements, but we'd like to split everyone into groups. So you can form relationships, discuss the Bible passage. After prayer, Irene will assign chores."

A large woman sprang to her feet and shot her arm in the air. "What if we gotta work? I got me a job starting Monday."

"That's wonderful." The man smiled. "Come talk with me, and we'll find a schedule that works for you. Which leads me to my next topic. I know many of you have suffered extreme losses, not just of homes, but of jobs as well. We want to help. Starting next week, a group from our financial counseling department will be available for one-on-one consultations. They'll help you create or update your resume, brainstorm potential career options, and determine a logical course of action."

Voices rose once again, praises merged with complaints and sarcasm. Gavin's mom joined the latter. "Right. Everyone's going to be fighting to hire a bunch of poor, homeless storm victims. Get real." She snorted. "Show me to the local welfare office, so I can get me my check and food stamps."

Baby Jaya started to fuss again, kicking her feet and reaching forward in an effort to break free from Gavin's grasp. With a sigh, he rummaged through his duffel bag, finding a small, bean-filled softball, the kind given in party favor bags. He handed it over. She shoved the thing into her mouth, drool dripping down her chin and onto Gavin's arm. Her peaceful chatter lasted all of one minute before she started writhing, trying to break free once again.

Planting his feet on the ground, he stood her between his legs and placed her plump hands on his thighs. She bounced and cooed. Laughing, he leaned forward and kissed her forehead. He glanced at Mom, wishing she'd care, like moms were supposed to. But it didn't matter. As long as they had each other, they'd be OK.

When the man concluded, voices grew louder as everyone returned to their usual places. Younger men moved to the far corner. Their coarse laughter carried across the gym. The older men, five or six in all, gathered around a bunch of chairs next to the coffee pots. As usual, someone placed a pile of toys on blankets spread in the eastern corner, and already women and children gathered around them.

Standing in front of Gavin, baby Jaya stilled, her face pinched and turning a deep shade of red. The stench followed.

Mom flicked his arm with a wrinkled nose. "Change your sister. She stinks."

"Yes, ma'am." No sense arguing, not unless he wanted to set Mom off. One of these times, she'd blow it and get them kicked out. What would they do then? His stomach soured and he shook the thought aside. So many what-ifs. Just once Gavin wanted something he could count on, something he could know for certain. Something good.

Grabbing baby Jaya under the arms, he whisked her up and laid her on the cot. He pressed his nose against the fat folds in her neck and pushed air through his lips. She squealed with laughter, feet kicking.

"Oh, no you don't."

He turned to find Mom glaring at him.

"Take her out in the hall."

With a nod, mouth shut, Gavin obeyed. He carried Jaya around cots and people to the hallway leading to the church's main level, an area that was quickly becoming his favorite hangout. Adele followed and knelt beside him. She clutched her doll in one hand, crayons and a coloring page given to her by one of the church ladies in the other.

After changing baby Jaya, Gavin let her crawl around, trailing close behind. He turned her around when she reached the wall. She was so close to walking, trying to pull up on everything from walls to legs and shoulders. Probably would be before they left this place.

Footsteps tapped, and a shadow fell over them. He glanced up to see Jacqueline's bright-eyed smile. She held a paper sack.

"What a cutie!" She squatted down beside them and pulled a package of glittery stickers and a shiny new comic book from her bag. She handed the former to Adele and the latter to Gavin. "You read this one?"

Shifting to act as a barricade for Jaya, Gavin studied the cover and shook his head. *The Comic Book Bible.* Beams of light spread from the lettering. An image of Jesus filled the cover. Gavin recognized the white robe, thick beard, and long wavy hair from pamphlets distributed on street corners back in Crystal Shores.

Jacqueline sat beside him, adding to the baby barricade and closing the distance between his left foot and the far wall.

She spread the comic book in front of them. "I saw this at the local Christian bookstore and immediately thought of you."

Although Gavin tried to act cool, a smile tugged at his lips.

As the woman opened the book, Adele inched closer and sifted through the pages, skimmed the text bubbles. She asked about a hundred questions.

Jacqueline smiled. "I'm kinda new to this Christianity thing." She snatched up baby Jaya, wrapping her in a hug. "But I'm learning." Jaya squealed and squirmed. Jacqueline tickled her beneath the chin before setting her back on all fours. She turned back to Gavin. "Maybe we could learn together."

He studied her soft smile and warm eyes then shrugged.

They flipped more pages, and Jacqueline began to read the stories to Adele while Gavin alternated between rerouting baby Jaya and peering at the page.

After two stories—one of a man named Noah, the other of a tower reaching to the sky—Jacqueline looked at her watch. "Guess I better check in with Irene. See if she needs any help." She ruffled Adele's hair and stood, leaving the comic Bible on the ground.

Gavin grabbed it and jumped to his feet. "You forgot your book."

She grinned. "It's yours."

Standing in the hallway, book clutched in his hand, he stared after her. When she disappeared around the corner, he turned to Adele. "We should probably head back, too."

He grabbed Jaya, calmer after her moment of freedom, while Adele gathered her things.

At their cots, Mom flirted with a couple guys. One had wavy blond hair cut short at the sides, longer on top. The other looked like he'd stepped out of an old *Rolling Stones* cover, with crunchy hair and small gold hoops poked through his nose and bottom lip.

Gavin placed Jaya on the cot beside him. He focused on his new comic book, trying to ignore the conversation in front of him. Mom used her too-sweet voice, giggling over stupid jokes. No, not giggling. Her fake laugh sounded more like a strained hyena.

"I've had enough of this place." *Rolling Stones* dude shoved his hands into his pockets and tongued his lip ring. "What do ya say we get out of here? Snag a brew or something."

Gavin's jaw clenched. *Say no!*

He watched Mom's raised eyebrows and cocked head. Nothing good came from conversations like this. Nothing good at all.

Mom pushed her chest out and twirled a lock of hair around her finger. "You got money?"

The guy gave a crooked smile. "Girl, I know how to get mine." His buddy laughed and the two slapped high fives. "You coming or what?"

With a glance at baby Jaya, Mom shrugged. "Sure beats sitting in this nasty place all day listening to a bunch of whiners." She stood and nudged Gavin's arm. "Take care of your sisters."

Gavin watched her leave, the pit in his stomach deepening as questions flooded his mind. When would she back? Where was she going? What if those guys were crazy, like—

He shuddered, remembering one of her previous boyfriends.

Lifting his chin, he offered Adele what he hoped was a calming smile and motioned her over. "Want to hear more stories?" She nodded and wiggled next to him.

The two spent the rest of the afternoon reading and watching baby Jaya. Each time Gavin turned the page, he stared at the shelter door, hoping to see Mom, wondering what the church people would do if she came in too late or returned drunk.

What if Mom got them kicked out? Or worse, shacked up with another Ace?

WHILE IRENE EXPLAINED the new shelter procedures, including devotional "small groups," which would begin on Monday, Jacqueline watched Gavin and his sister slumped on their cots. The way both children watched the shelter door broke her heart. Who were they waiting for? And where was their mother?

She turned back to Irene, catching the tail end of a question. "I'm sorry, can you repeat that?" She really needed to pay closer attention.

"I wondered if you'd feel comfortable leading one of the Bible studies."

"I, uh . . ."

She felt the blood drain from her face and pool in her clenched stomach.

"We'll divide the room up based on cot positions." Irene bit her bottom lip and surveyed the refugees spread throughout the room. "Although I wish there was a way to group people by age and interest levels. Families, singles, teens, that sort of thing. In fact, that's what we should do. These women could really use a godly role model."

Clearly Irene had no idea who she was talking to. "I, uh . . . I'm not all that knowledgeable about Bible stuff."

Irene gave Jacqueline a sideways squeeze. "I'm sure you'll do great."

Ruckus exploded from the hallway, and a moment later, two volunteers ran toward them with wide eyes and pale complexions. When they reached Irene, the older of the two, a woman with silver hair pulled into a French twist, spoke between gasps. "Eugene is back, and he's off his meds."

A voice broke through the chaos, growing louder, frantic, almost shrieking. A crowd of shelter residents gathered near the hall, craning necks, peering, chattering.

Irene's lips compressed. Deep lines edged between her brows as the clamor continued. "Call Ron and ask him to send a deacon. Quickly." She turned back to Jacqueline. "I must attend to this, but I'll have the church secretary send your devotional materials to you by mail."

"Thank you." Jacqueline offered a weak smile while watching a resident with twice the patience she'd ever had rock a toddler to sleep.

Her, lead a Bible study? She was the last person these women needed as a role model. Her current relationship with Delana proved it.

CHAPTER 12

JONATHAN PARKED OUTSIDE a brick ranch house covered in ivy and cut the engine. This was ridiculous. Pathetic. Why did he let his sister talk him into these things?

His cell phone rang, and he checked the number. Speaking of the matchmaker. "Hey, Beannie." Probably calling to make sure he didn't back out at the last minute. Not that he hadn't considered it on more than one occasion. Now being one of them. "You can relax. I'm here."

"Oh, great! Are you taking her to the riverfront? It's so beautiful this time of night with the setting sun glimmering on the water."

"It may have been a while"—like, more than decades—"but I still know how to date a lady."

I think.

"Just trying to be helpful."

And she was, although Jonathan would never admit it. With Evie, their friendship had morphed into romance naturally. There'd been no awkward first dates. No, "Should I kiss her on the mouth or the cheek?" Merely a seamless progression from best of friends to soul mates. And although Jonathan longed for a close companion, he'd never find another Evie.

Especially if he didn't get out of his car.

A bundle of chrysanthemums lay across the passenger seat, their petals smashed, thanks to a near rear-end collision. His attempts to unsmash them only made things worse, littering the floorboard with bruised petals. Didn't matter. Flowers were a bit much for a blind date. It'd make it that much harder to run if Godzilla answered the door.

He chuckled and shook his head. At least Sharon, his date, liked the Cubbies, so she couldn't be that bad.

As he stepped out, the hot southern air pressed down on him and clung to his face like a sticky film. He paused on the stoop to check his breath and smooth his hair then rang the bell. Footsteps followed.

The door creaked open.

Nice.

Jonathan exhaled and offered a genuine smile. A lovely woman with sandy blonde hair and emerald green eyes stood before him wearing a purple sundress with yellow flowers. A wide belt encircled a trim waist, accentuating soft curves. Pink colored her delicate cheeks. For once, Jeanne-Anne came through.

"You must be Jonathan."

"Yes." His arms hung at his sides as his brain searched, unsuccessfully, for something clever to say. "You look nice." *Brilliant.*

"Thank you." She stepped aside. "Would you like to come in?"

He nodded and meandered into her living room filled with country-style furniture. His mind went blank, like a blue computer screen.

Say something, idiot. "It's a nice evening." He shoved his hands into his pockets, feeling like a chess geek on prom night.

"It is. Have a seat." She motioned toward a floral couch, her perfume wafting toward him. "I'm almost ready."

His nose twitched, and a tickle crawled up his throat. Covering a cough with his hand, he plunked into the cushions, his lungs constricting as a puff of dust filled the air. By the time Sharon disappeared down the hall, he'd started to sneeze. Profusely. Not the best way to start a first date.

Was he having an allergic reaction? Twining his fingers in his lap to keep from clawing at his itchy skin, he scanned his surroundings. His puffy eyes widened as a mound of fur sidled next to him, rubbing its fat body against his leg. *Oh, no!* A low mew sounded behind him, and a moment later, another cat jumped onto the couch, zeroing in. Followed by another, until four cats surrounded him, tails twitching, cat fur flicking into the air.

As tears gushed, he bolted for the door. He stood on the stoop, sneezing like a machine gun until snot dripped from his nostrils and water poured from his grainy eyes. Mopping his face with an old, frayed handkerchief, he peered back through the torrent gushing from his tear ducts. Manners told him to stay, at least long enough to excuse his departure, but his bronchi screamed, "Run and don't look back."

Gulping air between nasal explosions, he dashed down the walk, pausing outside his car to fumble for his keys.

"Jonathan?"

He whirled around, stared at Sharon through tear-blurred eyes. She stood in her doorway, her porch light casting long shadows over her face and obscuring her expression.

"I'll call you," he squeaked out between coughs and sneezes.

She stepped forward, leaving her door ajar. "Is everything OK?" An orange feline slinked beside her.

Flicking his hand in what he hoped to be a parting wave, he lurched into his car. He cranked the engine and the air, sucking in the stale blast pouring from the vents. Suppressing the urge to breathe deeply, which would only aggravate his airways further, he exhaled slowly while searching for a drugstore.

A Wisco's Pharmacy stood on the corner. He eased into the lot. After buying an over-the-counter antihistamine and a bottle of water to take it with, he downed the pill. Staggering out of the store, his cell phone chimed.

He checked the screen while taking the call. "Hey, Jeanne. It appears news travels fast." Climbing into his vehicle, he switched the phone to his other ear and cranked the engine.

"Please tell me you did not pull a teenage ditch-n-run."

"I've got a better question for you, Bean. Why didn't you tell me your lady friend hosted a feline factory?"

"Oh."

Leaving the parking lot, he eased behind a silver Mazda. "Oh?"

"I guess I hadn't realized."

"Obviously." He stopped at a red light. "Where do you find these women?"

"They're both in my Sunday School class."

"Well, maybe you should stick to prayer groups and leave the matchmaking alone."

"Sharon's a lovely lady with a servant's heart. She would have been perfect if not for the—"

"Snot-inducing, throat-constricting cats."

"Right. I'll be more careful next time."

"Uh-uh."

"Come on. Don't give up so easily. Your happily-ever-after is but a few more dates away."

He sucked in a breath of air and let it out slowly. "Already found that. With Evie." Maybe a guy only struck gold once.

"I know. And you two had a beautiful thing. But it's been five years, almost six. You've got a lot of living left, Jonathan. She would have wanted you to be happy. You know that."

CHAPTER 13

A S NIGHT SETTLED over the shelter, people migrated back to their cots. Gavin snuggled baby Jaya in the crook of his arms and rocked gently. Sucking on her pacifier, she peered up at him through droopy eyelids. He smiled and kissed her forehead.

Adele rested her hand on his arm. "Where's Momma?" Her bottom lip poked out, and her chin quivered.

Gavin pulled her to his side. "She'll be back." He rested his chin on her head. "Want me to read you some comics?"

She nodded.

He set the now sleeping Jaya beside him and tucked the blankets around her. Rummaging through his duffel bag, he shoved aside dirty clothes and pulled out his favorite comic book.

"Uh-uh." His sister shook her head. "The other one."

A dull ache filled the back of his throat as he thought of Jacqueline, sitting on the hallway floor, reading to Adele. Like he'd seen other women do—in the library, sitting on park benches, even here in this shelter. He glanced around, pausing to watch a woman rub the back of a sleeping toddler.

What would it be like to have a mother like that? His gaze drifted to the shelter door, the one Mom left through hours before. What if she didn't return? What would happen to him and Adele? Would the church people kick them out? Call the police?

A chill crept up his spine as he remembered a conversation Mom and Stella shared only a few days ago about making money. He knew exactly what Stella meant.

Adele nudged him, so he turned back to his duffel bag, pulling out the comic book Bible. She leaned closer as he flipped the pages. He paused on a picture of a teenager crouched on a cavern floor while a group of men gathered near the top, laughing. One held a brightly colored garment.

Gavin glanced at Adele. "This one?"

Her head bobbed, so he read. "Thrown into a deep pit by his jealous brothers, Joseph waits helplessly while they decide his fate." Helpless, waiting for others to decide his fate. That was something Gavin knew well. But one day, things would be different. He'd go to college, earn a degree, and get a good job. He'd live in a big fancy house with lots of foods, bought with cash, not food stamps. And he'd never come to a place like this again.

He continued to read, moving through the story of a guy named Joseph to the birth of a baby hidden in the reeds along a river. Adele's head fell forward. She jerked awake and stared at Gavin through wilting eyelids.

He chuckled and gave her a squeeze. "Looks like it's time for bed."

Rubbing her eyes, she pushed her lips into a pout. "I'm not tired."

"Right. And Superman sucks lollipops. Come on, before you get me in trouble."

She looked at the empty cot beside them. "Mom's not coming back, is she?"

"You're talking crazy. Of course she is." After a quick glance to baby Jaya, he guided Adele to her cot and pulled the blanket under her chin. "Quit fretting and get to sleep, you hear?"

With a sniffle, she nodded.

He lifted baby Jaya into his arms, careful not to wake her, and wiggled onto his cot. Rolling on his side, he tucked her under his arm and watched the shelter entrance. A short time later, the lights clicked off. He continued to stare into the darkness, eyes trained on the faint glimmer drifting from the exit sign.

Murmurs filled the shelter, along with a few snores. Footsteps shuffled down the hall as people made their way to and from the bathroom. One of the church volunteers sat in a folding chair near the kitchen. Light tumbled out, glimmering on his bald head and casting weird, elongated shadows across his face. Gavin didn't recognize him, which wasn't odd, considering some churchies never seemed to come around twice. Except Irene and Jacqueline, who always had a smile and a kind word. And who might notice Mother was gone. Jolting to a sitting position, he scanned the empty cots beside him—one used by Mom, the other by Stella. What if one of the volunteers noticed and came asking questions?

Heart thrashing, he stared at the bald man. The man yawned, stretched, and stood. Gavin held his breath. When the man meandered toward the bathroom, Gavin bolted to his feet. They needed to find another place to sleep.

But what if their mom came back and couldn't find them? So she'd be mad, slap Gavin upside the head. Wouldn't hurt. But if these churchies got in their business . . . His blood went cold, bile souring the back of his mouth.

He made a visual sweep of the dim interior, packed wall to wall with cots and people. Dark forms filled the room. Snoring vibrated like a backwoods chorus. Someone hummed, low and soft, and fabric rustled as people flopped in their beds.

Along the left wall, catching the rays spilling from the overhead exit sign, lay two empty cots.

He inched closer to Adele and nudged her. "Wake up."

She moaned and buried her face deeper into the covers.

He nudged her again, then again, until her eyes popped open. "Why you bugging—!"

He clamped his hand over her mouth and leaned closer until his lips brushed her ear. "We need to move. Sleep somewhere else."

Wide-eyed, she surveyed her surroundings, her gaze landing on their mother's empty cot. "But why?" Her voice quavered. "Where are we going?"

Gavin shushed her and smoothed her hair. "No. Nothing like that. We're going to sleep somewhere else. Over there." He cast a quick glance toward the hall leading to the bathroom then pointed to the empty cots.

"I don't want to." She rubbed her eyes.

Gavin gripped her shoulder, fingers digging into her soft flesh. "Just do what I say. Now."

This spurred her into action, and she jumped to her feet.

"Grab your stuff. And my bag. And hurry."

She nodded and did as she was told. He slid his arm under baby Jaya and carried her around sleeping mounds, careful not to disturb anyone. Adele shuffled along behind. They reached the empty cots as a shadowed form emerged from the hallway. Holding his breath, Gavin threw the blanket over Adele, clutched baby Jaya against his chest, and dove into the blankets. He peered over the hem, pulse racing as the man scanned the room.

After what felt like hours, the man ambled back to his chair. Gavin spent the rest of the night watching the entrance and fighting sleep. He must have lost the battle because he awoke to the sound of hushed voices and stirring.

Reality came rushing in. He turned to Adele, jostling her awake. She peered at him through droopy, sleep-encrusted eyes.

"Leave me alone." She started to roll over then her eyes snapped open. She bolted to a sitting position and stared all about her, face pale. "Where's Momma?"

"Shut up!" Every nerve in Gavin's body fired. He gripped Adele's arm and leaned closer until his face hovered an inch from hers. "Don't answer nobody's questions. Don't say nothing to nobody, you hear?"

Her lip protruded, and her chin dimpled. "But why?" Tears welled behind fluttering lashes. One escaped and slid down her cheek.

Gavin longed to soften his tone, to pull her close and wipe her tears, but now wasn't the time. She needed to be scared. Otherwise she'd blab, and who knew what would happen. "Because if you don't, they'll send you away. All of us. So do as I say, OK?"

She blinked again, releasing another tear. Baby Jaya started to fuss.

Gavin snatched her up, keeping his gaze locked on Adele. "OK?"

She nodded and swiped at her face, her small torso shivering.

Jaya's fussing mounted to a wail. Cradling her in his lap, Gavin grabbed her diaper bag and searched for a pacifier. As his hands swept against the cool plastic lining, encasing little more than a container of wipes and a few chew toys, his stomach bottomed out. No more diapers. Which meant he'd have to ask Irene for some, the very person he hoped to avoid. They needed to come up with a story, and fast.

His fingers closed around the small plastic hoop of Jaya's pacifier, and he exhaled. One problem solved. Pushing the pacifier into his sister's mouth, he cast another glance toward the shelter entrance.

Mom, come back. Please.

ANGLING INTO THE CHURCH parking lot, Jacqueline checked the clock on her dash. Thanks to an excessively long train blocking traffic on Main Street, she was late. OK, so not late exactly, but not as early as she wanted to be, considering this was her first morning as Bible study leader—if Irene actually followed through with her great intentions. Not that Jacqueline blamed the woman for her lack of organization. After all, she'd never run a shelter before. Hurricane Gita had jolted everyone into a frenzy. As chaotic as things were, Irene was doing the best she could. But even so—Jacqueline? A Bible study leader? Who was she kidding? Clearly Irene was operating on faulty perceptions.

Jacqueline looked at the leader's guide on the passenger seat, sent through priority mail. A quick glance verified she was the last person to lead such a study. Die to self. Living as sojourners, unblemished by the world. Radiating the contagious love of Christ. She snorted. *I'll make a great leader, all right. Follow me, and I'll show you how to shred relationships and the hearts of those you love in pursuit of a failing career.* And what did she have to show for it? A deluged home and a resentful daughter. Quite the role model.

She pulled around back and parked in a near-empty lot. Most refugees had arrived by bus. Those with cars had already found more pleasant accommodations, or family. The others, like Gavin's family or the rough looking men and women who gathered in the shelter corners, had nowhere to go and no jobs to return to. Most of them spent their days at the library filling out applications for Federal Emergency Management Agency (FEMA) assistance. Something Jacqueline couldn't do. From what she'd read, disaster relief wasn't available to her, considering her insurance policy. Not unless her claim was delayed, but even then, she'd have to pay it back.

She parked in the shade of a magnolia tree and tucked her purse under the seat. As she reached for her things, a hot flash hit, triggering nausea. A burst of anxiety followed. It was like being jolted with a nine-volt wire.

Not now.

Opening the door wide to allow maximum airflow, she waited until her pulse slowed before stepping out of her vehicle. With her study material in hand, she caught a glimpse of Gavin lugging a bulging trash bag across the lot. It snagged on the asphalt, leaving a trail of trash behind him.

"Let me help you." She set her guide on the roof of her car and approached him.

He stopped and glanced at the line of garbage stretched behind him. Faster than maggots on a carcass, flies swarmed and buzzed. Puffing air through pressed lips, Gavin squatted and began picking up the scattered trash.

Jacqueline helped, swallowing back a gag reflex as the smell of rotting meat flooded her nostrils. "Does this mean you're having a bad day?"

He shrugged and tossed a gooey napkin back into the bag.

"Where's your sister?"

His head jerked up, and his eyes widened. He studied her for a long moment before turning back to the trash. "With Adele and Ami, my friend."

"Where's your mom?"

"Around." He paled, and his gaze fell to the asphalt.

As Jacqueline continued to watch him—his jerking movements and the way he avoided eye contact—a heavy weight settled in her gut. Something wasn't right. "You wait here while I get another bag."

"K." He rocked back on his rear, legs apart, knees pulled up. Dull eyes rose slightly before angling down again. Jacqueline resisted the urge to ruffle his hair and strolled across the lot and into the shelter.

She wove around cots and people, searching for Irene. Halfway across the room, she paused to glance down the hall. Adele, the baby, and another girl she'd seen with Gavin on occasion, occupied the hall. They glanced up and held Jacqueline's gaze until she took a step toward them. Then they angled away from her and stared at the floor, as if hiding something. She'd seen the same behavior in Delana plenty of times. Enough to know there was no sense trying to talk to them. They were hiding something, and she intended to find out what.

Quickening her step, she headed to the kitchen.

She found Irene in the pantry, sifting through various dry goods. "Anyone hear from Family Foods today?" She pulled three soup cans off the shelf and handed them to a brunette standing behind her.

The handful of women gathered around answered in the negative.

Irene sighed and kneaded her forehead. "We knew the donations would run out soon enough, once the hype wore off." She glanced at Jacqueline and waved her over. "Morning." She held her hands out to the women on either side of her. "Let's pray."

After the prayer ended, Jacqueline motioned Irene aside. "Can I talk to you?"

Irene regarded her with a wrinkled brow. "Is everything OK?"

"I think so. First, where do you keep the trash bags? I forgot."

Irene exhaled, her tense expression smoothing into a smile. "Now that's a question I can handle. There should be a box under the sink." Her smile wavered slightly. "Any chance your next question is equally simple?"

Jacqueline glanced past Irene, through the kitchen archway, and into the crowded gym. "You wouldn't happen to know if Gavin—" What was his last name? Why hadn't she asked? "The boy with auburn hair. He's got two sisters, one elementary age, the other an infant. Their mom's on the heavier side."

"Right! I know who you're talking about." Irene grabbed one of four clipboards off the counter and flipped through the pages. Her face fell as her finger scrolled the sheet. "I really wish we'd been more organized about checking people in. Less panicked." She shook her head and grabbed another clipboard, moving through it sheet by sheet. "What were their names again?"

"Gavin, Adele, and a baby . . ." She closed her eyes and pinched the bridge of her nose. "Jenna? No, Jaya. Baby Jaya."

"The mom?"

"I don't know."

Irene dropped the clipboard on the counter. "We really should have done better." She glanced to a woman with sandy hair pulled back in a fabric headband. "Let's make sure we have an accurate list of all our refugees. We might need to start assigning cots, doing bed checks, that sort of thing." She turned back to Jacqueline. "What's this about anyway? You seem . . . worried. Did something happen?"

"I'm not sure, but I think the mom might have left."

"Left—as in how?"

"Left left."

Irene's eyebrows shot up. "You mean abandoned her children?"

Jacqueline shrugged. That was a heavy accusation, one that would bring devastating consequences to all involved. She hoped she was blowing things out of proportion.

CHAPTER 14

JACQUELINE STOOD AT the sink, elbow deep in sudsy water. The scent of roasted beef and onions surrounded her as she scrubbed crusted gravy from the rim of Delana's slow-cooker.

"Thanks for dinner. It was great." Delana dropped a plate into the dishwasher.

Jacqueline smiled. "My pleasure." Staring through the window toward a puff of clouds drifting across the horizon, she thought of Gavin and his sisters. Had his mom come back? And what if she hadn't, didn't? What kind of mother could abandon her children?

Acid surged through her stomach, squelching her thoughts. She had zero business judging other mothers. None.

Having conquered the gravy ring, she set the washed and rinsed pot to dry and drained the suds. She wiped her hands on a towel and studied Delana, torn between a desire to extend their surprisingly pleasant evening and wanting to dash down to the shelter. And yet, how many times had she pushed Delana aside to chase after something else—namely her career?

Not tonight.

She draped the hand towel over the stove handle. "So, wanna hit a movie?"

Delana glanced at her watch. "I've got plans. I think."

"Yeah? Where you going?"

Delana shrugged. "Downtown." She ran a rag over the counter then draped it over the faucet. "You're not really thinking of buying that boutique, are you? Of moving here?"

"Yes, I am. I know I haven't always been the mother you needed." Delana snorted and Jacqueline grabbed her hand, searched her eyes. "But I'm here now. I'd like to start over. See if we can't become friends."

Her daughter jerked her hand away. "Just like that, huh?" She snapped her fingers. "A storm hits, and suddenly you want back into my life."

"That's not how it happened."

"Right." She scoffed. "Because you've always been the involved parent."

"I'm sorry. I should've done better."

"Yeah, well."

"I wish could undo the past, sweetie. I really do." Tears stung her eyes. "I'm not proud of the choices I made."

"As a mom or a slut?"

Jacqueline flinched, heat climbing her neck, as shameful memories resurfaced. "Either." She took in a deep breath. "But I've changed."

Delana laughed, a low, bitter sound that sliced through Jacqueline's heart. "Right. I forgot, you found Jesus. Convenient." Her cell chimed, and she checked the screen. "As delightful as this evening's been—" She spun around and pressed the phone to her ear, "Hey. Give me a minute," and left.

Jacqueline rubbed the back of her neck. Their relationship was like the Gulf of Mexico, calm one minute, white-capped waves the next. *Lord, I need Your help on this one. Remove Delana's bitterness, and bring back the sweet, giggly girl that used to crawl into my lap—when I gave her the chance, anyway.*

Not wanting to mope around an empty house all night, Jacqueline grabbed her purse and headed back to the shelter. The place she felt wanted, needed. Significant. She arrived at the tail end of dinner, while men and women were nibbling on cookies or drinking coffee. An odd aroma filled the air—a mixture of coffee, sweat, and stinky feet. After allowing her eyes to adjust to the pale florescent lighting, she searched the area for Gavin and his sisters. They weren't on or near their cots, and their mother was nowhere in sight. A group of women and children gathered in the east corner, toys scattered among them. A few men sat in chairs along the far wall. Old women occupied an area near the center of the gym.

As she strolled past numerous cots and clusters of people, a thick locker-room stench wafted toward her. She made a mental note to talk to Irene about doing some linen washing.

She found Irene in the pantry stacking cracker boxes on shelves. An opened crate stood beside her next to three bags of oranges.

The woman dusted her hands and turned toward Jacqueline. "Can't get enough of this place, huh?"

Jacqueline smiled. "I could say the same for you. Have you been here all day?"

"Almost." She craned her neck side-to-side and rubbed her shoulders. "Our volunteers are dwindling. Along with our supplies."

"Is there someone you can call? Like FEMA?"

"Not sure." Irene smoothed a lock of hair off her forehead. "I'm a Sunday School teacher, not a shelter director. Well, I was, anyway. But I'll figure it out, one box of crackers at a time."

There was no point asking if Irene had seen Gavin's mom yet, as they'd already established with her fruitless clipboard searching she had no idea who the woman was.

Irene studied Jacqueline. "Is there something else?"

Why add more stress to the woman's life without information to back it up? "No. I think I'll go see if any of my Bible study ladies want to chat."

"Oh, I love it! That's just what these people need—community. How'd your first discussion go, by the way?"

"Good, minus the fact that I rarely know the answers to their rapid-fire questions." Not for lack of trying. She'd done enough Bible reading over the past week to earn a seminary degree. OK, maybe not. But at least she was learning her way around in the Book. She had even started to memorize a few verses. A habit she hoped her Bible study ladies would want to pick up.

"I'm sure you did great." Irene gave her a sideways hug. "I heard you were in the church bookstore the other day, depleting their stock."

Jacqueline blushed, remembering how she'd accidentally spilled her large stack of books—a concordance, study guides, and a beautiful prayer journal—across the counter, frightening the poor cashier. "I'm learning."

"That's wonderful." Irene's eyes shone. "Never under-estimate what God can do with a willing heart and teachable spirit. And just as important, you showed those ladies, by sitting with them, talking with them, praying with them, that they weren't alone." Her smile widened. "Maybe seeing that will encourage more shelter residents to join a group. How many did you have in yours?"

"Three."

Irene nodded. "A start." She returned to unloading cracker boxes, and Jacqueline meandered back into the gym.

She found Gavin, Adele, and their newfound friend sitting in the hall while baby Jaya, beginning to walk, toddled between them.

The children glanced up when Jacqueline approached, but Gavin and Adele quickly dropped their gaze. He stared at the comic book Bible spread before him while Adele fiddled with her doll, casting frequent glances Jacqueline's way.

She plopped down, back against the wall, knees to her chest. "Whatcha reading?"

Gavin shrugged and flipped the page.

She slid closer. "Mind if I join you?"

Again he shrugged and slid the comic book toward her. She looked at Adele and found her watching with a tight expression, doll clutched in a frozen hand.

"Where's your momma?"

Heads jerked up, eyes wide.

Gavin's expression soured. "Why?"

Jacqueline tried to keep her voice and expression casual. "Wanted to invite her to join my Bible study group. She hasn't joined any yet, right?"

"Don't know." Gavin flipped two pages. "Doubt she'd want to. She's not into Bible stuff."

"Yeah, well, I'd like to ask anyway." She stayed by Gavin's side for several minutes.

He flipped pages in between rerouting Jaya—Adele watched, almost twitching. Jacqueline couldn't shake the feeling that the girl wanted to tell her something, or ask her something.

The longer Jacqueline sat, the more she became convinced that something indeed was wrong, terribly wrong. "Listen, Gavin, is—"

"We better go." He grabbed his comic book and stood. Snatching baby Jaya, he threw Adele a pointed look. "Come on."

She scrambled to her feet, looking from Jacqueline to her brother.

Jacqueline reached for her hand. "If you guys need any help—"

"Come on!" Gavin's voice deepened, and Adele startled. She scampered after him while their friend hung back.

Jacqueline approached the girl. "Your name's Ami, right?"

She nodded.

"Can I talk to you for a minute?"

She nodded again.

"Is everything OK with Gavin's family?"

"What do you mean?"

"Have you seen their mom?"

She shook her head.

"When did you see her last?"

"I don't know. I guess I didn't pay that much attention."

"Right." Jacqueline turned back around and stared through the now empty hall to the mass of people gathered throughout the gym. So many shattered lives, holding on to mere threads of hope. And it looked like Gavin's thread was beginning to unravel.

Oh, Lord, please let me be wrong.

It was like reliving the pains of her past, her worst mistakes, through someone else. Only this time, she would do something about it. Although she had no idea what.

CHAPTER 15

THE REST OF the evening, Jacqueline visited with residents, helped clean up after-dinner clutter, and located deodorant and other necessities for those in need. By 9:30, Gavin's mom still hadn't appeared, and unfortunately, Irene had already left.

A young woman Jacqueline didn't recognize emerged from the kitchen lugging a bulging laundry bag. Long, beaded earrings dangled beneath amber hair streaked with blonde.

Jacqueline approached her. "Hi, I'm Jacqueline."

"Mia." The girl flashed a smile, revealing a mouth of braces twined with neon green rubber bands.

"Who's in charge tonight?"

"In charge? Here?" Mia laughed. "Now that would be nice. Seriously, though, not sure. Irene left about thirty minutes ago. Told me to call her cell phone if I needed anything."

"Think she'd mind if you gave me that number? I had it. Well, it was on the bulletin, but I don't have it on me."

The girl angled her head, frowned. After a moment, she shrugged. "I'm sure it'd be OK." She fished in her back pocket and pulled out a yellow sticky note, which she handed over.

"Thanks." Dialing the number, Jacqueline moved to the corner of the kitchen.

"Irene Ford. May I help you?"

"Hi, it's Jacqueline. I hate to bother you."

"No bother. What can I do for you?"

"I'm calling about that kid we talked about—Gavin. I haven't seen his mom all night, and the kids are acting pretty weird."

"You're afraid she won't come back."

"Right. So now what? How long do we wait?"

"Wow, I don't know. It's almost a quarter till ten. The shelter doors lock up in fifteen minutes. Maybe she'll still show?"

"Maybe." Jacqueline crossed the room to the doorway, searching the many heads and faces for Gavin. He and his sisters occupied a far corner, surrounded by old women. Their mother wasn't one of them. "But they've got a baby."

"Oh." A pause. "I'll call the pastor."

An hour and a half later, Irene, Jacqueline, and the pastor gathered in the church lobby, waiting for the police and child protective services (CPS). to arrive. Questioning Gavin hadn't helped. The boy only grew increasingly defensive until he quit answering altogether.

The pastor rubbed his face. "How many children we got down there, Irene?"

"Ten. Maybe fifteen." She raked a hand through her hair. "It's so hard to keep track, what with people coming and going."

"We're still getting refugees?"

"A few. And some homeless folks that heard we have a shelter."

According to the news, the Coast Guard continued to pull survivors from flooded homes, depositing them in the already stressed towns throughout the South.

The pastor rubbed his face again, his skin turning a purplish-red.

"Should we turn the homeless away?" Irene asked.

"Yes. I mean, no. I don't know." The pastor exhaled. "No. Of course not. I just wish we had had more time to prepare, to plan."

"We all wish that, sir."

Jacqueline felt like an outsider intruding on a family crisis. She wasn't even a church member, had only attended a couple services, and yet here she stood, poking into things that weren't any of her business. Except Gavin had become her business. He and his sisters had wiggled and giggled their way into her heart. Although she could do nothing to help them, she couldn't leave until she knew the children would be OK.

Someone rapped on the church door, but the light reflected off the glass shrouded the exterior. The pastor lumbered across the foyer. Irene and Jacqueline followed.

He pulled the door open, ushering in the sticky, mid-summer air and revealing a deceptively peaceful starry night. A uniformed police officer and a tall, lanky woman with a square jaw and bob haircut stood under the awning. A hint of sadness filled her pale blue eyes, as if she expected the worse.

The police officer looked from one face to the next before addressing the pastor. "You must be Pastor Suggs?" He had broad shoulders and jet-black hair cut in a military style.

The pastor nodded and moved aside to allow the city officials in.

"I'm Officer McCallen, and this is Jesseca Mansfield from child protective services."

The woman nodded, hands clasped in front of her. "Where are the children?"

Florescent lighting glimmered on his badge, reminding Jacqueline of the seriousness of this call. Had she done the right thing? Was it even her business? A news article of a foster child beaten to death flashed through her mind, chilling her. Would strangers really do a better job caring for these precious children? But if not them, then who?

The pastor cleared his throat. "They're downstairs. Come with me."

They traveled past the nursery and toward the stairwell leading to the basement. Their footfalls echoed through the hall, each step landing with the force of finality. When they reached the gym entrance, the pastor turned to Irene. "Where are the children?"

Tears stung Jacqueline's eyes as she watched Irene scan the shadowed forms stretched out before them, countless heads poking from multicolored sheets and blankets. Each person ripped violently from his or her home. They had already suffered so much! What would happen to Gavin and his sisters now?

Irene frowned and shook her head. "I'm not sure I would recognize them. There are so many refugees. So many children. I spend most of my time in the kitchen and directing volunteers." She turned to Jacqueline. "Do you see them?"

Jacqueline nodded, a shudder running through her. "I believe so." She faced Officer McCallen, searched his hazel eyes. "Can I talk with them? Explain what's happening and bring them to you?"

The officer and social worker exchanged glances. She nodded. "That would probably be best."

Their faces grew solemn, and Irene squeezed Jacqueline's hand. "May God's love and grace flow through you. We should pray."

Still holding Jacqueline's hand, Irene reached for the officer, who stared at her like she'd just asked him to make a public profession of faith. But then he nodded and took her hand, offering his to the social worker, who stared at it, took it, and then offered hers to the waiting pastor.

They bowed heads, and Irene's voice filled the hall, soft yet powerful, like a soothing balm. "Holy Father, how Your heart must break when You look at our sin-ravished world, when You see Your children, Your precious children, in such pain. Please go before Jacqueline, before each of us. Hold these children close to Your heart. Watch over them, wherever they may go from here." Her voice cracked. "Help them to find a safe, loving, forever home, if not with their mother, then with someone who can love them as their own. Protect their hearts, Father, and place Your seal of ownership upon them."

After she concluded, everyone stood as if frozen or perhaps weighted, hands still interlocked, heads still bowed.

Clearing his throat, the pastor broke the silence. He looked at Jacqueline with firm yet compassionate eyes.

Breathing deep, Jacqueline nodded and began the long trek along the perimeter of the room, searching the shadowed forms around her. She passed an old woman with matted hair, a man too big for his cot with socked feet poking out from under his blanket. Two toddlers shared a cot, curled nose-to-nose. In the dark, Jacqueline struggled to make out faces, so she wove through the room bed by bed, crouching low, peering, searching.

A boy with shaggy blonde hair and slight shoulders sat up and stared at her with a wrinkled, heavily-shadowed face. "What you doing?"

"I'm looking for someone. Name's Gavin." She gave his age and a description of him and his sisters. "Have you seen him?"

Metal screeched, followed by a bang. Jacqueline glanced up to see Gavin bolting for the door holding the baby in one hand and dragging Adele with the other. This created quite a stir, and people murmured, swore, sat upright.

"Gavin, wait!" Jacqueline took off after him, edging around cots and extended limbs. "Stop him! Please!"

People jumped to their feet, funneling toward the entrance and the running Gavin. About ten feet away, he tripped and fell. Baby Jaya started to howl. Jacqueline reached them to find Gavin clutching the baby to his chest while his sister crouched at his side. His wide eyes flashed in the pale beam of light drifting from the door exit.

Jacqueline squatted down and reached for him, but he flinched and jerked away. By now a crowd had gathered with more murmurs, questions. Jacqueline ignored them and focused on the only thing that mattered—allaying Gavin's fear before he hit fight mode. "Hey, we're on your side. We're not going to hurt you. We just want to talk."

"Who's we?"

Suddenly she longed for less light, more shadows, so she wouldn't have to see the hollowed look in the boy's eyes. A hush fell over the gym, and Jacqueline slid to the floor. "There's a police officer."

He clutched his sister tighter.

"And someone from child protective services. They just want to talk, to find out how they can help you. To make sure you're safe, and to help you find your mom." So much for breaking the news to him gently.

He sat stock-still, head angled toward the ground.

She lowered her voice. "Please, Gavin, help us out here. Talk to us. Tell us what's going on. For your sisters' sake. These people aren't going to go away."

People stirred, and Jacqueline held her breath. What if Gavin wouldn't come willingly? Would the police force him? Drag him?

"Gavin?" She offered but the faintest whisper.

He looked up and nodded. He nudged his sister. "Come on."

Adele stood, trembling, staring from Jacqueline to her brother. "Where are we going? Where will they take us?"

If only Jacqueline had answers. "They're going to make sure you're safe."

"They'll find our mom?" The child's voice squeaked, laden with unshed tears.

"They're going to try, but you need to help them." She lifted Gavin by his elbow. "Both of you." She looked at baby Jaya, still crying. "Is she OK?"

Gavin nodded. "I think so."

Jacqueline felt like part of a funeral procession as they made their way through the gym. Everyone stared and spoke in hushed whispers. Children clung to their mothers.

Upon reaching the rest of their group, the social worker stepped backward, drawing everyone further into the hall and away from watching eyes and listening ears. "I'm Jesseca Mansfield. I work for child protective services. I have a few questions I need to ask you. It's my job to keep you safe." She glanced at the pastor. "Is there someplace we can all go to talk?"

Gavin's eyes shot left, and his stance widened, as if considering making a run for it.

Jacqueline laid her hand on his shoulder. "She's on your side. We all are."

Then why did she feel like she was about to betray him into the hands of strangers?

CHAPTER 16

GAVIN'S THROAT constricted, and tears pricked his eyes. Inhaling, he squared his shoulders and lifted his chin, shoving his emotions behind an impenetrable wall. He stared Jacqueline in the eye—a woman he once considered his friend.

She offered him a soft expression and a tender smile—one that said, "I'm here," even though she wasn't. Wouldn't be. Like Mrs. Rust, his friends from school, the gray-haired lady he passed on his way to school. People he'd probably never see again. In a year, a month, maybe even a week, they'd forget all about him and his sisters, because that's what adults did. And yet, as Jacqueline reached out for him, watched him, held his gaze in her own, he longed to believe she was different.

"Can I?" Mrs. Mansfield reached for baby Jaya.

Gavin clutched her all the tighter, icy sweat pooling in his palms and snaking between his shoulder blades. Jaya cried out and clung to his neck, burying her nose against his cheek, her fingers digging into his skin. Swaying slightly, he soothed her to a low whimper then shifted her to one side. With his now free hand, he grabbed hold of Adele and deepened his voice. "Come on."

She peered up at him, her bottom lip poked out, her shriveled chin quivering. "Where are we going, Gavin?"

Before he could answer, the tall, ugly child protection lady weaseled in and grabbed Adele by the shoulders. "We're going to talk, you and I, in the pastor's nice office." Hunched over, Ugly Lady glanced at the old man in a polo shirt and nudged Adele toward the stairwell.

Adele stumbled forward, looking from the adults towering around them to Gavin. They were outnumbered. Trapped. He exhaled, allowing his tense shoulder's to slump. He gave her a quick nod. What else could he do? Once again, they were at the mercy of the adults, only at least this time no one screamed or swore.

The man in the polo shirt led the way, walking like a steel bar had been jammed down his spine, while the others shuffled behind him. Gavin and the police officer took the lead. Apparently the dude thought Gavin might make another run for it, because he hovered like a barracuda, watching Gavin from the corner of his beady eyes. Dude's arms hung like knotted tree trunks, and his feet fell heavy. His presence sent chills up Gavin's spine, but he'd never show it, wouldn't give the guy satisfaction.

They reached a room with glass walls, and the polo-shirted, balding guy flicked on the lights. A wood desk stood against the far wall, leather furniture on either side of the entrance. Religious magazines and a thick, leather-bound Bible rested on a fancy glass coffee table.

"My office is down this way." The bald dude motioned to a dark hallway.

Ms. Ferret Face nodded. "We'll need to speak with you each separately." She released her grip on Adele's shoulders and turned to Gavin. "You ready?"

He stared at her for a while, feet glued to the floor, heart stuck in his throat. Adrenaline shot through his veins like tiny razor blades. But running wouldn't help. Nothing would. He swallowed, jutting his chin and narrowing his eyes like he did when Ace smacked him around.

Jacqueline stepped forward and held out her arms. "I'll take the baby."

He looked at Jaya. She'd fallen back asleep. Her head flopped to the side, mouth parted slightly, breath quavering with the remnants of tears. He reluctantly handed her over, a chill filling the void where her warm body once rested.

Ferret Face led him into a fancy office lined with books. The cop followed and hovered, pencil in one hand, pocket notebook in the other. His thick torso cast a bulky shadow across the desk.

To avoid the dude's steady gaze, Gavin scanned his surroundings. Picture frames—the fancy silver kind—collected dust on a large desk in front of him. Baldy and a blonde lady dressed in a frilly pink blouse. A family of four clustered around a tree—probably Baldy's kids and grandkids. The brass nameplate read Pastor Rick Suggs.

Cheesy inspirational sayings printed over mountain and ocean scenes were hung all over the walls. Stupid stuff that made people feel good saying them but fell flat in real life. Like, "I can do all things through Christ who strengthens me," and, "Be still and know that I am God." Gavin snorted. He was still, all right. Sitting like a fool waiting for some lady with yellow teeth dressed in grandma clothes to decide his life. Not much he could do about it, though. Never was.

"I imagine this has been a rough couple of weeks for you." Weasel-breath leaned forward and rested her pointy chin on folded hands. She offered a sappy smile, and for a moment, Gavin's resolve started to waver.

He wanted to tell her how frightened he was—for Mom, his sisters, himself. He wanted to ask what was going to happen next, where they'd take him. What if they didn't find Mom? But he didn't want to know. As if not knowing could prevent the worst from happening. More than anything he wanted to run out of the office to Jacqueline, with her kind eyes and soft voice, to let her wrap her arms around him and pull him close. Only that wouldn't do him any good. Most likely, after tonight, he'd never see her again anyway.

"Do you know where your mom is?" Ferret's eyes softened, and Brutus hooked his thumbs in his holster.

Gavin swallowed. Shifted. Swallowed again. If he said no, would they lock her up for child abandonment or something stupid like that? If he said yes, they'd want to know where she was. And if he kept his mouth shut, he'd be here forever. Didn't matter. Where else did he have to go? Back to the nasty smelling shelter? Except then at least he'd be with baby Jaya and Adele— and Ami. His chest went hollow as he thought of Ami and the very real possibility that he might never see her again. Just like Mrs. Rust—and his best friend Daniel. Daniel's mom liked Gavin, too. He could tell. She always sent him home with cookies or roast beef sandwiches wrapped with tinfoil.

Ferret Face leaned back, and the chair squeaked. "Where's your dad?"

"Don't got one."

"Do you have any family members we can call?"

Gavin stared at the cubicle wall—a velvety blue, covered in sticky notes. Mom hadn't popped into the world out of nowhere, but last he'd heard of his grandparents, they weren't any better than the gunk that got caught in the treads of your shoe. Far as he knew, his mom ran away when she turned seventeen. Once she'd mentioned a sister she hated.

"Is there anyone we can call, Gavin?"

There was somebody once, one of his mom's boyfriends, and the only one who didn't act like a complete jerk. His mom dated the guy for a month, maybe two, and during that time, Gavin had actually dreamed about what it might be like to have a real dad. Dude's name was Robert. He and Gavin used to throw a football around, and sometimes Robert took them all out for ice cream. In the end, his mom had driven him off and latched on to an angry drunk instead.

But what if Ferret Face managed to find him, called him? Would Robert come get Gavin and his sisters? His heart pricked as the old fantasy reemerged and all the images that came with it. 'Cept he was older now. It was time he quit daydreaming.

"Gavin, I'm trying to help you. Does your mom have a cell phone number?"

He held her gaze, unblinking. Telling her it got shut off 'cause Momma didn't pay the bill wouldn't help.

The clock on the wall ticked. Her chair squeaked again. His lungs screamed for air as he fought to keep his breathing steady.

"I know this is tough, but I need to make sure you're safe. And I want to find your mom."

"Yeah, well, maybe you should come back tomorrow."

Ferret Face glanced at the clock and frowned. When she looked back at Gavin, her eyes were going all misty. She didn't have to say it. She didn't think his mom would come back, at least not anytime soon. What if she was right? His mom always said her kids drug her down, drove her boyfriends away, ate up all her money.

Ferret stood and rounded the desk. With one last glance at Gavin, she opened the door and held it.

He exhaled, tension draining from his neck and shoulders, only to reignite when they made it to the outer office where Ferret summoned his sister. Adele's eyes widened, and she stared at Gavin as if asking for help or permission. Or maybe a command not to go. A desire to protect her, to fight for her, welled within but there was nothing he could do. Temperature rising, he turned to her with fisted hands. "Ferret-fa—" He clamped his mouth shut, staring at the CPS worker with wide eyes.

But the woman only smiled at him, a sad, pitiful smile. "It's OK. I know you're angry. It's only natural that you'd want to lash out at those you believe responsible for your pain, but we truly are trying to help you."

With caved shoulders, he looked away and slumped into an empty chair. Elbows propped on his knees, he stared at the carpet. Although he fought against them, tears blurred his vision as swooshing footsteps receded. Then a door clicked shut.

He watched Jacqueline from the corner of his eye, studying her face, her clasped hands, the way she rubbed her thumb over her index finger knuckle.

She gave a heavy sigh then sprang to her feet, turning to Baldy. "Do you have a slip of paper and pen I can use?"

Baldy nodded and crossed the room. He returned with the requested items and handed them over. Jacqueline plopped back into the chair beside Gavin and hunched forward, scribbling something. When finished, she gave it to Gavin. She'd written her name and phone number down. Swallowing back tears, he met her gaze.

She leaned toward him, placed her hand, warm and soft, over his. "If you need anything, anything at all, please call me."

She breathed deep, exhaled slowly. "Everything's going to be OK. God's going to turn all this to good."

His throat closed as he looked at the slip of paper again, then toward the hallway leading to the pastor's office and Adele. "I hope so."

JACQUELINE PULLED INTO Delana's condominium complex in the nearest available slot. She glanced at her phone. It was 2:15 a.m., and most likely, Gavin and his sisters' night was just beginning.

Her message light blinked. Three missed calls, all from her daughter. Normally that would have cheered her. She played the first one. "Mom, I'm worried. Where are you? Listen, I'm sorry about all those ugly things I said. I don't want to fight."

Jacqueline listened to the next one. "Mom, please come home, or at least tell me where you are. I'm starting to get really freaked out."

Dark shadows enshrouded the corners of the lot, clung to the trees, and hung around the building like an impenetrable fog. Her car idling, she dropped her phone in her lap, draped her arms over the steering wheel, and cried.

Delana had been frightened by Jacqueline's absence after but one night. She couldn't imagine how terrified Gavin and his sisters were. Not only had they not seen or heard from their mother in who knew how long—but to be taken away from the shelter by complete strangers?

Oh, Father, please hold those children tightly tonight.

CHAPTER 17

JONATHAN ROLLED ONTO his side and pulled the pillow around his ears, trying to drown out the less than pleasant noises seeping through his hotel wall. Maybe he should've taken Beannie up on her offer of her guest room.

He glanced at the clock radio on his nightstand—2:30 a.m. And thanks to Party All Night next door, he'd managed maybe an hour of sleep. But at least tomorrow was Saturday, and he could sleep in—except that he had to meet the realtor at 8:00.

Throwing off the covers, he jumped to his feet and grabbed his laptop. As long as he was pulling an all-nighter, he may as well make the most of it. He clicked to LakeView Realty then typed his criteria in the search engine. One acre, ranch, log cabin. He skimmed through the images that filled the screen. On the third page, his breath caught, and his hand froze on the mouse. His dream house, from the old-growth trees to the wraparound porch and stone chimney.

He and Evie used to sift through architecture magazines and travel brochures, contemplating where they would retire. Within driving distance of family, in the mountains, hidden from the world but within reach of it.

He glanced back at the screen. Would Evie have chosen this house? She always wanted to live in the mountains, surrounded by all God's creatures. Of course, that was before he teased her about the bears and coyotes lurking through the pines. He chuckled at the memory. Funny how he could laugh about it now, even smile when he thought of her. Was this what healing felt like? It almost scared him, as if in losing the ache, he'd be losing her all over again.

The noise in the adjacent room settled to a dull hum, and Jonathan's eyes grew heavy. After writing down the multiple listing service (MLS) reference number for the cabin, he closed his computer, flicked off the lamp mounted in the wall, and crawled back into bed. As he pulled the blanket around his shoulder, his cell rang. With a sigh, he fumbled for his phone, grabbed it, scanned the screen. Great. Someone from the railroad, which meant one of two things—there'd been a derailment or an injury.

"Hello?" He turned the light back on.

"Sorry to wake you, sir. This is Floyd, down at the shop."

"Whatcha got?"

"Burt Meyers. He fell off a ladder, landed on his arm. I think it might be broken."

"All right." Jonathan kneaded the tight muscles in the back of his neck. "Take him to the hospital. I'll meet you there."

He called Darren on the way to the hospital. Got his voice mail. The guy didn't call back until after Meyers took his drug test and underwent x-rays.

"Hey, got your message." Darren's voice sounded thick, throaty. "How's Meyers doing?"

"The doctor looked at him. It's not broken, but they're making him wear a brace. I'm heading to the office now to fill out the injury report."

"Don't put the brace on the paperwork."

"Excuse me?"

"I said, don't put the brace down. Leave that part off."

"I can't do that."

"You can, and you will."

The line went dead. Jonathan needed to talk to Shaffer or labor relations before Darren wove an even bigger mess. His stomach soured as he thought back to the planner, the other managers, the foreman. How many had Darren involved, and how many would lose their jobs over this? And if this became a he-said, he-said deal, which man would Shaffer believe—the newbie or half his crew, some with thirty years' experience to back them up?

GAVIN SAT IN A WAITING ROOM a few paces from Ferret's cubicle. Her assistant/babysitter, a lady with long, black hair that hung over her shoulders in loose ringlets, sat kitty-corner to him, glancing from the television screen to the cubicle. Brutus occupied the remaining chair, arms crossed, face slack. Gavin snorted. So now they had two babysitters. Stupid.

He glanced at his duffel bag lying at his feet, filled with everything he owned—which wasn't much. He chewed a fingernail, a war raging in his stomach. Ferret's back faced him, phone pressed to her ear.

Adele slept beside him, head draped over the arm rest, feet tucked under her. Baby Jaya lay on his other side tucked against the back cushions, wrapped in a blanket. Stupid cartoons played on an old television screen in front of him. The cartoon character's laugh drowned out Ferret Face's words, but Gavin caught enough to figure out what was going on. She was finding someone to take them, and by the sound of it, wasn't having any luck.

The cartoon ended and the babysitter stood. She sifted through movies spread across a cheap coffee table, much like the one they'd had at home. She held up a case with a picture of limbless vegetable people. "Do you like VeggieTales?"

He swallowed back a sarcastic remark and shrugged instead. Babysitter pulled out the old movie and started to slide the new one in when Ferret's chair squeaked. Gavin turned his head, his blood turning cold when her sad, apologetic eyes met his. She walked over with her hands pressed together in front of her, inhaled, then gave a tight smile.

She knelt in front of him. "I found a family to take baby Jaya."

His stomach curdled. "What do you mean?" Blood swooshed past his eardrums like a pulsating current. He looked from Ferret to Babysitter. "What do you mean?"

"This is temporary." Ferret nodded her head to her assistant, who moved to the couch and leaned toward baby Jaya.

"No!" Gavin lunged for the woman, yanking on her arm, digging his nails into her flesh. "Don't touch her!"

Baby Jaya's eyes popped open, and she started to cry. This only fueled Gavin's panic, tightening his grip, igniting his pulse. Firm hands gripped his shoulders, and a deep voice cut through him, reminding him of how little power he had. "Let go. Don't make this any harder than it is, son."

Gavin stood, trembling, gripping.

"Son," Brutus said.

Gavin glanced at Adele.

She stared back with wide eyes, face pale. Her shoulders trembled. "What's happening, Gavin?"

His hands went slack, numb, as a thick, suffocating cloak encased him. There was nothing he could do. Nothing.

"I'm going to find a safe place, for all of you." Ferret crossed the room. "So you can get some rest. And we'll try to find your mom. I promise." She knelt in front of Adele, and stroked her hair. "It's going to be OK, sweetie. Trust me."

Gavin thought about Jacqueline's promise that God would turn this into good. He thought about the posters in the pastor's office, and about words from a song he'd heard the previous Sunday. He shot a plea to the sky then held his breath, waiting, listening. Nothing. Because like his mom said, his kind didn't belong in church. God had better things to do than pay attention to some loser homeless kid.

The officer pulled him backward, and Gavin stared from Adele's tear-streaked face to baby Jaya, clutched in Babysitter's arms. And then Babysitter left with baby Jaya and all her things. A cartoon and a half later, the woman returned for Adele. Only this time, Gavin didn't fight. Couldn't. Hopelessness had rendered him paralyzed.

CHAPTER 18

GAVIN'S HEAD DROOPED forward as conscious thoughts gave way to dreams. A gentle breeze stirred, carrying the sweet scent of freshly cut grass. Laughter bubbled on the air as families spread blankets beneath the shade of trees and filled the picnic tables that dotted the park. Gavin leaned forward, hands propped on his knees, legs spread shoulder distance apart. He tried to catch his breath while Robert fished through a cooler, their football tucked under his arm.

Robert winked and tossed Gavin a cold sports drink. "You're fast, bro." He came to Gavin's side, and the two sat in a patch of shade next to Mom and his sisters.

Gavin gave a dopey smile, the kind he couldn't suppress if he tried.

Something nudged his shoulder, and a distant voice cut through his dream world. Scrunching his face, he tensed, trying to grab hold of the fading image playing through his mind.

"Gavin, wake up." Another nudge.

The scene vanished, replaced by black, and yet, he continued to squeeze his eyes shut, as if doing so could bring back the moment.

"Gavin."

The hand, soft and warm on his shoulder, the voice gentle but firm, incessant. A hint of light pressing through his eyelids, bringing with it cold, harsh reality.

He opened his eyes and stared at Ferret. She stood over him, dark circles shadowing her eyes.

He searched for a clock. "What time is it?"

"It's 7:30. I'm taking you to a children's home on the other side of town."

He bolted upright, a sharp pain shooting through his neck, his spine sore from sleeping in a contorted position. Circulation had left his left foot, and pins and needles pricked his skin as he stirred. "How long? When do I get to see my sisters?"

She shook her head and touched him under the elbow, urging him to his feet. "I'll know more this afternoon, but right now I want to get you to a safe place."

His teeth ground together, sending shock waves through his jaw. *Safe place*—if he heard those words one more time, he'd lose it. The shelter had been a safe place, until these people came and wrenched him and his sisters from it, and from one another. They weren't looking for a "safe place" but instead somewhere they could pawn off a couple of kids. Somewhere they didn't have to deal with them.

He clutched his duffel bag and rose on wobbly legs. With her hand still on his arm, Ferret guided him out of the building and to her car, a silver sedan. She held the passenger door open for him. He glanced toward the street, considered running. Where would he go? Besides, he had no idea where they took his sisters, but this woman knew. And he needed to find out. To make sure they were OK. To get them back.

Ferret slid behind the wheel, offered a stupid smile, and cranked the engine. As she drove, she talked about the place she was taking him to and what he could expect.

He shook his head, his fingers digging into the vinyl seat cushions. "I bet my mom's back, probably pretty mad, too."

Ferret looked at him with soft eyes—like he'd lost a hamster or something. "She hasn't returned."

"Yeah, well, maybe something happened." His stomach lurched as a thousand what-ifs came to mind.

What if she never came back?

They drove the rest of the way in silence, through town, past a convenience store with shoppers going in and out, across intersections and a railroad track. Gavin held his breath and pressed his forehead to the glass, searching every parking lot and street corner for Mom.

He thought of Adele, her tears and trembling shoulders, the pleading in her eyes when they took her from him. His throat closed, and a burning pressure welled within his chest. *Keep it together.* No time for tears, what-ifs, or pity parties. He'd fix this, somehow. Like he always did. When they found Mom, she'd be all freaked out at having almost lost them. She'd pull them all into a big hug, bawling and saying how sorry she was, and everything would go back to normal. No, better than normal, because Mom would finally realize how much she loved them. She'd promise to change, to quit drinking and hanging out with sleazy guys. Maybe she'd even find another Robert.

Ferret Face pulled up to a security gate and punched in numbers. The metal doors screeched open, and they continued up a long road cut between rolling hills. This turned into a gravel lot positioned in front of a two-story brick mansion. Windows framed by white shutters stretched across the front of the building, and four porch pillars gleamed in the early morning sun.

Ferret parked in the shade of a padlocked storage building and turned to Gavin with a stiff, sickly sweet smile that set his nerves on edge.

"We're here. Let's get you checked in." Her overly sweet tone only made him madder, but he kept his mouth shut. Causing a stink wouldn't help him find Mom or get his sisters back. But maybe if he played the good kid, like he did in school, these people would help him out.

A woman dressed in jeans and a T-shirt met them at the front door. The skin hanging from her bony face looked about two sizes too big, and gray roots spread from her scalp to a mess of blonde hair. In bright red letters, her T-shirt read: "Whatever you do for the least of these."

"Good morning, Jesseca." Skin Flapper extended a saggy arm, shook Ferret's hand, then turned to him. "You must be Gavin." She wore the same stupid expression Ferret wore, only with more wrinkles. Apparently they attended the same sappy-face, how-to-freak-kids-out-with-a-psycho-smile class.

He nodded, his hand growing slick around the rough fabric of his duffel bag straps. He followed her into an office that reminded him of his sister's old state-paid preschool. Except instead of stick figure pictures, poorly painted abstracts decorated the walls.

"I'm Roberta Roberts, director of Orange Blossoms Children's Home. Are you thirsty? Hungry?"

Settling into a folding chair beside Ferret, Gavin shook his head. Acid ate away at his stomach lining and climbed up his tightened throat.

Flapper ignored him and reached into a metal cooler pressed against the wall. She pulled out a soda and bagel wrapped in cellophane and slid both across the desk. Gavin watched a droplet of water slither down the can. Grabbing the drink to occupy his hands, he let his gaze drift from Skin Flapper's gray-splotched eyes to a laminated poster tacked behind her.

He skimmed the poem printed on it while flapper talked about rules and expectations. Stupid stuff like no fighting, no swearing, doing chores, keeping your room clean. Her voice droned on like the guy from the eye drops commercial: blah, blah, blah. When finished, she handed Gavin a thick stack of papers and folded her hands on top of her messy desk. "Please take the time to review the rules, and note the schedule printed on page four."

Ferret stood, and back went the saccharine smile. "I'll be in touch." She and Skin Flapper shook hands once again then she left.

Skin Flapper pushed herself up, a slight grimace flashing across her slackened features, then rounded the desk. "I imagine you're exhausted. Come. I'll show you to your room."

She led Gavin through a large multipurpose area with kids of all shades and sizes spread throughout. Heads swiveled in his direction, scowls darkening hardened faces like German shepherds guarding their territory. On one wall, a western played on a flat-screen television, and on another wall were nearly empty bookshelves.

A pack of teens crowded around a foosball table stopped playing, eyeing Gavin as he walked past. Another dude lounged in a recliner, arm draped over the back, ball cap shading his eyes. Forcing his shoulders square and his chin up, Gavin ignored the knots twisting through his intestines and added a swagger to his step. If he'd learned anything living in dive apartments among crackheads and prostitutes, it was not to show fear. Fear attracted alpha males like maggots to rotting meat. Oh, make no mistake, he was already a target—with a big ol' bull's-eye slapped on his back, but even so he'd take it with his head held high. Besides, Mom would come for him soon. She'd barge in waving her fist and cursing like the crackman, all bug-eyed.

They continued through a locked door and up a narrow flight of stairs that smelled like a thrift store then down a hall lined with doors. It reminded Gavin of a cheap hotel right down to the musty carpet and dingy walls. Only this one had rules and schedules plastered everywhere.

Skin Flapper slid a plastic card through an electronic lock then opened the door. "This is where you will sleep."

The room was sparsely furnished—a bed covered in a faded blue blanket, empty wooden shelves where a dresser should have been, an end table like the kind kids make in eighth grade shop class, empty wooden shelves. Two security cameras filled opposite corners, and probably the hall as well, although he hadn't noticed them. They comforted him, in a creeped-out sort of way, assuring him this was one place the alpha dude from the rec room couldn't go.

"I'll let you get settled, catch up on your sleep. The door's left unlocked until lights out, and there's a bathroom down the hall. It's clearly labeled." She pointed. "Please let me know if you need anything. I'll be back in an hour to check on you."

The click of the door echoed through his brain. Dropping his duffel, he shuffled across the room and slumped onto the bed, letting his head fall in his hands. Exhaustion pressed on him, enveloped him, but his raging mind refused to slow.

Where had they taken his sisters? And where was Mom? Did anyone even care? His blood turned cold, pooling in his raging stomach, as he stared at the barred windows draped by striped curtains. Trapped, like a prisoner.

Jacqueline's soft face came to mind, her words replaying like a faint mist. He pulled the slip of paper with her number on it out of his pocket. Stared at it. Studied it. Memorized it. Wouldn't do him any good, though. Not without a cell phone. And he doubted this prison allowed personal phone calls.

CHAPTER 19

JACQUELINE AWOKE TO the sound of birds chirping and the sun streaming through her window. Shuffling from the room in slippered feet, she found Delana nestled in the corner of the couch, feet tucked under her, a steaming coffee mug in hand.

Upon seeing Jacqueline, she planted her feet on the ground and set her cup on the coffee table. "Hey." A hint of smudged mascara shadowed her eyes.

Jacqueline sat beside her. "Morning, sweetie. I got your message. I'm sorry I worried you. I should have called."

Delana eyed her, working her bottom lip. Jacqueline considered telling her of Gavin and his sisters, of how their mom had ditched, and all the events that followed, but painful memories from the past stopped her. Although she'd never left Delana helpless in a shelter, she had left her nonetheless. She'd told herself she was doing what was best, but in reality, all she'd thought about, cared about, was chasing the next big sale. And it'd come, for a while, when the market was booming and houses were selling like funnel cakes at the fair. Until the economy tanked, leaving Jacqueline with a large mortgage and a trail of broken relationships.

Delana wrapped her hands around her mug. "There's coffee. Caramel roast."

Jacqueline inhaled the rich aroma. "It smells wonderful." She plodded to the kitchen, returning with a mug of cream-filled coffee.

Once again, Delana studied her. "What are you doing today?"

Jacqueline shrugged. There were countless things she needed to do. She could check with her insurance, reroute mail, pay the bills shoved in her overnight bag, find a new herbal remedy to counter her hormonal flare-ups. Or sit here with Delana.

"You want to go for a bike ride?"

Jacqueline raised an eyebrow.

"Or not." Delana sipped her coffee.

"No, that's a great idea. Except I don't have a bike."

"I've got an old ten-speed that's been collecting cobwebs in the garage for about a year now."

"Then I guess we have a problem, because I'm not riding piggyback." She chuckled at an image of herself, legs flying, clutching her daughter's waist as they flew down a hill.

"We could rent one. There's a bike rental place down by the river."

"You're serious, aren't you?" She set her mug on the coffee table.

"Why not? Better than watching soap operas all day."

"You know what, you're right. Let's do it. It'll be fun." Jacqueline nestled deeper into the couch cushions, watching her daughter from the corner of her eye, resisting the urge to wrap her arms around her. Instead, she leaned her head against the cushions and closed her eyes. *Thank You, Father.* Now she needed to make sure she didn't do anything to mess this up.

An hour later, they stood outside Mike's Bike Rentals, neon pink helmets strapped on, Delana straddling a racing bike. She let Jacqueline take her ten-speed—an older, less streamlined model with enough gears to give her a headache.

"Don't shift and you'll be fine." Delana made a face and tugged on her helmet strap. "And remember, the brakes are on the handlebars, not the pedals."

They each wore backpacks filled with sunscreen, an extra water bottle, and a few snacks.

Jacqueline pushed her smashed bangs off her forehead, shoving her locks into her helmet. "You know we're going to have some serious hat hair after this, right?"

"Sounds like an excuse to hit the spa."

Except spas cost money, and until her insurance came through—assuming it would, in fact, come through—Jacqueline needed to watch her spending. With a slight smile, she averted her daughter's gaze and gripped the handlebars, her toes digging into the sidewalk for support.

Squinting, she surveyed the long stretch of pavement in front of her. "You know, I can't remember the last time I rode a bike. What if I've forgotten how?"

With one foot on the ground and one on a raised pedal, Delana pulled a water bottle from her drink holder. "You'll get the hang of it. Besides, it burns a killer number of calories. Enough to justify a scoop of ice cream when we're done."

"Really? Then I guess we better get pedaling." She lifted her foot onto the pedal. The bike swayed, and she planted both feet back on the ground, strangling the handlebars with sweaty fingers. A family of five passed by, a girl with blonde braids bringing up the rear.

"OK, now that was plain embarrassing!"

Delana's smile widened. "Right. Gotta show up the kiddos. I always knew you were pretty studly." Her chain zipped as she spun her left pedal backwards.

After a few more wiggles and waggles, Jacqueline managed to lift both feet off the ground. A few tries later, she wobbled down the path while her daughter coasted a few feet ahead. Soon, she relaxed enough to carry on a conversation. By the time they passed the playground, she'd slackened her death grip on the handlebars.

Delana glanced over her shoulder, wisps of hair blowing in her face. "Wanna take five? My rear's getting a little sore."

Jacqueline nodded and coasted to a stop. Inhaling the sweet scent of lilacs and honeysuckle blossoms, she propped her bike in the grass and followed Delana to the shade of a weeping willow.

"Hungry?" Jacqueline plunked down and dropped her helmet onto the grass, sweaty hair plastered to her temples. She rummaged through her backpack until she found the chewy, extra chocolaty, granola bars.

"Starving." Delana accepted the snack Jacqueline offered and tore off the wrapper's corner. "And more than ready for ice cream. Like a whole tub of it. I'm not buying that exercise to lose weight slogan. If anything, it pushes me in the other direction by sending my hunger in overdrive. Which is the last thing I need."

"You're beautiful, and you know it."

"Whatever." Rolling her eyes, Delana took a drink from her water bottle. "So, where'd you go last night? You had me pretty freaked out."

"The shelter."

"All night? I guess you wanted to get away from me pretty bad, huh?"

"No." Jacqueline straightened the wrapper of her granola bar, set it down, and wiped crumbs from her hands. "I met some kids there. Kind of started mentoring them, well, trying to."

"I see." Delana's smile faded.

"Their mom never showed, so we called child protective services."

"Wow." Delana's expression hardened. "A mom who ditched. Sounds familiar. Guess there's no point asking the obvious question, right?"

What kind of mother could walk away from her kids?

Jacqueline swallowed. "I'm sorry. I never meant to hurt you."

"No. In fact, I doubt you thought of me at all." Delana scooted back and rested against the tree trunk.

"You're right. My behavior was unacceptable. But I'm here now, and I'm trying. What's it going to take for us to move past that?"

"You know what? Forget about it. That was a long time ago." She popped the last of her granola bar in her mouth and stood. "I'm ready to head back."

So much for their pleasant mother-daughter day. The best thing Jacqueline could do now was keep her mouth shut and wait for Delana's bitterness to wane. Eventually laughter would outweigh the fights, right? At least that was her goal.

CHAPTER 20

JONATHAN PEELED THE COVERS back, rubbed his dry eyes, and checked the bright red numbers on the clock radio. 10 a.m. He hadn't slept that late since college, and if not for the car alarm blaring in the parking lot below, he probably could've remained in dreamland for a few more hours.

He grabbed his phone off the bedside table. Five missed calls. His pulse quickened as Darren's icy voice, laden with unspoken threats, replayed through his mind. After sifting through a list of potential rebuttals should Darren push the matter further, he skimmed through the return numbers. One call from a foreman, another from his sister, and one he recognized but couldn't place. He returned the call.

"Good morning, Jonathan. Thanks for calling me back."

He rubbed his forehead, a dull ache spreading across the interior of his skull. That voice—

Oh! His realtor. "Mrs. Nelson, I'm so sorry. I completely forgot about our appointment this morning."

"I understand." The edge in her tone countered her words. "I've made a few phone calls, juggled some things around. How soon can you be here?"

"Um . . ." Maybe buying a house wasn't the smartest thing to do, considering he could very well be out of a job soon. How much would a breach of contract cost him, anyway? "Can I get back to you?"

The realtor sighed. "Yes. Yes, of course. And in the meantime, how about I reschedule our appointments for tomorrow afternoon?"

"I'll call you." He hung up before she could finagle him into a commitment. Was it too late to ask Bart for his old job back? Jonathan started to dial the man's number then put his phone away. No sense disrupting Bart's weekend. He'd call Monday, after he had time to sort a few things out. Figure out a life plan, hopefully one able to salvage his retirement without ticking off labor relations.

He ambled across the room and pulled back the heavy wine-colored curtains. Maybe a good, long run would help clear his brain clutter.

Five minutes later, dressed in sweat-wicking running gear and aerated shoes, phone strapped to his arm, he began the long, arduous task of uncoiling his fifty-plus-year-old muscles. Muscles that apparently preferred to go back to bed.

The midmorning sun filtered through the thick row of trees lining the path, splotching the concrete with light. After a half mile, muscle memory kicked in and he settled into a steady rhythm. He quickened his pace until his footfalls matched the beat of an old Hank Kelvins song.

Sweat dripped from his forehead and into his eyes. Didn't bother him. He swiped it away and pushed harder. Suppressing a smile, he passed a guy at least ten years his junior. *This old coon's still got a giddyup in his step after all, thanks to all Evie's nutritional nagging.*

And for what? So he could prolong his lonely, rerun watching life? It wasn't supposed to happen this way. He should've gone first. Better yet, they should've gone together. In a car crash. Blam. Quick end, whisked to heaven hand in hand.

He gazed at the bright blue sky. "Wait for me, babe. I'm coming. Don't know when, but I'll be there."

Why worry about finding a companion, anyway? They said everyone had their soul mate, or more accurately, helpmate. He'd found his. Lonely or not, there wasn't going to be another Evie, and he wasn't the type of guy to go looking for cheap substitutes.

Maybe he needed to take up bowling or something.

He turned the corner. There was a flash of metal, a scream, followed by a *thunk* that sent him skidding across the pavement. A sharp pain shot through his knees, palms, and elbows as he slid across the asphalt.

A crowd was quickly gathering. On the ground lay a woman tangled in a bike, helmet drooped to one side.

"Jacqueline, is that you?" He blinked, his scraped jaw going slack. "Is that you? You OK?"

She glanced around her, cheeks going from blanched to pink. "Yes, thank you. Fancy meeting you here." She worked to untangle herself from the bike while the spectators hovered, some offering to help, others repeating Jonathan's question.

Holding the bike in one hand, he reached out with the other, helping her up. "I'm so sorry. I didn't see you coming."

"Even with my radioactive neon helmet?" She rubbed her shoulder and offered a slight smile. "But that's OK. I hit a decline and kinda whizzed around the corner. I'm not used to brakes on the handlebars. Or bikes." Her blush deepened. "Delana, Jonathan goes to my . . . uh . . . the church I visited. Jonathan, this is my daughter, Delana."

He and Delana exchanged acknowledging nods, hers stiff with a hint of attitude.

She leaned over her handlebars and rested her chin on her forearm. "It looks like we're going to have a long walk back."

He followed her gaze to Jacqueline's sagging front tire, a shard of glass poking into the rubber.

Jacqueline frowned as she stared down the path. "How long have we been riding?"

Delana shrugged. "Not sure. An hour?"

Jacqueline moaned and shook her head. "I'm sorry, Del."

The girl exhaled through tight lips. Her cheeks were rosy, puffy, like they'd been pressure-cooked. "Guess this wasn't such a great idea after all, huh?" She swiped the back of her hand under her neck.

Jacqueline rummaged through her backpack and pulled out a change purse, fished around, and produced a bill. "You go, get yourself a soda or something. I'll meet you there. Or better yet, I'll call a taxi and will meet you at home."

Jonathan cleared his throat. It was probably the time to politely excuse himself, except there was no sense in this woman taking a cab. Not when he had a perfectly good vehicle sitting in the hotel parking lot less than a mile away.

"I can give you a ride. Where you headed?"

"That's nice of you, but," Jacqueline looked from him to her daughter, whose expression was anything but cordial, "I'd hate to put you out."

"It'd give me something to do. Besides, I could use the cool down. These old legs lost some of their steam."

"Yeah, crashing into a crazy woman on a bike has a way of doing that to a body." She laughed, soft and sweet.

"Well, then." Delana propped a foot on a pedal. "If you're sure." She glanced at a silver watch strapped to her wrist. "Because I need to jet."

Scraping her teeth over her bottom lip, Jacqueline looked from Jonathan to her daughter.

"Go." Jonathan waved Delana on. "I'll see she gets home in one piece." Before the last word passed his lips, Delana whirled her bike around and pedaled in the other direction. *Quite the concerned daughter, that one.*

He picked up Jacqueline's ten speed. "I got this." He moved to the side of the path to make room for a pair of bikers dressed in spandex and strolled back toward his hotel.

Jacqueline fell into step beside him. "I appreciate your help."

"No big deal. I gotta head that way anyway."

"And to Twenty-ninth and Vine? Because that's where my daughter lives."

He shrugged. "My momma always told me never leave a damsel in distress."

Jacqueline cocked an eyebrow. "Is that what I am?"

"Just kidding."

They walked in silence for a while, the chains zinging, their footsteps scraping against the pavement. He cast frequent glances her way, noting how her hair bounced on her shoulders and the way the sun hit her cheeks.

Jacqueline gave him a sideways glance. "So, how are you liking Willow Valley? You tried any fried armadillo yet? I hear it's a community favorite."

He chuckled. "Did you now?"

She gave a half shrug. "That and Uncle Jed's famous white chili."

"You must be hungry."

She blushed, the soft pink in her skin accentuating her delicate cheekbones. "Just making small talk."

"I see." Poor woman was wound tighter than a flywheel.

She straightened, her features relaxing, and cast him a sideways glance. "You have children?"

He nodded. "One. She lives four hours away. Engaged to a nice guy from Louisiana."

"That's sweet. When's the date?"

He scratched his head and gazed toward the horizon. "You know, I can't remember. They've changed it four times now. I lost track awhile ago."

"I'm guessing she's a nervous bride?"

"To put it mildly." He smiled, his chest warming. "Just like her mother."

Jacqueline gave him an odd look before turning her attention back to the path in front of her. The rest of the walk, they talked about random stuff—Willow Valley, the hurricane, and clean up efforts, and finally, the shelter in the church's basement.

"It's pretty sad, you know. Seeing so many people who lost so much." She told him about the woman who left her three kids—one of them a baby.

"That's crazy." He shook his head. "Some people don't deserve to have kids."

She frowned and stared at the ground. Great. Now he'd offended her. Maybe it'd be best if he kept his mouth shut.

When they reached the hotel grounds, he loaded the bike in the back of his company truck—something else he'd lose if he quit this job—and hopped in. Jacqueline slid in beside him, her hair windblown, cheeks rosy, green eyes sparkling.

"I'll find us the nearest bike shop." He cranked the engine then flicked on his GPS.

"You don't have to do that."

"Might as well. No sense carting this thing to your house, then you lugging it back to a shop, right? Besides, it's probably on the way." And indeed, it was, in the center of town between a coffee and floral shop, the scents of roses and dark roast merging.

He rounded the truck, pulled her bike out, and hefted it over his shoulder. She followed him into the store and to the counter where a wiry man with long hair pulled in a ponytail stood. A shiny blue name tag read "Rupas from Chicago." "Can I help you?"

"We got a flat."

The man inspected the bike, the skin around his pug nose crinkling. "Gonna need a new tire."

Jacqueline nodded and reached for her purse. "How much does that cost?"

She'd just come out of a major storm, probably lost her home, maybe all she owned. The Christian thing to do—

"I've got it." Jonathan pulled his wallet, and plucked it on the counter.

She frowned. "Now why in the world would you do that?"

He blinked. "I figured, I mean . . . what with the storm and all . . ."

She crossed her arms. "You thought I needed charity."

"No. I mean . . . this was my fault, considering I ran into you."

"Put your billfold away. I'm perfectly capable of paying for a flat tire."

"Be my guest." He swiped the wallet off the counter and shoved it back into his pocket. *Give a gal a ride, and she turns Dr. Jekyll.*

When they got back in the truck, her demeanor softened. "Look, I'm sorry I snapped like that."

"It happens." Evie never acted like that. Well, not after her morning coffee, anyway. He chuckled and cast Jacqueline a sideways glance.

"What's so funny?"

"Just thinking of my wife." He paused, spoke more softly. "She died. Five years ago."

"Oh. I'm so sorry."

"Me, too. But I'm OK, minus the date dodging my sister's forced me into." He told her about Jeanne-Anne's attempts to get him hitched by the time he retired.

"That's crazy. And sweet."

"It's something, that's for sure. But she means well."

That killed the conversation, the hum of the engine filling the void. As he followed his GPS past the grocery mart, his cell phone rang. He glanced at the return number. Jeanne-Anne. "Speaking of." He answered. "Hey, Bean."

"You coming over for dinner tonight?"

"Whatcha making?"

"Like that makes a difference."

"What time?"

"Six sound OK?"

Something in her voice got his hackles up. "What's going on, Beannie?"

"What do you mean?"

"I know that tone."

"What tone?"

"Uh-uh. No games. What do you have planned?"

"Lasagna."

"With whom?"

No answer.

"With whom, Jeanne-Anne?"

Her breath swooshed out, followed by a tidal wave of words spoken so fast it left Jonathan breathless just listening to them. "Her name's Mary, and you'll really like her. She's in my quilting class and leads a women's Bible study at Harmony Sacred across town. She—"

"Nope."

"She's really—"

"Uh-uh."

"Nice. Works for—"

"No."

"The water department—"

"I will hang up."

"Come on. Give this a chance. Besides, I've already invited her."

"Not my problem, sis. I told you last time no more blind dates."

"Jonathan, stop being so stubborn."

"I would, really, but . . ." Life would be so much easier without the "thou shalt not lie" commandment. He held his hand over the receiver and turned to Jacqueline. "You got plans for tonight?"

Her eyes widened, her lashes fluttering, as her mouth went slack. "I, uh . . . tonight? I'm not sure."

"Wanna get something to eat?" That would still leave a few hours of evening, a few hours Jeanne-Anne would find a way to weasel out of him. "Then hit a movie?"

"Uh . . ."

"What do you say?"

"I guess I can check—"

"Great." He pressed the phone to his ear. "Like I was saying, I'd love to, but I've got plans. I'll call you tomorrow?" He hung up before she could press further then glanced at Jacqueline. Had he just asked a woman out? Laughter bubbled in his throat. Maybe this whole dating deal was easier than he thought. Not that he really wanted to date the woman, although she wasn't that bad. Besides, it was one night, and it sure beat spending another evening in the hotel.

CHAPTER 21

GAVIN STARED AT the tray of mushy food in front of him. The peas rested in a puddle of slime. A slab of what he assumed to be meat but looked more like a dehydrated sponge soaked in coffee grounds sat next to a lump of pasty mashed potatoes. They came from a box, gauging by the small flakes that weren't mixed in. No dessert, no soda. Nothing but rehydrated paste accompanied by a pint of sour-smelling milk.

With fork in hand, he glanced at the surrounding tables. Kids gathered in packs of four and five, according to style and ethnicity. Skateboarders hunched over one table, flicking long bangs from their eyes. The rappers sat across the room, scowling. Three wiry guys huddled in the middle of the cafeteria looking like stalking victims with the way they eyed the place.

And Gavin? He sat alone two tables down, a long empty bench stretched on either side of him. A few of the other guys shot him fierce glares. One with a unibrow set in a square face, arms barricaded around his tray, stared him down. Gavin stared back, shoulders and biceps flexed, left hand fisted, right strangling his fork.

When a tendon in the kid's jaw twitched, Gavin broke the alpha stare first and focused on his plate. He stirred the peas. His stomach vacillated between growling and lurching. Hunger won, and he shoved a glob of goo into his mouth. It clung to the back of his throat. He grabbed his milk and took a gulp, then another, until the gunk slid into his gut. Stealing a glance toward the stare-down kid, he exhaled. The dude was gone. Probably found someone else to creep on.

A fight broke out across the cafeteria, and the few adults manning the room rushed to referee. Apparently some kid was having a mental breakdown, screaming, swearing, flailing. Great.

Gavin was surrounded by a bunch of crazies. What was this place, anyway? A community drop-off, like those clothing recycle bins stuck in parking lots, except this was for kids?

Footsteps approached, and a shadow fell over him as a pack of foul-smelling guys hovered around him. One of them pressed against Gavin's back, thick hands landing on either side of him. His hot breath, which smelled like curdled milk and garlic, flowed over Gavin's right ear.

His chest squeezed when he looked to the empty table where the stare-down kid once sat.

"Lookie here." Jo-Jo, an ugly dude with one-inch gauges in both ears, slid beside Gavin, straddling the bench. "We got ourselves a new pansy." His posse copied the guy, hedging Gavin in. "You a crier or a whiner?" He grabbed Gavin's milk and poured it over his food. The dude's friends made slurping noises while he swirled the paste into a multicolored mass. "Waste not, want not." He plunged his spoon into the goop and raised it to Gavin's face, green sludge dripping back onto the tray. "Open wide, dweeb boy."

Gavin smacked his hand, splattering the dude's friend in the face. "Lay off me."

"You want to play, nerdo?" Jo-Jo yanked Gavin by the hair and thrust his face into his tray, grinding until goo squeezed into his nose and seeped through his compressed lips.

Gavin sputtered. Gripping the edge of the table, he fought to turn his head, but the kid pressed harder, crushing Gavin's nose.

The pressure lifted, and Gavin raised his head as Jo-Jo's voice lightened. "What are you doing, dude?" Gavin wiped the gunk from his eyes, staring from one face to the other, a staunch form passing through his peripheral vision. Heels clicked on the linoleum, and a woman in a stained apron approached.

She jabbed her hands on her hips, face pinched. "What's going on over here?"

Jo-Jo laughed. "This kid challenged us to some eating contest, puppy dog style." He handed Gavin a napkin. "Said he'd clear his plate in thirty seconds." He checked his watch. "Got fifteen left, bro."

The woman crossed her arms and narrowed her eyes. "Why do I find that hard to believe?" She pulled a pen from her apron and scrolled something on a clipboard. "Gavin, do you care to tell me what happened here?"

Gavin swallowed. A quick glance confirmed what he already knew. He had two options: keep his mouth shut and play along, or raise the stakes and head to round two. He chose the former. "Just trying to be funny, ma'am."

The woman stared at him for a minute longer, but then more drama broke out across the cafeteria. Another fistfight, this time two on one as adults tried to tug them apart. Gavin quickly forgotten, the woman spun around and pulled a walkie-talkie from her front pocket. With the contraption pressed to her ear, she stalked away, plump hips swaying.

Jo-Jo and his gang broke out in laughter. "Show us what you got, dweeb boy." He hacked up a wad of phlegm and spit it into Gavin's tray. With his gaze locked on Gavin's, he stirred, grabbed Gavin's spoon, and held it up. "Like I said, you got fifteen seconds." His eyes darkened and a tendon in his jaw twitched.

Gavin's stomach lurched, flooding his throat with bile.

"Go."

JACQUELINE CHECKED HER phone. No missed calls, from Gavin or Irene. And there was no sense calling the social worker, not today. Hopefully Jacqueline could find out more Monday, although something told her it wouldn't be good. Based on what she read on the Internet, the system was overloaded with unclaimed kids. Hurricane Gita had only made things worse, such a sad truth with no apparent solution. So many lives destroyed. So much irreversible destruction.

All that remained of her worldly belongings was piled along the far wall. Bills and other junk mail poked from the outer pocket of her suitcase, demanding her attention. She'd deal with them tomorrow, right after she contacted her insurance company.

The clock radio read 5:40 p.m. Jonathan would be here any minute. A slight giggle popped out. Had she really agreed to a date with that man? Technically no, although she hadn't turned him down either. She blamed it on the sun, the deflated bike tire, and her tumultuous interchange with Delana. A woman could only handle so much before the mind started to fade. And apparently, when the mind faded you ended up dating uncouth railroaders who wore flip-flops to church and had hardhats crammed into the back of their pickups. Nothing like the steak and champagne her previous date Kelvin had offered, but then again, Kelvin nearly put her to sleep with his endless droning.

She glanced in the mirror and flashed her teeth to check for lipstick stains. Like usual, a glob clung to her right central incisor. More fanned into the wrinkles around her lips. Grabbing a tissue, she rubbed it off, opting for gloss instead.

She smoothed foundation around her crow's feet, tucked extra sweat dabbers, aka wet wipes, into her trendy little case, and started to leave.

Her cell phone rang. She glanced at her screen and smiled. Elaine.

"Hey, there. How's Grammaville?" She strolled out of the room, closing the door behind her.

"Great!" Giggles and a household full of voices seeped across the line. "But I plan to go back to Crystal Shores next week to survey the damage and pick up the pieces, whatever's left of them anyway. Wanna join me?"

"I don't know, Elaine. Maybe." Truth be told, that was the last thing she wanted to do. Seeing the devastation on the news each morning was hard enough.

"You still thinking about relocating to Willow Valley?"

"I was, although I'm not sure that's such a great idea." She told her about the bike ride with Delana, the brief stretch of laughter, followed by an extended period of bitterness. "If I didn't know better, I'd say she's bipolar."

"Or riding the emotion tidal wave as she trudges through life without Jesus. We both know what a crazy ride that is." Elaine paused. "I hope this doesn't mean you're going to spend the evening moping around."

"Actually, I've got a date."

"Get out."

"No, really. In fact, he'll be here in about fifteen minutes."

"Girl, you move fast! But good for you. A bit of fun will do you good." Her tone tightened. "Where'd you find this guy anyway?"

"Relax. He's not a psycho. At least, not that I can tell." Laughing, Jacqueline told her the whole story, from their bicycle fiasco to Jonathan dodging his sister.

"Ah, so a relationship of convenience, huh?"

"Necessitated by sheer boredom. Probably not the best reason to spend the evening with a guy I barely know."

"He sounds harmless enough. I say go for it."

Jacqueline moved into the kitchen to make a cup of tea while waiting for her knight in not-so-shining armor. The doorbell rang at the same time as the kettle shrieked. "I gotta go. I think he's here. I'll call you later this week?" She turned off the stove and strolled out of the kitchen and toward the door.

"Sounds good. Have fun—the G-rated version, of course."

Shaking her head, Jacqueline hung up and dropped her phone into her purse. She slung it over her shoulder and answered the door. Jonathan stood on the stoop, feet shoulder distance apart, hands shoved into his pockets, a crooked grin on his face.

"Hi."

"Hi."

The two stared at each other like gawky tweens at their first dance. He wore a Louisiana State University (LSU) T-shirt with a ball cap, cargo shorts, and flip-flops, a sharp contrast to her mint green sundress and matching sandals.

He stepped aside and angled toward the parking lot. "So, you hungry?"

"Starved." She stepped out, locking the door behind her.

He cast her a sideways glance. "I kind of thought you'd cancel."

She smiled. "Almost did."

"Yeah, me, too. Except then I'd have to face my sister and another blind date. Never been one to lie."

"Right. Asking strange women to go out with you is so much easier."

"Exactly. Where do you want to go? For dinner, I mean?"

She glanced again at his flip-flops and the hairy toes protruding from them. The Golden Olive was out, as was the Errege Mahai. "I'm up for anything."

"Chinese it is. A machinist at work told me about a great place across town. Wok-n-Walk. I figured we could get it to go and head to the river. What do you say?"

Like a picnic? She glanced down at her designer dress and swallowed. She was about to protest when his phone rang, and based on his emerging scowl, it wasn't good. By the time he got off, they'd already pulled into Wok-n-Walk's drive-through, and she decided it wasn't worth pressing the matter. This date probably wouldn't make her top ten, but at least she wasn't sitting in an empty house or tiptoeing around a bitter daughter. Not that she could avoid Delana forever. But come tomorrow, their little one-sided spat would be forgotten, and awkward tension would return.

While they drove to the river, the rich smell of garlic and ginger permeating his truck, they talked about sports. He wasn't really an LSU fan, but their T-shirts had been on sale. He grew up in Los Angeles but developed a taste for country music and collard greens after spending a summer on his grandfather's farm in central Iowa. They talked more about the shelter, the kids, and how food donations dwindled along with the media hype. By the time they reached the rectangular parking lot in front of the boat launch, Jacqueline started to relax until he cut the engine, draped his hands over the steering wheel, and turned his hazel eyes on her.

"I'm not looking for anything serious. I might not even be here in a few months, the way my job's going."

"Same here, on both counts."

"I'm not into casual sex either."

Heat seared her cheeks, and her mouth dropped. "Excuse me?" She pulled her spine straight.

"Not saying you are or anything. Just laying it all out so there's no misunderstanding."

Was this guy serious? Although his blunt honesty was better than the stupid lines most men shoveled. Slightly.

"But maybe we can hang out once in a while, seeing as how we're both new in town. Hit a movie, picnic." He swept his arm toward the river. "Whatever." The corners of his eyes crinkled, the green flecks dancing in the sun. "Sound doable?"

She stared at him for an extended moment. "Why not? Might be fun, as long as bicycles aren't involved."

CHAPTER 22

GAVIN SAT IN the recreation room, paper, pencil, and markers in front of him. He wanted to give Adele something to hold on to, but a picture seemed cheesy. Besides, he couldn't draw. Maybe a poem? Except that was stupid, too. Only poetry he'd ever written was those haiku things, which were easy, if you knew the formula. One word followed by three, or maybe three then five. He couldn't remember. So instead, he wrote a simple letter. Something to give Adele hope.

Poor baby Jaya. There was nothing he could do for her. Nothing she would understand. Was she scared? Of course she was. She didn't understand what was going on, where she was, or why the strangers took her. All she knew was she didn't have Momma, him, or Adele. Did she cry at night? Did her foster parents hold her, comfort her? Or did they get frustrated and stick her in a crib? Or worse?

He couldn't think about that now. Wasn't nothing he could do about it anyway.

He picked up his pencil and chewed on the eraser. Words flowed through his mind, promises he longed to give but knew he couldn't keep. He wrote the first sentence, erased it, then tried again. In the end, he retold a story from the comic book Bible. It was the one about a guy named Joseph, sitting as second in command of all Egypt, reunited with his family. It was her favorite. His, too.

Harsh laughter came from behind, and Gavin flinched.

"You writing a love letter, dweeb boy?" Jo-Jo planted his hands on the table directly in front of Gavin, his posse surrounding him. "Let me guess, you and one of your locker-room buddies getting friendly?" He snatched up the paper.

Gavin lunged for it. "Leave me alone!" The sheet tore.

The boys laughed, and Jo-Jo held the ripped page in the air. "Ah, so sad." He turned it toward him. "Adele? Who's Adele, lover boy? Is she a hottie? You won't keep her all to yourself, will you?"

A sharp pain shot through Gavin's right ear as his teeth ground together. He gripped his pencil in one hand and fisted the other. His muscles itched for release, to pound the smile off Jo-Jo's face, hear him whimper like a baby.

"Is there a problem?"

The posse moved as everyone turned to look.

Ms. Roberts approached, face stern. She crossed her arms and looked from one face to the next. "What's going on here, boys?"

Jo-Jo gave an easy smile. "Nothing, ma'am. Just being friendly with the new boy."

She frowned. "Are you, now?" She looked at Gavin. "Is everything OK?"

With muscles stiffer than frozen taffy, Gavin forced a smile. "Jo-Jo here was telling me . . ." Sweat pooled under his palms as a spicy comeback hovered on the tip of his tongue. How he'd love to humiliate Jo-Jo in front of his loser friends. "We were talking about . . . stupid stuff."

Ms. Roberts's eyes narrowed on each of them in turn. Then, as if giving up, she sighed. "Gavin, you've got a visitor."

A smile tugged on his mouth. "My sisters?"

"No, sweetie, not today."

Gavin exhaled, wilting, but then someone else came to mind. Mom? Maybe she'd finally come to take him out of this nasty place. Bring him to stay with her, wherever that was, or to the shelter. Any place was better than this dump with its psychos. Only this time he kept the question to himself, preferring to hold on to the hope it offered as long as possible.

Ms. Roberts touched her hand to Gavin's back. "Remember we talked about this? About the Lewises?"

He stared at the table and pushed up on stiff legs.

"They're here to meet with you. They're a nice family. I'm sure you'll like them."

A few heads turned and conversations stilled as he followed her out of the room and toward the administration's office. Gavin knew the questions behind everyone's watchful eyes because he'd asked them, too, every time Ms. Roberts pulled a kid. Sometimes the kids returned, scowling, throwing junk into a bag. Others got real quiet. Only one came back smiling, talking about going home with his Mama while everyone else placed bets on how long his "reunion" would last. Most gave him two weeks.

Their footsteps echoed in the empty hall, mirroring the thud of Gavin's racing heart. As they walked, he held tight to his fantasy, played it in his mind. Maybe Mom didn't come this time, but she would—soon—once whatever jerk she ran off with found someone else. When she did, Gavin would act mad at first, not talking. He'd make Mom think he might not want to come home, like he liked this dump or something. She'd cry, tell him what a terrible mom she'd been, how much she loves him, and how badly she wants him back. She'd promise never to hurt him like that again. His sisters would be with her, too, hugging and laughing. Adele would be talking so fast her words would all jumble together.

Soon. They'd all be together again soon.

Ms. Roberts stopped outside a closed door near the end of the hall, three rooms down from her office. Although Gavin had never been there, he'd seen enough kids slip inside, acting all jittery, to know it was where big things happened— important things.

Ms. Roberts brushed a hand across her forehead, smoothing imaginary locks of hair. Then she turned to Gavin with a weak smile. Her gaze swept over him as if doing a mental inventory. This made Gavin's stomach clench all the more.

When Ms. Roberts reached for the doorknob, Gavin sucked air into tight lungs. The door swished open with a creak, and he stared at a couple plucked straight from one of those old black-and-white movies. Ferret Face was there, too, dressed in brown.

The woman had hair the color of mud and translucent, almost vampire-like skin. She stared at Gavin through dull gray eyes, chin raised, back straight. Her husband had black hair slicked to one side. He wore a plaid collared shirt, buttoned to the top, and forest green shorts. A girl with long brown hair that flowed over her shoulders in loose ringlets sat kitty-corner from them. Pink filled her cheeks when she glanced at Gavin.

They rose and Ms. Roberts made introductions. "Gavin, this is Mr. and Mrs. Lewis."

The man stepped forward and reached out a thick, hairy hand.

Gavin stared at it, then at the man's narrowed eyes, before giving in. The man's skin was rough, callused.

"Good to meet you, son. The missus and I have been taking in fosters for over ten years."

"And this is their birth daughter, Emma Rose." Ferret motioned to the teen, who nodded, then studied the floor.

The man returned to his seat and propped his elbows on the armrest, hands steepled. "We understand the issues involved with . . . foster parenting and have developed a successful program."

He glanced at his wife, who nodded, her lips pressed so tight that white lines fanned out from her mouth.

Gavin sat in a faded chair, the kind with sagging cushions that nearly swallowed a body, forcing kneecaps to chin level.

Ferret sat to Gavin's right, her face contorted like she and her lips battled over whether or not to smile. All four of them huddled around a scuffed coffee table.

"As I said, we've had many a kid in our home over the years." Mr. Lewis's Adam's apple bobbed when he spoke. "Those who follow the rules, contribute to the family, do well. There will be no television—it dulls the brain and provokes irrational thinking. No video games—they lead to violence and antisocial behavior. As you may know, corporal punishment is not allowed, so we utilize a behavior modification system based on reality discipline. It is quite effective."

He went on to talk about unity between the body, mind, and spirit, and the importance of a well-balanced diet in proper proportions. "Soda pop rots the teeth and contributes to attention deficit disorder." He followed with an explanation of the need for consistent "times of silence."

Didn't matter. Gavin could deal with anything so long as this guy got him out of here and provided access to a telephone.

Mrs. Lewis shifted and crossed her ankles. "We operate on a three strikes system."

Her husband nodded. "We simply do not have the time or energy to deal with problem children who have no desire to obey."

The prickly pair laid out a few more rules and expectations, using words plucked straight from the dictionary. They asked Gavin some questions and ended with a lame motivational speech about rising above your circumstances. Gavin understood that. He'd been doing that all his life, not that it'd gotten him anywhere. But he wouldn't give up. Not yet. Four more years and he'd be free—an adult—paying for no one's dumb choices but his own.

After they left, Ferret Face talked about his "case." Apparently, a court date approached. If his mom showed, she'd learn what she needed to do to get Gavin and his sisters back. But since no one knew where she was—

Like they cared. Had they even looked?

Ferret leaned forward. "The Lewises are a great family, and they'd like to take you in. They might be a little more regimented than you are accustomed to, but you'll adapt."

"What about my sisters? Are they coming too?" A dull ache filled his chest as he fought to keep his voice steady.

"I'm sorry, but no."

"Where are they? When can we all live together?"

Ferret's eyes got all misty. "We're doing the best we can, Gavin. It's very difficult to find individuals willing to take babies *and* teenagers. Most of our families are too full to take on multiple children."

An old fable called *The Mitten* came to mind. In the story, an animal found a glove to winter in. Page after page, more animals arrived seeking shelter. Each one received the same response: "There's always room for one more."

In storybooks, maybe.

Ferret stood, face all droopy, like she stared at some bony kitten found under an abandoned car. "It might take you some time to get used to living with another family, to learn their rules, but give it a chance. I'll be back on Wednesday to pick you up."

CHAPTER 23

JACQUELINE PACED THE kitchen, phone pressed to her ear, repeating her policy number for the third time in under two weeks. "I've left several messages but haven't heard back yet."

"I apologize for that. As I'm sure you can imagine, we've received a large number of claims, and our agents are doing their best to get in touch with every client as quickly as possible. I can look it up. What's your name?"

"Jacqueline. Jacqueline Dunn."

Clicking came through the line. "2389 Olive Boulevard?"

"Correct." She probably should've paid more attention to the insurance salesman when he droned on about coverage and liabilities. And clearly opting for the higher deductible and lower premium hadn't been her smartest move, considering she lived on the coast.

"I'll have a claims officer get back to you. Is this a good number?"

She sighed, massaging her temples. "Yes. When should I hear from him?" More importantly, when would she receive her cash payoff? In time to make an offer on the boutique?

"As soon as possible, ma'am."

That was informative.

Forcing a thank you, she hung up and tossed her phone onto her bed. Why did it feel like she kept running into one slammed door after another? Lord, Elaine told me You never promised Your followers rainbows and unicorns, but an occasional ray of sunshine would be nice about now.

She moved to a small box buried under a mound of junk. She cleared everything off and sifted through the contents until she found a stack of pictures secured by a rubber band. Her heart clenched at a hand-drawn image of her and Delana—stick figures, holding hands. A round, yellow sun hovered above them. *Best mommy ever* was scrawled in childish handwriting across the top.

Where would they be now if Jacqueline had been a better mother? If she'd stood by Delana through the rebellion, the bulimia, the anger, instead of passing her off to Delana's father? A man who had proved completely irresponsible—neither one of them had seen or heard from him in over a decade—leaving their daughter more wounded than ever.

If only she could start again, with Jesus standing beside her. She'd be a great mom. Patient, loving, nurturing, the kind kids confided in and wanted to hang out with.

Her thoughts drifted to Gavin and his sisters, and of their time sitting in the hall, the comic book Bible laid between them. The way he and Adele watched her—no bitterness or contempt, merely curiosity and perhaps even a hint of admiration. And in that moment, it was as if God had given her a do-over, a chance to make amends through another child.

But now they were gone. Only this time she wouldn't walk away. Even so, there wasn't much she could do except commit to pray for those kids. That, and she could stand behind them, let them know she was here. Like she should've been for Delana.

She grabbed her phone and the social worker's business card off her dresser. She punched in the social worker's number.

"Jesseca Mansfield, child protective services. May I help you?"

"Hello, this is Jacqueline Dunn. We met the other night. At the shelter."

"Yes? Is there a problem?"

"No. No problem. Actually, I'm calling about the children you interviewed. Gavin, Adele, and Jaya?"

"Yes?"

"Are they OK? Have you found a safe place for them to stay? Can I visit them?"

"Irene told me you've formed a relationship with the children. Were you wanting to learn the steps involved in becoming a foster parent?"

"What? No! I mean . . . I'm fifty-one years old." And single, unemployed, basically homeless. Besides, she'd already messed up her own kid.

"What can I do for you, Ms. Dunn?"

"I just want them to know someone cares about them. That they're not alone."

"I'll call the group—I mean, I'll see what I can do."

"Group what? Group home? Where are the children staying, Mrs. Mansfield?"

"I'm sorry, I can't discuss their case with you, but I will work on arrangements. You aren't an approved guardian, so your visits will need to be supervised."

Jacqueline's stomach soured as more questions filled her mind. She knew so little about the foster care system and abandoned children. "OK. I understand."

After ending the call, she turned to her computer, looking for answers. Mrs. Mansfield's guarded voice concerned her. Where did kids go, once they were taken from their parents?

She found a foster care support group on a social media website, read a few stories. She followed a link to an article discussing the problems of an overburdened system. Children ripped from their families, sibling groups separated, some stuck in group homes. Some even sent to juvenile detention facilities where they underwent strip searches.

The article quoted a man raised in the system, placed in ten homes before spending the remainder of his adolescence in a place for troubled kids. Not because he'd done anything wrong but because there was nowhere else for him to go.

She slumped forward, holding her head in her hand. What about Gavin? Had he and his sisters been split up? How many homes would they be cycled through? Worse, how long before the system broke them?

Lord, please fix this. Place those children in a loving home. Keep them together. All they have is one another.

She grabbed her purse, tucked her phone inside, and headed out. En route to her car, she sifted through foggy brain matter in an effort to recall the name of her daughter's dental office. A quick Internet search jogged her memory, and she pulled into the parking lot of Dazzling Smiles fifteen minutes later.

A handful of people filled the lobby, and a woman with curly black hair manned the receptionist counter.

When Jacqueline approached, the woman lifted a fleshy chin and peered at Jacqueline through leopard print glasses. A thick gold chain dangled from the rims to her ears. "Can I help you?"

"Yes, I'm here to see Delana Dunn."

"May I tell her who's visiting?"

"Her mother."

"Oh." The woman studied Jacqueline a moment longer then left.

A short time later, Delana appeared wearing powder blue scrubs. A paper mask dangled around her neck. "Mom . . . Is everything all right?"

"Yes, of course." Jacqueline flicked her wrist. "What time's your lunch?"

"Normally 12:30, why?"

"I thought it'd be fun to catch a bite. I saw a cute little bistro down the road."

"That's a lovely thought, but unfortunately, I'm working through lunch today. We had a messy filling that set us back."

"That's crazy. How many hours are you working today?"

Delana shrugged. "Nine. No big deal."

"It is a big deal. You deserve a break, and you should take it. You can't let your boss take advantage of you like that."

"Like I said, it's no big deal. And no one's taking advantage of anyone. Things happen. We're a team here, and we deal with things like a team."

Jacqueline turned as a tall man dressed in a crisp white lab coat emerged through a side door. A blonde woman with gold earrings and a matching pendant necklace accompanied him. She was trim, petite, and matchy matchy from her pink sandals to her designer purse and rose-tinted lipstick.

"I'll see you at home, then." The woman rose on tiptoes and planted a kiss on the man's cheek.

With a strained expression, he glanced at Delana. She blanched, and her right cheek twitched as her plastic smile reemerged.

Jacqueline's gaze darted between them, fighting a scowl. Clearly the man intimidated Delana. Could she—?

No. Of course not.

The woman left, and the dentist turned to Jacqueline, thick lips stretching over straight, white teeth. "I'm Dr. Layton." He extended his hand and they shook. "I hear you're Delana's mother." He wore his sandy-blond hair short, spiked in the front, and had eyes the color of cappuccino. "Your daughter is a wonderful addition to our team."

"Really? If that's the case—" Jacqueline was about to push for Delana's lunch break when a hygienist poked her head through the door.

"Dr. Layton, I have a question." Soft curls framed the hygienist's face.

"I'll be right there." He excused himself with a nod.

Delana looked from the door to her mother. "I've got to go. I'll be home around 6:00. Maybe we can rent a movie or something?"

Jacqueline blinked. In a flash, her daughter's tone went from stale to sugared, but hey, she'd take it. "Sounds great. I'll rent a movie this afternoon."

She ambled back to her car, squinting in the bright morning sun. Trying to reconnect with Delana was like riding a roller coaster in the dark. Only amusement rides had an expected end, returning exactly where they started. Oy.

She slid behind the wheel and cranked the engine. Music poured from her speakers, and hot air blasted her face. It turned goose-bump cold by the time she made it to the first stoplight.

Her cell phone rang. She flicked off the radio and glanced at the return number flashing on the screen. It was local and vaguely familiar.

"Good afternoon, this is Jacqueline."

"Yes, hello. This is Sky Rainbows from Silver Sky Boutique."

"Yes?" Jacqueline felt a flutter of excitement.

"I've received an offer and wanted to give you a chance to counter."

Could be the woman was bluffing to force her hand, a common trick. But if not—

"How much did they offer?" Only a newbie would answer that question.

"Not as much as I'd hoped, which is why I'm calling."

"I see."

"Are you still interested?"

"Yes, I mean . . ."

Delana would hate her. Or begin to trust her, once she saw Jacqueline wasn't going anywhere. But unless her insurance company came through, the down payment would eat what little savings Jacqueline had. Her retirement funds. If it failed, she'd be the oldest burger flipper in the South.

CHAPTER 24

GAVIN SAT WITH his knees up, spine pressed against a hot brick wall. The midmorning sun loomed over him like an angry ball of fire. The late-August heat caused sweat to drip down his back, making him itch. Sighing, he wiped his forehead with the back of his hand and started across the soccer field. The drinking fountain beckoned him, but reaching it meant passing Jo-Jo and his gang. Gavin wasn't that thirsty.

Four adults "supervised" the recreation area, two deep in conversation beneath the shade of an old, knotted tree. A man the kids nicknamed Captain Hook because of his hooked nose and deep-set eyes, refereed a football game turned fighting match. A lady called Dorothy-Do talked with a wiry kid called Slopstick, who walked with a permanent hunch, gaze locked on the floor.

Rumor had it the staff found his sheets smeared with feces, which created a ripple effect of snickers throughout the dorm. Everyone knew the culprits, probably the staff did too, but clearly ignorance made things easier.

Oh, they held their investigation—lined all the kids up, making threats like they actually had the power to follow through. But no one messed with Jo-Jo—not the kids or the staff. Besides, why point fingers at the psychos when Slopstick offered to take the blame? Yeah, the kid had a party with the toilet and brought it to bed with him. Course, half the guys up in here were crazy enough to do just that. Gavin almost envied them. Maybe being crazy made things easier, helped them forget they were stuck in a people pound.

Only Gavin wasn't stuck, least not forever. All he needed was a plan. He touched the slip of paper tucked in his back pocket, remembering the look on Jacqueline's face when she gave it to him. She said he could call her any time, if he needed anything. Did she mean it?

A shadow passed over him, and he glanced up to see Roberta Roberts wearing one of her creepy smiles that always made her eyes bulge. He swallowed, a cinder block settling in his gut. Nothing good ever came from a smile like that, especially not in a place like this.

The wind stirred the hair around her face, and she smoothed it back with thick, knobby fingers. "Mrs. Mansfield is here to take you for your transitional visit."

He suppressed a snort. Transitional visit? Like speed dating? *You've got two hours to decide if you want to mooch off this family, except you don't really get to decide. Nope. Strangers do that for you.*

He stared at her, throat dry, and wiped sweaty hands on his shorts. "They found my mom yet?"

Her smile hovered near a frown. "I don't think so. Your case worker will talk about that, I'm sure."

Touching his shoulder, she guided him around unit B, a two-story brick building that housed twenty, maybe thirty kids, most they called lifers—those who'd been in the system so long, they'd started to grow moss. They continued past two more housing units to Gavin's.

He stopped. "What if my mom shows up? They'll tell her where I'm at?"

She nodded and nudged his arm. "Of course."

He didn't budge. "And Jacqueline?"

"Who?"

"The woman from the shelter. My friend." *Friend* was pushing it. So the lady gave him her number. It was probably nothing more than a blow off. She wouldn't care that he looked at it every night, read it so many times the numbers replayed in his sleep.

"I'm not sure. You can ask Mrs. Mansfield." She nudged him again, with more force this time, and he complied.

They reached the sitting room to find Ferret Face waiting for them, dressed in her usual brown, dark circles under her eyes. Her hair hung limp around her pale face, adding to her droopy appearance.

She stood. "Gavin, how are you?"

He studied her, stomach turning back flips. "Where are my sisters?"

Mrs. Roberts touched the small of Gavin's back and pushed him forward. "I'll leave the two of you to talk." The door clicked behind her, instantly thickening the air.

Ferret Face motioned toward the couch then sat back down. Gavin stared at the coffee table to avoid her shadowed eyes. He knew he was pathetic. Didn't need her pity to remind him. What he needed was a way out.

"As you know, there's been a court hearing." She folded her hands and sat like one of those stone statues outside public libraries. "We haven't located your mother. The judge is giving us time to do that and would like me to ask you some questions."

Gavin studied the lace doily on the coffee table. Counted the holes.

"Do you have any relatives we could contact?"

He stayed stock-still, unblinking, barely breathing. She'd asked this question half a dozen times, but today he considered answering. If only to get her off his back. He didn't buy their "We're doing all we can to find your mom" garbage. Maybe so they could lock her up for being an unfit mother. Or maybe they thought she was dead or something. His stomach soured as an image of the guy she was last seen with came to mind.

"I'm trying to help you here. We're doing all we can to find your mother, but we're running out of places to look."

"I got an aunt." Admitting his grandma kicked his mom out at the age of fifteen wouldn't help.

Ferret smiled. "Good. Wonderful. What's her name?"

"Gigi."

She wrote on a yellow notepad. "Last name?"

"Not sure. Maybe Kross, like me. But I think she got married."

"Do you know where she lives?"

"Up north. I think."

"When was the last time you saw her?"

"Six or seven years ago. Only met her twice." Although she'd tried to help. Came toting a Bible talking about Jesus and living right. The visit ended in blows and his mom chasing Gigi out, wielding a broom and shouting curse words.

"What about your dad?"

Gavin stared at the table, traced a crack with his finger. Admitting his dad was probably a one-night deal wouldn't help. But there was Robert. "Never met my dad. Don't know his name." Except for what his mom called the guy, which would turn Ferret's cadaver complexion tomato red. "But there is a guy who used to hang out. His name's Robert. I bet he'd take us. All of us."

Ferret looked at him for a long time, wrinkles deepening on her forehead. "Do you have a last name?"

Slumping, Gavin exhaled. He shook his head.

They talked for another ten minutes, Ferret babbling on about court dates, lawyers, and a bunch of other junk.

When she started talking about his "transitional meeting," he cut her off. "What about my sisters? Have you found anyone to take us all?"

"I'm sorry, but we haven't."

"When do I get to see them?"

"I'm working with the other foster parents to arrange a visit." She checked her watch. "Are you ready? The Lewises are anxiously waiting." That horror movie smile returned below hollow eyes.

He shrugged. Did it matter?

She gathered her things and guided him out of the group home and to her car. Leaving the city, they continued down a two-lane country road, past faded barns and long stretches of pastureland. On the way, Ferret asked a bunch of dumb questions like what kind of music Gavin liked, how he liked the group home—seriously? It was a real party. Like juvie with ice cream. But he told her what she wanted to hear, then pressed his cheek against the window and watched the power lines blur together.

They turned onto a gravel road encased with trees. Branches scraped the side of Ferret's car, and potholes made Gavin's teeth clash together. A sour smell, like rotting corn mixed with horse manure, filled the air. The trees cleared and a two-story farmhouse surrounded by cornfields came into view. Three silos stood in front of a weathered barn, and a sagging fence surrounded a bunch of pigs.

Ferret pulled behind a rusted pickup and cut the engine. She flashed her fake smile. "You ready?"

And if he said no? He shrugged and touched his door handle. This place couldn't be that bad. Anything had to be better than the kid pound with Jo-Jo and his loogie-hurling, feces-smearing gang. Besides, the Lewises had a cute daughter.

A hot wind swept over him as he stepped onto the gravel drive. Nearing the lopsided wooden steps leading to a covered porch, he stopped, eyes wide. A fat chicken waddled in front of him, clucking and pecking the ground. Scattered across the dirt-packed yard, two more chickens and an ugly rooster did the same.

In the shade of the front porch, an old golden retriever sprawled, front legs stretched in front of him. He looked up, swished his tail, then dropped his head. Gavin fought a smile. He'd always wanted a dog, but Mom said they stank and ate too much.

The door creaked open as Ferret reached for the doorbell. Mr. and Mrs. Lewis stood before them, him in coveralls, her in a yellow dress and floral apron. They flashed matching smiles, then moved aside to allow Gavin and Ferret in. The house smelled like chocolate chip cookies and pine-scented cleaning fluid.

"Welcome." Mrs. Lewis twined her hands and held them near her naval.

Gavin nodded and scanned the dim interior. His pulse quickened at the sight of Emma Rose, sitting in a rocker. He squared his shoulders and puffed out his 5-feet-4-inch, 110-pound frame.

Light drifted from a dome in the ceiling and two lamps centered on ancient-looking end tables. An old chest, like those found in thrift stores, acted as the coffee table. A hodgepodge of furniture placed around it—a green recliner, plaid love seat, another rocker made from knotted branches and thick twine.

Ferret Face hovered near the door. "I'll be back in a few hours."

Don't leave me here!

Gavin tensed, fighting against a sudden urge to bolt. Not a bad idea, really, if Mr. Lewis didn't outsize him by a foot and one hundred pounds. Ferret left, the door banging behind her, and he considered making a run for the cornfields. Plenty of food, as disgusting as it would be. An option, if things got weird. Minus losing contact with his sisters.

Mr. Lewis sat in the plaid chair and jerked his head toward the couch. "Have a seat." He looked at his wife. "Barb, bring the cookies."

Gavin flinched at the man's throaty voice. Mrs. Lewis nodded and scurried away. The clatter of closing cupboards and clanging dishes followed.

Gavin perched on the edge of the seat cushion and focused on a brass lock on the chest. Rust lined the hinges.

The man crossed a booted foot over his knee. "You're a freshman, right?"

He nodded. "Going to be."

"Mrs. Mansfield is tracking down all your records together. Barb'll get you registered."

That was the best news Gavin had heard all summer. Maybe he'd make it to college after all.

"We've got a great school here. You and Emma Rose might share some classes." He cocked his head and pressed his folded hands under his chin. "Course, she's taking advanced place-ment courses."

Gavin didn't mention that he planned to do the same. Nor that he maintained a 3.5 grade point average. Wasn't worth the effort.

"But if you work hard, study, you can do well. Make a future for yourself." He went on to share a story about some foster kid they housed a while back. Came in a trouble-maker, left ready to go to college, thanks to some good old-fashioned sweat work like mucking stalls and feeding pigs. What did horse dung have to do with chemistry and college admission tests? But Gavin nodded and smiled at the appropriate times.

"Here we are." Mrs. Lewis swept into the room carrying a plate of cookies—four, and an equal number of saucers. She set them on the chest, dashed out, and returned with a tray of milk. After distributing everything, she settled into the rocker, resuming her normal old church lady pose.

The rest of the afternoon, Mr. Lewis dominated the conversation while his family murmured and nodded. Mrs. Lewis acted like a politician while Emma Rose sat quietly with her knees pressed together, spine straight, looking from Gavin to her father. The family was weird, but nothing Gavin couldn't handle. There certainly were worse things than sharing a house with a girl like Emma Rose. In fact, this place wouldn't be so bad. Not bad at all, and maybe they'd even let Adele and baby Jaya join him.

TRAIN BRAKES SQUEALED through the yard, the thick stench of burning diesel seeping through Jonathan's office window. He studied the reports spread across his desk. The numbers didn't make sense, unless the guys managed to release a slew of locomotives the night before. He'd talk to the command center later.

Swiveling to the computer, he sifted through his e-mails. Ten forwards, a request for overtime, a long list of complaints from the union rep, and one from his daughter. Ignoring the others, he clicked on the latter, a smile forming as he read.

> *Thanks for the check. I thought you'd like to see the dress I chose. I've attached pictures, along with some of the reception hall. I know the price is higher than we talked about, but it's so beautiful! Give me your yay or nay. We need to pay the reservation fee by the end of the month, although the sooner the better. Places like this go fast. See you soon! Which reminds me, any ideas on what to get Uncle Walter for his birthday? Maybe we can go halves?*
>
> *Love ya!*
> *Stephanie*

Smiling, he pulled up a photo of his daughter wearing an elegant gown covered in ruffles and lace, her cheeks rosy. Her soft smile and lowered eyelashes mimicked the expression Evie made when he slipped the ring on her finger, declaring his love. *Till death do us part.*

His cell phone rang, jarring him back to the present.

"Hey, Gary, thanks for calling me back. How are things going?"

"Great! Absolutely great! How about you? Sign the deed on your dream home yet?"

Jonathan chuckled. "Not quite. Gotta sell my old one first. How are things at the shop? It didn't crumble after I left, did it?"

"Almost, but we made do. Got Barrick working your job."

"Barrick? Really?" Jonathan's stomach sank. "How's he doing?"

"Excellent. The man's like a sponge, with enough enthusiasm to keep this place popping. Come to find out he's always wanted to work in management."

"No kidding."

"Yeah. He approached me the day after you left, asked if he could bid on the job. Says he's been taking night classes, even. Plans to finish his business degree in a year and a half."

"Wow, what timing, huh?"

"Exactly. I was about to hire a guy from EMD, but the fella wasn't going to be able to come out here for another month. Plus he lacked shop experience."

They talked for a few more minutes, about Stephanie's upcoming wedding, golfing, Gary's kids, but Jonathan only half listened. With plan A shattered, two options remained—turn snitch or snake.

CHAPTER 25

THE HOT, MIDMORNING air clung to Jonathan's skin, producing a sheen of sweat almost as soon as he stepped onto the blistering asphalt. Walter was in his garage loading golf clubs into his trunk.

He set them aside and greeted Jonathan with a wide smile and a firm shake. "You up for a game? I'm playing nine holes down at Palm Whispers."

"Wish I could, but I'm on my lunch."

"Jeanne-Anne's inside, although I gotta warn you, she's been cleaning out the fridge."

"Leftovers, huh?"

"For two days now." Walter shook his head. "Don't mind pork roast the second day. But by day three, I'm starting to squeal."

"Guess I better help you then."

"Please do. And you may as well start coming to dinner on a regular basis. She cooks enough 'just in case' as it is."

Jonathan laughed and rubbed his stomach. "Happy to oblige."

The door was unlocked, so he let himself in. Stuffed garbage bags and boxes sat stacked on either side of the foyer. The faint aroma of cinnamon drifted from candles placed throughout the living room.

He inhaled deep and sauntered toward the kitchen. His sister stood with her head in the fridge, singing off tune. Another candle burned on the center island, and soft music poured from the living room.

"It smells like a bakery in here."

She startled and spun around, her eyes going from wide to crinkly. "Jonathan." She met him with a hug. "What a pleasant surprise. If I'd known you were coming—"

He shook his head and settled at the kitchen table. "Uh-uh. No more. Nada."

"Can I get you something to drink? Coffee?" He nodded, and she poured him a cup before darting to the cupboard. "You haven't eaten yet, have you? Because I've got a mess of food on my hands."

"So I heard, and I promised Walter I'd help you out."

Her grin widened, and she filled him a plate, chattering on about some new recipe she'd tried and loved but Walter had hated.

"Too much ginger, I suppose. But I keep telling him it's good for his joints. They say it's a natural anti-inflammatory, you know." She paused. "Speaking of, you really need to reduce your fast-food intake."

"What makes you think—?"

She set a heaping plate of baked squash and pork loin slices, fresh out of the microwave, in front of him. "I know you—before, during, and after Evie. If not for that sweet wife of yours, God rest her soul, you would've had a heart attack a long time ago."

"I'm a railroader, Beannie. We eat steak and potatoes. It's what we do."

She harrumphed, plopped a mountain of greens onto a salad plate, and shoved it in front of him. "Like I said, you need to eat here more often."

"Looks like I won't need dinner." He shot her a wink, then inhaled, his saliva glands kicking into overdrive. "But hey, I'm not complaining. Not at all."

"So, tell me about your date the other night."

"Wasn't a date per se. More like two adults hanging out. Friends. You know." He shoved a forkful of pork into his mouth. Moist and salty. Just like he liked it.

"And did your friend happen to be female?"

He shrugged, and her eyes danced.

She squeezed his shoulder then plopped into the chair beside him. "Good for you. Maybe now I can quit worrying about you so much."

"And quit trying to set me up with everyone from your crochet class."

"Sunday School class."

"Them, too. And anyone else you might have on your list."

"For now, anyway, but there's always room for a backup plan."

"You're impossible." He shook his head and shoveled in another bite.

Minutes later, plate cleaned, he swallowed the last of his coffee and checked his watch. "Hate to eat and run, but I've got meeting this afternoon and need to go over some reports before then." He started to carry his plate to the sink, but she took it from him.

"I'll see you tonight then. Unless you've got a hot date with your new lady friend."

"Ha, ha."

She deposited his dishes onto the counter then walked him to the door.

He eyed her mound of clutter once again. "Doing some spring cleaning?"

"That's for the shelter. Why let it clutter my closet when others can use it?"

"That's very kind of you." An image of Jacqueline's smiling face and bright eyes came to mind. He pushed it aside. "I can drop this stuff off if you want."

"Isn't that out of your way?"

"Not really." Heat seeped up the back of his neck. OK, slightly. He shifted and cleared his throat. "Consider it my way of saying thanks." He grabbed a box then paused. "Do you know if the church is doing anything to help those folks get back on their feet?"

"What do you mean?"

"I don't know, like life skills—teaching them a trade—that sort of thing."

"I'm not sure, but that's a great idea."

"Do you remember Mr. Tethers?"

Jeanne-Anne offered a slow smile. "I do. Such a sweet man."

"And probably the reason I stayed in school. And out of juvenile detention." He looked at the box in his hand, the sides bowed by the weight. "Guess I'm wondering if maybe it's time I started giving back. Find a way to serve."

Later, driving to the shelter, his thoughts turned to Jacqueline again, and the image of her sprawled on the ground, entangled in a bike, neon pink helmet strapped under her chin. A smile tugged at his lips. Poor woman. She was lucky she hadn't busted something, and that he hadn't snapped his knee.

A handful of cars dotted the church parking lot, most of them looking ready for the scrap pile. He pulled in, slowed, then let the engine idle.

Was that Jacqueline? Yeah, standing with her head ducked under the hood of a shiny sedan, one hand on her hip, the other holding a cell phone. A water jug, motor oil, pile of hand towels, and—he strained to read the label on the bright blue container glimmering in the sun—washer fluid, littered the pavement.

He stepped out of the car and into the heat of the day, the thick air clogging his lungs. "Can I help you?"

She startled and whacked her head on the hood. "Ouch!" Rubbing her head, she stared at Jonathan with a flushed face. She glanced at her engine, her phone, then back to him, that cute little chin pointing upward.

Stubborn woman would rather stand out in the 90-plus degree weather then receive help from a man.

He stepped forward anyway and peered at the engine. No steam, no heat except what the sun generated, radiating from it. "What's it doing?"

"Won't start."

"Can I have the keys?"

She frowned, and a bead of sweat trickled down her temple. She stared at him for a moment, as if going through some internal war. Like he was asking her to join him in the Bahamas or something.

He was about to leave her with her trendy cell phone and variety of car fluids when she shrugged and handed over her key ring. "Yeah, sure. I'd appreciate it."

He slid into the car, hotter than an inferno, and cranked the engine. It turned over but didn't start. Glancing at the fuel gauge, a chuckle tickled his throat. On E. He stepped back out and returned her keys.

"What do you think? Am I going to drain my savings for this one?"

"Nope. It's a cheap and easy fix. In fact, I can get it running for you in about fifteen minutes."

She cocked her head. "Yeah?"

His bottom lip twitched as he suppressed a smile. "You're out of gas."

"Oh." The red in her face deepened, and her pretty little mouth rounded, adding a sense of childlike vulnerability. "You're kidding me."

"Nope. Why don't you hop in my truck, and I'll take you to the gas station? There's one about half a mile down." He glanced at her shoes—leather flats. "Unless you want to walk." Looked like he might not have much time to look over those premeeting reports like he'd wanted. Even so, he couldn't just leave her here.

She turned, looking toward the street. He looped his thumbs through his belt loops and waited. Sun reflected off the pavement and passing cars bit at his skin.

She swiped at her forehead with the back of her forearm. "If you don't mind."

"Not a lick." He returned to his truck, her footsteps clicking behind him. After opening the passenger door for her, he rounded the hood and jumped behind the steering wheel.

They made it to the gas station and back in under ten minutes, and he returned to his task—dropping off Jeanne-Anne's donations—while she climbed into her now running car.

Lugging three boxes stacked one on the other, he strolled past her.

She rolled down her window, glanced from him to his pickup bed where more boxes and filled garbage bags sat. "Can I help you?"

"I've got it, but thanks."

She jumped out and reached for the top box. "Let me return your favor. It's the least I can do."

Something told him she wouldn't give up easily. "Yeah, all right." He tipped his head toward the truck. "You can grab one of those bags. Be careful. They're heavy."

She did, and they crossed the lot together. They entered the church through a back door and descended stairs leading to a large open area crammed with cots, people, and piles of junk. A thick stench of body odor filled the air, along with voices—male, female, angry, laughing, all jumbled together. Florescent lighting flickered from long beams stretched across the ceiling. Three were burned out, two more heading that way.

A large woman with thinning hair and wearing a pink tank top approached with arms outstretched. "Ms. Dunn, let me help you." She wiggled the plastic bag from her hands. Two other ladies approached, offering assistance.

"That's very kind of you." Jacqueline handed her bag over and glanced at Jonathan. "I assume these are donations?"

Regarding her with a raised brow, he nodded. This woman made no sense. Balked to high heaven when he offered to help, but didn't blink when these ladies did.

Jacqueline turned back to the women. "Can you take these to Irene and ask her to write out a donation slip?" Then to Jonathan. "You and I can get the rest of the stuff."

When they got outside, he wanted to ask her about her contradictory behavior, but she beat him to it.

"Those are ladies from my Tuesday morning Bible study. They've lost everything, including their dignity. Giving them something to do, something to be part of, helps bring it back."

He studied her a moment longer, thinking back to her gasless car and the way her face had worked itself to a tizzy when he'd offered to help. Was that what she was fighting for? Dignity?

But why? An intelligent, beautiful woman like her? She probably lost quite a bit in the storm. Maybe everything. Yeah, that'd level a person pretty quick.

They made two more trips, handing the items over when they reached the gym. With their last bag unloaded, Jacqueline led him through the shelter in search of Irene. They found her in a storage room picking through various janitorial items.

She straightened, a lock of hair falling over her eyes. "Jacqueline, you haven't left yet?" She glanced at Jonathan. "I'm Irene, the shelter director/plumber/Bible study leader, and whatever else you want to throw in there." She extended her hand.

They shook. "Jonathan Cohen. I'm new to the church."

"He brought in a bunch of donations," Jacqueline said. "I'm not sure where the ladies put them."

"Probably piled everything in the kitchen, where everyone else does." Irene turned to Jonathan. "You wouldn't happen to know how to fix a running toilet, would you?"

"Um . . ." He shoved his hands into his pockets. Not exactly how he wanted to spend the rest of his afternoon, and showing up late after lunch would only fuel Darren's fire. If the guy was even there, which half the time, he wasn't. "I do."

Irene beamed. "Great! Because one of our toilets isn't working, which is a real problem when housing this many people. I tried to call the church janitor, but he's not answering. Poor guy. He's running ragged as it is, without the increased demands of the shelter. He's almost eighty years old, you know. But if we don't get the toilet fixed soon, I'm afraid we'll have a riot on our hands."

"No problem. Where is it?" Another ten minutes wouldn't hurt.

Irene handed him a rusted toolbox then led him to a bathroom near the back of the gym. Jacqueline followed. A sign with the word *men* was taped on the outer wall. The lady waited outside while he went in. He stepped over a trail of water seeping from the sink to a grate in the center of the tile. He'd fix that before he left, too. Probably as easy as tightening a loose coupling joint.

When finished, he and the women returned to the storage room where he deposited the tools, leaving his business card with Irene in case another emergency arose. "I might not be able to get out here until after work, but I don't mind stopping in once in a while." Considering what these refugees went through, it was the least he could do.

He started to leave then turned back around, an idea simmering. "Do you think any of these guys would like to learn marketable skills? Like how to turn a wrench or change motor oil?"

Irene glanced over his shoulder toward the gym entrance. "Maybe." She rubbed her knuckle beneath her chin. "You know who could really use a class like that?"

"Who?"

"The boys at the group home."

Jonathan and Jacqueline exchanged glances.

"Group home?" Jacqueline's face fell. "For kids? Like an orphanage or something?"

Irene shrugged. "No. Well, kind of. Sometimes. It's for . . . troubled youth . . . and others awaiting placement with foster families. It's pretty much a catchall."

Jonathan shook his head and let out a slow breath. "That's rough." What difference would a male role model make to those kids? Personal experience said a lot. He'd have to check that place out, see if they needed volunteers. Not knowing what else to say, he turned to Jacqueline. "I'll walk you out?"

She studied him with a slight smile on her pink lips, a hint of a dimple emerging in her right cheek. "That would be nice." Passing through the shelter area, she paused to hug a few women. "Don't forget about your Bible reading."

When they hit the pavement, a hot breeze met them, stirring Jacqueline's hair. Walking beside her, Jonathan caught a faint whiff of coconut and citrus. Upon reaching her car, she opened the door then lingered with her hand on the frame. "You ever go to the concerts in the park?"

"Can't say that I have."

"They've got a bluegrass band playing this Friday. From Houston I believe. Maybe Austin."

"Uh huh?" Was she hinting at something? Was this how people dated?

She shrugged and slid behind the wheel. "Thanks again for the gas."

Jonathan watched her leave then ambled to his car. Dating. Who needed it? Course, if Jeanne-Anne and Walter wanted to listen to some bluegrass . . .

CHAPTER 26

JONATHAN AND WALTER SAT at the kitchen table while Jeanne-Anne loaded food into a wicker basket—enough to feed the South twice over. She chatted as she worked—of Stephanie's upcoming wedding and the photos Jonathan had forwarded. Filling a thermos at the counter, she glanced over her shoulder. "More importantly, how do you feel about the groom?"

Jonathan considered her question. "Honestly, I've only met him maybe a handful of times, but he's coming with her for—"

Her eyes widened, her gaze flying to her oblivious husband.

"They're both coming to visit . . . soon." Considering his near blunder, mentioning the date would only reveal Walter's surprise that Jeanne-Anne had been planning. Not that Walter would clue in, regardless of how much Jonathan flubbed it. The man barely remembered his anniversary, let alone his own birthday.

"Wonderful." Jeanne-Anne shot Jonathan a pointed look. "I'll give her a call to see if we can't plan a day and time for dinner. I have a new recipe I can try. Does he like mushrooms? I can't remember."

He suppressed a chuckle. *Smooth conversation change, Beannie. Not obvious at all.* Chirping like a toddler full of sugar, she flitted about the kitchen, doling out picnic supplies.

She must have seen his mirth because when her gaze met Jonathan's, her smile hardened and her left eye began to twitch. "How about you help me load the car?" She shoved a roll of paper towels into his chest with enough force to pop his suppressed laughter right out.

He coughed to cover it then cleared his throat. "Happy to."

When they reached Rolling Hills Park, colorful blankets dotted the lawn and music poured from two large speakers centered on the concrete stage. Scanning the crowd for signs of Jacqueline—for curiosity's sake only—he followed his sister to an open area near an older couple nestled on a baby blue quilt.

The silver-haired woman leaned into her husband, legs stretched out, chin angled upward. She smiled. The man, wearing a straw hat that shaded the top two-thirds of his face, glanced at Jonathan and nodded. He did likewise then helped his sister spread a checkered tablecloth on the ground.

While she and Walter scooted closer together, Jonathan turned his attention to the band—a group of five dressed in wide-collared shirts and tan slacks. A smattering of people danced in the grassy area in front of the stage while children scampered between them.

Jonathan propped his hands behind him and leaned back, observing the surrounding area.

His sister flicked his arm. "Looks like we're about to have company."

He followed her gaze, blinked, and bolted upright. Dressed in a tie-dyed sundress that clung to her legs like plastic wrap to chicken wings, came raw-potato-eating, parsley chewing, Maggie. And based on the numerous phone messages she'd left him, she wouldn't go away quietly. Something told him hitting call ignore hadn't been his wisest move.

JACQUELINE SAT ON Delana's couch sifting through an *Omaha Lifestyle* magazine, dreaming of boutique displays. She had a meeting scheduled with her insurance appraiser later this week. Although she wasn't looking forward to returning to Crystal Shores and viewing all the destruction, she remained hopeful. If her home were leveled, she'd receive a cash-value check, according to her policy, up to $500,000. With that kind of money, she could almost buy the boutique outright. An action that could work like cement or bug repellent to her relationship with her daughter. So many what-ifs, all beyond her control.

She dropped the magazine into her lap and rubbed her temples. Did she really need another failure on her long list of shoulda-couldas? But what else could she do? Go back to school? Degree or not, nobody would hire a fifty-something flub-up.

The front door clicked open, and she held her breath. Her daughter entered wearing her scrubs and a grin.

Delana dropped her purse onto the coffee table and kicked her shoes off. "Hey."

"Hey. Good day?"

She tilted her head, lowered one brow. "You could say that." Laughter danced in her eyes.

"You got plans tonight?"

Delana checked her watch then glanced toward the living room window. "Probably not." Plopping beside Jacqueline, she grabbed the remote. After flicking through all the channels and consulting the TV guide, she turned off the television. "So lame. Wanna do something?"

Jacqueline's heart pricked. "Sure. Yeah, that sounds great. Like what?"

"I don't know. Maybe hit a movie or something."

Jacqueline grabbed a newspaper and leafed through the pages until she reached the community section. A picture of three smiling children with rosy cheeks splattered with ice cream stared back at them, adults lounging on blankets in the background. The headline read, "Concerts in the park bind the community together." A list of dates and bands followed.

"I can't believe I've never taken you to our community concerts." Delana dropped the paper on her lap. "They're a big deal around here. Practically the whole town goes." She smiled. "You still like bluegrass?"

"Uh . . ." Would Jonathan be there? Her stomach fluttered, her face growing warm, as she remembered their previous—and quite awkward—conversation. One that made her seem like a desperate teenager fishing for a date.

Do you like bluegrass?

Lucky for her, the man appeared clueless. Or uninterested.

"You OK?"

Jacqueline looked up to find her daughter watching her. "Of course! And I think the concert in the park is a great idea. Want me to pack a picnic dinner?"

"Don't bother. We can grab a burger on the way." She stood and padded to her room.

Jacqueline followed suit, shucking her jeans and T-shirt for a cute sundress that accentuated her tan and deepened the blue in her eyes. She ran a brush through her hair, fluffed her bangs to counter their late-afternoon wilt, and added a dash of gloss to her lips. And none of it was for Jonathan's benefit. She probably wouldn't even see him, but that didn't mean she needed to traipse around town looking frumpy.

She returned to the living room to find her daughter dressed in a pink top with thin straps and jean shorts that hit an inch below her panty line. Jacqueline kept her opinions to herself.

Extending her legs one at a time, Delana slathered on blackberry-scented lotion then offered the bottle to Jacqueline.

"I'm good, thanks." Although an extra layer of deodorant wouldn't hurt, in case a hot flash hit. "Give me a minute." She dashed back to her room, increased her body-odor defense, then returned with unscented wet wipes tucked inside her clutch.

As they drove, Delana was in a chatty mood, reminding Jacqueline of the tween that once followed her around. It was nice. By the time they arrived at the park, laughter filled the car and Jacqueline's heart.

The grassy area fanning from the stage was packed with people sitting in folding chairs or spread on blankets stretched on the grass. Jacqueline and Delana stood on the fringe. "Where do you want to sit?"

Delana planted her hands on her hips. She pointed to an area near a concrete half wall. "How about over there?"

Weaving around blankets and feet, they meandered across the grass, dodging running children. Halfway there, Jacqueline paused to watch a toddler devour a mound of pink cotton candy, his nose and cheeks stained. Clumps of melted sugar dangled from his chin. A memory of her and Delana, twenty years ago, flashed through her mind, weighing heavily on her heart. What she wouldn't do to go back in time, back to when she and Delana shared butterfly kisses and giggles. *Lord Jesus, give me my baby girl back.*

Nearing the stage she turned, her pulse quickening. Jonathan Cohen sat on a picnic basket with a group of people. Four in all . . . two couples. Apparently the man had a date. No wonder he'd evaded her bluegrass question. Not that it mattered. He'd made it clear; he wasn't looking for romance. Merely someone to hang out with. Clearly, he'd found that.

Smoothing her silk blouse with her one clean hand, she nodded and put on her best smile. "Hello, Jonathan." She smiled at each of his friends in turn, her gaze lingering on a woman with short black hair. Her tie-dyed dress reminded Jacqueline of a trippy, late-1970s music film.

Jonathan stood with a school-boy grin. "Jacqueline, good to see you."

The rest of his party rose and gathered around, as if awaiting introductions. The tie-dyed lady studied Jacqueline with narrowed eyes, face pinched so tight it looked ready to swallow itself.

Avoiding the woman's glare, she stepped aside, motioning Delana closer. "I'm Jacqueline Dunn. And this is my daughter, Delana."

Jonathan's sister raised an eyebrow, and a hint of a smile formed as she looked from Jonathan to Jacqueline. "I see." She and the man standing beside her exchanged glances. "You go to our church, right?"

Jacqueline nodded, noting the bags of potato chips, containers of fruit, and partially eaten sandwiches on their picnic blanket. An awkward pause followed.

She cleared a nervous tickle from her throat. "Well, I suppose we should leave you all to what's left of your dinner."

"Please, join us." Jonathan's sister swept her hand toward their blanket. "I'm Jeanne-Anne by the way, and this is my husband, Walter, and this"—she motioned to Pickle Face—"is Maggie Barrick. She goes to Abiding Fellowship as well."

"Nice to meet you." Jacqueline shook each person's hand in turn. "I'd hate to intrude."

"Oh, no intrusion." Jeanne-Anne elbowed her husband, who coughed.

"None at all." Mirth danced in Jonathan's eyes. "We always love connecting with church family."

"Yes, please." Jonathan touched the small of her back.

A bolt of electricity shot up her spine. She studied him, frowning. Such a sudden show of enthusiasm, and with his date standing but a few feet away. Before she could protest further, Jeanne-Anne and Walter had rearranged their blanket, clearing room for Jacqueline and Delana.

Jacqueline glanced over her shoulder at Delana who stared toward a pack of twirling kids. "This OK?"

"Beats sitting next to bouncing toddlers."

Not wanting to appear impolite, and more than a little curious about Jonathan and his stiff, pucker-faced date, Jacqueline accepted the invitation and helped Delana stretch their blanket next to Jeanne-Anne's. Once arranged, she and Delana sat between Jonathan and his sister. Jacqueline sat in front of Maggie, who seemed interested in a staring contest. Fighting a giggle as ninth-grade cheerleading tryouts came to mind, Jacqueline leaned back on her hands and watched clouds drift across the sky.

"So, how do you like Willow Valley, Jacqueline?" Jeanne-Anne plucked a grape from the bunch.

"You have a nice town, cozy. And your church seems very friendly."

"Oh, it is. Have you had a chance to check out the women's ministry?" Jeanne-Anne grabbed a purse sitting beside her and rummaged around inside. "We have a game night coming up." She pulled out a yellow flyer, which she handed to Jacqueline, then held an additional one out to Delana.

She frowned and studied the paper. Jacqueline held her breath, praying the event could be a first step of many. But she wouldn't push. She'd leave the heart nudging to God.

As the conversation continued, Jacqueline began to relax. So did Delana, going from tight-lipped to chatty by the time the fourth song ended. She talked about her favorite bands and some of the concerts she'd been to, none of them Sunday School listening, but Jeanne-Anne didn't seem to mind. In fact, her easy questions turned what started out as an awkward moment into an enjoyable evening. A rare night, free of temper flare-ups and biting words. Maybe Jacqueline needed to borrow Jeanne-Anne for her next mother-daughter event.

The sky turned velvety blue as the sun dipped below the horizon, a fringe of purple stretching across the horizon. The crescent moon poked from behind a cluster of wind-stirred trees, and stars emerged.

Jeanne-Anne checked her watch. "Walter, we should probably head out. I still have to prepare for my morning Bible study." She glanced from Jacqueline to Delana. "I'd love for you to join us. We're talking about God's abundant grace, the kind that can turn a murderer like Paul into perhaps the greatest missionary of all time."

Jacqueline's heart stirred. "That sounds interesting."

"It is! We're diving into all the bad guys of the Bible—the murderers, adulterers, liars—evaluating their lives in light of the Cross. We meet at nine."

Pickle Face stood and inched closer to Jonathan, her lips twitching as if words bubbled behind them. She stared from one face to the next, cheeks pink, before turning back to him. "Do you enjoy musicals?"

"Er . . . no."

"There's a poetry reading at the Grandview Center."

He shook his head. "Thanks for the offer, but I'm not much into poetry."

"How about lunch? We could meet at—"

"Jacqueline and I have plans." He lunged toward Jacqueline and wrapped his arm around her shoulder, yanking her closer.

Blinking, she stumbled over her purse, gaze flitting from one wide-eyed face to the next. "Isn't that right?" He gave her shoulder a squeeze while shooting her a pointed look.

"I, uh . . ." So this must have been the woman Jonathan evaded the other night and the reason for their dinner excursion. Pulling her lips over her teeth, she fought a giggle.

"Oh!" Jeanne-Anne pressed her hands together. "I see."

Maggie's face and shoulders fell. "Well, I understand." She turned to Jacqueline with a stiff smile. "It was nice meeting you." The edge in her voice belied her words. She flicked a hand in the air, "Have a nice night," then strolled away, stiffer than if she'd been dipped in plaster.

As soon as she left, Jeanne-Anne practically pounced on Jacqueline. "So you're the reason my brother's been—"

She looked from Jonathan to Jacqueline, her smile growing, then grabbed Jacqueline's hand. "So very good to meet you."

Jacqueline looked at Jonathan. "I'll see you at lunch. Call me." Pressing her tongue to the roof of her mouth, she didn't release her laughter until she and Delana were halfway to the parking lot.

Delana glanced over her shoulder. "What was that about?"

"That, my dear, is called giving a railroader a taste of his own diesel fuel."

CHAPTER 27

"UP AND AT 'EM."

A bright light flicked on, slicing through Gavin's dreams.

He rubbed his eyes then squinted at the thick frame standing in his doorway. Mr. Lewis. What time was it?

"Got cows to milk and chickens to feed."

Gavin glanced from the empty nightstand beside his bed to the partially opened blinds across the room. A layer of pink pushed back the gray sky. and beams of light extended from the horizon.

"You got five minutes. Meet me in the kitchen." Mr. Lewis' heavy footfalls receded, followed by the sound of banging cupboards, rattling dishes, and distant voices.

With a heavy sigh, eyes grainy, he lugged himself out of bed and shuffled toward the bathroom. The door was closed—behind it, the sound of running water. Yawning, he leaned against the wall and waited, straining to catch bits of the conversation drifting from the kitchen. No luck. A moment later, Emma Rose emerged wearing jeans and a T-shirt, with her hair pulled into a ponytail. Brown wisps framed her smooth forehead, and a loose strand rested on her collarbone.

Upon seeing Gavin, her cheeks colored. "Hi."

His stomach flip-flopped. "Hi."

They stared at one another. Gavin's arms hung like limp string cheese, feet anchored to the ground, while his heart ricocheted in his chest.

Footsteps thudded toward them, and Emma Rose straightened, her face growing pale. "Excuse me." With head dipped and gaze locked on the floor, she entered the hall and hurried past her approaching father.

Mr. Lewis stopped a few feet from Gavin, dark eyes locked on his. A tendon in the man's jaw twitched.

Swallowing, Gavin nodded then dashed into the bathroom, closing the door behind him. Staring at his reflection in the mirror, heart still thudding, he gripped the sink and shook his head. That was the last man he wanted to make angry. Best thing he could do was stay as far away from Emma Rose as possible, unless he wanted to be cannon-fired back to the group home.

He splashed water onto his face, brushed his teeth, then followed the scent of sausage to the kitchen. Mrs. Lewis stood at the stove wearing a floral dress and an apron. Her hair wound in a ball on top of her head like the lady from an Old Maid's card game. Emma Rose sat at the table sipping a glass of milk.

Mr. Lewis sat beside her, a stack of books and a tablet spread before him. Jaw set, he locked eyes with Gavin. "Good morning, son."

Gavin nodded and settled into the nearest open chair, squirming under the man's intense gaze. Mrs. Lewis marched across the kitchen and set a plate before him with two eggs, two orange slices, two links of sausage, and half a piece of toast. She set an identical serving in front of Emma Rose then placed a double portion in front of her husband. After handing Gavin a glass of milk and refilling her husband's coffee, she returned with a fourth plate—hers—that mirrored Emma Rose's and Gavin's.

Mr. Lewis sipped his coffee then cleared his throat. "School will be starting soon enough. However, your case worker is still attempting to locate all of your old records and such." He folded his hands on the tabletop. "In other words, you might get registered late."

Gavin frowned. That meant he'd start out behind, which could hurt his grades. And what if they didn't register him for the right classes? He'd earned the right to take honors courses. Stupid storm.

"But that's no reason to declare defeat, you hear me?" The man's voice deepened as if he expected a challenge. "You're in charge of your destiny, understand?"

Gavin nodded, poking at the yoke of his egg. Yellow goo seeped across his plate, pooling around the bacon.

"Each day is an opportunity to man up." He slammed a fist on the table, causing Gavin to jump and his plate to rattle. "To find and use our inner grit. You," he pointed to Gavin, "determine your future. But you've got to grab it, you hear me, boy?"

Gavin squirmed. Staring at his food, he gave a slight nod.

Mr. Lewis slammed his fist on the table again. "Look me in the eye when I'm talking to you, boy."

Gavin raised his head, jolts of adrenaline shooting through him and souring his stomach.

"I know your kind. Think you can skate through life, live off the system, 'get what's yours.' Well, let me tell you something: ain't nobody gonna give you anything. You hear me? You gotta earn it."

Again, Gavin nodded, fighting to maintain eye contact.

"We don't house freeloaders, do we, Ma?"

Mrs. Lewis looked up, gave a weak smile that resembled a grimace, then studied her plate.

Her husband stacked egg in the center of his toast. "You're going to have to earn it through hard work and sweat. That's what's wrong with teenagers these days. They don't know how to sweat. How to put in an honest day's work." As Mr. Lewis continued, talking about felons and murders and all other forms of human depravity, Gavin's already knotted gut continued to cramp. The last thing he wanted right now was a slop of eggs, but he certainly wasn't going to give Mr. Lewis any indication of that. Shivering, he gripped his fork tighter, hoping the mass of food would make it down his tightened throat.

Mr. Lewis concluded with a story of an immigrant who worked his way from poverty to riches. He asked his daughter a few questions about some biography he'd assigned her to read, gave his wife a list of commands for the day, and then shoved up from the table.

"Let's go."

Gavin looked from his half-eaten plate to Emma Rose's, also half-eaten, and shrugged. He wasn't that hungry anyway. Not after Mr. Lewis's "pep talk." Something told him this visit wasn't going to be a dip in the lake. More like an upstream swim at flood season.

Four more years. All he had to do was make it four more years. Then he'd find a college dorm room far away from adults telling him what to do and why he wasn't good enough to do it.

JACQUELINE DROVE DOWN the streets of Crystal Shores. Planks of wood, shingles, and chunks of brick and concrete piled along the sidewalk next to jagged branches. An uprooted tree dissected a caved-in building, and shop owners swept glass from the cluttered sidewalk.

As she neared her neighborhood, murky water pooled in trenches and glistened from swampy grass. Wires draped from bent and broken electrical poles. A layer of mud covered the road.

Tears stung her eyes as she surveyed the shattered properties all around her. Homes with roofs torn off, fences left in shreds, people's belongings scattered. A man and a woman sifted through the rubble of what once was a beautiful two-story, custom-designed home with bay windows.

A horn blared, and Jacqueline glanced in her rear-view mirror. Behind her, two men scowled from the cab of a trash truck.

Wiping a sweaty hand on her thigh, she turned the corner, inching toward what was left of her house. A navy Volvo parked along the curb. Blobs of dried mud caked on the sidewalk and across the road. A blond man wearing jeans and heavy boots trudged across her yard, stepping over tree limbs, chunks of roof, and what appeared to be planks of siding. Not hers. They were blue, and her house was a forest green—but splattered with grime, it looked olive.

She parked behind him and glanced at her sandals. Probably not the best choice of footwear. She offered up a prayer asking for divine favor and slid out, careful to avoid the mud. Unfortunately, there was nowhere else to step and she soon gave up. By the time she reached the man, goop seeped into her shoes and between her toes like hot, slimy snot.

"You must be Jacqueline Dunn?" The man tucked a clipboard under his arm and shook her hand.

She nodded.

"I'm Martin Humford with Security Assurance. I've inspected the exterior of your property and am ready to take a look inside."

Shielding her eyes, she scanned what remained of her house. A painful lump filled the back of her throat. Blinking back tears, she dug in her pocket for her house key. Once inside, she stood frozen in her living room while the appraiser examined the interior. Her feet sank into the damp carpet, and a yellow water line extended to the top of the baseboards. Her leather furniture, ruined. Glass coffee table, shattered. The partially packed boxes that hadn't fit in her car lay beneath mud and shards of glass, warped and water stained. The product of long hours and even longer work-weeks, destroyed.

Footsteps clomped and Mr. Humford rounded the corner. He paused in the center of the room to scribble something on his clipboard.

She took in a slow breath then exhaled. "What's the damage?"

After explaining her policy, what was covered and what wasn't, he handed her a check for $50,000. "You'll receive the rest once you make repairs and submit the receipts."

"And if I don't make repairs? I mean, what if I want to relocate?"

"In that case, you'll keep the $50,000, but we can't reimburse you for money not spent."

"Isn't there a cash-value option?"

"The cash-out option is only available if your house is beyond repair, which it isn't."

Now what? Hire someone to fix it up so she could sell it? No one would buy here. The once beautiful town looked like a junkyard. Cut her losses and pay two mortgages? Moving back wasn't an option. She'd closed her heart on Crystal Shores the day she evacuated.

STANDING OUTSIDE HIS truck, Jonathan surveyed the brick buildings comprising Orange Blossoms Children's Home. The blooming myrtles and lush magnolias lining the plantation-style structure gave the appearance of peace and stability. The stately columns gave the façade of strength. Although Jonathan had only spent a week in such a facility, he knew life inside was far from Disneyland.

Entering, it was as if he'd ventured back in time, reducing him to that scared and lonely teenager searching for hope. A laminate counter stretched before him with two chairs positioned in front, one behind—all empty. He strolled forward and scanned the area for a receptionist. Clearing his throat, he propped his elbows on the counter and waited.

And waited.

And waited.

He was about to leave when the phone rang, ushering in a woman—a child, really, most likely a college intern—with long black hair and porcelain skin.

"Oh! Hello." Glossy lips rounded before smoothing into a beauty pageant smile. She held up a finger and answered the phone. After the call concluded, she turned back to Jonathan. "Sorry to keep you waiting. May I help you?"

"Yes, uh . . . Is there someone I can talk to about volunteering?"

The girl nodded and picked up the phone receiver. "Mrs. Roberts, there's a man here who'd like to talk with you."

A moment later, a woman with two-inch roots and more wrinkles than an underweight pug emerged from the hall. "Good afternoon. I'm Roberta Roberts, director of Orange Blossoms. And you are?"

"Jonathan Cohen." They shook hands, hers cold and rough, like it'd been soaked in acetone.

"I'm happy to meet you, Jonathan. How about we talk more in my office?"

He nodded and followed her down a narrow hallway into a room barely bigger than a bathroom stall. Files, documents, and slips of paper cluttered her desk.

He sat in a metal folding chair while she settled into a squeaky leather one that looked almost as old as her.

"What can I do for you, Mr. Cohen?"

"I'm here to learn about your volunteer opportunities."

"Lovely." She swiveled to a green filing cabinet and pulled out a pack of stapled papers. "What type of volunteering would you like to do? Lawn care? Facility maintenance?"

"Actually, I was thinking more in line with offering some kind of life skills class."

"What kind of class did you have in mind?"

"Mechanics."

Mrs. Roberts studied him, her expression tight. She was cautious. He understood that, expected it even. "Have you worked with troubled youth before?"

"No, but . . . I understand them."

"And why's that?"

"I used to be one of them."

"You spent time in a children's home?"

He nodded.

"May I ask why?"

With a nervous chuckle, he rubbed a hand across his jaw. "Because I was a stupid, angry kid."

"Was your stay court ordered?"

"No. More like mom ordered." He chuckled. "I was raised by a single parent. She did her best, bruised her knees praying on my behalf, but she couldn't be around all the time. When I hit fourteen and started cutting classes, she decided it was time to call in the big dogs."

"I assume it helped."

Actually, the group home nearly broke him. It sapped what little hope and dignity he'd had, and he'd only been there for a week. But he wouldn't tell Mrs. Roberts that. It wasn't her fault places like this were understaffed and sterile. The sheer number of residents required rigid scheduling with limited personal interaction. "What helped was someone took the time to reach out to me, give me something I could be proud of. A sense of accomplishment."

He smiled, remembering Mr. Tether's unruly eyebrows and bushy hair, his underchin that jiggled when he laughed, and the way he'd puff his cheeks out when frustrated. Beneath the man's gruff appearance laid a heart softer than wax. "A retired man taught me to work with my hands, gave me an outlet for my anger. I believe I owe a lot of who I am today to him."

Mrs. Roberts took notes while Jonathan laid out his plan. Thirty minutes later, they agreed to start a pilot program focused on a small group of boys.

"You know this won't be easy." With a grimace, she pushed to her feet and handed Jonathan her business card with a start date scrolled on the back. "A lot of these kids come from rough places." She led the way out of her office and to the lobby. "They may not want to learn, some might even hate you."

"I understand."

She glanced toward the young receptionist who'd returned to her book. "Many come in here wanting to change the world, but they're not willing to drudge through the muck in order to do so. These kids have been shuffled through enough systems. They need someone to stand by them. What they *don't* need is someone else to bounce in and out of their lives."

The implication of her words sank deep as Jonathan stepped into the parking lot. If he started this program, he needed to stick with it. No matter how hard these kids fought against him.

Could he do it? So he'd been rebellious, angry. For what? Because he didn't have a dad and his mom had to work a lot? His minor demons were easy to fix, but with these kids? God only knew what some of them had endured, how many people had walked out on them, convinced them they were worthless.

This wouldn't be easy, but he was determined to try.

CHAPTER 28

MUSIC DRIFTED FROM the sanctuary into the church lobby, and a few couples milled around the information tables. For once, Jonathan wasn't late. He'd even traded his flip-flops for tennis shoes and his shorts for jeans. That was as fancy as this railroader got.

Would Jacqueline come today? Did he care? He smiled, remembering their encounter at the park. As dolled up as that woman was, with her trendy shoes and matching purses, she had a sweet shyness about her. One she tried hard to hide. He laughed remembering the wide-eyed look she gave when he used her as an excuse to keep old Maggie Moo off his back. Except using her as an excuse sounded too harsh. But she had arrived at the perfect time.

"Jonathan!" Jeanne-Anne breezed in clutching a Bible, polka-dotted tote tossed over her shoulder. Walter shuffled in behind her looking like he needed a few more hours of sleep. "No flip-flops?" She regarded him with a crooked smile. "What's the occasion?"

"No occasion. Figured I'd follow orders for once." He winked at Walter.

"Mm hm." She gave him a knowing look then scanned the lobby. "So, where's your lady friend?"

"She's not my—"

He clamped his mouth shut. Two horrific blind dates were enough. Besides, what'd it matter if his sister thought he was dating Jacqueline?

"I haven't talked to her."

But he had considered calling her half a dozen times, as stupid as that was. Still, it wouldn't hurt to hang out with her for a while, until she moved back to Crystal Shores, anyway.

Jeanne-Anne looped her arm through his and guided him to the sanctuary. "Oh, my! I really do need to teach you a few things about winning a woman's heart, don't I?"

Nope. He wasn't interested in heart issues, or any issues for that matter.

They entered the sanctuary, his sister waving to people as they passed. They reached a row of empty seats. Walter filed in first, Jonathan followed. Jeanne-Anne turned to drape her tote's strap over the back of her seat then straightened, hand shooting into the air.

"Jacqueline!" She reached around Walter to flick Jonathan's shoulder. "There she is. Now, scoot." She nudged Walter, who nudged Jonathan, then dashed back into the aisle. "Jacqueline, over here."

Walter chuckled. "How about you and I change places, my man?"

"This isn't high school."

But Walter pressed past him and into the aisle, joining Jeanne-Anne and Jacqueline, who now stood beside him.

Not wanting to act like a jerk, Jonathan ambled over. "Good morning."

Jacqueline wore a slim sleeveless dress, salmon against her sun-kissed skin. Her golden hair brushed against her smooth shoulders, and her glossed lips parted in a soft smile. "Good morning, Jonathan. How are you?"

"Wonderful. And you?"

"Doing well, thanks."

The sanctuary filled as more people found seats, and the choir filed onto the stage. The worship leader took the microphone, and Jonathan moved into the row, leaving room for the others. Jacqueline stood beside him, her arm mere inches from his. The scent of coconut wafted from her hair. As she sang, she swayed slightly, her face lifted, voice sweet as a hummingbird's.

The music stopped, and the pastor came on stage.

"Please be seated." He waited until everyone complied. "Let's pray."

As the service continued, Jonathan forced his attention from the beautiful and intriguing woman sitting beside him to the pastor. He spoke on Genesis 2, of all things. "It is not good that man be alone. We all need a helpmate. A team player, someone to partner with us and help us fulfill the mission Christ has for us."

Only problem, Jonathan didn't have a mission. Except to retire, something he'd been planning for, saving for, since he was twenty-five.

The pastor moved to the front of the stage and made a slow sweep of the audience. "Why are you here, Christian?"

People shifted. Someone coughed.

"Why doesn't God whisk us all to heaven the moment we're saved?"

Jonathan cast a sideways glance at Jacqueline who leaned forward, pen in hand, frantically writing notes on her church bulletin.

"You're here to point others to Jesus. That's it. That's what your life is all about—knowing God and making Him known. If you're not doing that, if you're not actively demonstrating the love of Christ, then you're missing out on your life's purpose."

Jonathan chewed on the pastor's words, not sure how they applied to railroading, but God would show him in due time. He always did. Course, soon enough he'd be a grandpa. The name had a nice ring—Grandpa. His baby girl, getting married. If only Evie were here to see it. He glanced at a beam of rainbow-colored light streaming through a stained-glass window and imagined Evie sitting with her Savior. He had had his helpmate, a faithful wife, great mother. God had been good.

His mind drifted to Jacqueline, her smile, her slender neck, her soft laugh.

Could a man find love twice in one lifetime?

THE SERVICE ENDED, and Jacqueline grabbed her purse as people thronged the aisles. Once again, she stood sandwiched between someone and Jonathan, not that she minded. The man was starting to grow on her. He was so unlike the businessmen she normally dated—less stuffy and puffed up. Besides, it was nice being around a man who wanted absolutely nothing from her. No stupid lines and empty promises.

Still blocked from the aisle by a steady flow of people, Jeanne-Anne turned to face her. "You hungry?"

"I . . ." Jacqueline checked her watch. Maybe she should call Delana, see what she's doing, perhaps invite her along. Which would be rude. Besides, Delana's attitude the night before suggested she might need some space. "Sure. Where would you like to go?"

"How about if everyone comes to my place." Jeanne-Anne glanced at her husband who shrugged. "I've got chili simmering in the slow-cooker, more than Walter and I could eat, that's for sure."

Jacqueline bit her bottom lip. The offer was tempting, if not awkward.

"Come on." Jeanne-Anne slung her tote over her shoulder. "You and Jonathan can ride together. And I can show you some material for the Bible study I lead. Are you still planning on coming? We missed you last week."

"I had to meet the insurance appraiser."

They filed out of the sanctuary, Jonathan walking by her side. He emitted the faint scent of cedar.

"Did everything go all right?" The soft expression in his hazel eyes stole her breath.

She swallowed and nodded. "It did, thank you. Although the meeting left me with quite a few decisions to make."

"I see."

That seemed to end the conversation, and they drove to Jeanne-Anne's in awkward silence. Her house sat near an algae-covered pond, surrounded by mature trees. Cheery roses lined the walk, and wooden planters filled with orange and red lilies bloomed beneath the front windows. The interior smelled of fresh baked bread and garlicky beef.

Jeanne-Anne dropped her purse on an accent table. "Walter, will you help me in the kitchen?" She flashed Jacqueline and Jonathan a smile, sweeping her arm toward a country-style living room decorated in shades of blue and yellow. "You two relax. It'll be just a moment."

She pulled her husband down the hall, her sandals clicking on the tile floor. Jacqueline crossed to the couch, paused to look at a photo attached to the wall. She recognized Jeanne-Anne, Walter, and Jonathan. A petite woman with wavy brown hair and high cheekbones stood beside Jonathan, nestled beneath his arm. A cluster of cattails sprouted behind them, and wispy clouds stretched across an aqua sky. The woman gazed up at Jonathan who peered back at her, his expression soft. They looked so in love, something Jacqueline had never experienced. Not truly. She'd thought she'd been in love once, but all she got out of the deal was a lot of heartburn and a series of migraines. And Delana, the only sweetener in an otherwise sour romance.

Jonathan came to her side. "That's Evie, my wife."

Jacqueline studied his face.

"She's beautiful."

"Inside and out."

"I'm so sorry for your loss."

He shrugged. "Me, too, though it's gotten easier. I miss her, for sure, but my heart doesn't ache anymore. Not like it used to."

Footsteps shuffled behind them, and Jacqueline turned.

Jeanne-Anne crossed the living room carrying two glasses of soda. "I'm so sorry, but it looks like lunch will be a little while. Apparently I set the temperature on warm."

Speaking of warm—Jacqueline's neck and face began to tingle as heat crawled through her skin. *Not now!* She scooted to the edge of the seat cushion to allow maximum airflow around her flaming body. "It's no big deal." She grabbed her drink. Watching a bead of water slide down the glass, she longed to rub it against her face, her neck, her blazing stomach.

Walter joined them, taking the recliner. He initiated a conversation on a recent dry spell wreaking agricultural havoc in

East Texas. Jacqueline held her smile intact as sweat trickled down her spine and pooled between her legs and behind her knees. Switching her glass to her other hand, she casually pressed her chilled fingers against the back of her neck.

Jonathan didn't seem to notice. He leaned back, ankle propped on his other knee, sipping his soda. "How are things at the shelter?"

"Good." She took a drink, funneling in a cube of ice, which she ran over her tongue then pressed against her cheek. "Thank you for solving our plumbing issues. We've had more fights over bathrooms than anything else." Something she could use right about now. Oh, how lovely it would feel to splash cold water on her face. She was about to excuse herself to do just that when Jeanne-Anne initiated further conversation.

"It's such a wonderful thing the church is doing. I've been meaning to go down there myself. Thought maybe I could read a few of those kiddos some stories, give their mommas a much-needed break."

Jacqueline frowned and studied her hands, thinking of Gavin and his sisters. She needed to call the social worker tomorrow, see if she'd set up a meeting yet. Or found their mother. Someone—anyone—to love them unconditionally. Every child deserved that.

A snippet of a song flashed through her mind, pricking her heart. "What if you're the hand, the heart, the answer you've been praying for?" She shook the thought aside. There were a million others more qualified, much more godly, to care for those children. Someone younger, married, not plunged into the throes of menopause with a history of broken relationships and a shameful past.

CHAPTER 29

JONATHAN CRUMPLED HIS burger wrapper and tossed it into the fast-food bag. He checked his watch. Ten minutes early, which might give him time to relax. Seriously, what was he so freaked out about? These were kids, not hardened criminals. Not yet, anyway. But according to statistics, half of them would be. Another chunk would age out of the system and spend the rest of their lives on the streets, unless someone intervened. And yet, did Jonathan really think he could make that much of a difference? By teaching these kids how to change a tire and perform a lube?

Wouldn't know if he didn't try.

Entering the facility, he encountered a different receptionist, a male, dressed in a faded T-shirt.

The guy glanced up and acknowledged Jonathan with a nod. "Can I help you?"

"I'm here to teach the auto-mechanics class."

The guy angled his head and frowned, as if trying to decipher Latin. "Auto-mechanics class?"

"Mrs. Roberts is expecting me."

The kid flicked his hand toward the hall entry. Jonathan found Mrs. Roberts in her office flipping through a stack of papers.

He poked his head into the doorway. "Good evening."

She startled and her reading glasses, attached by a chain, fell from her nose to her chest. "Jonathan, hello." She rose to greet him. "I've prepared an area for you in the east parking lot, with a pop-up tent and a pitcher of ice water." She shook her head and blew out air. "Ninety-seven degrees. I don't envy you, my friend."

He shrugged. "We'll manage." He followed her out into the parking lot, melted asphalt sticking to the bottom of his shoes.

"I'll let you set up while I gather the students."

"How many?"

She folded her hands and pressed them against her chin. "Four, although I must be honest, they don't want to be here. Their counselor strongly recommended they come. He thought they needed a positive outlet for their . . . energies."

Which meant they were the troublemakers. An intimidating thought, but nothing Jonathan couldn't handle, right?

Ten minutes later two men flanked a pack of sneering teens, two of whom walked with exaggerated swaggers. A blond kid with broad shoulders and thick veins snaking his arms occupied the lead, gaze locked on Jonathan.

Upon reaching him, the kid stopped with his feet planted shoulder distance apart, arms crossed. With head tilted back, smirking, he surveyed Jonathan's truck. "You looking for a major rewire, old man? Because we'll hook you up." His gaze flicked to his friends who started to laugh.

One of the staff members, a guy with a buzz cut and onion-bulb head, stepped forward. "You boys better not start any trouble."

A kid with black, curly hair snorted and muttered something under his breath that provoked more snickers.

Glancing at Jonathan, the staff member shook his head. "Good luck, bro."

When he and his colleague left, the teens jumped on the water and ambled into the shade, where they plopped onto the ground.

Jonathan moved in front of them, hands shoved in his pocket, forcing himself to look into the kids' eyes. It was like standing in the middle of a high school locker room, surrounded by laughing, towel-snapping jocks. Only he was an adult now, with a good paying job and people who respected him. He snorted. A man intimidated by a bunch of hurting kids. Pretty pathetic.

"I know what it's like to live in a place like this."

The blond kid cursed and rolled his eyes. "Here we go."

Jonathan shifted. "Didn't care about myself or life. Was on a fast track to juvie—"

"Or reject land." The curly haired guy spit on the ground and wiped his mouth with the back of his hand. "Dude, do you think we care?" His friends laughed and he and the blond kid gave each other a high five. "How long's this little sob story gonna take, anyway?"

Jonathan's well-planned speech swirled through his mind, the words clogging his throat. What was he doing? These kids didn't care—about his testimony or themselves. Only thing they cared about was finding a snide comment. Sweat trickled down his back as the afternoon sun bore down on him. Here he stood in the sweltering heat, wasting his time, when he could be watching sports on cable TV. Maybe this ministry wasn't for him.

What they don't need is someone else to bounce in and out of their lives.

JACQUELINE STOOD IN a dimly lit hall, clutching her purse. She stared through the glass window at couples gathered around a rectangular table. A woman with long blonde hair and rosy skin. A man, most likely the woman's husband, with a military cut and a goatee. Another couple, round faces lit with laughter, a sprinkling of acne on their faces, suggesting they recently emerged from puberty.

"Are you going in?"

She spun around. A man dressed in a mint green shirt and silver tie reached for the door and held it out for her. "I'm Howard from Healthy Connections." He extended his free hand to her and they shook. "And you are?"

"Jacqueline. Jacqueline Dunn." She stepped inside then hovered near the door.

"Good to meet you. I love it when the grandparents get involved and show their support."

"I, uh . . . I'm here by myself." She scanned the faces turned toward her, the talking now stopped. "To learn."

"Good for you. There's no age limit on helping a child, right?"

No age limit? Wow. "I guess I'll find out."

He gave a hesitant chuckle then started to leave, but she called out to him. "Excuse me?"

He turned back. "Yes?"

"I have some questions. I mean . . ." She chewed on her bottom lip, her stomach catapulting. "I'm not even sure I'm eligible."

He nodded and stepped closer, listening as she told him about the hurricane and her situation. "I still have my realty license, but all my listing are . . . submerged." She gave a nervous laugh. "And well, I'm staying with daughter at the moment. Is that a problem?"

"Not necessarily, though if you plan to stay with her long-term, she'll need to have a background check done."

"And my job situation?"

"If you decide to go through with the certification process, your case worker will evaluate all that, including your history. You've had reliable employment up until now?"

"Yes, of course."

"That will be taken into account." He smiled. "Obviously you'd need a job and stable living environment in order to foster. But you can complete everything else, including the classes and background checks, in the meantime." He touched her arm. "Don't worry. We'll work with you." He looked at the clock. "If you'll excuse me." With a slight nod, he grabbed a stack of information packets and began to distribute them.

Jacqueline moved to an empty seat next to the postpubescent woman and tucked her purse under her chair. What was she doing here? Foster care at fifty-one? So she could fall in love with those sweet kids only to have them ripped from her when their mother decided she wanted to parent again?

But what if their mom didn't come back and they grew up in separate homes, their only sense of family severed?

Oh, Lord, show me what to do. I bailed on Delana. I don't want to repeat myself with these kids. They've already been through so much. Only I can't do this. Foster care? At my age?

After the meeting, she meandered through town, processing all the information, the video images, the personal testimonies shared by kids who'd spent ten, twelve, seventeen years shuffled through the system. But what could she do? She might not even be here by the end of the year.

She grabbed her phone and checked missed alerts. One call from Elaine. None from the boutique owner. Was the place even still for sale?

Cutting down Main Street, she drove to the shop, then idled near the curb. Her heart sank. A sale pending sign hung in the window. In her effort to hear from God, to wait for confirmation before jumping into another mortgage, she'd blown her chance.

You promised. Whether we turn to the right or the left, remember? So where's that voice that's supposed to be behind me? Where are You?

My ways are not your ways. The words flowed through her, stirred her heart, and stilled her thoughts. For half a second.

Lord, show me Your ways, then, because I feel like I'm hanging from a cliff without a landing mat.

SATURDAY EVENING, the sun descended and a faint crescent moon glimmered against a pale blue backdrop, but the squelching temperature remained. Sweat plastered Gavin's hair to his forehead and slicked his T-shirt to his itchy skin.

Setting his bucket aside, he lifted the lid of the pig feed. He recoiled at the acrid stench. Angling his face to avoid the smell, he grabbed the scoop and plunged it into the dry pellets. Five scoops, right? The memory of his morning chores rang clear and strong, but he checked the directions in his pocket anyway. He pulled out the slip of paper, now splotched with water stains and smudges of dirt. Mr. Lewis's handwriting was as tight and crisp as his face had been when he handed it over.

Every detail, from breakfast to chores to lights out, recorded in precise detail.

*Feed the pigs: four scoops, level with the rim,
spread across the base of the trough—4:30 a.m.,
6:30 p.m. Clean the pig stall.*

Gavin sighed and glanced toward a mud-packed, fenced-in area and grimaced. Snorts and squeals filled the air as filthy pigs poked slimy snouts through the fence, screeching piglets sandwiched between them. Even from this distance, the stench of urine-saturated hay filled the air, making him gag.

Back stiff and muscles tight, he filled his pail, counting each scoop, then lugged it to the pigpen. Squeals grew louder, more fervent, as he shoved his way into the pen, closing the door behind him. His boots—two sizes too big—sloshed in the mud, suction sounds popping with each step. Three pigs, weighing at least 100 pounds each, clamored around him. A sow with sagging teats waddled closer, nipping at his legs, her slimy, dripping snout jabbing at him.

"Get back!" His right foot slipped, and he grabbed onto the wooden fence. His fingers strained to hold tight to his bucket.

Giggling sounded behind him, and he turned to see Emma Rose watching him, long hair stirring in the wind. Even in her faded jeans and stained T-shirt, she looked soft and sweet, like she ought to be on one of those *Country Living* covers and not mucking around chickens and mules. "Better watch your step. One slip and they're likely to eat you."

"So I see." Gavin continued to press through until he reached the trough, gooey remnants slathered to the bottom. Next to this, straw and feed fragments floated in cloudy water lining the edges of the watering trough.

With a grunt, he heaved the bucket and poured its contents on top of the remaining slush. He returned to the barn where he exchanged one bucket for another and proceeded to a rusted spigot poking from the ground. An east wind stirred, momentarily thinning the air, and Gavin gulped it in. But then it shifted, bringing with it the sour scent of manure and animals.

Lugging the water bucket took quite a bit of effort, his hands sore and rubbery after a week of farm work. Water sloshed over the rim onto his boots and pants with every step. Next time he'd need to do this in two trips. Upon reaching the pen, he set the bucket down and wiped his hands on his dusty pants. He wiped the sweat from his brow with his forearm.

The pigs stood shoulder to shoulder.

"Hold on, I'll help you." Emma Rose flashed a smile, pink-tinged cheeks shining beneath aqua eyes. She dashed to his side then held the pen open for him. A lock of hair stirred across her forehead. Gavin suppressed the urge to brush it away.

"Thanks." Her eyes reminded him of sunlight drifting through ocean waters, long lashes curling beneath thin brows. A few freckles dotted her nose.

"Emma Rose!" A voice bellowed behind them, and Gavin whirled to see Mr. Lewis stomping toward them. A heavy shadow extended below his thick eyebrows. "Don't you got something to do?"

An icy chill crept up Gavin's spine.

"Yes, Poppa." She scurried away, the gate clanging shut.

Mr. Lewis closed in, a tendon twitching in his jaw. "Keep your mind on the job, boy." His voice, deep and throaty, grated against Gavin's nerves.

Figure out what he wants and obey. That's all you have to do.

"Yes, sir." He gripped his water bucket with one hand, his shoulder joint pulling against the weight, and reached for the gate with the other.

Mr. Lewis beat him to it, pressing through the herd. Gavin hurried to keep up, hands slick with sweat, water sloshing onto the thick mud. When he reached the watering trough, he heaved his bucket, ready to pour it in.

"Whoa, there." Mr. Lewis grabbed Gavin by the wrist, his thick hand cutting the circulation to his fingers. "Check your paper."

Blood swooshed past Gavin's eardrums. Muscles trembling, he eased the bucket to the ground, narrowly missing his toe. He pulled out his wrinkled sheet of paper.

Remove settlement and debris, which apparently meant residual pig slime.

"Yes, sir." He carefully folded the paper and slipped it back into his pocket, then scanned the area for something to scrape the gunk out with.

"What's the holdup?" Mr. Lewis's chiseled expression told Gavin this wasn't the time for questions.

"I . . . I . . ." Gavin plunged a hand into the tepid water and sloshed it over the side, swiping again and again. Senses overloaded by the thick stench and the feel of warm slime clinging to his flesh, he swallowed a gag reflex. Another rode on its tails, and another, so that he convulsed as he sloshed the water into the trough. Finished, he clung to the bucket.

Mr. Lewis inspected the feeding trough, scowling. The man hated him, no doubt about it. Gavin just needed to find a way to please him, before he got kicked out.

Obey, keep your mouth shut, remember your manners.

Only four more years.

CHAPTER 30

JONATHAN PACED HIS hotel room, flicked on the television, turned it off. He was acting stupid. Beyond stupid.

Just call the woman. She won't think anything of it, which begged the question: why did he? He'd already resolved not to dabble in heart garbage. Realized there weren't any more Evies out there. Besides, she was probably as bored and ready for company as he was.

He grabbed his phone and searched his contacts, then stopped. What were they going to do? Go to dinner? No. That seemed too formal. Too datey. They weren't dating. He'd clearly established that. You can't flip the rules once they're laid. Coffee sounded easy enough, something two chums might do. Two chums in college, anyway.

Wait a minute. Today was Friday, which meant there'd be another concert in the park. Perfect! Maybe he should invite Jeanne-Anne and Walter to come along.

You're pathetic, Jonathan Cohen. Grown man and looking for a hand-holder. Just call the woman already.

He grabbed the newspaper off the desk and flipped to the community pages. Tonight's concert: Mountain Melodies. How did Jacqueline feel about country music?

He dialed her number, feeling like a freshman trying to find a date for homecoming.

"Jonathan, hello."

"Hey, Jacqueline. How are you?"

"I'm good."

"You have a good day?"

She paused. "Quiet but yeah." She sounded tired, or perhaps deflated. Maybe she'd rather spend her evening alone. "What about you? Did you fix lots of trains today?"

"That we did," which surprised him, comparing the final reports to the work orders, something he'd investigate more fully come Monday. This action would only increase the tension down at the shop, but at least things seemed to be settling down a little. "You like country music?"

Another pause. Not the best start to an already awkward conversation.

"Yeah, sometimes. As long as it's not too sad and twangy. Why?"

No encouragement there, but it was too late to pull back now, unless he wanted to look like a complete idiot. "There's another concert in the park."

"Oh, how lovely."

He exhaled at the lift in her voice. "You want to go?"

"Great. I'll pick you up in hour."

"Sounds perfect. And tell your sister I'll bring the fruit this time. And some fresh baked brownies with thick, gooey, fudgy frosting."

Heat inched up his neck. "Er . . . She's not coming." Maybe he should've called her after all. A verse from an old song, "Big boys, put your drawers on," played through his mind and he clenched his jaw.

"Oh, OK."

"And I'll handle the food." Would that make this a date? If so, was that a good thing? Women! Someone needed to write an instructional manual: *How to Enter the Dating Arena for Old Men.*

The lot in front of Rolling Hills Park was filled by the time they got there, so Jonathan pulled to the curb to let Jacqueline out. "I'll park then meet you."

Dressed in white capris and a soft, lavender blouse, she stared out the window then turned to him with a wrinkled brow. "But how will you find me?"

From the looks of it, half the town stretched out on the grass before them. "Right." He eased back around, circling the lot before heading back to the street. He found an open spot on the curb two blocks down then edged between a Volkswagen bug and a black Mercedes.

Loaded down with a heavy basket, Jonathan and Jacqueline hiked back to the park, hot, thick air pressing down on them. A bead of sweat trickled down his temple. More slid down his back. He probably looked—and smelled—like a Neanderthal.

He cast a sideways glance at Jacqueline—her high cheekbones tinged pink, her slender nose, her long lashes that curled upward. So incredibly beautiful.

She glanced up, and when her gaze met his, the color in her cheeks deepened. Clearing his throat, he squared his shoulders and looked away.

JACQUELINE'S PULSE QUICKENED. He'd been watching her, his eyes filled with what? Admiration? Curiosity? How did he feel about her?

For that matter, where was their relationship headed? Where did she want it to go? There were too many uncertainties to even think about that right now—her foster care efforts, the insurance money, the boutique, Delana.

She cast him a sideways glance, studying the firm set of his jaw and the way his eyes intensified when he was deep in thought. Handsome, honest, and kind. Not a combination she encountered often.

What if this was her shot at love, and she passed it by?

His words, spoken the day she broke her bike, resurfaced. *I'm not looking for anything romantic.*

"You OK?" Jonathan watched her.

Blushing, Jacqueline forced a nervous chuckle. "Yes, just . . . thinking." She regretted her words the moment they came out.

"Care to share?"

"I, uh . . ." Still walking, she searched for a thought—anything to allow her to answer honestly. It was hot. The park was busy. She could use a cold glass of sweet tea?

Her sweaty feet slipped in her sandals, a blister forming under her big toe. "I'm wishing I'd brought tennis shoes."

"So go barefoot." He winked, the skin around his eyes crinkling.

Jacqueline studied him for a moment then looked at the soft grass beneath her. A giggle bubbled in her throat as the idea took hold. But, no. That'd be silly. Fun but silly.

When they returned to the stage area, Jonathan stopped in an open patch of grass and surveyed his surroundings. "This look OK?"

"Looks great." She planted her hands on her hips and looked around. "Did you bring something for us to sit on?"

Jonathan's eyes widened. "Hold on." He dropped the picnic basket and wove around people on blankets, heading back to the truck.

She glanced from the grass to her white pants, debating whether or not to test the stain-be-gone detergent commercials. A bee buzzed around her head, and she swatted it with her purse, stirring a welcome breeze to her exposed armpits.

The band switched songs, the singer's baritone pouring over the crowd. To her right, children danced in the city sprinklers, water gushing from a stretch of concrete. Oh, to be a kid again, running through an icy sprinkler.

Jonathan returned carrying an armful of yellow vests reminiscent of school crossing guards.

"Sorry, but this is all I have." He spread them on the grass, and Jacqueline bit back a laugh.

Safety vests? Still smiling, she sat on one then waited for Jonathan to settle beside her.

He grabbed a soda, still cold, and handed it to her. "You hungry?"

"Starved."

He unloaded his basket. Everything was store bought, still in their packages. A container of veggies, a bag of chips, wrapped sandwiches, beans, and a tub of coleslaw. He opened the lid of coleslaw, glanced around, and then frowned, blushing. "Guess I forgot the silverware." He continued to analyze the food with a lowered brow. His face brightened, and he grabbed a cylinder of veggies. "Perfect dipping tool." He flashed Jacqueline a boyish smile. "You mind?"

She giggled. "Not at all. No need to recycle."

"That's what I'm talking about."

He leaned the cylinder toward her, and she pulled out a carrot stick. "So, how's your week been? You like your new apartment?" He'd moved out of the hotel the week before, signing a six-month lease. Hopefully that meant he'd decided to stay in the valley.

"I do. It's quiet. Homey."

"Things still tense at work?"

"It's awkward to say the least." He took a sip of soda. "It's getting so I don't know who to trust. At first I thought it was just management, but I'm not so sure anymore. Maybe I'm a conspiracy theorist."

"What are you going to do?"

"I've got a class next week in Denver. The big dogs'll be there, including the man who hired me. I'm thinking of telling him about it, although I'm not sure I have enough specifics. Nothing but a bunch of reports that make zero sense and one unreported injury that I know of."

"What do you think he'll say?"

"I guess it depends on if he believes me or not. The way my boss tells it, I'll do anything to win his job."

"He said that?"

"Not to me, but word gets around. Railroaders are worse than church ladies in that regard."

"Wow, I'm sorry."

"It happens." He frowned and gazed toward the stage.

"You regret taking the job?"

He looked at her for a long moment before shaking his head. "I don't believe in regrets. Life happens. It's all about pushing through, you know? Like the Bible says, 'Forgetting what's in the past and straining toward what's ahead.'"

Jacqueline stared at her hands. She could use a little forgetting of the past right about now, but the straining to what lay ahead? That was the tough part, especially since she had no clue what she was straining toward, or even if God was leading. But one thing she knew, she wasn't ready to leave Willow Valley.

GAVIN SHUFFLED IN, muscles sore, hands blistered, after completing his evening chores. His stomach grumbled, his dinner burned off by farm work, but Mr. Lewis's scowl didn't invite questions.

Emma Rose sat at the kitchen table, drawing in a notebook. She glanced up, meeting Gavin's gaze. Blushing, she looked first to her father then to her paper, growing visibly tense.

Mr. Lewis eyed Gavin. "Jump in the shower. Lights out in thirty minutes."

Gavin checked the clock on the microwave—8 p.m., and it was still light out. Didn't matter. He needed to keep his mouth shut and do as he was told. "Yes, sir." At least school started Wednesday. Except he still hadn't been registered yet. How hard could it be for them to sign a kid up? Most likely Ferret wasn't even trying. Why should she care whether or not Gavin got an education?

He showered quickly then hurried to his room where he spent the next hour staring at the wall, wishing he felt sleepy. Wishing his brain had an off switch. Where was Adele right now? What was her room like? Did she sleep by herself? She was afraid of the dark, liked to keep the hall light on and her door open. And what about baby Jaya? She always liked it when Gavin rubbed her back and sang the Oscar Mayer bologna song.

With a sigh, he rolled over, his face smashing into his flat pillow. His room was crazy hot. Crickets and frogs croaked outside. A spider crawled up his wall. He counted his pulse then clouds. Nothing helped. In fact, the longer he lay, the more awake he felt. And stiff and itchy, despite—or maybe because of—his shower with the homemade soap that smelled like acetone and made his skin tingle.

He threw off his sheet and slipped out of bed. Without a clock or watch, there was no way to know what time it was, except that the evening sun still hovered near the horizon. But lights out was lights out, and Gavin had a printed schedule to prove it. If only he could get his body on the same schedule, maybe the before-dawn wake-up call wouldn't be so brutal.

He slid open his door and tiptoed down the hall toward the bathroom, cringing when a wooden plank squeaked. Not that relieving himself was a crime, but the way Mr. Lewis eyed Gavin's every move—

He shook his head. If the guy thought Gavin was such a thug, why take him in? Not that Mr. Lewis's motives were a secret. Gavin was nothing more than a project.

He finished quickly, holding when the toilet flushed, then eased the door open. Faint voices drifted from the kitchen. Although he couldn't make out the words, nausea gripped his stomach.

He tiptoed closer and pressed against the hall wall, keeping his breathing shallow.

"I shoulda known better 'n to take in a hormonal teen." Mr. Lewis said.

"But we talked about this with Mrs. Mansfield in great detail. You said—"

"I don't care what I said. The boy's got his eyes on Emma Rose."

"He'd never—"

"How would you know what that kid would or wouldn't do? You know his history. No daddy and a mom with a new boyfriend every month. Or did you forget where they found him?"

Gavin flinched, Mr. Lewis's words stabbing him in the gut as memories from the shelter came rushing back—the scent of urine mixed with body odor, men covered in grime and tattoos, a few crazies twitching on the outskirts. Not much different than his Crystal Shores apartment, really.

"But Mrs. Mansfield said no one else would take him."

"Yeah, well, maybe there's a reason for that."

A dull ache seeped into Gavin's soul, weighting his limbs and numbing his mind. *No one else would take him. No one wanted him.*

"So, what do you want to do?" Mrs. Lewis's voice came out barely above a whisper.

"Don't know."

A chair scraped against the floorboards and Gavin scampered back to his room. He left the door ajar—Mr. Lewis's rules. No closed doors except in the bathroom. He dove into his bed and rolled on his side, rigid. Heavy footsteps neared then stopped outside his room. The door creaked open wider and Gavin held his breath, his heart ricocheting against his ribs.

The footsteps receded, but Gavin's pulse refused to settle.

No one wanted him. Not the Lewises, not Mom. No one.

He stared through the window toward a smattering of stars poking through shadowed clouds. *Don't send me back to the group home. Please. Send me anywhere but there.* He didn't know much about God, but who else could he turn to? He reached into his pocket, touched the slip of paper with Jacqueline's number. She'd probably forgotten all about him anyway.

Oh, Momma, where are you?

CHAPTER 31

JACQUELINE AWOKE TO an empty house, freshly brewed coffee, and a note on the counter.

Should be home early today. Want to try bike riding again? Seems to be a great way to meet men. LOL.

Laughing out loud—and a large smiley face filled the rest of the page.

That it had, Delana. That it had. Chuckling, she poured herself a cup of coffee, savoring the rich aroma. Of all the places to meet men. She walked to the counter, where her cell phone lay plugged into the wall, and sent her daughter a text.

Thanks for the note. A bike ride sounds lovely.

After her visit with Gavin and his sisters . . . and the Willow Valley Police Department.

Her stomach fluttered as she thought about her upcoming fingerprinting appointment, one of many self-exposing requirements laid out by the foster care system. And to top it off, she needed Delana to write a letter of reference.

Oh, Lord, please let her be in a halfway decent mood when that happens.

Mug in hand, she moseyed back to her bedroom for some Bible reading. She flipped to Philippians 3:13 (NLT), the verse Jonathan quoted. "But I focus on this one thing: Forgetting the past and looking forward to what lies ahead."

I'm trying, Lord, but the past keeps rising to the surface. And this home study—the fingerprinting, the reference checks—blur the lines of redemption. You may be merciful and forgiving, but I doubt Mrs. Mansfield offers such grace. And rightly so.

What was she thinking? She wasn't. When it came to those kids, her heart took over, and memories from the past submerged her. A past where her daughter lay crumpled in a hospital bed, dark circles under her eyes, intravenous needles attached to her thin arms.

She'd walked away from one child. She wouldn't do it again. They might expose her, judge her, deny her, but she wouldn't give up. Not this time.

JONATHAN LINGERED AT the back of the meeting room, near the door, and scanned the crowd for Mr. Shaffer. He stood near a table covered in coffee pots and water pitchers, talking with an older gentleman. The seat to Mr. Shaffer's right remained open. Weaving through the gathering crowd, Jonathan squared his shoulders and approached the man.

"Good morning, Sir."

Mr. Shaffer's cracked lips stretched across crooked teeth. "Cohen, good to see you. Have you met Mr. Scott? He runs the car department out in Hatworth."

"I don't believe I have."

Mr. Shaffer made introductions before continuing with a story on a discrimination complaint. "So, Kelvins listened to his messages, and it's this guy, running his mouth on what he should've done to the girl." He laughed. "The guy butt-dialed him. Spilled it all on voice mail."

The elderly gentleman shook his head. "Unbelievable. I'm guessing the idiot didn't appear for his investigation."

"Oh, he showed up all right. We didn't tell him about the recording until questioning."

"Good morning." A voice boomed through the mic, ending Mr. Shaffer's conversation and quieting the room. A man dressed in all gray stood behind a podium, pointer in hand. "Thank you for coming. This morning we'll talk about LEAN. It's all about reducing waste by eliminating defects, overproduction, wait time, nonessential tasks." The man continued reciting the list projected on the big screen.

Jonathan jotted down notes, trying to keep his mind on the presenter while his thoughts drifted to Shaffer and the conversation he hoped to have during break. Assuming he could catch the guy alone. Unfortunately, when break time hit, Shaffer's phone rang. With a sigh, Jonathan followed a steady flow of men out of the room. Nodding to a few in passing, he found a quiet place to check his messages while watching for Shaffer. He last saw the man entering the restrooms, still on the phone. Not the place to initiate a conversation.

Jacqueline sent a text with an attachment: *Look what I found. Picnic time. What do you say?*

Hilarious. She'd taken a picture of a bag of fried veggie sticks sitting beside a bucket of beans with one stick plunged in them.

He replied: *Sounds great. I'll call you when I get back into town.*

At least he had something pleasant to return to. More than pleasant, and almost worth sticking it out at the job for, if he didn't get fired.

Still waiting, he moved from checking texts to reading e-mails.

Rubbing his forehead, he clicked on a message from Darren. A safety feed, to celebrate no injuries. Gift certificates given to foremen along with a half day off, paid. So Darren had deleted the injury report Jonathan had filled out, and if word got out, most likely Jonathan would take the fall. Unless he could talk to Shaffer. Assuming the man believed him.

Lunch came at 1:00, and Shaffer immediately reached for his phone.

"Excuse me, sir?"

With his cell to his ear, Mr. Shaffer raised a finger, clutching a briefcase with his other hand. Jonathan followed at a polite distance as the CMO strode out of the room and toward an open area filled with linen-covered table clothes. Wait staff bustled, holding water glasses and green salads.

"Jonathan? Jonathan Cohen?"

He glanced at a man to his right. He had curly, black hair that looked like it needed a bit of taming. They shook hands, Jonathan sifting through mental images, trying to put a name to the face.

"Peter. Peter Nelms from RailServe."

"Right. Good to see you." He glanced at Shaffer, now off the phone and surrounded by a group of men.

"I heard you switched to Central Rails. How's that working out for you?"

Jonathan forced a smile, gaze shifting between Peter and Mr. Shaffer. He needed to catch the guy before he made it to his table. "Great. It's going great. Listen I—"

Too late. Mr. Shaffer moved to the front of the room and sat between the class presenter and a man in a blue blazer. Jonathan turned back to Peter. "I'll have to catch you later."

Peter's smile wavered, no doubt his contractor's sale pitch burning to be released. "Sure. No problem." He pulled a business card from his front pocket. "Give me a call. I'd love to talk to you about our replacement engine parts."

Jonathan nodded and tucked the card in his pocket with no intention of calling and pressed his way toward Shaffer. He took an open seat across the table and offered a casual smile. Once again, the CMO was in the middle of conversation.

"Figured, might as well enjoy life while I can." He stabbed his salad and shoved a forkful into his mouth.

The man sitting beside him lifted his glass. "You taking a buyout?"

Shaffer shook his head. "Don't offer it at my level, but that doesn't matter. I've got my thirty years in, my pension, some stock options that come due this year."

Jonathan leaned forward, fighting to maintain an appropriate smile. The man was planning to retire, which meant Jonathan needed to have that conversation now, today. Otherwise he might not get the chance, and with Shaffer gone, his job was as secure as a chlorine spill on a windy day.

Unfortunately, the opportunity never arose, and after class, Shaffer was once again surrounded by men sharing railroad stories and plans for retirement. Only this time Jonathan didn't wait quietly.

"Excuse me, sir?" He edged between the CMO and a balding man with a bloated stomach. "Can I speak with you for a moment?"

Mr. Shaffer's expression twitched, as if hovering between curiosity and annoyance. "Certainly, Cohen. What can I do for you?"

Jonathan swallowed, his palms growing slick. "In private, sir?"

Mr. Shaffer glanced around, frowned, then shrugged. "Excuse me, gentleman."

The other men mumbled a few good-byes and catch-you-laters before resuming their conversation. Mr. Shaffer led Jonathan to a sitting area with leather chairs, a few end tables, and an accent table at the end of the hall. Neither of them sat.

"What can I do for you?"

Jonathan cleared his throat, shifted. "I'd like to talk to you about the shop."

"Whatcha got?" The corners of Shaffer's mouth dipped, and he looked on the verge of a yawn. Not surprising. The man's head was already in his retirement, not rail drama. Which is exactly what Jonathan was about to unload—major, Equal Opportunity Employment, Federal Railroad Association, labor relations drama. Labeling himself as a whiner in the process.

"Did you see the reports this morning?"

"Haven't had a chance. Why? Something wrong?"

Jonathan took in a deep breath, expelling his concerns on the exhale.

When he finished, Mr. Shaffer crossed his arms. "You got proof?"

Jonathan rubbed the back of his neck with a clammy hand. "Maybe." Computer records that could be erased. A hospital visit that could implicate himself. His word against the general director backed by loyal, maybe even paid-off employees. And if headquarters launched an investigation, what would they find? If Darren could erase company records, lie about injuries and work orders, he could easily point evidentiary fingers at Jonathan.

CHAPTER 32

GAVIN SAT AT a plastic table splattered with gobs of dried ketchup, watching the Burgers-n-Frenz entrance. Mr. Lewis sat beside him, face stern, staring at his phone. The man had said a total of four words on the drive over. Commands, barked out like an officer to a felon.

A woman dressed in jeans and a Mickey Mouse T-shirt sat near the window, a toddler bouncing in the seat across from her. More children spilled from the tube slide on the other side of a glass wall.

Ferret Face pulled into the lot, and Gavin sat straighter. His gut rolled, a bead of sweat breaking out on his forehead. She wore a blue dress suit and carried a large tote bag.

Upon entering, she approached Mr. Lewis, and they shook hands. "Thank you for coming." She acknowledged Gavin with a hollow smile. "Good morning. How are you doing?"

Having a party. "Fine." He stared back to the lot, heart pricking each time a new car pulled in. "My sisters?"

Ferret set her tote on the ground and checked her watch. "They should be here soon."

"Can we talk for a minute? Alone?" Mr. Lewis's hardened gaze shifted from Gavin back to Ferret.

The corners of Ferret's mouth dropped as if fighting a frown. "Sure." She squeezed Gavin's hand.

Her soft expression sliced at Gavin, threatening tears. He gritted his teeth and lifted his chin. *Four more years. Four more years.* So long as he could see Adele and baby Jaya. That's all he cared about.

Mr. Lewis and Ferret moved a few feet away and spoke in hushed tones. Gavin held his breath and strained his ears.

Couldn't hear nothing. Fighting against an overwhelming sense of defeat, he turned his attention back to the entrance.

Jacqueline approached. She came! Gavin bounced on the balls of his feet before he could catch himself. A smile tugged at his lips but he fought it off, planted his feet firmly on the ground, and stilled his wiggling legs.

Upon reaching him, she wrapped him in a tight hug. Stiff, arms pinned to his side, the ache in Gavin's heart intensified. He blinked, tears springing to gritty eyes, but he squelched them.

Releasing him, Jacqueline turned to Ferret and Mr. Lewis. "Good morning. Thank you for letting me come." She scanned the lobby. "Where are the girls?"

Ferret glanced at her watch. "They should be here any—"

"Gavin!"

His head snapped up as he looked toward the door. *Adele!* He raced toward her, barreling into her with enough force, it knocked the air from him. They clung to each other, her soft hair tickling his chin, her fingers digging into his sides. The adults gathered, standing, staring. Jacqueline approached with open arms. Adele tumbled into them. Cupping the back of Adele's head, Jacqueline watched Gavin, her eyes moist. He held her gaze, studied her expression.

Help us! Please.

A moment later, the door swooshed open again. A woman with waist-length hair shuffled in carrying baby Jaya.

He lurched forward, arms outstretched. "Jaya!"

Baby Jaya writhed in the woman's arms, pudgy hands grasping at air. "Gab-Gab! Gab-Gab!"

The woman grimaced and dropped Jaya on her feet, and she toddled forward. Gavin blinked. She'd learned to walk! He scooped her up, Adele clinging to his side, and buried his nose in her neck. She smelled like baby powder and curdled milk.

Pulling on his arm, Adele leaned over his shoulder and smothered Jaya with kisses. Jaya squealed, fat fingers grabbing at Adele's face.

The longhaired woman cleared her throat. "What time should I be back?"

Ferret looked from the woman to Adele then to the other adults gathered around. "An hour?"

A heavy weight crashed on Gavin's shoulders. An hour? He hadn't seen his sisters in almost a month, and they'd only have an hour? Why? Because the adults were bored? Had better things to do than let a bunch of loser kids hang out?

"Call my cell phone if you need me." Stepping toward Jaya, the woman patted her on the head then tenderly stroked her chubby cheek. "Bye, little one." Then she left.

Jacqueline edged closer and placed a hand on his back.

Ferret glanced at a distant table. "Why don't we give the children some space?"

With mumbles of assent, the adults ambled away. Lingering, Jacqueline looked from Gavin to his sisters, her face downcast. Like maybe she really cared—wanted to be with them.

"You can stay." Gavin turned to Ferret. "Can't she?"

Ferret studied Gavin and his sisters for a moment. "If you'd like."

Gavin shrugged, hiding the faint flicker of hope that niggled in his heart. "I don't care."

Clutching Gavin's and Adele's index fingers, baby Jaya lunged toward the play equipment.

Gavin laughed. "What? You want to slide? Huh? Huh?" He tickled her ribs, longing to scoop her up again, to hold her close. Instead, he and Adele led her to the playground.

Adele paused near a row of cubbyholes to kick off her shoes. "I'll take her."

Gavin did the same. "I'm coming."

Jacqueline hovered near the playground entrance, and for a moment, Gavin thought she'd join them. *Grandma in the tubes.* He swallowed back laughter and smiled instead.

He and Adele climbed up ten or twelve times, bringing baby Jaya with them. Going down, they took turns holding her in their laps. Adele's laughter and baby Jaya's happy squeals echoed in the slide and made Gavin's heart swell. For the moment, he forgot his life stunk.

But then Ferret approached. "Adele, it's time for you to go."

Gavin looked at the clock, stomach souring. He clutched baby Jaya with one hand, fingernails on the other digging into his palm. "We got twelve more minutes." He looked through the window to see the other adults lined up shoulder to shoulder. No smiles. No frowns. Nothing but emotionless faces. Like they were watching some documentary.

"I'm sorry, but your foster mom is ready to take you home." Ferret reached for Adele.

She flinched and clung to Gavin, cheek pressed against his arm. "No! You can't make me!"

But she could. Ferret and all these adults could do whatever they wanted, make him and his sisters do whatever they wanted. Didn't matter how they felt about it.

Jacqueline touched Gavin's back, her other hand around Adele. "Sh. It's OK. It's going to be OK."

Heat surged through him. "You're a liar."

Ferret pried Adele from Gavin's arm. "It's time to go."

Gavin's blood pumped fast and hot. Still holding baby Jaya, he reached his free arm around Adele and pulled her close. "We've got twelve more minutes."

Baby Jaya started to cry.

Ferret's eyes misted. She glanced behind her as the woman with long hair approached, face firm. She checked her watch and threw her hands up. "Fine. Five more minutes."

The others entered the play area.

Mr. Lewis held Gavin's gaze, his thick brows darkening the shadows under his eyes. "No arguing, boy. When it's time to go, it's time to go."

Gavin glanced from one adult to the next, a sudden urge to grab his sisters and run pulsating through him. But it wouldn't do any good. Nothing would. *Keep my mouth shut and do what I'm told.* It'd always worked before. In school, at home. Only it wasn't working now. Things were only getting worse.

A searing pain ripped through his chest as he released his grip. He looked Adele in the eye. "Do what they say, Adele. You hear me? Don't sass now."

Tears spilled over her lashes and slid down her cheeks.

"We'll see each other again. Right, Fe—Mrs. Mansfield?" His voice squeaked the question, desperation gripping his gut.

She touched Adele's shoulder. "That's right. I'll arrange for another visit."

With a shuddered breath, Adele dropped her arms and followed her foster mom out. Next went baby Jaya, howling, until Gavin was left alone with Ferret, Jacqueline, and Mr. Lewis.

"Well, boy." Mr. Lewis lowered a brow.

Gavin nodded then turned to Jacqueline who stood in front of him with a pitiful frown.

"I'm sorry, Gavin." She reached for him.

He jerked away. "Yeah? How sorry? Sorry enough to help us?" His temperature rose as tremors shot through him. "You told me to call if I needed anything, remember?" Hands fisted, his nails dug into his palms. "We need you. Can't you see that?"

Face pale, she made a sobbing gasp and stepped back, hand to her mouth.

Ferret touched Gavin's arm, and he recoiled.

"Let's go." Mr. Lewis jerked his head toward the exit.

PALMS SWEATY, Jacqueline drove through the streets of Willow Valley. Buildings drifted through her peripheral vision, horns honked. But nothing registered except Gavin's trembling voice, which replayed again and again.

We need you. Can't you see that?

The memory of his pleading eyes merged with an image of her daughter from ten years ago.

Jacqueline shook her head and death-gripped the steering wheel as if strangling the memory. *Oh, Delana, I'm so sorry! Please forgive me. Father, help her forgive me.*

She thought of Delana's note, decorated with a large happy face, and her stomach soured. She didn't deserve forgiveness. Didn't deserve love. Not from Delana nor from Gavin and his sisters.

But they deserved it. She glanced at the manila folder, labeled "foster care licensing requirements," sitting on the passenger seat. *Keep stepping. I can do this. I have to do this. Those kids need me. They don't have anybody else.*

Her phone rang, a welcomed distraction. The number flashing on her screen brought a smile. "Jonathan, how are you?"

"I'm good. Just got in." His voice was like a balm, low and soothing. "Thought maybe you'd like to try out those veggie sticks you showed me. What do ya say? You up for some good old country music down by the river?"

That was exactly what she needed right now. To sit beside him, soaking in his calm. To lose herself in the warmth of his laughing eyes beneath a setting sun. But first she needed to walk through a long prayed for opened door. "I wish I could, but Delana asked me to hang out with her tonight."

"Wow, really? That's awesome. Sounds like you two are heading in the right direction."

"I hope so." She stopped at a red light and watched a pack of kids dressed in cleats and shin guards spill from a pizza parlor. "What about you? Did you get a chance to talk to your boss?" The more important question was: are you staying in Willow Valley?

"I did."

"How'd it go?"

"To be honest, I'm not sure. The guy's retiring. Probably focused on Jamaica or something, not the railroad."

"But still, he'll do something, don't you think? I mean, it's the right thing to do."

"I hope so. If he believes me."

Another call chimed in, and Jacqueline glanced at the screen. Elaine, probably calling to share more cute grandchildren stories. Jacqueline would call her back later.

"You free tomorrow?" Turning on her blinker, she headed right on South Eighteenth Street. "I hear there's an amazing ice cream store across town."

"Now that's something I can't turn down."

They chatted for a while longer, dragging out the conversation like a couple of teenagers. At least they didn't pull a, "You hang up first," "No, you," "No, you." But it felt good—right. No pretending. No expectations.

A mile from Munchester Boulevard, a crossing train held up traffic. Looking for a roundabout, she wove her way through side streets. Unfortunately, she got lost. Crazy, considering the town stretched less than five miles across. But she wasn't ready to return to an empty condo anyway.

She stopped at a red light near a rundown hotel. Now what? It was too hot for hiking. Too late for lunch, although her growling stomach disagreed. Mexican food sounded awesome, and according to late-night commercials, Rosita's boasted the best burritos in town.

She searched for the restaurant using her GPS then glanced around to orient herself. A woman emerging from a second-story hotel room caught her attention. She blinked, leaning toward her side window for a better look. Trim, petite figure, blue scrubs, gold purse. Jacqueline studied the cars in the parking lot, found one identical to Delana's glistening in the sun. "What would—?"

She waited, watched, holding her breath as Delana descended the steps and climbed into her car. A moment later, Delana's boss emerged. He paused outside the door, glanced right, left, then dashed down the stairs and into a black Mercedes.

Delana was having an affair? With her boss? Jacqueline felt ill, remembering the slinky red lingerie she'd found in Delana's laundry. Exhaling a gust of air, Jacqueline massaged her temples.

Now what?

CHAPTER 33

JACQUELINE PACED HER room, Delana's note clutched in her sweaty hand. Bits of an old memory verse played through her mind. *People who wink at wrong...*

She shook her head. What right did she have to say anything?

The front door clicked, followed by Delana's cheerful voice. "Mom?"

Squaring her shoulders, Jacqueline took a few calming breaths. It didn't help. She tucked Delana's note into her pocket and strolled out.

"Hey, you ready for some more two-wheel wobbling?" Grinning, Delana dropped her purse onto the coffee table.

Her rosy cheeks and sparkling eyes—signs of a woman in love—weighed heavy on Jacqueline's heart. The man was using her, would devastate her.

"Oh, before I forget. I mailed that reference letter."

"Thanks." Jacqueline stepped forward, hands clenched in front of her.

Delana studied her with a frown. "Is everything OK?"

People who wink at wrong...

The man would destroy her. Scenes from the past came rushing back. The phone call. Delana in the hospital. The bottle of pills, empty. Her ashen complexion, but a few shades darker than the sheets pulled around her. Her hateful tone and explosion of curse words: "Like you care. Get out of here, and leave me alone."

"Mom?" Delana's voice sliced through Jacqueline's thoughts like a paring knife.

Trembling, she stumbled to the couch, fell into it. She knew what came from sleeping with married men. She knew what it felt like to be used and discarded. To soak up their empty promises. "Oh, Delana."

"What is it?" Her daughter sat beside her. "Did you have a rough visit with the kids?"

She shook her head. Struggled to maintain eye contact. "I got lost today. Downtown. Stopped along the side of the road on Hollistar and Elmwood by the Tree Lodge Inn."

Delana's face blanched then reddened. She jerked her hand away and stood. "So use your GPS next time." Walking away, she pulled her cell phone from her back pocket.

"I know." Jacqueline could barely whisper the words. "I saw you."

Delana whirled around, eyes flashing. "What I do is none of your business."

"He'll use you, sweetie. I know. I've been there."

"Right. I remember. Half the town heard all about your afternoon rendezvous."

Heat seared Jacqueline's face, urging her to retreat, but she fought against it. This wasn't about her or her past. She crossed the room and reached for her daughter. "You need to stop seeing him."

"Get out."

"Delana, I—"

"Get out! Now! And take your junk with you."

Delana stormed into her room and slammed the door behind her.

Dropping her head, Jacqueline closed her eyes and rubbed her face. She'd blown it. It was none of her business who Delana saw, except that she was her mother.

Right. Some mother—but she was trying now. Except maybe it was too late.

She slumped to her room, gathered her things and carried them to her car, box by box. Everything she owned minus the rubble that remained in Crystal Shores. Car loaded and rear window blocked, she glanced at her daughter's condo one last time. They'd come so close and, once again, Jacqueline had messed everything up. But then, that's what she always did.

She searched for a hotel using her GPS. A handful pulled up. Too many for her frazzled mind. The hotel Jonathan had stayed at seemed nice enough. Clean, and he never complained.

She called him en route.

"Hey, I was just thinking about you." His soothing voice lifted her heart. "When's your mother-daughter deal?"

"It's not going to happen. Delana threw me out."

"You serious? Why?"

"I kind of meddled."

"You're a mom. That's what moms do."

She let out a long sigh and rounded a corner. "Yeah, well, we don't really have the relationship to support that." *Nor do I have the credibility.*

"So where're you going?"

"I figured I'd try your old hotel." She stopped at a red light. A lady in jean shorts and a baggy T-shirt crossed in front of her, pushing a rosy-cheeked toddler in a stroller. "I'm headed there now."

"I'll meet you with Kung Pao chicken."

Food was the last thing on her mind, but Jonathan meant well, and she needed the company. "Sounds great."

Upon reaching the hotel parking lot, she cut her engine and sat, watching cars pass on the street in front of her.

Delana wanted nothing to do with her, and the boutique was sold. Maybe she needed to return to Crystal Shores. Rebuild her house, resurrect her old career.

But what about Gavin and his sisters? Jonathan?

And yet, Jonathan could move at any time—if he quit or lost his job. Leave it to her to fall for the one potentially unavailable man in Willow Valley.

A blur of color flashed through her peripheral vision, and when she turned, an instant sense of calm washed over her. Jonathan—strong, undemanding, goofy-cute—pulled up beside her. He jumped out carrying a large bag labeled Hong Lee's Buffet.

"Hey." He gave her a shoulder hug then pulled out a handwritten slip of paper. "Check your fortune."

She did, reading his words out loud. "A strong, paunch-bellied, hunk of a man bearing greasy carbohydrates will soon cross your path." She smiled. "Cute."

He glanced at her box-filled car. "You want help unloading this stuff?"

"I don't think so. I'm hoping this is temporary."

He studied her, the laughter fading in his eyes. "Are you going to go back to Crystal Shores?"

She watched a minivan pull into the lot. "I don't know."

"How about we go for a walk? Find a quiet picnic bench to sit at?"

"That sounds lovely. After I check in?"

"Right."

He walked her inside and waited near the entrance while she reserved a room. Then, looping her arm in his, she matched his stride. They continued in silence. The gentle breeze rustled fallen leaves, and a woodpecker drummed in the distance.

"How about there, in the shade?" Jonathan pointed to a picnic table under a large oak draped in Spanish moss.

"Perfect."

They sat side by side. Jonathan spread a few napkins in front of them and unloaded the contents of his bag. The rich aromas of garlic and ginger filled the air, making Jacqueline's reluctant taste buds water.

He handed her a box of fried rice. "Does your daughter normally lose her temper? Any chance this'll all blow over by the weekend?"

She wrapped both hands around the warm container and watched him through the rising steam. He was such a good man. Faithful father, honest worker, good Christian. Would he still want to be with her if he knew about her past? He had a right to know, didn't he? But then again, he could be gone tomorrow. And yet, she needed to find out how he felt now, before he stole her heart.

The wind picked up and blew her hair into her face. She smoothed it away.

"Delana's got a lot of bitterness, anger. I wasn't the best mom."

She lifted her chin and stared into his warm eyes, analyzing every blink.

"Before I came to Jesus, I did a lot of things I'm not proud of. I barely knew her father, and once I got pregnant, I hated him. Made it my mission to make sure Delana hated him, too. I didn't let him see his daughter unless it fit my schedule, which it started to do once the housing market hit a boom. Then I started calling him all the time, telling—not asking—him to pick up Delana after school, take her for the weekend. She became my ammunition, my manipulation tactic."

Her heart ached as memories from the past rushed back. The hateful words she spoke, in front of Delana, talking like she was an obligation instead of a child.

"She got moody, and she and I began to fight all the time. Looking back, I know she was begging for attention, for me to show I cared." She shook her head. "Only I was so consumed with making that next sale. Instead of holding tight to her, fighting for her, I passed her off to her father. I turned my back on her when she needed me most. A week after she moved out, I got a phone call. She went to a party with a bunch of college kids. Overdosed on a drug cocktail. I almost lost her."

And instead of caring for Delana, instead of reaching out, she'd spent the next weekend shacking up with a married man. A guy she expected to sweep in and fix everything but who left her empty and more alone than ever. The images swirling her brain became too much. Inhaling, she closed her eyes and pinched the bridge of her nose. Tears welled in her throat and fought for release, but she shoved them down. Until Jonathan placed his arm around her shoulder and pulled her close.

"It's OK. We all make mistakes we're not proud of. That's what grace is all about."

His gentle strength became her undoing, and for the first time in more than twenty years, she released her tears. "I abandoned my daughter, my baby. I don't deserve grace."

Jonathan turned her face toward him and looked into her eyes. He offered a soft smile. "No one deserves grace, darling. That's why it's grace. As far as the east is from the west, remember?"

"What?"

"When we come to Jesus, that's what God does with our sins. He removes them from us, as far as the east is from the west. You know how far that is?"

She swiped at her tears, sniffling. "I guess it depends on where you're standing."

"Uh-uh." He leaned closer and traced the back of his hand along her jaw. "No matter where you're standing, the east is as far from the west as you can get. Because there's no condemnation for those who are in Christ Jesus. If you're a Christian, the only condemnation you'll get is right here."

He tapped her temple then ran his knuckles along the curve of her face. "No condemnation. Nothing but glorious grace."

His lips brushed hers, one hand lifting her chin while the other cupped the back of her head.

She leaned against him, losing herself, her worries, her pain, in his strong yet soft embrace.

Don't break my heart, Jonathan Cohen.

CHAPTER 34

HEAVY FOOTSTEPS AND gruff voices passed in the hallway outside Jonathan's office door. One of them sounded like Rustin, one of the few machinists Jonathan trusted.

He jumped to his feet and poked his head out. "Hey, Rustin, you got a minute?"

The guy, a stocky man with a thick beard that reached midchest, stopped, glanced back. "Sure boss, whatcha got?"

Jonathan motioned him into his office then closed the door. "You've been working here a long time, right?"

The man hunkered into the chair in front of Jonathan's desk. "Going on thirty years. Why?"

Jonathan sat across from him. Rustin appeared trustworthy. He always gave an honest day's work, looked Jonathan in the eye when they talked. "One of the new hires said something about spraying parts. You know anything about that?"

Rustin brought folded hands under his chin, his knuckles rubbing against his jowls. "Heard a thing or two about the night shift, but don't have proof."

Maybe Jonathan needed to show up during third shift, check things out for himself.

"Heard something else from a bro-in-law from the FRA."

"They coming for another inspection?" According to Darren, the Federal Railroad Administration had nosed around a few months ago. Although they could come unannounced at any time, they tended to be predictable.

"He told me they launched a big investigation. Said they've been looking through records three years back. Don't know the details except to say, my bro-in-law said it was bad."

Jonathan massaged his forehead until his skin tingled. "OK. Thanks. You can go, and close the door behind you, will you?"

If things were as bad as Jonathan expected, they were all in a heap of trouble. The feds weren't people you wanted to mess with. It didn't matter that Jonathan had only been here a month and a half. Didn't matter who was behind the mess, either. As senior manager over the repair shop, Jonathan was directly responsible for the repairs made by 120 machinists.

This mess could cost him his job and his retirement. What then? He could always call Bart Lanquist, see if he'd take him back as a foreman. Pipefitter—whatever he needed.

But then Jonathan would lose Jacqueline. Sweet, beautiful Jacqueline.

GROGGY-EYED, Gavin rolled on his side and gazed through the blinds to the farm beyond. The morning sun poured in, casting long beams across his floor.

What the—?

He'd overslept. But how? Why hadn't Mr. Lewis woken him?

Gavin threw off his sheets and sprang to his feet. Yesterday's clothes lay in a mound on the floor, covered in dust and hay fragments. He pulled the shirt over his head, jumped into his pants, and shoved his feet into his too-small sneakers. No time to find clean socks, and yesterday's were still wet with sweat. Besides, he only had one other pair.

The faint scent of sausage hovered in the air, the house quiet except for the occasional clink of dishes. In the kitchen, he found Mrs. Lewis standing at the sink, arms in sudsy water.

She glanced over her shoulder when he entered, her face tight, eyes droopy. She grabbed a hand towel and turned around slowly. Her creased brow and down-turned mouth made Gavin's gut tighten.

"I'm sorry I overslept." He scanned the tidy kitchen. No carefully measured servings of breakfast on the table. No sausage or eggs frying on the stove. "Where's Mr. Lewis?"

Her eyes softened. "Are you hungry?" She pulled a plate of food from the fridge and placed it on the table. Two sausage links, two fried eggs, and half a slice of buttered toast.

"Where's Mr. Lewis? Why didn't he wake me up?" His voice squeaked.

"There was no need. After you eat, you are to pack your things. Mrs. Mansfield will be here in a couple hours to pick you up and take you back to the group home."

Unwanted. Unlovable. "But why? I want to stay. I'll work hard. Harder. I won't eat much. You'll hardly know I'm here." *Don't send me back! Please.*

Mrs. Lewis returned to washing dishes. She started to hum.

Gavin staggered to his room, mind and limbs numb. He stared at his dirty shirt then to his soiled clothes piled in the corner. All he owned amounted to little more than three outfits, which would've been cleaned tonight. And his comic book Bible with Jacqueline's phone number carefully tucked inside.

Call me if you need anything. . . . I need a home. That's what I need.

He searched under his mattress for the comic book, pulled it out, and removed the slip of paper. Standing in his doorway, he poked his head into the hall. His pulse quickened as he held his breath, straining for the sound of approaching footsteps. Dishes continued to clank. Tiptoeing, he scurried toward Mr. and Mrs. Lewis's room and scanned the area. An old rotary phone sat on the bedside table. He crossed the room and dialed Jacqueline's number. Her voice mail picked up, followed by a long beep.

What could he say? Come get me? Don't make me go back to the kid pound? It wouldn't matter. She didn't care. At least not enough to do anything about it.

JACQUELINE SAT AT a coffee shop table near the window. Jazz music mingled with the conversations around her. The scents of vanilla and cinnamon espressos wafted over her, almost soothing her jumbled nerves. She checked her watch then glanced out the window. Her fear of being late brought her here ten minutes early. Ten long, excruciating minutes.

She drummed her fingers on the table. Jiggled her foot. Watched a young lady with long blonde hair grind coffee beans.

What kind of questions would Mrs. Mansfield ask, and how much should Jacqueline divulge? The Bible said to forget the past, but something told her the state wouldn't agree. She sighed and turned back to the window in time to see Mrs. Mansfield pull into the lot.

With a deep breath, Jacqueline smoothed her hair behind her ears and straightened. Grabbing her purse, she rose to meet Mrs. Mansfield at the door. The social worker wore all gray, a matching briefcase slung over her shoulder.

"Good morning." Jacqueline flashed her best smile, her cheeks tight. "Can I get you a latte? A mocha?"

"That's not necessary."

"I insist. Have you ever tried the white chocolate mousse?"

"Oh, that sounds wonderful."

"It is." Jacqueline glanced at the line, which extended along the counter and almost to the door. "You want to hold our seats while I get the drinks?"

"Sure."

Jacqueline turned, back and neck stiff, stomach queasy. She'd be denied. No doubt. Mrs. Mansfield would ask some probing questions, and Jacqueline would be forced into self-exposure.

Can't we focus on the greater good here, Lord? A small fudge to help these poor children? Who would it hurt?

Her relationship with a holy God.

She sighed. That's where trust came in, right? Christianity was about doing things God's way and trusting Him to take care of the rest. If only so much wasn't at stake.

Five minutes later, she returned with two steaming, aromatic cups of coffee. She set them on either side of a manila file resting on the table. Her name was printed on the tab in black permanent marker.

"Thank you for meeting me here." She perched on the edge of her seat, trying to look professional and relaxed.

"My pleasure." Mrs. Mansfield pulled a checklist, printed on a sheet of paper, out of her briefcase. "I'd like to discuss where you're at in terms of employment. Also, your daughter still needs to complete her background check, and I'll need to inspect your home before finalizing the study. Would you like to schedule a time for that now?" She opened a leather-bound planner and waited, pen poised.

Jacqueline shifted, the sip of coffee sitting heavy in her gut. "Actually, I'm in the process of finding an apartment."

"Are you still at your daughter's?"

"No."

"Was there a problem?"

"I . . ." She swallowed, her stomach clenching. "We needed a little space." She tried to chuckle, but it came out strained. "Neither one of us are accustomed to roommates."

Mrs. Mansfield's mouth flattened. "And you want to take in three demanding children—one a teenager at that? Are you sure you're prepared for this?"

"Yes, of course." She raced through a slew of thoughts, searching for the most logical, the least incriminating. "There's a difference between living with your grown daughter who's fighting for independence and caring for children who need a mom."

"These children will probably fight for independence as well. At least, on the surface. They will test you, push you, rebel against you. Are you prepared for that?"

Jacqueline nodded. "I've raised a teenager." *And failed.* "I understand completely."

Mrs. Mansfield studied her a moment longer and scrawled notes on a legal pad. Jacqueline pressed sweaty hands on her thighs and prepared for more condemning questions. Luckily, the conversation shifted to generalities, like her view on discipline and the characteristics of good parenting. At least bombing things with Delana taught her one thing—what not to do.

Mrs. Mansfield set her pen down and grabbed her coffee cup. "How are the classes going?"

"Great. I'm learning a lot."

A slight smile. Point one.

The social worker flipped through the stack of documents in front of her, the smile fading. "You're fifty-one, correct?"

Jacqueline swallowed. "Yes." Setback number two.

"How would you describe your health?"

"Excellent." Minus the occasional hot flash and night sweats.

"Energy level?"

"Great." With large quantities of caffeine.

"You feel capable of caring for a toddler? Waking up in the middle of the night if necessary? Helping the older children with homework, teaching them to ride bikes, taking them to the playground?"

Jacqueline nodded to each question, self-doubt waging war with an overwhelming sense of love for those children. By the time the social worker left an hour and a half later, she felt like she'd been stretched across the asphalt and flattened by a garbage truck. Twice.

What if Mrs. Mansfield denied the home study? Would Gavin continue to be shuffled from place to place? Would he and his sisters ever find a home they could stay in together? And what about their mom? Icy fingers gripped her heart.

What if she went through all this, aired all her sin and shame, and their mom came back?

CHAPTER 35

JONATHAN GRABBED HIS suitcase and slammed the trunk shut. He deposited it on the sidewalk to free his hands. Slipping an arm around Jacqueline's trim waist, he pulled her close. She gazed at him through long, dark lashes, a hint of a dimple emerging on her right cheek.

The wind stirred her golden hair, and he brushed a lock from her face, tracing his knuckles against her smooth skin. So beautiful. So soft and tender, like a fragrant cherry blossom on a spring day.

He kissed her, and an electrical current shot from his lips to his heart. Pulling away, he stared into her blue eyes flecked with gray. A darker ring encircled each iris, the pupils large, reflecting his face. "Thanks for the ride."

"My pleasure." She looked past him and gave his hand a squeeze. "Wait here." She darted back to her car, which was parked near the curb, and returned with a brown lunch sack. "Here. Airplane food stinks."

He smiled, wanting to kiss her again, to hold her close indefinitely. But he needed to catch a plane and close the last chapter of his life. "I gotta go. I'll call you?"

The skin around her eyes crinkled, the blue sparkling. "You better."

He opened the lunch sack as soon as he boarded the plane. Packed inside were ziplock bags of fried vegetables, a sandwich, and a disposable container of coleslaw. A small note lay at the bottom. He pulled it out, unfolded it.

Maybe hurricanes aren't so bad after all. As they say, every storm cloud has a silver lining. You're mine.

He folded it carefully then tucked it into his back pocket, the reality of an FRA investigation souring the moment. If he lost his job, he could lose Jacqueline, too. But he couldn't stay with things like they were. Central Rails couldn't hold him and Darren. One of them had to go.

God, You sold my house and closed two doors in Alta Loma. You brought me from Southern California to Willow Valley and gave me Jacqueline. I'm going to trust You to work out all the details. And yet, God never promised candy and caviar.

No sense worrying about things he had no control over. Shoving a pillow under his head, he slept for the remainder of the flight. A rough landing and the sound of chattering voices woke him three hours later.

He rode a taxi home, high-rise buildings giving way to the tree-lined streets of Alta Loma's planned communities. As they neared his old house, they passed a playground he and Evie used to take Stephanie to. Cars filled the lot, and children dressed in soccer uniforms scurried across the field. Decades worth of memories.

At one time, the memories were unbearable, the darkness enshrouding his heart impenetrable. But today, they brought him joy, like when friends watched old home movies. Slices of life cherished. Was it wrong that he no longer mourned for Evie? That he cared so deeply for Jacqueline?

"Turn here." Jonathan pointed to a road ahead then directed the cabbie to his house.

A sale pending sign stood in the yard next to a tall palm tree with long fronds in need of trimming.

He checked the meter as the cabbie idled in the driveway. "Do you have a business card? I'll need a ride back to the airport." The movers the relocation company hired said they'd have everything packed and loaded by late afternoon the next day. They'd have everything at his new apartment three days later. Still feeling unsettled at his job, Jonathan had finally decided to sign a lease rather than a mortgage agreement. That way, if things at the railroad went south, he wouldn't have to refund the relocation company for realty and closing fees.

"When you call for a cab, just make sure to ask for Reggie." Grinning, the man handed over his contact information.

"Thanks." Jonathan paid him, adding a generous tip, then stepped out.

He entered through the garage. It was dim and quiet, as was the house. Everything looked the way he'd left it, tidied in preparation for the selling. A few picture frames decorated end tables and walls, but most had been tucked away.

In the den, a Thomas Kincade print hung above the mantle, vibrant reds and oranges splashed on trees. A cobweb stretched from a crystal cross Stephanie gave him and Evie for their twentieth wedding anniversary.

Till death do us part. Those were the vows he'd spoken, and he'd honored them. Treasured them. Evie's words, uttered weeks before her death, replayed through his mind. He sat on the couch and closed his eyes, reliving that day.

"You're a good man, Jonathan. Any woman would be blessed to have you." She touched his hand with a soft smile.

He recoiled, a knife slicing through his heart. "What are you talking about? I have you. Fight this, Evie. You can fight this."

She shook her head, her eyes searching his. "No, my love. I'm ready to go home. To see Jesus. To be well, healed. But I need to know you'll be OK. Happy. That you'll find someone else, when you're ready."

"Don't say that."

"Someone who will love and support you. It's not good for man to be alone, remember?"

Tears spilled from his eyes, his chest burning as his heart wrenched in two. "No, Evie. You can't leave me. I don't want anyone else. Fight this. Please, fight this."

"My fight's done, my love. I'm ready to rest." She reached up a pasty hand, translucent skin stretched over purple veins. "I love you, Jonathan. More than life itself."

"And I love you." He held her hands and leaned so close he could feel her wisps of breath on his face.

"If you ever find someone else, I want you to know you have my blessing."

JACQUELINE SAT ON the edge of the bed in her hotel room. With her laptop open and cell phone in hand, she began calling the realty management companies listed by her Internet search engine. Her results were less than optimal.

"Sounds lovely. Where is the property located?"

"Crystal Shores."

Silence stretched across the line, followed by the realtor's tight voice. "I'm sorry, but we're not taking new clients right now."

Two more calls ended with the same unenthusiastic response.

At least the third guy feigned interest. "Let me make sure I understand. You need someone to manage the property from repair to sale, correct?"

"Precisely."

"And you understand there will be a fee involved. Most likely a commission on repair charges with an additional commission on final sale."

"Right."

"Our office doesn't handle these sorts of projects."

A sigh blasted out before she could contain it.

"But I can give you a few contacts."

She jotted down four numbers, mumbled a thank you, and hung up. Ten minutes later, having left messages on four voice mails, she rose to catch some fresh air. No one wanted to take on a toxic property located on a storm-ravaged beach. But she wasn't going back.

Please, God, don't make me return to Crystal Shores. Send a bolt of lightning, if You have to. Burn that place down. But do something! Please?

GRABBING THE MOP HANDLE, Gavin pushed the wheeled bucket into the locker room. The thick stench of urine emanated from the row of stalls lined along the far wall. The grout between the tiles was caked with black mildew, the metal drains on the floor rusted.

It was already September, and Ferret had just registered him for school, two weeks after the official start date. It hadn't helped matters that they kept shipping him around. And of course, no one had even thought to sign him up for honors classes. Which was probably for the best, considering how behind he'd be. Who knew how long he'd stay at LaVerne Middle School, anyway? According to Ferret, they were still working to find some family to pawn him off on. *News flash, Ferret Face, no one's gonna take me.*

He paused to swipe sweat off his forehead with the back of his arm. Across the way, a handful of boys scrubbed the shower area, a large cinder block room with spigots circling ten or so metal poles. No privacy there. Little safety, either, depending on who supervised. Most staffers were college interns who thought they could solve the world's problems by saving a bunch of troubled kids. Few made it past the first week.

Today a lanky dude with hair the color of old coffee grounds stood near the door holding a clipboard. His gaze darted about like a cornered rodent. Outnumbered and outmuscled ten times over, he kept his back to the concrete wall. He wouldn't last long. Maybe not even through the day.

Gavin tensed when Jo-Jo and his gang slithered in. A kid maybe ten or eleven years old, their runt-slave as the others called him, accompanied them. He carried an armload of rags and cleaning supplies. Hunched forward, the dude stared at the ground.

Jo-Jo's dark eyes shifted to Gavin, and his face contorted into a crooked smile. "Look who we have here. You miss us, Dweebster?"

Gavin lifted his chin and held Jo-Jo's gaze. He clenched his teeth together and scowled, muscles flexed. They might outnumber him, could smash his face into the tile quicker than he could catch his breath, but he wouldn't go down easy. And not without inflicting serious pain.

Harsh laughter grated his ears. He looked at the kid with the clipboard. The dude's face paled, and he looked away. No help there. But everything would be fine if Gavin stayed out in the open. Skinny supervisor or not, Jo-Jo wouldn't do anything in front of the staff.

Still snickering, Jo-Jo and his gang strolled into the shower area, and Gavin returned to his mop. He sloshed chemical-saturated water onto the floor and swirled. Halfway across the tile, gobs of hair and slips of tissue paper floated on blackened water.

The clipboard dude left the wall long enough to peak into Gavin's bucket. "Looks like you're ready for fresh water."

Gavin suppressed an eye roll. "Yes, sir." Lifting the bucket, hands clutching the slimy bottom, he poured the dirty water into the drain. A layer of slime clung to the sides of the container, the stringy mop stained gray. The bucket was too heavy to lift to the sink, but there was a hose in the janitor's locker.

"Excuse me?" A kid in a faded T-shirt poked his head out of a stall. "I think I need some help." Water seeped under his feet. "I kinda accidentally flushed my rag. I've got the plunger, but it's not working."

Clipboard kid huffed and crossed the room, stepping over a rivulet of water. Gavin allowed a slight smile. At least he didn't have toilet duty. Today. But according to the schedule, his turn was coming.

Unless he found a home before then.

Who was he kidding? No one would take him. Mr. and Mrs. Lewis taught him that much. Bucket upright, he rolled it out of the locker room and down the hall.

En route, he passed a kid from C block vacuuming. Or more accurately, yawning and pushing the machine across the same stretch of carpet. A teen with black hair that hung in his face cleaned a window at the end of the hall. No one monitored the area, least not at the moment, which wasn't surprising, considering they were always short-staffed. From what he overheard at breakfast, almost half the workers had called in sick. They were sick, all right. Sick of reject kids.

The door to the janitor's office stood open, the room dark. Gavin ran his hand along the wall, feeling for the light. He caught cobwebs instead and jerked back, tried again. The bulb was out.

He strained his eyes to find the cleaner amidst the shadowed clutter. Three industrial-sized bottles stood next to a bunch of brooms. He didn't need to read the label. He grabbed the nearest jug, poured some in the bucket, and added water. The scent of sour mop fumes billowed toward him.

Heavy footsteps fell, and he froze, pulse thudding in his eardrums. A shadow fell over him, blocking the light from the hall.

"Look who I found. A rodent in the storage closet. What do you say, boys? Think it's cleanup time?"

Gavin straightened. Muscles flexed, he spread his feet shoulder distance apart and bent his knees. Hot blood throbbed through his fisted hands. Four against one. He didn't stand a chance.

He stepped backward, his heel hitting something hard. Jo-Jo laughed, and one of his thugs lunged at Gavin. The next thing he knew, someone had him by the hair and shoved his face into the bucket. His forehead connected with the rim, sending a stab of pain followed by a dull ache through his skull. He clamped his mouth and eyes shut, catching his lip between his teeth. His lungs screamed for oxygen. The skin on his scalp stung as they jerked him out. He sputtered and gasped for air. They plunged him under again and again until his lungs burned and his skin itched.

Someone yanked his hair again. On his knees, he pushed against the sides of the bucket, gasping.

"I'm thinking he needs the salon treatment, boys. What do you say?"

Gavin gripped the hard plastic, muscles trembling as he braced himself for the unknown. A zipper unzipped. More laughter. Then something hot snaked down his head and across his cheek before drizzling off the corner of his clenched mouth. The stench made him gag. Urine.

"Now for the rinse."

CHAPTER 36

ON THE PHONE, Jonathan pulled into the hotel parking lot and waited for his sister to finish her instructions.

"You know how Walter is with surprises." Jeanne-Anne smiled. "You'd think the guy reads minds or something."

"Or your highly emotive facial expressions. Admit it, Beannie, you're not exactly a good liar."

"I guess that's a good thing, except when I'm trying to throw a surprise birthday party for my husband. So, will you help me out or what?"

"Spend a day on the golf course with a great friend? Torture me some more. How long should this punishment last?"

"Think you can keep him until 5:00?"

"Not a problem."

"You talk to my favorite niece?"

"Uh-huh. Stephanie will be there." The engine continued to run, the gust of air blowing through his vents fighting against the intense sun pouring through his windshield. "And she's bringing her fiancé."

"Oh, good! Wonderful!"

He checked the time on the dash. "Listen, I've got to go."

"Another hot date?"

Warmth spread through his face. "Something like that."

Jeanne-Anne paused. "You bringing her to Walter's party?"

"I don't know." How would his daughter feel seeing another woman on his arm?

"Have you told Steph about her yet?"

"No."

"You might want to do that. Sooner rather than later."

"Yeah, I know. I will, when the time is right."

"Just pick a time, and make it right."

He ended the conversation and tucked his phone into his front pocket. Steph would understand, right? He'd loved Evie with every ounce of his being—still did—but it'd been five years. And like she'd said the day she'd died, it was not good for man to be alone. It sure wasn't good for Jonathan. Jacqueline was like fresh air on a muggy day. He'd spent enough time watching reruns and lame commercials.

He arrived at Jacqueline's hotel to find her waiting in the lobby wearing a draped-neck summer dress with peach flowers. Her hair was pulled back. A few wisps framed her face. Her lips shimmered a light pink. Jonathan paused, taken aback by her beauty, and for a moment, he was overwhelmed by God's goodness. He'd carried Jonathan through Evie's illness, held him through her death. And now, after he'd given up on ever finding love again, God had brought him a delicate rose.

"Jonathan." She walked toward him with grace. He took her hands in his and kissed her cheek, her skin soft as down feathers. Stephanie would love her. How could she not?

And if she didn't? Staring into Jacqueline's sparkling eyes, he shook the thought aside. He'd deal with that when the time came. If it came.

"You hungry?" Twining his fingers in hers, he led her out of the lobby to the parking lot.

"Very."

They decided to spend the evening downtown, beginning with dinner at a quaint little café. The sun set, stretching purple and golden beams across the horizon. As summer drifted into the first hints of fall, the normally stifling temperatures turned pleasant. Soft music poured from hidden speakers, the aroma of garlic butter permeating the air.

They sat outside under the café awning.

Jacqueline nibbled a piece of focaccia. "How was your trip? Did you get everything moved?"

He nodded. "Most of it will go in storage until I figure out what I want to do."

Her face fell, and her gaze fell to her plate.

He knew she was thinking of his job and probably shared his question. If Central Rails fired him, would he, could he, stay in Willow Valley? There wasn't much of an economy outside the railroad, and if he lost his pension . . .

He leaned forward and cupped her chin in his hand, running his thumb across her bottom lip. "I missed you." More than he'd expected.

She smiled. "I missed you, too."

"Remember what I said when we first met? About not looking for anything?" *What are you saying? Talk to Stephanie. Don't make promises you can't keep.*

She nodded, her mouth parting ever so slightly.

He moved closer until her breath mingled with his. As his lips touched hers, movement stirred in his peripheral vision. He glanced up to see their server standing beside them, looking awkward.

She offered a sheepish smile, revealing a row of braced teeth. She held a tray of steaming food.

Jonathan chuckled and leaned back. Jacqueline's lashes lowered, and color sprang to her cheeks, making him want to kiss her again.

Trance broken, he let his proclamation drop. He'd talk to Stephanie this weekend. Maybe even introduce the two.

JACQUELINE WATCHED JONATHAN while she ate, the feel of his lips still fresh on hers. He wanted more, they'd become more, but something held him back. Was it his deceased wife? They'd been married for a long time. How could she compete with that? She didn't want to. And yet, Jonathan had never made her feel like a replacement. Not at all. He made her feel beautiful, cherished.

But her home, in shambles as it was, remained in Crystal Shores. To make matters worse, Delana still refused to return her calls. It'd been over a week. How long would her daughter remain angry? Their relationship was now more strained than ever. Maybe Jacqueline never should've come to Willow Valley.

No. There was no sense second-guessing herself. Besides, her heart was here, with Jonathan and the children.

When she and Jonathan finished eating, he suggested they walk past the storefronts. She readily agreed. They stopped in a gift store, laughed at "over the hill" trinkets, and flipped through birthday cards. For once, Jacqueline's hormones behaved. Not a single hot flash to spoil the evening. After selecting a boot that doubled as a vase—a gift Jonathan was sure Walter would find hilarious—they strolled toward a coffee house. En route, they passed Sky's boutique. Jacqueline stopped, blinked. A for sale sign hung in the window.

Jonathan looked at her. "What is it? You OK?"

"This is the boutique I told you about. The one I wanted to buy."

"The one that sold?" He turned toward the window. "Think maybe the sale fell through?"

She grinned, a giggle tickling her throat. "Must have. You mind if—?"

"Please. Go. I'll keep that bench over there grounded."

She squeezed his hand. "I won't be but a minute."

Pushing through the door, she scanned the interior for Sky. The woman sat behind the counter, hair mussed and streaked with gray. Jacqueline approached with a smile.

"Ms. Dunn." The woman grunted to her feet, a faint glimmer of hope lighting her dull eyes. "I planned on calling you next week." Dark circles shadowed dull eyes, and her slacken skin had a grayish tint. She had aged five years since Jacqueline last saw her. Was she ill?

"You may have noticed, the sale fell through. The buyers, a young couple from Arizona, broke up, of all things." She shook her head. "Thought they were a bit young, green behind the ears. Should've listened to my gut." She tottered around the counter, favoring her right leg.

"You OK?"

Sky nodded. "Fibromyalgia and old age keep beating down this haggard body." With one hand clutching her hip, she glanced about the store. A stack of partially unpacked boxes sat in front of a jewelry counter. A few shelves needed straightening. "Finally got a shipment in I ordered six months ago. Tried to return it, but I bought it on clearance." She leaned against the counter. "You still looking to buy?"

Oh, she wanted to. But what about her home? Her mortgage? She had the insurance check, but that needed to go into savings—to pay back some of the money she'd depleted.

Lord, if I take a leap of faith here, will You catch me?

Silence.

"I need to check on a few things. Look at my finances."

Sky frowned. "Honey, I need out of this thing as soon as possible. Make me an offer."

"I'll call you tomorrow. Next Friday by the latest."

GAVIN SAT IN the visiting room of Orange Blossoms Children's Home. He stared at his hands, avoiding Ferret Face's pointed gaze. Mrs. Roberts sat across from him, sighing loudly and carrying on. He didn't look at her, either.

"Gavin, we can't help you if you don't tell us what happened."

They couldn't help him if he told, either. Not with how Mrs. Roberts was understaffed all the time. "Don't know. Maybe it's the laundry detergent or something." Least now he knew he was allergic to toilet bowl cleaner. When his face was shoved in it, anyway.

A soft knock sounded on the door. It creaked open, and Rissa, an office intern, poked her head in. "There's a Jacqueline Dunn here. She says she has a scheduled visitation."

Mrs. Roberts rose. "Send her in. Gavin's sisters should arrive with their foster parents at any moment. When they do, please escort them down."

Rissa nodded and closed the door. Jacqueline entered a moment later.

"Gavin, what happened?" She stared at him with a slackened jaw.

He scowled and shook his head, gaze shooting to the floor.

Mrs. Roberts cleared her throat. "One of the staff saw him return to the locker rooms with drenched hair. We suspect something happened, but he won't tell us."

Gavin watched Jacqueline from the corner of his eye, the only person in this place he halfway trusted.

Her face blanched, and she clutched a hand to her neck. "Something like what?"

Although the red in his eyes had diminished, a nasty rash covered his face. The downfall of being a redhead with sensitive skin. A purplish lump had formed on his forehead, and his lip, once clenched between his teeth, swelled.

"We have no idea," Ferret said. "Please, have a seat. Can I get you a cup of coffee?"

Jacqueline sat beside Gavin and gave him a sideways squeeze. "No, I'm fine, but thank you." She turned his face toward her. "Honey, did someone do this to you?"

Gavin kept his mouth clamped shut. A tendon in his jaw twitched.

"Honey, we can't help you if you don't talk to us."

"You want to help me? Then get me out of here."

"I'm trying to do that, sweetie."

Another knock sounded, and the intern reappeared, frowning. "Mrs. Roberts, I received a phone call from a Mrs. Dyer. She said Gavin's sister is sick, and they won't be able to make it."

Gavin scowled. Sick his toe. This was the second time baby Jaya's foster mom had canceled this week.

"I'm sorry, Gavin." Jacqueline pulled a pocket comic book out of her purse and placed it in front of him. "I saw this in the grocery store and thought of you. I figured you might be due for more reading material."

"Thanks." Gavin stared at an image of a viking with a horned helmet and red cape.

Like he cared about horned brutes. He checked the clock on the far wall. Adele wasn't coming. He knew it. Her foster mom would cancel just like baby Jaya's. Ten minutes later the intern stepped in and confirmed his suspicions.

He sprang to his feet. "I wanna go back to my room." He stomped toward the door.

"Wait." Jacqueline grabbed his arm. She held out the comic book. "Here." Her eyes softened, tears building behind her lashes. "It'll get better. I promise."

"The only way it'll get better is if someone takes me out of here. Let's me be with my sisters. That's all I want."

"I know."

"So help us."

"I'm doing all I can."

"Yeah, well, good luck with that. No one wants me."

She grabbed his hands and turned him to face her. "That's not true."

"Not my mom, not the Lewises or anyone else on that long list Ferr—Mrs. Mansfield calls all the time. Not even you."

"I do! I want you, Gavin."

"Then get me out of here. Can't you do that?"

She stared at him, mouth quivering.

He jerked his hands away. "That's what I thought."

He reached the door.

"Gavin, wait. I'm doing all I can."

Right. Along with everyone else. A lot of good that did.

CHAPTER 37

GAVIN SAT ON his bed with his comic book Bible opened before him. He studied a picture of the man named Joseph, dressed in rags, kneeling on a dungeon floor. Normally the end of the story brought Gavin hope, but not today. What was the point? He couldn't see his sisters, couldn't help them. None of them would probably ever see their mom again.

Coarse laughter drifted down the hall, and he tensed, hands fisted. Sweat beaded on his forehead and pooled in his palms. He stared at his open door. Stupid Mrs. Roberts and her open door policy. For his safety, she said. In case he tried to hang himself or something stupid like that. With what? The blanket?

Whatever. Didn't matter. Nothing mattered anymore. Why should it? Wasn't nothing he could do about anything anyway.

The voices drew closer, and Gavin leaned forward, ready to lurch to his feet. Could be Jo-Jo and his gang looking for another chance to pick on the newbie. Gavin would be outnumbered, but at least this time he'd see them coming. He glanced at a security camera in the corner of his room. Were those things even on? Even if they were, he doubted anyone paid any attention to them. When three kids he didn't recognize passed by without glancing in, Gavin exhaled. The tension eased from his shoulders. For now.

He grabbed his duffel bag from under his bed and pulled out a folded sheet of paper. Opening it, he smoothed it flat on his bed. He read again the words carefully printed on it. A bunch of stupid promises he couldn't keep. Telling Adele everything would be OK, to keep her chin up, to be good. For what? So some stranger could slam on her, tell her she wasn't worth nothing? But maybe it'd be different for her. She was sweet, cute. So was baby Jaya, only Jaya cried too much. People didn't like that. It made them angry. A chill crept up his spine as memories of his mom and her many boyfriends, came flashing back. People did crazy things when they got angry. Only now, Gavin had no way to protect his sisters.

A knock sounded on his door, and he startled.

Mrs. Roberts poked her head in. "Hey, there. You ready for auto-mechanics class?"

Gavin heaved a sigh and shrugged. Beat sitting in his room waiting for someone to pound on him. He stood and followed her down the hall and out into the muggy afternoon air. The sun reflected off parked cars, stinging his eyes. Didn't help he hadn't slept more than a few hours the night before. Or the night before that, or any night since he'd been in this stupid kid pound.

His pulse quickened when they reached the class area, his adrenaline-saturated muscles twitching. Jo-Jo and his gang sat on the asphalt in the shade of a work shed, all eyes trained on him.

"Look who's here." Cruel laughter danced in Jo-Jo's narrowed eyes.

Gavin ignored him and the sarcastic murmurs slung by his gang. He focused instead on a man with silver-streaked hair and smiling eyes.

"I'm Jonathan Cohen, and I'll be teaching this class." The man extended a hand and Gavin stared at it. The dude dropped his arm to his side, his smile wavering.

Mrs. Roberts nudged Gavin forward. "Behave and mind your manners. I'll be back in an hour."

As her footsteps receded, Gavin moved to a sunny area near a long table holding a pitcher and water cups. This provided distance from Jo-Jo and his gang and kept him in Mr. Cohen's direct line of vision.

The man handed Gavin a sheet of paper with what appeared to be a bio followed by a bullet list printed on it. So the guy had a college degree and a bigwig job. Were they supposed to be impressed?

Dude fidgeted as he read the page out loud, each sentence punctuated with a bunch of ers and ums. He acted so nervous,

Gavin almost felt sorry for him. For once, an adult who didn't pretend to know it all.

The man cleared his throat and folded his paper in half. "I never was much good in school. Had a teacher tell me I wouldn't amount to anything if I didn't get my act together." He looked from one face to the next before focusing on Gavin. "I tried, but all those formulas, dates, literature books." He shook his head. "OK, so maybe I didn't try as hard as I could, but I didn't see the point."

Gavin swallowed as a lump lodged in his throat.

Using his arm, the man wiped sweat from his forehead. "One day I got caught shoplifting in a local convenience store. Not sure why the guy didn't call the cops, but he didn't. He reached out to me instead. Taught me to change a tire, to check washer fluid. No big deal, right? Except it was for me. It gave me something I could do besides landing in trouble. Today I help run a locomotive repair shop east of town, all because someone took the time to work with me. Look me in the eye and give me something to shoot for."

The man's eyes softened as he held Gavin's gaze, as if trying to infuse him with hope. Gavin looked away and stared at the tiny pebbles on the pavement. Hope only got you one thing— bigger disappointment. This guy could spin a great speech, but that's all it was. Once the class ended, he'd be gone. Just like everyone else.

CHAPTER 38

JACQUELINE LEFT A MESSAGE on Delana's voice mail then dropped her phone on the hotel bed. How long would she stay angry? Maybe Jacqueline should have stayed in a hotel from the beginning. What she'd hoped to be a bonding experience had only widened their rift.

Lord, please soften her heart. Heal her wounds. Show her, somehow, how much I love her.

Redirecting her thoughts, Jacqueline scanned her foster licensing requirements checklist. Classes finished, background check completed. All she needed was a home. And a job. Buying the boutique would solve both problems, while potentially adding another—a second mortgage. Not the smartest move at her age.

She pulled her individual retirement account statement from her computer bag and studied the numbers. Withdrawing funds would land her a heavy tax penalty. Two mortgages, meager savings, tanked stocks. *Brilliant. Way to plan ahead, Jacqueline.* Staying in Willow Valley could turn into financial suicide, but she couldn't leave Jonathan. Or the kids. The image of Gavin's blotchy face, swollen lip, and slumped shoulders wouldn't fade.

Lord, give me something. If You say jump, I will.

Nothing but divine silence.

As her anxiety level rose, so did her temperature. After plunging the thermostat as low as it'd go, she grabbed the ice bucket. She marched down the hall, returning with as much ice as she could carry. Flipping Bible pages with one hand, she rubbed ice against her neck with the other.

What am I thinking? I'm in the throes of menopause. Old enough to be Gavin's grandmother, not his mother.

But he's got nowhere else to go, and clearly that home isn't a good place.

Give me a sign, Lord. Show me something.

More silence. She moaned and pounded a fist on her bed.

Why won't You talk to me? Tell me what to do?

Closing her eyes, she flipped the thin pages of her Bible. She landed on 1 Samuel 8:1 (NLT). "As Samuel grew old, he appointed his sons as judges over Israel."

What, You want me to go to court?

She huffed and turned the pages again. This time she landed on Leviticus 21. Rules and regulations for priests. Not helpful. Plunking her ice back in the bucket, she wiped her hand on the comforter and shoved the Bible aside. She jumped to her feet and paced.

You promised to guide me. To speak to me. Or does that only apply to Your saintly Christians?

A sense of failure washed over her as shame from her past rushed in. Her temperature spiked again, her pulse quivering. Grabbing the bucket, she carried it into the bathroom, emptied it into the tub, and turned on the cold water.

With a defeated sigh, she slipped in and closed her eyes. Water dripped from the faucet in a soothing rhythm. The heat dissipated from her body, taking the tension with it. In the aftermath of an emotional day, fatigue drew her into a light sleep.

Jeremiah 29. The words drifted softly, stilling her heart.

She opened her eyes, held her breath. Strained her ears. *Is that You, Lord?* What did God's voice sound like?

Jeremiah 29.

She stood, grabbed a towel from the rack, and wrapped it around her. Water dripping from the ends of her hair, she pattered across the carpet to her Bible lying on the bed. She flipped to Jeremiah 29. Verses five and six caught her attention. "Build homes, and plan to stay. Plant gardens, and eat the food they produce. Marry and have children. Then find spouses for them so that you may have many grandchildren. Multiply! Do not dwindle away!"

An image of Gavin as a grown man, holding a child flashed through her mind. *"Wives for your sons . . . so that they too may have sons and daughters."*

One day Gavin could have a family, a wife who loved him. Children following in his footsteps, encased by his love. With Christ's help, the cycle of abuse could be broken.

Releasing the Bible, she slipped to her knees as intense emotions swept over her.

Oh, merciful Father!

The God of healing longed to make these children whole, and He wanted to use her to do it.

AFTER THE LAST of Walter's birthday guests left, Jonathan, his daughter, and her fiancé, Hugh, migrated to the living room. Walter and Jeanne-Anne joined them, sipping mango-flavored tea and sitting with hands twined. Stephanie nestled next to her fiancé, her green eyes sparkling with laughter and love.

Hugh sat rigid, chin raised, like a job applicant wanting to make the best impression. Whenever Jonathan spoke to him, the kid practically jumped, his Adam's apple bobbing, his words measured. His brown hair, spiked in the front, and his boyish features robbed him of at least five years.

Jonathan liked the kid. Quiet, hardworking. A good Christian man who'd lead by example, not by force. And Hugh adored his daughter. That was obvious. He'd be a devoted husband.

"How's the wedding planning going? Were you able to reserve the facility you emailed me about?"

Stephanie squeezed Hugh's hand and nodded. "We did, thank you." She went on to talk about flower arrangements, song selections, and table decorations. Laughter filled her voice. Jonathan's heart squeezed. How many years had he and Evie prayed for this moment, and the one that would soon follow? For Steph's future spouse, that God would mold her into the woman He created her to be. God had been faithful. Beyond faithful.

Ceremony, reception, and honeymoon sufficiently discussed in rapid, animated succession, Stephanie sucked in a breath of air and reached for her iced tea. "Enough about us. How have you been, Dad? Do you like Willow Valley?"

"I do." For more reasons than one, but was now the best time to tell her about Jacqueline? Would there ever be a *best time?* And yet, if he wanted to bring her to the wedding, he'd need to tell Stephanie eventually. Preferably not over the phone.

"The job's crazy, but it's nice to have someone to beat in golf now and then." He shot Walter a crooked smile.

The man raised an eyebrow, and Jonathan knew why.

Jonathan propped his elbows on his knees and clenched his linked hands. "This has been a great move in many ways. Things were getting pretty quiet in Alta Loma."

Stephanie smiled and squeezed his knee. "I worried about you spending so much time alone in that big old house. I'm glad you're here. That you have Auntie Jeannie and Uncle Walter."

Jeanne-Anne set her glass down. "The Bible tells us it's not good for man to be alone."

Jonathan shot her a warning glare. He didn't need her help. Not this time. But how did someone start a conversation like that? Would Steph understand he wasn't trying to replace Evie? No one could do that. Nor did loving Jacqueline mean he no longer loved Steph's mom.

"You OK?" His daughter looked at him. "You seem . . . worried." She stared at her hands, working her bottom lip. "Is it the money? Jeanne-Anne told me about what's been going on with your job. How you're worried about getting fired." Her voice quivered. "We can cut back on some of our expenses. We've still got six months, so I'm sure we can find a cheaper place to host the reception. Maybe we can make our own decorations or—"

"Oh, no!" Jonathan lifted her chin so her eyes met his. His heart clenched at the tears welling behind her lashes. "I want this wedding to be everything you envisioned."

She'd dreamed of her special day ever since she was a little girl. She and Evie used to talk about the long, white gown she'd wear, what kind of flowers she'd have, what colors she'd choose.

One weekend they had made an event out of it. Jonathan took Stephanie out for dinner—just the two of them—and gave her a purity ring. The same one Evie's dad had given to her. The same ring Stephanie would one day give to her daughter. "We always told you true love waits, and once it came, we'd celebrate with all of heaven behind us."

Her soft smile returned as she glanced at her fiancé. "And you were right." When she looked back at Jonathan, her eyes sparkled. "There's nothing like it. To know you've found the person God created just for you." She frowned. "Are you thinking of Mom? Wishing she were here?"

He inhaled, lifting his torso. "I do, but . . . there's something I need to talk to you about." Was now the right time? But if not now, when? He needed to get it over with. To give her time to process.

Walter stood. "Jeanne-Anne, how about I help you clean up in the kitchen."

"I'd like to hear what Jonathan has to say."

Walter narrowed his gaze. "Jeanne-Anne."

"All right." She rose, and turned to Hugh. "You want to join us? I'd love to hear about your accounting firm. You opened it a year ago, correct?"

"I did, with the help of a longtime mentor." Their voices drifted as they disappeared into the kitchen.

Stephanie scooted to the end of the couch. "What is it, Daddy? Are you sick?"

"No, nothing like that. Quite the opposite." He chuckled, although it came out grainy. "I'm doing really well. Happier than I've been in some time."

"And why's that?"

It was too late to change his mind now. "I've met someone."

She stared at him. "You what?"

A distant clock ticked. Jonathan felt like a snake slithering among desert rocks. *Oh, baby girl, please understand.* And if she didn't? Would he have to choose between her and Jacqueline? Would he, could he, walk away from such a precious, unexpected treasure? "You'd like her."

"I don't want to hear about it." The laughter drained from her eyes. "What about Mom? Huh?"

"Steph, it's been five years."

"Oh, so that makes it better? What happened to forever, huh?"

He touched her hand, but she jerked away. "She's a good woman. A sweet, Christian woman." He breathed deep, exhaled slowly.

"I can't deal with this right now."

Standing, he reached for her, but she pulled away. She stared at him, tears springing to her eyes. "Not now." She turned around. "Hugh?" Her voice sounded strangled.

"Steph, wait."

She stopped and turned back around. "I need a minute."

Jonathan settled back into his chair, his heart wrenching at the wounds he had just ripped open in his daughter. Except it'd been five years. Was he never allowed to date—to love—again?

The door to the kitchen swung open, and Jeanne-Anne rushed out, the men trailing behind. Crossing the room, Walter's eyes softened when he looked at Jonathan.

Hugh looked from one face to the next, forehead creased, mouth slightly ajar. "Is everything OK?"

Red crept up Stephanie's neck. "It's time to go." With shoulders slumped, she slipped out, the door banging closed behind her.

Hugh made a move to follow her, but Jeanne-Anne blocked his path. "Wait. Give me a minute with her."

He glanced from one face to the next then did what any smart soon-to-be-in-law would do and sank into a chair. Walter sat next to Jonathan as Jeanne-Anne chased after Stephanie.

He leaned back and propped an ankle on his knee. "I take it you told her about Jacqueline?"

Jonathan nodded, glancing toward Hugh.

The guy looked more than a little uncomfortable. "Maybe I should leave."

"Welcome to the family, boy." Walter punched Hugh's shoulder. "Might as well get used to the drama now. Right, Jonathan?"

Jonathan shrugged. "Not like I got any secrets. I'm sure Steph'll tell you all about it later, anyway."

Hugh stared at the floor. "Mind if I get a soda?"

Walter waved a hand. "Be my guest."

Hugh bolted from the room, the door swooshing behind him.

Walter laughed again. "Poor kid. Guess we welcomed him in good, huh?"

"Guess so."

A moment of silence stretched between them. Jonathan watched the front door, praying Jeanne-Anne could talk some sense into Steph. Only it wasn't sense she needed, but healing. Just because he was ready to move forward didn't mean she was.

"What are you going to do if she doesn't come around?"

Jonathan raked his hands through his hair. "Don't know. I mean, she's gotta come around eventually, right?"

"Who knows? We all deal with death differently, you know?"

Jonathan tugged at a hangnail.

"Is Jacqueline worth fighting for?"

He looked Walter in the eye. "I never thought I'd hear myself saying this, not after Evie, but I think she is."

"Are you ready to accept the whole package?"

"What do you mean?"

"Those kids from the shelter—what're their names?"

Jonathan blew air through tight lips. "I'm not sure."

"I thought you said she was trying to become a foster parent or something."

He nodded, shrugged. "Yeah, maybe. We don't really talk about the kids much. I mean, she's mentioned taking a few classes and stuff, but I guess I never gave it much thought."

"Maybe it's time you start thinking about it. Are you really ready to start over, to take on a ready-made family, so close to retirement?"

Walter was right. If he wanted a future with Jacqueline, he'd need to accept a future with the kids, too. Diapers, late-night virus attacks, teen rebellion. He'd done all that before, except this time he was older, tired. Settled.

"You have no idea what you'll be up against, either. What kind of emotional baggage those kids'll bring with them. Before you step into their lives, you need to make sure you're there to stay. Those kids don't need any more rejection. Something to think about. Pray over."

Walter glanced toward the front door, checked his watch, then handed Jonathan the remote. "Let me go check on our buddy hiding in the kitchen." He rose and squeezed Jonathan's shoulder.

Jonathan flicked on the television and tried to focus on the sports highlights, but Walter's words replayed through his mind. He loved Jacqueline, right? He thought about her all the time, enjoyed being with her, started thinking in terms of a future. But did he love her enough to make promises, not just to her but to those kids?

A short while later, Walter and Hugh joined him with a pitcher of iced tea and a bowl of chips. Together they watched two commentators fight over which team would be the best in the National Football League this coming season. Walter tried to initiate small talk, but apparently, Hugh wasn't a football fan. Or baseball or basketball fan, either. Which left two options: talk about accounting or Steph's blow up. They opted for weather. Safe, neutral.

Stephanie and Jeanne-Anne returned half an hour later, Stephanie's eyes red, her nose pink and puffy. She glanced at her aunt who smiled and gave her a sideways hug before motioning for Walter to follow her into the kitchen.

Hugh went to his bride, took her hand. "You OK?"

She nodded and tucked her hair behind her ears. "Can you give me a minute? I need to talk to my dad."

He nodded and trailed the others into the kitchen.

Jonathan scooted forward, swallowed. Stephanie sat across from him and stared at her hands. After a minute, she looked up through teary eyes, sucked in a breath of air. Let it out slowly.

"I'm sorry I reacted like that."

"It's OK. I understand. I probably shouldn't have . . . this wasn't . . . .I know this is hard." He leaned forward, wishing he were close enough to grab her hands in his. He'd never been good at these sorts of things—talking about emotions. Seeing her cry, knowing she hurt but not knowing how to fix it. Only this time was worse because he'd caused her pain.

"Do you love her?"

"I think so." What about the kids? Parenting was hard, but with Stephanie, his intense love got him through the late nights, temper tantrums, eye rolls. These children were strangers. How could he love kids he didn't know? Why have this conversation? Why break Stephanie's heart and make her deal with all this when he didn't have the rest worked out?

She pulled a thread in her shorts. "I don't know what I'd do if you didn't like Hugh. If you told me not to see him. I know you've been lonely. I want you to be happy. Mom would've wanted that, too." Her voice trembled. "If this woman makes you happy, then I won't get in the way of that." She stood and waited for him to do the same. "I guess I better go."

He hugged her then watched her leave, feeling as if a slab of concrete settled on his shoulders. He had a lot of thinking to do. And he needed to do it quickly, before anyone got hurt.

CHAPTER 39

JACQUELINE STARED AT the bright yellow file in front of her. A tiny voice niggled: *How in the world will you pay for two mortgages?* She shoved it aside. She wouldn't let any fears or doubts dampen the moment. She was now officially a boutique owner.

"I believe this is yours." Sitting beside the notary-signing agent, Sky Rainbows dangled a feathered keychain with a glimmering gold key. "Congratulations."

Jacqueline fought the urge to jump up and hug the woman. "Thank you! And I hope you enjoy your retirement."

Sky smiled. "Oh, I will. I leave for Anacortes, Washington, tomorrow morning, as a matter of fact." She stood and tugged on her static-charged dress. "If you need anything, don't call." Her eyes danced above a toothy smile. With a wiggle of her fingers, she thanked the signing agent and ambled out of the office.

Jacqueline maintained composure until she reached her car. Then she let her laughter loose. Was this what it meant to surrender without reservation? Without a backup plan or safety net? She needed to call Elaine. She would be ecstatic!

Jacqueline grabbed her phone and dialed.

"Well, if it isn't my long lost friend!" Elaine chuckled, and as usual, giggling voices could be heard in the background, along with what sounded like a dying tuba. "I was getting ready to file missing person charges."

Jacqueline laughed. "It's been a while, huh?" She relayed the recent events, sharing in Elaine's high-pitched squeal.

"I guess your done stuck in Willow Valley now, huh?"

"Seems that way." She cranked her engine and eased out of the parking lot. "And to think, I believed that door had been slammed shut."

"Sounds like another door I know of."

Tears pricked. "Delana."

"Uh-huh." Elaine's voice softened. "Don't give up, sister. Keep praying. Remember how long it took you to come around?"

Jacqueline laughed. "Well, if I'd known you were praying for my salvation all those years, maybe I would've listened sooner."

"Either that or you would've been spooked." The tuba noise sounded again, and Elaine moaned. "Music lessons and grandkids. Maybe not the best combination."

"I'll keep that in mind. If I ever have grandchildren, that is."

"Speaking of kids, how are Gavin and his sisters doing?"

A lump lodged in her throat, and she sighed. "OK I guess. Adele's been shuffled around again, and Gavin's—" Her voice cracked. "I just wish God would provide a stable home for those kids, you know? Someone to love them, help them heal."

"Someone like you, you mean?"

"I'm pretty sure their case worker's given up on me by now."

"Oh, don't be so sure about that. Have you told her about your boutique purchase?"

A glimmer of hope sparked. "I need to do that. Right now, actually. Love you, girl."

"Only because I send you chocolate."

"Um, no you don't." She stopped at a red light, watching thick clouds invade the horizon. "But I can text you my new address."

Elaine laughed. "You do that. I'd love to mail you a housewarming gift, one sure to stay with you—and your hips—for decades."

"Such a friend."

"The best you have. And Jacqueline?"

"Yeah?"

"I'm proud of you."

"Thanks, Elaine." Ending the call, she clicked to her call logs and engaged Jesseca's number.

Ten minutes later, she ended the call, a niggling of excitement rising.

Or rational thinking, apparently, but God had made His will clear. Hadn't He? Settle down, build a profitable home, marry. Her heart skipped as an image of Jonathan on bended knee flashed through her mind. She stretched her bare hand in front of her, envisioning a diamond ring. In fifty-one years, not one proposal, but that was about to change. Everything was changing, falling into place.

Unless that verse came not from God, but instead from her. What if she'd been so desperate to receive an answer, her subconscious produced a passage? Jeremiah 29 wasn't unique, after all. In fact, one of her favorite promises came from that chapter, "'For I know the plans I have for you,' says the LORD. 'They are plans for good and not disaster, to give you a future and a hope'" (NLT). She often recited it when she felt anxious or discouraged. It wouldn't be surprising for her to think of that same chapter during a stressful moment. How could one tell if random thoughts came from God or their own will?

She groaned and slapped her hand against the steering wheel. This Christianity thing, following God's leading, was so hard. It'd be much easier if He'd provide step-by-step directions! But no fretting. Not today. She'd made her decision, signed on the dotted line. Now she needed to make the best of it.

Don't leave me hanging, God.

With the fluttering stomach of a teen in love, she dialed Jonathan's number. *Oh. He's at his brother-in-law's birthday party.* She started to hang up, but he answered before she got the chance.

"Hey." His deep voice, normally filled with laughter, sounded heavy. He was probably tired. A party following eighteen holes of golf could do that to a man.

She turned onto Eighth Avenue. "You're not going to believe what I just did."

"What's that?"

"I am now the proud owner of A Ray of Light Books and Trinkets." A partially stocked boutique, no less, since the sale had included whatever inventory remained in the store—half of which Jacqueline would keep. The rest would be tossed or maybe sold on clearance. "Is Walter's party over? Because I'd sure love company to help me celebrate. I'm thinking this calls for fudge."

Jonathan paused, his breath echoing through the line. "Can I meet you somewhere?"

That didn't sound good. "Is everything OK?"

"Yeah, I mean, I don't know. We need to talk."

A queasy sensation seeped into her gut. It'd been a long time since she'd heard those words, but she didn't need a history lesson to tell her what was coming.

Give me one day, Father. Just one day of joy with no hurdles or disappointments. Is that too much to ask for? "Sure. Where do you want to meet?"

"Espresso and Cream?"

"OK. Yeah. I'll be there in a few minutes."

PULLING TO THE CURB, Jacqueline angled between Jonathan's pickup truck and a pink Cadillac. She sat with the cold air blowing in her face, fighting against a nervous stomach. He sat near the window, hunched forward, rubbing his forehead. Two plastic foam cups of coffee emitted steam in front of him. She knew the contents—a skinny, decaf mocha for him, a low-fat, chocolate raspberry with extra whipped cream for her. Because he knew her. Even in their short time together, he knew her.

The door chimed her entrance, and he looked up with a tight smile. He stood to greet her, his embrace stiff, almost formal. He brushed his lips across her cheek like one does for a distant relative, all signs their relationship was over.

Ending as abruptly as it had began. Like always. She hadn't had a serious relationship since Delana's dad, and look where that got her.

He turned his cup, straightened the edge of his napkin. "Listen, I've been doing some thinking."

She grabbed her coffee to keep her hand from trembling. "You don't have to say it. You told your daughter about me, and she got upset. I get that."

"That's not it. I mean, yeah, she got upset. But she got over it."

She released the breath she'd been holding, only his pained expression caused her to suck it right back in.

"I've been doing some thinking. About us, and . . . the kids."

Oh, no. She worried this might happen, had tried to convince herself it wouldn't. But what could she expect? It was crazy enough she wanted to adopt a bunch of kids—including a baby— at her age. To expect someone else to do the same?

"This is a big deal. I came here to retire, to start a new chapter. I'm not sure if I'm ready to be a father again. To commit to that."

She'd heard that one before, too. Delana's dad had said the same thing before giving her money for an abortion. Money she used to buy maternity clothes. And a pair of earrings.

She sipped her coffee then set it down. "I understand." Standing, she forced her best smile despite the stabbing pain in her chest. "It's been fun. You take care."

He said something about calling her, but she barely heard him. So much for her Jeremiah 29 revelation. Obviously she'd heard God wrong.

THE TELEVISION DRONED while Jonathan paced his small apartment living room. Women. Things were never this complicated with Evie. Everything just fit. Surely all these problems—his job, foster kid issues, Stephanie's pain—were signs that this wasn't right. Besides, how could he commit to anything when he wasn't even sure he'd stay in Willow Valley? The way things were going, he'd be hitting the unemployment lines soon enough. Though Darren tried to hide it, Jonathan knew the man was still fudging the numbers, and Jonathan continued to stumble on questionable work orders. But whenever he questioned the guy, he became evasive. And the rest of his cronies weren't any better.

He needed a nice, long, lung-burning run to clear his head. And some divine wisdom, because he needed to make a decision—this week. It wasn't fair to keep Jacqueline hanging on. His heart wrenched at the memory of the pain in her eyes, the tremble in her voice. Could he really let her go?

He changed into running gear, dropped his cell phone into his fanny pack, and hit the pavement. A few tenacious runners and bikers, slick with sweat, cheeks puffy, traversed the pavement. A hot breeze swept over him as he began his warm-up, provoking his sweat glands. Despite the humidity, he pounded hard, fast, a summer's worth of frustration fueling each step. Had he made a mistake in coming here? Was it too late to go back? He couldn't do kids. Not now. He was too old, impatient. Had lived alone for too long. Three kids, three college tuitions, doctors' bills, hormonal outbreaks when puberty hit.

I came here to retire, Lord. To enjoy the fruits of my labors. Not to start over.

Rounding the corner, he slowed, his heart pricking. In front of him, an older couple with silver hair walked hand in hand, while two children pedaled in front of them. The kids, one on a tricycle, the other on training wheels, looked between five or six years old, probably the couple's grandkids. Their laughter spilled behind them.

Jonathan shook his head and weaved around them. Grandkids were one thing. Raising children at his age was another.

By the time he finished his run, he knew what he needed to do. He loved Jacqueline but not those kids. How could he? He hadn't even met them. They deserved someone who loved them for who they were, not someone who accepted them as part of a package. It wouldn't work. It'd only hurt them and his relationship with Jacqueline.

He stopped at a drinking fountain and gulped until his stomach bulged. Then he splashed water on his face and neck to cool the hot blood coursing through his veins.

His phone chimed and an image of Jacqueline's smiling face came to mind. Pathetic. He'd made his decision, and here he was, waiting for her phone call. But that would pass. Maybe they could be friends. No. That wouldn't work. Not anymore. It was time to say good-bye.

He wiped sweaty hands on equally sweaty shorts and wiggled his phone from his fanny pack. A quick glance at the number deflated him. In more ways than one.

He stifled a sigh. "Hey, Rustin, what's up?" Another road failure? An injury Darren would find a way to weasel out of? More federal inspection drama?

"The FRA is crawling all over the place."

Bingo. The prize? Most likely a demotion or worse. Heading back to the hotel for a shower, he sopped his face with the end of his shirt. "I'll be there in a minute."

"Darren and his shadow are with them now. Heard him send one of the managers home. Told him he had it covered."

Sounded like something Darren would do. And as asinine as that was, Jonathan wasn't in the mood for a battle today. He had enough wars waging within himself as it was. Wasn't anything he could do, anyway. They'd fire him, and he'd go crawling back to Lundquist begging for a job. "What're they looking at?"

"They found a bunch of spray-painted air brake valves."

"What?" His grip tightened on the phone. "What are you talking about? Why would the machinists do something so stupid?" The very reason Jonathan needed to leave. Why wait to get fired when he could save his dignity and walk out with his head held high?

"I guess they couldn't get the parts or something."

The day he tried to order the parts, Darren insisted the shop release the engines anyway. Now he knew why. "So they spray painted them? How many were involved? You know what? Forget it. I don't want to know. Thanks for the heads-up."

He hit call end, sifted through his contacts, and dialed Bart Lundquist's number. The guy's voice mail picked up. "Hey,

Bart. It's Jonathan. Can you call me back? I'd like to talk to you about—"

Pride squelched the words. It was one thing to beg your old boss for employment, to openly admit you'd failed and made a terrible decision. It was another to record your loser status on voice mail. "I'd like to talk, when you get a chance."

And if Bart didn't take him back?

CHAPTER 40

THE PHONE CHIMED, and Jacqueline's pulse quickened as her mind leapt to thoughts of Jonathan. She shoved them aside. He wouldn't call. He didn't even know this number, and even if he did, it wouldn't matter. He couldn't commit, and she wouldn't bring another potential rejection into the children's lives. They needed security, unwavering devotion, unconditional love. Not that she blamed Jonathan. Kids weren't something you could force on a person. She'd learned that when she conceived Delana.

The phone trilled again. "I'm coming!" She placed a ceramic figurine on the shelf and dashed across the boutique. Rounding the counter, she stepped over a mound of clutter and lunged for the phone.

"Hello? I mean—"

Her mind went blank. Scanning the counter, she reviewed notes and to-do lists scrawled on slips of paper. She caught a glimpse of an ad graphic she'd been working on. Right! "Good morning, A Ray of Light Books and Trinkets." Wow, that was wordy. Maybe she needed to come up with a new name. "How may I help you?"

"Good morning, Jacqueline. This is Mrs. Mansfield."

Jacqueline froze, her breath catching. "Yes?"

"I'm calling about your home study."

She'd been denied. She knew it and braced herself for the bad news. It'd sting, add one more glob of mud to her already murky heart, but she'd get over it. "OK." What about the children? Oh, those poor children. Why did her past have to hurt them? Blinking, she fought back tears.

"You've been approved."

The air expelled from her lungs, and she fell against the counter, her legs turning to melted marshmallows. Approved?

"Ms. Dunn?"

Laughter bubbled from within. "Yes, I'm here." She released it, along with an onslaught of tears. After all the interviews, classes, background checks, it was finally over. Or more accurately, it was just beginning. "I can't believe it! What does that mean?"

"It means you are now the foster mother of three beautiful children."

"And the adoption? Is that still a possibility? When does that happen?"

"We're still looking for their mother, but if she doesn't show up within the next six months, the judge will terminate her parental rights."

"And then?"

"Then there will be a court date to finalize your adoption."

Mrs. Mansfield continued with details, along with when the foster placement would occur, but her words barely registered. After almost three decades, Jacqueline was going to be a mom again. A fifty-one-year-old, menopausal mom. Hilarious!

Lord, Your ways truly are not like my ways, but I like them.

After the call ended, she started to dial Jonathan's number then stopped. With an extended sigh, she tucked her phone back into her purse. He'd made his decision. She'd lost her daughter and the man she loved, but God was faithful. Like His Word promised, "And everyone who has given up houses or brothers or sisters or father or mother or children or property, for my sake, will receive a hundred times as much in return" (Matthew 19:29 NLT).

Although she wasn't looking for a replacement, she'd take whatever blessings God chose to give. And this time, with God's grace, she wouldn't mess up. Her stomach twisted as the full reality of her situation pressed down on her.

Just over a year with Christ following fifty-one years of sinful living marring her past. Could she really do this? Be the kind of mother these kids needed? But God wouldn't have brought them her way if she couldn't, right?

I'm trusting in You, Lord, and I'll be leaning hard. Please show up strong on my behalf.

Fifty-one years old and raising a toddler. And a teen. Oy. She wasn't sure which was more intimidating.

Thank goodness she had Irene. Sweet, nurturing, mentoring Irene.

Grabbing her purse, she dashed out to her car, leaving an excited message on Elaine's voice mail en route.

At the shelter, her Bible study girls met her with hugs, smiles, and long-winded stories. Although anxious to find Irene, Jacqueline listened patiently to each in turn, offering words of encouragement and praising their spiritual growth.

These women, once broken and consumed with rage, had come a long way. As had many in the shelter. In fact, most of the storm refugees had found jobs, apartments; some had returned home. But the doors remained open. The church had been touched by the work God began, not only in the lives of the residents but in the lives of the volunteers as well. They knew they couldn't stop His daily display of grace. Nor could Jacqueline. She'd never felt God's love so intensely as when it poured through her to the wounded.

When the conversation dwindled, she scanned the shelter. "Do you ladies know where I might find Irene?"

Leza, a pudgy woman that always smelled like garlic, nodded. "I believe she's in the kitchen getting things ready for lunch."

An intense task, and one that often occupied most of the morning.

Jacqueline thanked Leza then meandered through the shelter, pausing to greet residents on the way. She found Irene with her head in the pantry, as usual.

"Hey, there." Jacqueline spoke through a smile, barely keeping her giggles at bay.

Irene whirled around, eyes bright. "Hi!" She gave Jacqueline a hug. "It appears boutique ownership suits you well. Look at you. You're practically glowing."

"Must be motherhood."

Irene cocked her head, lines forming on her forehead. "Motherhood?" Her gaze fell to Jacqueline's less than flat stomach.

Jacqueline laughed. "No immaculate conception here. But I did get a call from Mrs. Mansfield."

Irene squealed and squeezed Jacqueline's hands, bouncing like a toddler infused with sugar. "Oh, Jacqueline! You've been approved?"

She nodded, the two embracing with enough force to cause mutual suffocation.

"See, you worried over nothing. I knew they'd accept you."

"Yeah, well. I'm just glad it's over. Mostly over, anyway, pending the final adoption hearing, but I'm not worried about that one. The only thing that could stop that is if their mom suddenly reappears, and we know the chances of that happening." Jacqueline glanced at two teenage volunteers manning the stove behind her. "But don't let me keep you. We'll talk later. Over coffee or something."

"It's a deal."

She returned to the gym area to chat with a few more of her ladies. One of them started a new job across state the following week, so the two prayed for blessings and travel mercies. It was a bittersweet moment, in many ways like sending your first born off to college.

She started to leave when the front door crashed open, and Teresa, the woman who'd walked out on her kids almost two months ago staggered in dressed like a whore and smelling like cheap booze.

She stood near the back of the gym, scowling, head swiveling. "Gavin! Adele!" As she stumbled forward, she cupped her hands around her mouth. "Gavin, you best get your sorry self out here." She ended with a slew of curse words, pushing through cots and tripping over people's belongings.

Jacqueline's heart wrenched, her feet frozen. *No, Lord! No more disappointments!*

"Watch where you're going, lady!" A man wearing a sweat-stained T-shirt leapt to his feet, blocking Teresa's path.

She pushed on his chest. "Out of my way, creep."

He shoved back, knocking her on her rear. Sprawled on a cot, she fired off more curses while struggling to her feet.

"Nothing but white trash." The man flicked his hand and turned to walk away.

"What'd you call me?" Teresa lunged forward and clawed at the man. He whirled around and grabbed her round the neck, the veins in his arms bulging.

People screamed and rushed to the scene. Two men clamored over cots and bags. One latched onto the man while the other gripped Teresa. Both yanked them off one another while Jacqueline continued to watch in a daze.

"What's going on here?" Irene appeared, face white, with the other kitchen volunteers.

More men gathered, muscles twitching as if itching for a fight.

Irene brandished a cell phone as if it were a gun. "Do I need to call security?"

The man in the T-shirt raised his hands and backed away. "Don't got time for crazy women no how." Shaking his head, he grabbed a faded duffel bag and moved to an empty cot.

Irene jabbed her hands on her hips and glared from one face to the next. "There's nothing to see here. Go back to what you were doing."

Once the crowd dissipated, she turned to Teresa. "Calm down, and tell me what you need."

Teresa crossed her arms. "I *need* my kids. Where they at?"

Irene and Jacqueline exchanged glances and Irene's eyes softened. A jagged knife twisted in Jacqueline's gut. She clamped her mouth shut, hands trembling at her sides. This woman had walked out on her kids. She had forfeited her right to be a mom. Jacqueline sure wasn't going to tell her where they were. If Teresa wanted them back bad enough, she'd find them.

Unfortunately, Irene felt differently. "Hold on. I've got their social worker's card in my purse."

"Social worker?" Teresa rolled her eyes, firing off another mouth load of curses. "My kids ain't nobody's business." With hip shoved out, gnawing on a nail, she watched Irene.

Jacqueline didn't wait for Irene to return. Heaving a sigh, she shuffled out of the gym and into the bright sunshine. A good Christian would ask for God's intervention, restoration for Gavin and his family. She couldn't do that.

THE AIR IN the shop hung thick, charged with electricity. Questions zinged, spoken in hushed whispers with frequent glances over tense shoulders. Jonathan sat in his office, staring out his window, watching it all. The mess he'd caused trying to do the right thing, which in the end would only cost him his job.

Lundquist still hadn't called back. Jonathan couldn't blame him. They were friends, but Lundquist was a businessman. And businessmen didn't rehire quitters. Rubbing his face, he swiveled toward his computer screen to sift through emails. Anything to get his mind off the drama all around him. One from his daughter, one from a new hire, and a bunch of spam.

No sense waiting around for the big F. Maybe Walter would be up for a golf game.

He grabbed his briefcase and headed for the door when his phone rang. He glanced at the number. Tom Haukmen, the new CMO. Great. At least now Jonathan would know for sure. Could move on, hopefully with a severance package.

"Hello?" His fingers felt numb around the phone, like his blood suddenly stopped pumping.

"Security is escorting Darren off the property. You're up."

"What?"

"Consider yourself promoted."

Promoted? As in the new general director? The line went dead, and Jonathan stared at the receiver. Still dazed, he meandered to his doorway and peaked out. He stayed there, staring, waiting. Five minutes later the elevator doors opened, and two railroad police officers stepped off in full uniform. In all, they escorted eight people off property—Darren, two senior managers, four foreman generals, and the day clerk.

Before stepping into the elevator, Darren looked at Jonathan. They made eye contact, and a chill crept up Jonathan's spine. When the doors clanked shut, deep relief replaced his trepidation.

With a prayer of thanks, he returned to his desk to respond to his daughter. "Let the caterers know you want the steak. Nothing's too good for my baby girl." He hit send then reached for his phone, ready to call Jacqueline. He let his hand drop. His promotion didn't change their situation or his plans for retirement.

CHAPTER 41

GAVIN WAITED IN the group home lobby, duffel bag clenched in a sweaty hand. No more toilet scrubbing, no more getting his face shoved in spit-swirled food. No more being shuffled from place to place, waiting to see his sisters only to have their foster parents cancel last minute. They'd even found his mother. She had a long way to go before the judge would grant her custody, but things were turning around. He could feel it. This was the first step.

He stared at a magazine, a picture of a mother and son depicted on the cover. What if Mom didn't change? What if she changed for a while, but then went back to drinking and drugging. Or worse, took off again? Would Jacqueline still take them in? Would he even be able to find her? Knowing Mom, she'd drag him and his sisters to some man's house. Until he left, or told her to ditch her kids. Which was more likely. Mom always said men didn't like a bunch of leaches. But Gavin wouldn't think of all that. Today he got to see his sisters, got to go where someone actually wanted him.

The door slid open, and Mrs. Mansfield stood on the other side with a wide smile. "You ready?"

He nodded and smiled in return, a real one this time. Ms. Roberts stood behind her to the left, grinning like a kid with a Toys-n-Games gift card.

She ruffled Gavin's hair as he passed. "You take care."

Mrs. Mansfield chatted the entire way to Jacqueline's, about coming court dates, her conversation with Mom. "She's got some work ahead of her. Rehab, counseling. She'll need to prove she has steady employment. It'll be a long process and could take two years, maybe more."

He nodded. Mrs. Mansfield was always straight with him. He appreciated that. Enough to quit calling her Ferret, although he still liked the name. It made him laugh, on the inside at least. But now he had a reason to laugh for real.

They stopped by baby Jaya's foster home first. Mrs. Mansfield let Jonathan scoop her up. She squealed and clung to his neck, burying her tiny nose in his ear. He laughed and tickled her sides, breathing deep her baby scent. Next, they picked up Adele who ran out the door, nearly knocking Gavin over with a full-body hug. Her foster mom followed with her things—one bag and a worn teddy bear Gavin didn't recognize.

Adele talked and giggled the entire way, about Jacqueline and what it'd be like to live above a boutique. She wanted to know if Jacqueline liked ice cream and tea parties, and a hundred other things. Mrs. Mansfield gave each question the same response. "You'll have to ask her, sweetie."

She pulled next to the curb outside a frilly boutique. Porcelain figurines, a jewelry display, and brightly painted plaques with inspirational sayings decorated the window. Kinda like an overstocked greeting card store. Warmth radiated from the walls, from Jacqueline, from within Gavin's heart.

Was this what it felt like to be wanted? To be loved?

Would it last?

WITH THE STOREFRONT closed downstairs, Jacqueline rocked baby Jaya in her arms. The toddler rubbed droopy eyes then reached soft, plump fingers to Jacqueline's face. Jacqueline smiled, looking into Jaya's big blue eyes, so sweet, so trusting. Jacqueline didn't deserve such a precious gift. Her stomach soured as an image of Teresa, standing with fists and jaw clenched, flashed through her mind. What if she cleaned up, fought for custody? Jacqueline sucked in a breath of air and let it out slowly.

"The LORD gave and the LORD has taken away; may the name of the LORD be praised" (Job 1:21 NIV).

Right now, she swam in blessings. She wouldn't let what-ifs steal her joy. Besides, this wasn't about her. God would do what was right for these children.

She surveyed her apartment. Boxes cluttered the living room. The saggy furniture wasn't what she'd have chosen. The paisley wallpaper and dingy curtains needed to go, but it was home. A filled home.

Each child received a "house warming" gift to celebrate his or her arrival, although baby Jaya preferred the wrapping paper. Gavin sat near the window, glancing from the emerging stars to the new comic book Jacqueline bought for him. Adele sprawled on the floor cutting paper dolls from a book.

The scent of buttery grilled cheese lingered throughout the apartment, and old hymns drifted from a portable radio propped on an end table. Baby Jaya's hand slipped from Jacqueline's face. The child's head draped over Jacqueline's arm, her eyes closed, a slight smile playing across her tiny lips. Jacqueline brushed a kiss against the child's smooth forehead and carried her to her crib, a gift provided by Irene. Two bedrooms and a boutique. So perfect, it had to come from God.

A bunk bed occupied the far wall, another gift from a church member. A pink, floral comforter spread across the bottom bunk, and a football print decorated the top one. White dressers flanked a small closet.

Tomorrow, she'd see about getting Adele and Gavin transferred to their new schools. Mrs. Mansfield said they were already behind. They'd probably be even more so with yet another change, but they'd get through it. She'd make sure of that.

After plugging in a nightlight, she flipped off the switch. She shuffled back to the kitchen, separated from the living room by a laminate countertop bar. A card pulled from the boutique below lay near a vanilla candle. After almost an hour of sifting through cards and praying, she'd finally selected one. The clichéd words fell short, but it was the best she could do.

She grabbed a pen and pulled a chair to the counter. *Lord, what do I say? How can I show Delana I love her, that I'm truly sorry? What words will heal her heart, earn her trust?*

She set her pen down and grabbed her Bible. A slip of paper nestled between the pages, marking the verse from her morning devotions. She opened to it and read the highlighted verse again: Romans 12:18, "Do all that you can to live in peace with everyone."

The words provided a command with no guarantees. She could do all she knew to do, and her daughter could still reject her because Delana's response was out of Jacqueline's hands. God could woo, soften Delana's heart, and give Jacqueline eloquent words to write, but Delana had to choose to forgive. Without Christ, that would be a hard step for her to take.

She closed her Bible and turned back to her card.

My sweet, precious treasure. I love you. I've always loved you. But I failed as your mother. I wasn't there when you needed me most, and I'm sorry. Nothing I could say will take away the pain I caused you. You must have been so frightened. You must have felt so alone. Nothing can erase those lonely memories. You deserved better. You deserved someone who would've fought for you, held tight to you, demonstrated day-by-day, moment-by-moment, unconditional love. Not through words or cards, but actions.

Know I will always love you,
Mom

With one last prayer, she sealed the envelope and laid it on the counter. She'd mail it tomorrow.

"Miss Jackie?" A soft hand touched her arm, and Jacqueline looked into Adele's soft eyes. "Are you sad?" Her smooth forehead crinkled.

"How could I be sad when my home is filled with those I love?" She scooped Adele up and nestled her on her lap. The scent of berry shampoo wafted from the child's hair. "Would you like to hear a Bible story?"

Adele nodded.

Jacqueline gave her a squeeze. "Think your brother would like to join us?" She rested her chin on Adele's head and gazed across the room. "Gavin, Adele and I were going to see how Joseph's doing." The patriarch had become both children's favorite biblical character. "Want to join us?"

Gavin's head jerked up, and his face brightened before he could cover with a blank expression. "Yeah, sure."

Jacqueline grabbed the comic book Bible and the three moved to the couch. Adele wiggled under her arm and Gavin inched closer. Almost within hug range. Jacqueline cast one glance to the card lying on the counter then flipped the book open. The moment was perfect. Almost. One of Jacqueline's children was missing.

CHAPTER 42

EVENING SETTLED AROUND the boutique as Gavin finished the last of his math homework then set his book aside. He was still far behind, but thanks to Jacqueline, he was starting to catch up. Should even be able to get an A by the time the semester ended. Even better, his school counselor promised to get him into honors classes come January.

He stood and stretched, ready to help Jacqueline prepare the shop for the grand opening. The steady stream of cars passing by the storefront window lessened to a trickle. Throughout the day, a few shoppers poked their heads inside. Some stopped to chat. A hairdresser from a salon a few doors down popped in with home-baked bread and coupons. Buy one, get one free.

That made Gavin laugh. Who needed two haircuts? Or was that in case they messed up the first time? But Adele was pretty excited about it. She'd never had her hair done before, leastways, not by a professional.

Gavin swiped a rag over an empty shelf, watching Jacqueline from the corner of his eye. She knelt beside Adele and patiently helped her arrange jewelry on a rack. Chattering and making all sorts of crazy noises, baby Jaya toddled around, exploring empty boxes and tearing through discarded packing paper.

Each time Adele pulled a new necklace or bracelet from the box, she held it to her neck. "Is this one your favorite, Miss Jackie?" If not for Adele's "help," the task would've been completed an hour ago. But Jacqueline responded with gentleness. She'd cock her head and touch her chin before answering. "That's beautiful," she'd exclaim. And with each response, she gave a squeeze and a compliment, expressing over and over what a treasure Adele was.

Gavin tried to remember when their mother had responded with such patience, such love. He knew she must have held them, hugged them—all mothers did, right?

"OK, munchkin." Jacqueline stood with a moan. "What do you say we call it a day?" She grabbed Adele under her arms and pulled her to her feet. "Irene brought over a game I've been dying to play." She glanced around and stretched, palm pressed against her lower back. "Might as well play it here because I don't know about you young bucks, but I'm not ready to tackle the stairs just yet." She flashed Gavin a smile. "Care to join us?"

Gavin grinned. "If you don't mind losing, sure."

Jacqueline hoisted baby Jaya on her hip and jutted her chin toward a blanket scattered with toys. "Adele, can you grab Jaya's things? I'll get the game."

Adele nodded and hurried to do as asked. Loaded down a moment later, they strolled toward Gavin. He cleared an area on the floor and rested against an armchair placed beside a bookshelf. Adele spread out the blanket and set Jaya's toys in the corner.

They occupied her for all of five seconds before the little one began squirming against Jacqueline's embrace and reaching for the dice. But once she began to rock the tired child, humming softly, Jaya settles down and her eyes started to droop.

As did Gavin's, though he fought against it, not wanting the perfect night to end. Adele snuggled close to Jacqueline's side, draping a hand on her thigh. Seemed like his sister hadn't stopped grinning since they got here. Pretty soon she'd have a permasmile, a nice change from the constant sadness that used to fill her eyes. Even baby Jaya seemed happier, more relaxed.

They played two games, Jacqueline holding baby Jaya with one arm, encasing Adele in the other.

Gavin started to set up for the third game, but paused at Jacqueline's soft laughter. He glanced up. Baby Jaya's head drooped forward, a stream of drool trickling from her mouth. Beside her, Adele leaned against Jacqueline, also asleep.

"Guess it's getting about that time. Can you help me out? Take baby Jaya for a minute?"

He complied, lifting baby Jaya from Jacqueline's arms, returning her once Jacqueline lowered Adele to the blanket. "I'll be back for her."

When she left, Gavin moved to the chair and turned toward the window. His breath caught, his heart stopping. Mom stood beneath the outside light, hands cupped around her face, nose pressed to the window. An odd expression filled her face, one Gavin didn't understand. He stared, blinked, stared again. Mom held his gaze then looked past him, through the shop. When she turned back to Gavin, her expression changed. Softened. Then she touched her fingers to her lips and blew him a kiss. With a wave, she slipped out of the light and into the shadows.

"Mom!" Gavin jumped to his feet and raced to the store entrance. It was bolted, and it took his trembling fingers a moment to fight with the lock. A moment too long. Standing on the sidewalk, chest heaving, he watched Mom slip into an old lowrider. Beneath the faint glow of the streetlight, he could barely make out the form of a man sitting behind the steering wheel. She always left for a man.

"Mom!" Gavin ran toward the car as it backed into the street.

Mom blew another kiss, and then was gone, red taillights receding in the darkness.

"Oh, Momma, why do you keep leaving? Why don't you love me?" Gavin trudged back inside. Fighting tears, he watched the stars flicker. A half-moon peaked through an inky blanket of clouds, casting a warm silver glow onto the street.

Jacqueline returned a moment later. She ruffled Gavin's hair then picked Adele up with a quiet groan. She was a good woman, kind. Like the mother he always wanted. Except he had a mother, and she came back. So what that she'd left again? She wasn't ready. Like Mrs. Mansfield said, she had a lot of work to do. Had to prove herself to the court. It was only a matter of time before she returned for good, took them all home.

But where was home, and how long would they stay there?

Here, they had plenty of food. Adele and Jaya received lots of hugs. They had someone to tuck them in, read stories to them, answer their questions without getting mad. He loved Mom, wanted her back, but he didn't want to lose what he had. Adele and Jaya needed this, needed Jacqueline.

WITH THE CHILDREN tucked in their beds, Jacqueline gazed through the window at the stars. God had done so much—brought such hope out of her mess. Yet her heart still ached. She loved these children dearly, but they'd never replace her sweet Delana.

Will she hate me forever, Lord?

Go to her.

The thought flitted through her mind but she pushed it aside. It wouldn't help. Delana hated her. Nothing Jacqueline could say would change that.

Needing some words of encouragement, she grabbed a devotional from the shelf. She skimmed through the pages, the verses flitting through her mind but failing to take hold. Until she landed on Ecclesiastes 4:10 (NLT): "If one person falls, the other can reach out and help. But someone who falls alone is in real trouble."

A lump lodged in her throat. For years, she'd left poor Delana alone, vulnerable, at a time when she needed her most. What about now? As Jacqueline began a new family, who did Delana have? A married man who used her until he got bored. And then what?

Please watch over her, Lord. Bring her comfort. Keep her safe.

Maybe she should call. Try again. And again, and again until Delana's anger waned and she learned to trust Jacqueline again.

She grabbed her cell phone and dialed Delana's number. Voice mail picked up. Probably because she was asleep. Hitting call end, Jacqueline glanced at the clock on the end table—10:30. No. Delana wouldn't be asleep yet. Not on a Friday night. More likely, she was out with that man.

Or spending the evening alone wondering if anyone cared.

She dialed Irene's number.

"Jacqueline, are you OK?" Television played in the background. At least Jacqueline hadn't woken her.

"Yes, I mean, I think so." She rubbed her forehead. "I'm worried about Delana."

"What happened?"

Maybe she was doing some sort of regressed nesting. More likely guilt caused by her abundance of past failures. "Nothing that I know of. But I think she needs me. I feel it in my gut."

"I'm on my way."

Irene arrived fifteen minutes later, shushing Jacqueline's apologies and ushering her out the door. "You go."

Jacqueline gave her a squeeze. "You're a good friend."

At Delana's, she knocked.

No answer. Risking wakening an angry daughter, she rang the bell.

Footsteps pattered on the tile, and a quavering voice responded. "Who is it?"

Squaring her shoulders, Jacqueline braced herself for rejection. *Don't let her send me away, Lord. She needs me. I know she does. I can hear it in her voice, sense it in my soul.* "It's me."

"What do you want? Just go away."

The footsteps receded. "Please, Delana. Let me in."

Fight for her. Show her you love her.

She tried the doorknob. It was locked, but she still had her condo key. She rummaged through her purse, found the key, and slid it into the lock. It clicked, and she eased the door open. Light spilled from the kitchen into the dark living room. Delana sat on the couch with slumped shoulders, feet curled under her, wine glass in hand. A pregnancy test kit lay on the coffee table.

Jacqueline waited for Delana to throw her out, but she remained silent. Didn't move except for the occasional shudder, indicating she'd been crying. Or still cried.

Jacqueline's heart squeezed. She longed to go to her daughter, to hold her close, to smooth her hair and wipe her tears. But she'd lost that right. Worse, she feared rejection. Only this wasn't about her. Whether her daughter accepted her love or not, Jacqueline needed to give it. Freely, expecting nothing in return.

Stepping softly, Jacqueline crossed the room and slid beside Delana. She wrapped an arm around her daughter's shoulders.

Delana tensed under her embrace. "What are you doing here?"

"I was worried about you."

Delana huffed. "I'm too old for late-night checkups." She shoved Jacqueline's hand away, but Jacqueline held tight. "Get off me."

She continued to push, to shove, to fight, but Jacqueline maintained her embrace, speaking words of love over Delana. *Don't let go. Show her how much you love her. That you're here, no matter how hard she tries to push you away. She needs this. Needs you.*

Delana finally quit fighting and pulled her hands into her lap, working a wadded tissue. "Kind of late to play mom now, isn't it?"

"I'm sorry. You're right. I'm late. I wasn't there for you when you needed me. I wish I could go back, undo the pain I caused you. I can't. But I'm here now."

Delana snorted. "For how long?"

Jacqueline lifted Delana's chin and turned her face to look into her eyes. "I'm not going anywhere."

Delana stared at her, her iced expression melting as the face of a hurting child emerged. Crumpling against Jacqueline, she buried her face in her chest.

The dentist must have left her, but there was no point saying, "I told you so." All Jacqueline could do now was hold her broken daughter. "I'm here now, baby." She smoothed Delana's hair as warm tears seeped into her T-shirt. "I'm not going anywhere."

CHAPTER 43

JONATHAN SETTLED INTO a restless sleep. Splices of time flashed through his mind like rapid-rewind movie clips. Stephanie's prom night with her long, strawberry blonde hair spilling from silver barrettes. Her baptism and the radiant smile she gave upon emerging from the water. It was like stepping backwards through his life. Laughter and bright smiling faces filled each scene, with him in the middle, the sun radiating above him.

But then dark clouds moved in, blanketing everything in a foggy gray. The ground below spun then receded. He stood as if above it all, Stephanie moving farther away, growing younger. Six with a toothless smile, five with bouncy pigtails, four chasing after seagulls on the beach.

The scene shifted to a cold, stark white cafeteria manned by adults with clipboards. Dressed in all white, their faces were stern. Children filed around tables like marching soldiers, mouths set in grim lines. They wore orange jumpsuits with COS printed across the back. They all looked the same. Same height, same hair color, same girth, same rod-straight posture. Everyone looked ahead, footsteps pounding out a rhythm. Like a funeral procession.

A voice boomed. "Next!" Each time it spoke, a branding iron lowered from the ceiling, searing numbers into bare arms. 780,243. 780,244. 780,245. The children didn't flinch, but kept moving, like thousands of toy soldiers. Upon reaching the food counter, they stuck their arms out, elbows locked. Faceless people, men or women, Jonathan couldn't tell, slapped a tray in their hands, and the children moved on.

The line continued, filling bench seats row by row. Women with hair wrapped in netting, dressed in white aprons, stood on either end of the tables, holding stop watches. Click. Click. Click, like a thousand readied rifles.

"Next!"

The children grabbed their trays and rose, marching to an overflowing dish station while others took their place. Jonathan stood in the center of the room, spinning, looking from one hollowed face to the next. But no one saw him. He stared at the back of a girl's head facing the counter. Strawberry blonde hair cascaded over her shoulders, and unlike the others, she wore a pink shirt and blue jeans.

She turned around and locked eyes with him. His lungs closed, a stab of pain nearly knocking him over.

"Stephanie!" He ran towards her, but couldn't move past the slow procession of children. Their footsteps pounded against his eardrums, louder, louder. Thudded against his brain like a hammer. "Stephanie!" He pressed through, tripping over someone's feet. Sprawling on the ground, he reached for the girl who now stood with her back to him. She turned around, only it wasn't Stephanie. A stoic face set beneath red hair stared back at him and Jonathan gasped.

But what if it was? Would you save her? Those children are my Stephanies. My beloveds.

He bolted upright, panting, trying to orient himself in his dark apartment bedroom. Sweat clung to his back, slicked his forehead. Although he fought against it, the question continued to play through his mind.

What if that were Stephanie? To what lengths would he go to save her?

CHAPTER 44

J ONATHAN SAT AT the kitchen table, Bible spread before him, coffee growing cold in his mug. The images from his dream haunted him. He'd never put much stock into dreams before—thought Jung and Freud and all those other head examiners functioned a neuron short. But this one felt different, and the feeling refused to leave. The children, their faces, the sterility of that cafeteria. What did it mean?

Lord, if You're trying to tell me something, can you make it a little clearer? I've never been good at symbolism.

He'd never been good at studying the Bible, either. At least, not without notes and clearly defined questions, which was why he'd purchased a study guide last week. He grabbed the glossy booklet and flipped through it. Love. An action and a choice.

So You're not going to tell me about the dream after all.

With pen in hand, he read through the material, jotting notes.

Human love—based on emotion, which changes.

Agape (God's love)—sacrificial, unconditional, demonstrated by action.

Romans 5:8 (NIV), "But God demonstrates His own love for us in this: While we were still sinners, Christ died for us."

As recipients of such a radical act of love, we are to be beacons of hope, conduits, of this initiating, sacrificial, passionate love.

Question: How can you demonstrate the radical love of Christ? Who may God want to love through you?"

Jonathan's heart pricked as he thought of Jacqueline and the children he'd never met. He felt compassion for them, for all children shuffled through the system, but he didn't love them.

He continued reading.

> *According to Jesus, others will know we are His disciples not by how many services we attended, how much money we gave, or how many hours we've spent reading our Bibles. They will know we're His disciples when we live like He did, pouring ourselves out like a fragrant offering, expending ourselves on behalf of others.*

He massaged his forehead and stared into his coffee cup.

You want me to take in those children, don't You? I need Your help, Lord.

An image of one of the kids from his auto mechanics class came to mind—the same one he'd seen in his dream. Where was the kid now? There was no way of knowing. He might not be able to help him, but there were three children he could.

He knew what he had to do. And although it scared him to death, ignoring God's voice scared him even more.

Heaving a sigh that did little to soothe his nerves, he grabbed his keys and headed for Jacqueline's. But after how he'd treated her, would she listen to what he had to say?

JACQUELINE STUMBLED BACKWARD and onto the stool. She pressed the phone closer to her ear, waiting for the catch, the raincloud to swallow her rainbow. "I'm sorry, could you repeat that?"

The man on the other line cleared his throat. "Yes, I'm Harvey Freeman from Longville Commercial Realty. I'm calling on behalf of Vacation Escapades."

"Hold on, please." She jotted all three names down, a prick of anticipation quickening her pulse. But it was too early to get excited. More than likely this guy was a con. They came in droves after major disasters, promising miraculous, cheap repairs. Running off with storm victims' money. Evil. But an Internet search and a quick trip to the Better Business Bureau website would prevent that.

She pulled the phone away to study the screen and wrote down the guy's return number.

While the man continued to talk, reciting business licenses and website URLs, she turned to her laptop and started searching sites. *Oh, please be legit! Tell me you'll help me. You'll manage my property, repairs and all, for a reasonable fee.*

What was her bottom line? With two mortgages, she wasn't in a position to negotiate, but she didn't want to make a rash decision either. After all, she still had three college tuitions to pay for.

She switched the phone to her other ear and wiped a sweaty palm on her shorts. "Why are they interested in my property?"

"Actually, they are interested in three properties, your personal residence along with two of your listings. They plan to develop a resort and have already purchased numerous lots along Crystal Shore's coast. Your property and the property of three of your clients, if my records are correct, sit between the lots they've already purchased."

She touched her neck, fighting against a giggle. A resort company wanted her land? Unbelievable. "How much are they willing to offer?"

"Do you have a fax number?"

"Yes." Somewhere. She rummaged through the clutter on the counter. Where had she placed her contact information? "My fax . . ." papers fluttered to the floor as she sifted through them, "number . . ." invoices, three to-do lists, "is . . ." an inventory chart that needed filing. Her gaze landed on the store phone and the list of numbers taped to it. Duh! She recited the fax number.

"Great. I'll get a formal offer to you by this afternoon."

Jacqueline hung up the phone and started to laugh. Gavin and Adele glanced her way.

"What happened?"

Still laughing, she skipped across the room and swept Adele into the air. "When God guides, He provides." Everything was starting to turn around. She even had a lunch date with Delana next week. The two had a long way to go. It'd take time for Jacqueline to earn Delana's trust. But it was a first step—initiated by God. Faith said He always finished what He started.

Adele giggled, the others soon joining. Baby Jaya squealed and reached out her chubby fingers. Jacqueline planted Adele on her feet, kissed her forehead, then tickled baby Jaya's ribs. Her heart felt ready to burst. God guided, she leapt, trusting Him to catch her, and here she was. With three beautiful children, her own boutique, and a corporate realtor interested in her home and two of her properties. And yet, one potentially devastating thread remained—Teresa.

Breathing deep, Jacqueline held tight to her smile. She wouldn't think about that. Not now. Today, she'd rejoice and let God handle all the what-ifs however He saw fit.

Behind her, a man cleared his throat. She turned to see Jonathan standing with a raised eyebrow. One corner of his mouth lifted, as if amused. He held a yellow tulip in his hand. Red roses symbolized passion. Carnations suggested love and fascination. But a tulip?

Jacqueline tensed, a wave of sadness tugging at her heart. "Good morning." Why had he come? To reiterate the "I can't do this" speech he gave her—over the phone. Like a cowardly teenager.

He shifted then glanced around. When his gaze landed on the children, his smile vanished, and his eyes widened. Gavin leaned forward, staring back with a similar expression.

Jacqueline looked from one to the other. "Do you two know each other?"

Jonathan stood, as if frozen, mouth slackened. When he spoke, his voice wavered. "I—Can we talk? In private?"

What was this about? The kids? Clearly seeing them made Jonathan feel guilty for ditching, put a face to her stories. Good. Served him right.

No, not good. She couldn't fault him for his decision. He wanted to retire, not start a family. She got that. So why was he here? There really wasn't anything left to talk about. Even so, she wanted to get this painful moment over with. So she could heal, move on.

"We can go to my office." She turned to Gavin who now sat erect, watching. "Can you stay with your sisters for a minute?" Which was all it'd take. Jonathan would say whatever he needed to say to absolve himself of whatever guilt drew him here. Or to tell her he was moving. Which would be better? Then they wouldn't have those weird, after-the-break-up chance encounters. But first he'd leave her with his cheesy parting gift.

Walking on stiff legs, she led him to her office and motioned for him to sit. He didn't.

"I—" He glanced toward the door then back to her.

"I'm sorry I hurt you." He handed her the tulip.

She took it with a forced smile, shrugged. "Life happens. I understand how you feel. I'm not mad or resentful." *There. Is that the closure you need?*

"I—" His face scrunched as he cast another glance to the door.

"I changed my mind."

She snorted. "What?"

"I changed my mind. I'd like to . . . to try again."

She studied him, sighed. "It's not that easy, Jonathan. These kids have been through so much already. Moved from one house to the next. They don't know who to trust. They need stability. Commitment."

"I know. I can do that. I'm willing to try."

"Try?" She shook her head. "That's not good enough."

"Not try. That's not what I mean." He stepped forward and grabbed her hands. "Please, Jacqueline. Forgive me. Trust me."

The protective barrier around her heart began to quiver, but she wasn't ready to knock it down. Not yet. But oh, how she wanted to. How she longed to believe him, to accept his words without challenge. But she couldn't. She had to think about the children. What if she let him in, they grew attached, and he walked away? No, she couldn't allow that. They'd been hurt enough already. "Those children need unconditional, forever love. Can you give them that?"

GAVIN'S STOMACH QUIVERED as emptiness settled over him. It was the man from the group home, the auto-mechanics teacher. Had he come to take Gavin back there? Was Jacqueline getting rid of him, just like everyone else? Just like Mom. This man would change everything. Men always did.

Gavin fought to keep his voice steady. "Adele, can you watch baby Jaya for me?"

Adele nodded and cleared her toys to make room on the blanket. Gavin handed over his baby sister and stood on numb legs. He paused, taking in the image as if to store it permanently. How much longer did they have? A day? Hours? And then they'd be back to weekly visits when foster parents spared the time to make them happen. Hopefully Adele and Jaya could return to their old home. Although their foster parents had been crabby, kind of weird, they'd taken good care of Adele and baby Jaya. Those families would probably take his sisters back, if asked. Unlike Gavin. He'd already burned through all his options. They'd send him back to that kid-pound. With Jo-Jo.

A shiver crept up his spine as he tiptoed across the boutique.

Jacqueline's tight voice seeped into the hall. "Do you love them?"

"No, but I love you."

Gavin couldn't breathe. Couldn't move. The man was asking Jacqueline to choose. Gavin knew what would happen. Women always chose the man. Why should Jacqueline be any different?

"I want to be with you. Trust me." The man's voice was low, soft. "Give me another chance. Please."

"Oh, Jonathan." Her voice caught.

Gavin stumbled backward. It was over. Jacqueline had made her choice.

He bolted, as if by instinct, for his sisters, started to reach for them. But where would he take them? They were fine. Everyone wanted the cute baby and the sweet girl with the freckle-faced smile. It was him no one wanted. But he wouldn't go back to that home. He couldn't. Anywhere was better than there.

Trembling, tears lodged in his throat, he knelt beside his sisters and ran his hand along baby Jaya's cheek. "Love you, Jaya." He brushed a kiss along her forehead, inhaling deep the sweet scent of baby shampoo. Then he turned to Adele, pulled her in a headlock, rubbed his chin against her scalp. She giggled and squirmed. "Love you, too, you little pest."

And then he left.

JACQUELINE EMERGED FROM her office holding Jonathan's hand. She peered up at him. "I think it's time I introduce you to the children."

He gazed down at her, traced his knuckles along the contours of her face. "I'd like that."

When they reached the reading nook where she'd left the kids, she found Adele standing with her face pressed against the window. Baby Jaya clung to the back of Adele's legs, crying.

Jacqueline lifted baby Jaya into her arms and touched Adele's shoulder. "What are you looking for? And where's Gavin?"

Adele turned around, face crumpled. She pointed toward the window.

"What do you mean?" She rushed to look outside. "Where'd he go?"

Adele shrugged.

"What'd he say?"

"That he loved me and baby Jaya."

Jacqueline's blood ran cold. Those were leaving words. But why? Why would he leave? Everything was going so well. Unless—

Had Teresa shown up again? *Oh, Lord, no.* Why else would Gavin leave? If she had, and he chased after her, there was no telling where he'd end up. No knowing what or who she was involved with. "I need to find him. Oh, Lord, help us find him!" She whirled around to look at Jonathan. "Help me! Help me find him!"

"OK. Calm down. Everything will be OK." He placed a strong hand on her shoulder. "Is there someone you can call to stay with the girls?"

She nodded. "I'll call Irene."

CHAPTER 45

GAVIN RAN DOWN the sidewalk, casting frequent glances behind him. Faster, faster, faster! He spun around the corner, past storefronts, around another corner. Through an alley, then a parking lot. He wove through cars. Adrenaline pushed him forward, not knowing where to go. Not caring. Pushing harder, faster from the terror of his life, only it trailed him around every corner, down every street. Screams bottled in for months, years, crawled up his throat, turning to rage. Hot, searing rage igniting his heart, fueling his legs.

Loser. Unwanted. Worthless! Unloved.

Unlovable.

He jumped over a concrete partition, into another parking lot. He barreled into a woman carrying groceries. Tripped over her spilled items. His ankle wrenched, and stabbing pain shot up his leg. His skin scraped against the concrete.

The woman, sitting on her rump with her legs stretched in front of her, produce scattered around her, stared back with wide eyes. Tampons, makeup, and her wallet spilled from her overturned purse.

"Sorry!" But there was no time to help. He needed to find somewhere safe. Like another church shelter. Some place they wouldn't ask questions. Until he could think. Figure out what to do.

His ankle screamed, his lungs burned, but he kept going. He raced down sidewalk after sidewalk, turning corners and darting across streets. Horns blared as he dashed in front of cars, but he didn't care. Finally, with muscles trembling, he collapsed onto a park bench. Sticky saliva caked his dry lips. The hot summer breeze stirred his dampened hair. At the end of a paved pathway, a drinking fountain drew him. After gulping enough water to bloat his stomach, he returned to the bench and dropped his head in his hands.

What now?

JONATHAN STOPPED AT the end of an alley and raked a hand through his hair. This wasn't working. It was like searching for a penny on the railroad track. As night settled over Willow Valley, Jacqueline grew more frantic. They'd called the social worker, who came to the boutique to talk with the cops. But Jacqueline refused to stay. She said she needed to be doing something. To look. So Jonathan joined her, only he didn't hold out much hope. If this kid wanted to run away, he wouldn't stay out in the open.

"Where could he have gone?" Jacqueline scanned the shadowed street, clutching hastily printed flyers in one hand, a roll of masking tape in the other. They bore a pixilated image of Gavin, taken off her cell phone. So far they'd plastered them on at least twenty electric and street light poles.

Jonathan rubbed the back of his neck. "I don't know."

They studied a row of dilapidated houses. Long shoots of uncut grass shot up around patches of dirt. Rusted cars with flat tires, some with no tires, filled driveways and lined the street. Three rough-looking teenagers with sagging shorts sat on concrete stairs at the end of a cracked walk.

"I wish I would've gotten Teresa's phone number," Jacqueline said. "Asked where she was staying."

"She wouldn't have given it to you. Wouldn't have told you. She wouldn't even give it to Mrs. Mansfield, the one who had the power to help Teresa get her kids back." Probably because she had nowhere to stay. Or at least nowhere decent.

"We need to split up." Jacqueline squinted as she peered toward a distant streetlight.

"Uh-uh. No way am I letting you wonder around this area at night. Or in the day, for that matter." It wasn't safe for either of them to be here, not with night falling. "Let's head back toward the boutique. See if we can't try to trace his steps somehow."

"That makes no sense."

"It makes as much sense as anything else we've done." They were beginning to walk in circles.

"Fine." She threw her hands up and marched back toward Jonathan's car, parked at a corner gas station.

He drove to a safer area. "Now we can split up. But stay where it's well lit. Near the main road."

"OK."

Why didn't he believe she'd comply? "How about you focus on tacking up posters," which, hopefully, would keep her in lighted areas, "while I search the area?"

She agreed and grabbed her stack of papers. As she taped a poster to an electric pole, he headed to a residential area. His feet ached after hours of walking, jogging, searching, and his poor night's sleep started to catch up with him. It was a strong reminder of the sleepless nights parenting would soon bring. And yet, he made a promise to God and to Jacqueline. He'd love these kids as his own, because the Bible commanded it. Pure religion was to look after orphans and widows. It'd be hard, frustrating, and at times, exhausting, but it'd never be as hard as what these kids faced. They needed a home, and Jonathan had the means to provide that.

The longer he walked, the more confident he grew. Crazy, considering the circumstances. But for the first time since he came to Willow Valley, peace settled over him. The kind that told him he was walking in God's will. Nothing else mattered.

He rounded the playground, the swings still. The faint glow of the moon reflected off the silver slide. He started to leave when a shadow caught his eye. A hunched form, sitting on the bench. Could it be?

Stepping lightly on the soft grass, he moved closer. The kid's head jerked up, the park light shining on a tear streaked face.

"Gavin?" Jonathan stopped, not wanting to scare the kid away.

"Leave me alone." Gavin started to stand, winced, favoring one leg. He inched to the right as if ready to bolt.

"I'm not going to hurt you. I just want to talk."

"Right. I've heard that one before."

Jonathan fingered his phone in his pocket. If he called the cops, the kid would run. If he didn't, the kid might bolt anyway.

Lord, help me out here. Give me the words.

JACQUELINE STEPPED BACK and stared at her last poster attached to a wooden fence post. No one would connect Gavin to that blurry image. But it was all they had, and seeing them tacked in neighborhoods offered hope. Someone would see them, see Gavin, and call. Wouldn't they?

Lord, please, help us find him.

The back of her shoe ate into her heel, and the skin on the edge of her pinky toe burned. A blister. Probably one of many. If she'd taken the time to think, she would've worn tennis shoes. Wouldn't have left Gavin unattended in the first place.

Why now, Lord? Everything seemed to be going so well. One minute she praised God for His abundant blessings, the next, her heart wrenched. Did every blessing have to come with such heartache?

She blinked, her eyes dry, lids droopy. Her body longed for bed, but her heart propelled her forward. Maybe Gavin had returned? Would return? Dare she even hope for miracles anymore?

She grabbed her phone, dialed Jonathan's number.

"Hey."

His voice sounded strained, and her pulse quickened. "Did you find him?"

"Yes."

"Where are you?"

"At a park off of Jeffers. Hold on!" He hollered out. "I gotta go. Gavin, wait!"

"Jonathan?"

He didn't respond, but across the line, she heard heavy breathing, movement, Jonathan calling out to Gavin.

Jacqueline hung up and dialed Mrs. Mansfield. "Jonathan found Gavin. He's at Green Hills Park." Or was. Based on what she heard, Gavin ran again. Jonathan would catch him, right? The cops would find him. Or they would send Gavin over the edge. Then there was no telling what he might do.

Shoving her phone into her back pocket, she raced through neighborhoods to the park a few blocks away. She reached it out of breath, skin flaming, and scanned the shadows. The park bench was empty. So were the playground and the field. Where were they? She tried Jonathan's number but got a busy signal.

As she neared an old shed, a low voice stopped her. Jonathan's. She crept closer, lungs tight, heart thrashing. Gravel crunched beneath her feet, and she froze. Careful. Don't do anything to make Gavin run.

With raspy breath, she peered around the corner, tip-toed closer.

Gavin crouched behind a riding lawn mower. "Leave me alone."

"Everyone's looking for you, Gavin," Jonathan said. "We're worried about you."

Gavin cursed. "What do you care? I heard you. You don't care about none of us."

"I'm here, aren't I?" Jonathan took another step and reached out his hand.

Gavin swore again. "Sell me something else. I'm not going back to that home."

"No one's sending you there, Gavin."

"Where then? No one else will take me. Not the Lewises, not even my mom."

"That's not true, Gavin. I won't let you down. I promise. I'm here for you, buddy."

Jacqueline stepped forward. "We both are. Come home."

Gavin turned toward her, his chin puckering in the light.

She took another step. "You ready to come home?"

He didn't move.

"Adele and Jaya need you." Her voice cracked. She opened her arms, welcoming him but not forcing. "Come home, sweetie."

Tears streamed down his face, and he swiped at his nose with the back of his hand. "Home?"

Jacqueline nodded. "Home. For good."

He rose and hobbled toward her. Stepping into Jacqueline's arms, he buried his face in her chest, his body trembling.

Jacqueline held him close, smoothing his hair. She lifted her gaze to Jonathan and smiled.

He came forward, wrapping his arms around both of them so Gavin was sandwiched between them.

EPILOGUE

SIX MONTHS LATER . . .
With Jonathan by her side, Jacqueline guided the children into the courtroom. She smiled at Delana, who was now six months pregnant and was carrying a squirmy baby Jaya in her arms. Chattering voices followed them—Mrs. Mansfield, Irene, and Elaine, who had come all the way from Maryland. Elaine carried a video camera, ready to capture every moment.

Is this really happening? Jacqueline looked from one face to the next, grinned at Jonathan. Squeezed Gavin's hand. "You ready for this?"

He looked up with bright eyes and nodded. Beside him, Adele bounced, her braids swinging across her shoulders.

The judge rose. "Any photographers, anyone that's videotaping, you may walk around the courtroom during the proceedings."

A giggle popped out, and Jacqueline touched her hand to her mouth. *Calm down. It's not over yet. But soon. Oh, soon!* She sat beside the children's lawyer and pulled Adele onto her lap. Delana sat beside her and nudged Jacqueline's shoulder with her own.

With tears stinging her eyes, Jacqueline glanced behind her to where the others had settled.

Jonathan nodded, eyes glimmering. He mouthed the words, "I love you."

A photographer Jonathan had hired stepped in front of Jacqueline and clicked. She blinked against the bright flash then wrapped one arm around Delana and Jaya and stretched the other around Gavin and Adele. All her children—*Oh, Lord, Jesus, my children*—leaned closer, and the camera clicked again.

The judge sat back down. "Welcome, everybody." After swearing everyone in, he glanced at the children's attorney. "Mr. Kelvins, you may proceed."

"Thank you, your honor." As Mr. Kelvins rose, the camera flashed three more times in rapid succession. "We are here today in the matter of the adoption of Gavin Rallings, Adele Rallings, and Jaya Batron." After stating each case number, he held a formal document in front of Jacqueline. "Could you please state and spell your name for the record?"

"Jacqueline." Her voice squeaked. She cleared her throat. "Jacqueline Monique Dunn." She spelled each name, her smile widening.

She continued, listing her address, her occupation, and spelling the names of each of the children she wished to adopt.

"You understand we're here today to ask the judge to grant this adoption and make it final?"

"Yes."

Adele squealed and the camera flashed again. Jacqueline gave her a squeeze.

The attorney smiled, still holding his paper. "If the judge grants this order, these children will then be your children. You understand the permanency of this?"

"Yes."

Leaning forward, Gavin wiggled in his seat, leg bouncing. He placed both hands flat on the table as if sitting still required an unbearable amount of self-control. When he looked at Jacqueline, his face stretched in a toothy smile, eyes bright. So many words spoken in that one steady look. She longed to grab him, to hold him, hug him as he bubbled with laughter. That would come. *Thank You, sweet Jesus.*

"Are you prepared to take care of these children until they are eighteen, possibly older?" The attorney's tone deepened.

Jacqueline laughed. "Yes!"

"Can you briefly tell the court your reasons for adopting these children?"

A lump lodged in Jacqueline's throat, blocking her words. Suddenly, because God told her to was so insufficient. Initially, yes, it had been a step of obedience, an urge to help. To find purpose. But now. Tears sprang to her eyes as her gaze swept across her children—all of them. "Because I love them." She looked at each one in turn, squeezed their hands, a tear slipping from her eyes. "Because they are a part of me, each one."

When the proceedings ended, Jacqueline sat, frozen. Surrounded by her children. Strong hands rested on her shoulders. She glanced up to see Jonathan standing over her, smiling, eyes misted.

The others milled around them, taking more photos, offering congratulations, but Jacqueline barely heard them. Adele slid from her lap, and Jacqueline rose.

She slipped an arm around Delana's waist. "I think this is cause for a celebration. I'm thinking ice cream. What do you say?" She glanced at all the smiling faces gathered around her.

"I say . . ." Jonathan turned her toward him. He reached into his pocket and pulled out a small black box.

"Oh!" Jacqueline touched her neck, staring at the satin through misty eyes.

He dropped to one knee and took her hand in his. "I think it's time to make something else official." He winked at Gavin and the boy grinned. "What do you say? Jacqueline Monique Dunn, will you marry me?"

Jacqueline yelled and wrapped her arms around Jonathan's neck. She planted a long kiss on his smiling lips. Laughter filled her to the depths.

A camera flashed, and she pulled away, cheeks hot.

Jonathan's eyes twinkled. "Is that a yes?"

She laughed, opening her arms wide to include the children in her embrace. "Yes, Jonathan Edward Cohen. Yes."

"All right!" He gave Gavin a high five then slipped a glimmering ring on Jacqueline's finger.

WorldCrafts^{SM} develops sustainable, fair-trade businesses among impoverished people around the world. Each WorldCrafts product represents lives changed by the opportunity to earn an income with dignity and to hear the offer of everlasting life.

Visit WorldCrafts.org to learn more about WorldCrafts artisans, hosting WorldCrafts parties and to shop!

WORLDCRAFTS^{SM}
Committed. Holistic. Fair Trade.
WorldCrafts.org 1-800-968-7301

WorldCrafts is a division of WMU®.

More Than
Happily Ever After . . .

In *Beyond I Do* readers journey with Ainsley Meadows to discover how choosing a mate has eternal consequences. Ainsley does not want to become like her mother, cycling through jobs and relationships. She opts for a safe, predictable relationship with a socialite psychiatrist. But as her wedding nears, an encounter with a battered woman and her child sparks a long-forgotten dream and unlocks a hidden passion. A passion that threatens to change everything, if she can open her heart to the love that God intended.

Visit **NewHopeDigital.com** to purchase or call **1-800-968-7301**.

$15.99
N144123

New Hope® Publishers is a division of WMU®, an
international organization that challenges Christian believers
to understand and be radically involved in God's mission.
For more information about WMU, go to wmu.com.
More information about New Hope books
may be found at NewHopeDigital.com
New Hope books may be purchased at your local bookstore.

Please go to
NewHopeDigital.com

If you've been blessed by this book,
we would like to hear your story.
The publisher and author welcome your comments and
suggestions at: newhopereader@wmu.org.